ONCE ACCUSED, FOREVER TARNISHED

G. F. HUNN

BERNICE,
HOPE YOU ENJOY THIS.

Gene Hunn

❀ Created with Vellum

To Linda, whose support on this project means everything to me.

1

Monday October 15, 1984

Ali Thorein's hand shook as she dropped the empty soda can in her rented Ford Tempo's console. She swallowed hard to wash away the bitter taste in her mouth but failed to remove the anxiety causing it. Three days earlier in Minneapolis, Ali stood in a conference room, the youngest person present as well as the lone woman, and demonstrated her success at saving profit-challenged Robel's stores to forty-plus district store managers. That was easy. Facing her mother today after eight years of estrangement? Much harder, but Ali could no longer deny she needed closure. Her past wouldn't disappear because of a promotion, and no accomplishment would ever be enough to atone for the dishonor she brought to her family.

Ali took her foot off the gas, slowing her car on the gradual incline entering the village. At least once a day the local cop, Mr. Hancock, sat on the other side of the slight ridge ahead catching speeders. *Don't want to see him again.*

After she crested the ridge, Ali braked and pulled off the pavement, delaying the inevitable. Before her lie Rausburg, Wisconsin, population 846, home for the first eighteen years of her life. She had always pictured Rausburg as more functional than quaint or charming. Today she blinked her eyes in disbelief. *Good Lord, has anything changed?*

A long moment passed while Ali accepted her return as reality. *Why did I wait so long? Should have called instead. She's moved on, I'm sure. I disappointed her, and she's never gotten over it. Why else would she keep Dad's death from me until after his funeral?*

"Need help there, miss?"

Ali jumped. A brown van had stopped next to her on the highway. She rolled her window down. "I'm good, thanks."

The driver waved and pulled away. *That never happens in California.* She checked her mirror before pulling back on the highway to cruise Main Street within the thirty-five mph speed limit. *God, Rausburg is even bleaker than I remember.*

Ali slowed and turned left onto Colfax to drive the final three blocks to her childhood home. The closed garage door showed Mom was there, but Ali drove past and circled the block. Eight years of walling off her past life here made Ali reluctant to reopen old wounds.

Ali paused at the final corner while a dozen excuses to turn right and avoid the confrontation vied for her attention. But avoidance was not her style. Ali made the choice to resolve any remaining issues from her past with a clear, rational mind before she boarded the plane from San Francisco last week. Today she would face her problems head-on.

Pulling in the driveway, Ali noticed the faded mailbox still read Max and Helga Thorein. Her old climbing tree in the front yard had been reduced to a stump while the row of maples by the driveway remained, and frost-bitten marigolds lined the porch as they had eight years ago, when she fled to California. The house stood exactly the way she remembered it: a two-story farmhouse with separate garage in back, cream-colored aluminum siding, and a welcome sign by the front door. The porch swing hung out, faded but inviting. *How many hours did I spend sitting in that?*

She shut off the engine and stepped out, shivering once before adjusting her suit. Spongy knees forced her to grab the railing on the porch steps. She hesitated before the heavy wooden door. The door should be unlocked but she couldn't open it and yell, "I'm back," as if nothing had happened. She returned now as a stranger, asking permission to enter her former home.

She knocked firmly three times and seconds later soft footsteps approached from inside. Ali swallowed hard as the door opened. Helga's hair was streaked with gray now, her crow's feet were more pronounced, and her eyes lacked their mischievous twinkle. As a child, Ali once boasted she had the prettiest mom around. Now she realized her mother's face stared back at her every time she used a mirror.

"Yes?" Helga asked as Ali removed her wrap-around sunglasses. Helga shrieked and threw her arms around her only child. Ali returned the embrace, hoping she made the right decision.

2

Tommy Peterson studied the picture that hung by the back door before stepping outside. The photo was of Ma, Pa, and a five-year-old Tommy posing at the farm they owned until Pa died. With Ma gone now, Tommy alone remembered that sunny Easter Sunday when his world was right and complete. In his mind, the warm breeze tousled his dirty blond hair. As birds sang in the trees, the green grass of spring tickled his nostrils while his parents' reassuring hands rested on his shoulders. This was before he found his father's body in the barn and retreated into a private world few entered. *Things would be so different if only...*

"I'll make you both proud today," he said, placing his hand against the glass. "I'll be extra careful too, Ma." His morning ritual complete, Thomas Joseph Peterson, Rausburg, Wisconsin's one-man police department, started his workday.

He stopped by his office on Main first. Since there were no messages on the answering machine, he started the coffee brewing before driving to the school-crossing zone. Regular volunteers escorted the kids across Highway 72, Main Street in Rausburg, but he parked nearby to remind drivers to use caution. This Indian summer day he had another reason to be there. An unpleasant but necessary task to perform.

Most of the kids gave him a friendly 'hello' as he leaned against his squad car. A few of the youngest stopped to tell him about their weekend while the oldest kids smiled politely as they hurried by, too cool to be seen with the village cop. Tommy greeted them all while he watched for today's perpetrator.

Ryan Kranutz pulled into the school parking lot in his mother's '82 Camaro. The car looked fast, but with the standard four cylinders and automatic transmission, it did not live up to its appearance. Tommy jogged over, intercepting Ryan before he went inside.

Ryan rolled his eyes when Tommy mentioned the reckless driving complaints after the homecoming dance last Saturday night. "I was careful. You saw me. You know."

Tommy maintained his composure. "I know you weren't speeding, but when you floor it, you make noise and wake people. I heard about it yesterday after Mass."

"Mrs. Johnson?"

Tommy nodded. "Among others. We do have a noise ordinance, but I won't cite you for such a petty violation as long as you promise to cool it."

"Okay."

"I'll call your dad later today and tell him we talked."

"Oh, man."

"I won't make a big deal out of it. I'm sure he'll tell you life's easier if you don't bother Mrs. Johnson."

Ryan shifted. "Okay."

Tommy smiled. "I bet your mom's Camaro is fun to drive. You impressed the Whitmer girl when you drove her to homecoming in it, didn't you?"

"Yeah." Ryan smiled too. No one stayed angry with Tommy for long.

"Okay, easy on the takeoffs. I'll talk to your dad, then the matter is closed."

Ryan headed into school without further comment while Tommy strolled to his car.

With the kids safely inside the school, Tommy drove two blocks to his office and parked behind the building. Warm coffee aroma greeted him inside. He drew his first cup of the day, added sugar, and sat in his chair, opening the Wisconsin State Journal on his desk. A successful liver transplant at UW-Madison's hospital made the headlines.

Tommy was on page two when the phone rang. "Police Chief Tom Peterson. How may I help you?"

Uncontrolled, hysterical sobbing filled his ear. Tommy sat upright. "Take a deep breath, and get hold of yourself. Now who is this?"

"Mary. Mary Albright. Oh, Tommy…"

Mary's voice choked into another sob. As the school secretary, Mary dealt with minor emergencies all the time. Tommy had never known her to lose control.

"I'm here, Mary. What is it? Problem at school?"

"Mister Luetz … Blood everywhere."

Tommy rose, his heart hammering in his chest. "Mister Luetz had an accident at school?"

"No. His house … He's dead…"

Tommy grabbed his jacket. "I'll check it out. Keep everyone in the building."

3

Helga clung to Ali in the doorway, simple words of joy and regret passing between them. A long minute later Helga stepped back to gaze at her daughter.

"I'm a mess now," Ali said, wiping her cheek with her hand.

"You're the loveliest mess I've ever seen." Helga hugged her again. "Where are my manners? Come in, come in. No need to stand on the porch."

The living room had changed little. "New curtains?"

"I splurged. The old ones fell apart the last time I washed them."

Ali examined the fabric. "Nice. Did you paint?"

"Yes, I spruced things up last year. Everything had faded."

Ali fixated on the chair and ottoman that replaced her father's old recliner for a moment before surveying the entire room. "Looks great, Mom."

Helga bit her lip. Her eyes grew moist. "Mom. I've missed that word."

Ali put her arm around her mother's shoulder, and Helga twisted into her to hug her again.

Despite the warm reception, caution ruled the conversation as Ali sat at the kitchen table while Helga started the coffee brewing. She opened the refrigerator and held up a small plastic bag of cheese curds. "Hungry?"

"Curds! I haven't had one since I left."

Helga handed her the bag. "Finish them if you like. They're a few days old."

Ali's appetite had returned, and she gladly bit into one. "They still squeak. I can't believe I forgot about curds. You get these from Simonson's dairy?"

"Their kids took over the whole operation. They let Chet sell their cheese at the grocery. That's where I got these."

"Delicious." She took another, thinking the Simonson kids must be pushing fifty now.

"You were in Minneapolis?" Helga asked as Ali bit into another curd.

Ali swallowed before answering. "Yes. I gave a presentation to all the district managers at our annual sales meeting, demonstrating my techniques for saving profit-challenged stores."

"Did it go over well?"

"My statistics speak for themselves. All the stores I've worked with have increased sales."

"I'm not surprised. So you're on vacation now?"

"Yes. I've accumulated an excessive amount of vacation time. Accounting told me to use it or lose it. Since I was in the area, I wanted to see where we stand."

Helga's face fell. "Where we stand? The same place as always. You're my daughter, and I love you."

Ali averted her eyes. "I've avoided you for so long, I didn't know."

Helga sat and forced eye contact. "You needed to work things out." She patted Ali's hand. "Anyway, you're here now. Tell me more about your job. I want details."

Helga drank in each word while the coffee brewed. "The West Coast is my territory, from San Diego to Seattle. When a store fails to meet our minimum profit standards, I spend time on-site, assessing their situation and strategizing their recovery. Inferior management

is the most widespread problem, but each store has unique chal-
lenges. My job is to make them all profitable."

Helga beamed. "Sounds like that job was made for you. You travel
a lot?"

"Three or four days a week. I subsidize several hotel chains."

The interrogation stopped while Helga poured the coffee. Helga
offered sugar and cream, but Ali took hers black.

Helga mixed sugar and cream in hers as she asked, "Any men in
your life?"

No was the truthful answer, but Ali cushioned it. "Not right now.
The long hours I work make dating difficult."

Helga blew lightly into her cup. "You'll know when the right one
comes along."

"Maybe."

Helga took a sip and set her cup on the table. "You're happy in
San Francisco, aren't you?"

"Yes. No one knows about my past there. No judgmental stares."

"It's been eight years. People do change."

"Sometimes."

Helga flashed her best guilt-producing smile. "You will stay for
day or two, won't you?"

Ali exaggerated a sigh. "Oh, all right." She laughed. "I'll stay for a
couple of days."

"Great." Helga squeezed Ali's hand. "I need to buy groceries. Why
don't you come with me?"

Ali's stomach rolled, and she knew it wasn't from the curds or
coffee.

4

Tommy parked at the Luetz's modest house next to the school and sprinted across the yard to peek in the back door. Orville Luetz sat slumped over the kitchen table.

Tommy used his handkerchief to try the doorknob and found it unlocked, as he expected. Gun drawn, he inched inside and scanned the room in silence. Dark blood had pooled on the linoleum. Tommy took Orville's limp wrist in his hand and checked for a pulse. Already cool to the touch so Tommy holstered his gun. He peered over the body and saw the left side of Mr. Luetz's head had been bashed in. His stomach knotted when the metallic smell of blood entered his nostrils.

All activity ceased as Tommy stared at the body in disbelief. He'd seen murder victims before—some as gruesome—but he knew this man. He met him as a little boy on the first day of school. Twelve years later and three feet taller, Tommy shook Mr. Luetz's clammy hand before taking his diploma. "Good luck, son," Orville said, flashing an awkward smile.

Tommy staggered but caught himself before running outside to vomit in the bushes. Embarrassed afterwards, he checked to see if anyone was watching. He saw no one, walked to his car, found a stick of gum in the glove compartment and began chewing. *I can handle this. Never expected it would happen here.*

Now he faced a decision. He should call Sheriff Sinclair in Mineral Ridge and hand the investigation over to him, but Tommy did everything in his power to keep Sinclair out of Rausburg. He didn't want that man around his friends, and he didn't relish the thought of becoming Sinclair's errand boy.

Involving his friends Steve and Del, the state troopers who patrolled the area, would also open the door for Sinclair. They didn't like Sinclair any more than Tommy, but their superiors insisted on complete cooperation with the locals. Tommy would have to handle the investigation himself until he found the killer if he wanted to keep Sinclair out.

Tommy grabbed the mic in his car and called Kickapoo County dispatch. "Tom Peterson here, reporting a homicide in Rausburg. 711 School Street. Victim is the school principal, Orville Luetz. I'm on the scene now. Send the coroner here ASAP."

The dispatcher repeated the address and asked, "Do you need assistance?"

Tommy paused as the reality of his decision to go it alone hit home. *What if I can't solve it by myself?* The memory of last August's village board meeting flashed in his memory. Harv, the village president, had suggested they budget for a slight increase in Tommy's pay. A member of the board said Rausburg might be better off using the sheriff's department and eliminating Tommy's position entirely. That proposal was tabled along with Tommy's raise.

"Chief Peterson?"

"Notify the coroner. I can handle the rest myself."

He closed his eyes and said a short prayer. "Help me do this right."

Tommy trudged over to the school and found Mary, the school secretary, alone in the front office. She stood at the counter, a box of tissues next to her, checking attendance slips. He leaned against the counter. "I'm sorry, Mary. Mr. Luetz is dead."

She put her hand to her mouth and closed her eyes, struggling to control her sobs.

"The coroner will be at the house soon to remove the body. Farmingham's the assistant principal. He's in charge now, correct?"

Tommy covered her hand on the counter with his and waited for the sobbing to stop.

"Tell him Orville's dead. He'll have questions. I'll answer them later. If he keeps the kids inside for recess, they won't see us carrying out the body. I'm guessing he'll dismiss school early today. Have the teachers stay until I speak with them. They might have useful information."

Mary pulled her hand away to wipe her eyes with a fresh tissue. "Murder?"

"Yep. I need to secure the house now." She blew her nose. "Please keep it together for the kids' sake. I'll take your statement later."

Mary tossed the used tissue in the wastebasket and pulled another. "Such a shock."

Tommy stepped away. "I'll be back after the body is removed."

———

Tommy had secured crime scenes during the two years he served on the Madison Police Department, but he had never used yellow crime tape in Rausburg. He wrapped it around the trees, outlining the yard, aware that several people now watched him. He chucked the tape in his car, grabbed his camera along with latex gloves and evidence bags, and avoided eye contact with the few headed his way.

His composure returned as he did his job inside the house and accepted his responsibility to bring Orville Luetz's killer to justice.

A note prominently placed on the table caught his attention. He pulled the camera out. Two pictures left on the roll. "Darn, of all days. At least there's another roll in the bag." He took two pictures, recording the note's placement, and read it as he bagged it.

Eight years ago you lied,

I didn't forget, now you die.
Burn in hell.

The handwriting struck him as feminine and familiar, but he couldn't immediately place it.

He put the bagged note aside and changed film rolls, taking pictures as he maneuvered around the kitchen. The murder weapon was a blood-stained baseball bat lying on the floor that any rookie could have found. Tommy studied it, noticing a lack of scuff marks from prior use. He bagged it, hoping the county's forensics expert could tell him who used it. He took prints off doorknobs, the table, and any surface the killer might have touched. He searched for other telltale signs, such as muddy footprints or a piece of torn clothing but found nothing else.

Next he swept through the house. Nothing missing, so it wasn't a failed robbery. He checked the windows for signs of forced entry, but everything appeared normal.

Tommy surveyed the kitchen, piecing together the probable order of events. Blood spatter suggested the killer hit Luetz first by the door leading to the dining room. Orville must have awakened to noise in the kitchen and never suspected death waited for him. When he pushed the door back, it hid the killer. Orville was struck from behind and on the left, so he never knew his enemy.

Smeared bloodstains on the floor indicated Orville fell and was dragged to the table. Tommy examined the table. No spatter there. The first blow must have been fatal. But why drag Orville's obese body several feet to the table and sit it in the chair? Why not leave it on the floor?

Tommy combed the yard for evidence while he waited for the coroner, but the note was foremost in his mind. "What did Orville lie about eight years ago?" Tommy did a quick calculation. "1976." He slapped his forehead, remembering what made 1976 memorable. "Has to be something else. Just has to be."

The coroner arrived twenty minutes later. While Tommy led him around the back, he told him what he discovered and promised to return as soon as he informed the widow.

Madison's Channel 6 TV news van arrived as he walked next door to the school. He looked away as star reporter Martie Pepper jumped out. "Chief Peterson, Chief Peterson." He kept moving, but she didn't take the hint. "I need a statement from you. Was it murder?"

He turned to her without breaking his stride. "Definitely homicide. I haven't contacted next of kin so no names yet. That's all I can say now."

"Who discovered the body? Any suspects? How was he killed?"

Tommy raised his hand and hurried past. "Not now. I'll be back as soon as I can with the name." He broke into a jog, leaving her behind.

As Tommy entered the school office, Mr. Farmingham, Tommy's science teacher and now acting principal, leaned against the counter while talking to Mary. Farmingham extended his hand, his normal upbeat demeanor muted by the tragedy. "Is it true? Mr. Luetz was murdered in his own home?"

Tommy shook his hand. "Afraid so. I need to use your phone."

Tommy pulled out his little notebook, flipped back a page, and found the rehab clinic's number. Two weeks ago he jotted it down while arranging a visit with Margaret Luetz. She was vibrant and anxious to return home, readily admitting sobriety wasn't easy and expecting Tommy to be frank with her if she faltered. How would she handle this?

The clinic's receptionist transferred the call and the head counselor agreed to break the news to Margaret and prepare her for Tommy's visit later in the day. One difficult job was taken care of now.

Curious villagers clustered by the news van as he approached. Martie had learned the victim's name, so Tommy asked her to hold off the identification for another ten minutes. She agreed before asking him again to be on the air. He ignored her but confirmed Luetz's murder to the small crowd. The sad truth produced a collective gasp.

Tommy retreated inside the Luetz house and waited while the coroner finished. Both men grunted, lifting Luetz's heavy body on the gurney and struggling with it on the back steps before rolling it to the ambulance. On the way, Tommy glanced at the news van. Martie was interviewing villagers on camera.

After loading the body, the coroner estimated the time of death occurred close to four a.m. "I'll be able to swear to it after the autopsy, but my guess won't be far off."

"Four, eh? The neighbors were most likely asleep."

"Maybe you'll get lucky and find one who heard noises and investigated."

"I hope so. When can I expect your report?"

"Tomorrow, barring any other emergencies."

The coroner left. Tommy inspected the house again but found nothing more of interest. He shut off the outside faucets and set the furnace to come on if the temperature dropped before locking the back door.

5

"No reason to keep extra food around the house anymore," Helga said. "I have to shop before lunch. Come to the grocery with me and help carry the bags home. Maybe you'll run into an old friend."

Ali's smile vanished. "I came back to see you, no one else." She had made it clear in her occasional letters home she no longer had friends in Rausburg.

Helga bit her lip. "Chet asks about you from time to time."

"He's making small talk to keep you as a customer."

"True, but he asks."

Ali took Helga's hand. "Oh, all right. It's a beautiful day. I'll walk with you."

They hugged again. "It'll be fine. Eight years is a long time. You're a different person now. Freshen up and we'll go."

The warm breeze, clear blue sky, and bright autumn leaves put a bounce in their step as they strolled Colfax. Helga glowed as Ali held onto her hand, reminding her of a time when Ali needed her mother's reassurance.

A block from home, Ali answered another of Helga's questions and noticed a small shape following her. "Well, hello there, handsome," she said, stopping to face a tuxedo cat.

Helga laughed. "That's Mittens, Mrs. Anderson's cat. He's a wanderer. Doesn't know a stranger. I'll shoo him away."

"No need. My allergy isn't as strong anymore. I used to feed the strays that hung around our apartment building. I sneeze a little is all."

Mittens trotted to Helga and rubbed on her pant leg. Helga bent over to scratch Mitten's head. "You remember that kitten we got you?"

Ali ran her hand along the cat's back. "Cosmo? I felt so bad we couldn't keep him. I suppose he's in kitty heaven by now."

"He lived a happy life on George Olsen's farm. Died four or five years ago."

Ali sneezed once and straightened. Helga lightly pushed Mittens away with her foot. "Such a shame, as much as you love animals."

"Everything for a reason, I suppose. I donate to a local animal shelter, and the baby seal foundation as well. One of the perks of being well paid."

Ali and Helga continued to Main. Mittens followed another block before losing interest and veering off for a different adventure.

When they intersected Main Street, Helga pointed out the Channel 6 TV news van parked by the school with its portable antenna extended. Several of Rausburg's oldest citizens clustered nearby. Even from a distance, Ali saw they were troubled about whatever brought Channel 6 to Rausburg. "Oh, dear. Wonder what that's about?" Helga asked as she headed in that direction. Ali followed reluctantly.

As they approached the drug store, Fern Johnson stepped out, clutching a small paper bag. Ali tensed at the sight of the old biddy, same tight bluish-white curls as always, purse hooked over the elbow, navy blue dress, fake pearls, and black shoes. The last person she wanted to engage in chitchat.

"Fern," Helga shouted. "What's going on?"

Mrs. Johnson swiveled, wearing a sour look on her face. "Mary found Orville Luetz dead this morning. Met his maker in the kitchen."

Helga put her hand over her mouth. "Oh, no. Heart attack?"

"Murdered. Some young hoodlum clubbed him to death."

"Oh, what a horrible way to die."

Fern eyed Ali. Her stylish business suit, more expensive than what the women in Rausburg wore, made her stand out. "Your friend chose a bad day to visit."

"Oh, she's not my friend. Well, I mean she is, but I'm surprised you don't recognize her."

Ali took off her sunglasses. "Hello, Mrs. Johnson. It's me, Ali."

Fern's eyes widened in surprise. "Oh, so it is. Good to see you, Alicia ... after so many years." The strained smile did little to hide Fern's real feelings. "Once a criminal, always a criminal. Leopards can't change their spots," Ali overheard Fern say before she fled Rausburg.

"Fern, you want to walk with us?" Helga asked.

"You go on ahead. I'm going home. Safer there with the killer loose," Fern said as her eyes lingered on Ali far longer than necessary.

"Better lock your doors then," Helga said, taking Ali's hand and hustling away. Once they passed the vacant Gullickson Ford dealership, well out of Fern's hearing range, Helga leaned over and whispered, "Fern sure has changed for the worse as she aged."

Ali lowered her sunglasses and peered over them at her mom. "At least she's subtle."

Helga snorted once.

Approaching the school, Ali recognized Mr. and Mrs. Harmon, Olivia Tengblad, Harold Saunders, Irma Koepke, and Harriet Rowe by the TV truck. "Is it true?" Helga asked. "Was Mr. Luetz murdered?"

"Looks that way," Mr. Harmon said. "We were in the diner when the ambulance came. The news crew told us."

"That's horrible. Never had any murders since I moved here," Helga said.

"Last one took place in the thirties," Olivia said. "Man got knifed over a woman in the Railroad Tap. None of us could recall his name."

"Augustus Noble," Ali said, remembering the name from a high school discussion about how safe Rausburg was.

Mr. Harmon raised his eyebrows. "Hey, you're right." He offered his hand to Ali. "Don't believe I know you." Ali removed her sunglasses. "Oh, you're Helga's girl, aren't you?"

She shook his hand. "Yes. Good to see you again."

Ali let them carry the conversation while Channel 6's Martie Pepper prepared for a live broadcast. As Martie got ready, the group debated if that was her real name or a name she made up for attention. "Who'd name a girl Martie? That's a boy's name."

"Those television people always take new names. They think they're celebrities, I guess."

"She's shorter than I pictured."

"Bet she's not blond, either."

"Paints herself up pretty well, too. Not a girl you'd take home to meet the family."

When Martie finished using the van's mirror to put on her makeup, she reached into a bag and pulled out a brush and brushed her hair out as she faced the cameraman. "Live in five," he told her. The old women's eyes and mouths opened wide as they watched this spectacle of a young unmarried woman chatting with a man while primping. Once they recovered from their shock, they whispered to each other but not soft enough that others couldn't hear.

"Why I never."

"What has this world come to?"

"My parents would have disowned me."

Ali bit her tongue as the old hens continued to find fault with the attractive young reporter while remembering her own amazement at the wide assortment of people when she first settled in San Francisco.

Martie raised her mic and all whispering stopped as she began her live remote. The TV audience learned Orville Luetz was discovered that morning slumped over his kitchen table. The local authorities remained inside the house, gathering evidence. Martie held her hand to her ear for a moment, gazing straight at the camera. "No one is in custody. Authorities are optimistic the evidence gathered will lead to a quick arrest."

Martie held a big smile until the studio director signaled the interview over. "Let's get local reactions," she said to her cameraman. Ali took that as a cue to leave and gently tugged Helga's hand. They slipped away unnoticed and strolled to the grocery store as Martie interviewed her loyal fan club.

The metal siding of Chet's grocery had faded since Ali saw it last. She remembered how kids often stopped there to buy a soda or a snack on their way home from school. Today she wondered how Chet stayed in business with only one car parked in the lot.

While Ali held the door open for Helga, a woman's gossiping voice leaked out. Ali removed her sunglasses as she stepped inside behind her mother. The gossiping ended, creating an embarrassing moment of silence before Opal Olson, Helga's next-door neighbor, said, "Ali, that must be your car I saw parked in your mother's driveway."

Ali took a hand basket and handed another to her mother. "Nice to see you, Mrs. Olson."

"Opal," Helga said and followed Ali down the first aisle.

Mrs. Olson said little more as Chet checked her out while Helga and Ali shopped. As they finished, Ali busied herself at the small magazine display while Helga put the baskets on the counter. Chet made small talk while he totaled and bagged Helga's purchases. "Suppose you heard the awful news."

"Yes. Poor Margaret." Helga shook her head.

"A shame, over in Madison, drying out. Just the other day Orville said she's acting better than she has in years. I hope this doesn't send her back to the bottle."

Helga opened her purse. "She hasn't been much for socializing. I hope her friends don't ignore her."

Chet shook his head. "Time will tell. That's $24.86."

Helga paid in cash, and Chet made change. "You take care now." Chet nodded at them as Helga and Ali each grabbed a bag.

"You forgot something, didn't you, Ali?" Chet called out before they reached the door.

They stopped to look back. He held a glass bowl filled with

Tootsie Pops for the kids. "If I remember right, you liked the orange ones, but take whatever you want."

Ali eyed the bowl before walking back for an orange Tootsie Pop. "Thanks. I haven't had one in years."

Chet flashed a wide smile as she removed the wrapper and put the candy in her mouth. "Good to see you, Ali. Please come back anytime."

She waved over her shoulder as they stepped outside. By the school, concerned citizens gathered around Martie Pepper. Ali noticed one addition. Fern Johnson stood next to Martie while she talked into the camera.

Ali pulled the Tootsie Pop from her mouth. "Guess she feels safe enough now."

―――――

By the time Tommy stepped outside, the news van had left. Several villagers lingered by his squad car, eager to learn the latest. "Looks like someone held a grudge against Orville," Tommy said. "Too early to speculate who did this."

Fern Johnson waved her finger at Tommy. "No need to speculate. I ran into the killer just moments ago."

Tommy cocked his head. "Oh, who is that?"

"Ali Thorein was here. Amazing coincidence, wouldn't you agree?"

A wave of nausea engulfed Tommy. "Anyone else see Ali?" Yes, several. They hadn't recognized her at first. Kept her hair short and darker now. Wore expensive clothes with big sunglasses. Didn't appear remorseful. Tommy's heart sank.

"I'll talk to her, but there's no reason to believe she's involved. No reason at all. Many kids disliked Mr. Luetz, even me at one time, so don't go spreading unfounded rumors." Tommy suspected they would anyway.

He politely urged them to go about their business, and they left him alone by his car. "Wish I'd never seen that darn note. Points right to Ali."

She would never harm another, but Orville did destroy her life and drove her away. Now he knew why the handwriting looked familiar. It reminded him of the note Ali put in his sixteenth birthday card —the note he read at least once a week since she had given it to him.

6

Mary Albright sat idly at her desk, hugging herself, wearing the blank expression signaling tragedy when Tommy entered the school office. Her eyes lifted as he leaned against the counter. "People are calling. Asking if it's true. What do I say?"

"You're doing fine, Mary. Tell them the truth."

"I feel helpless."

"I understand. You can help me go through Mr. Luetz's desk now, if you like."

Tommy hadn't been in the principal's office in years. Little had changed. The furnishings came from the fifties when a new cafeteria and several elementary classrooms were added and Orville became principal. He was tight with a dollar and won the continued support of the old farmers who dominated the school board.

Mary plopped into the hot seat facing the desk while Tommy sat in the principal's chair and checked the drawers. He thumbed through the file drawer first, reading the file tabs. "Did Orville act different lately?"

Mary took her time answering. "Now that you mention it... The other day he asked if I ever did anything I regretted later."

"How did you answer?"

"Haven't we all experienced at least one moment of regret?"

Tommy finished with the file drawer and pulled a pile of papers out of the top drawer to leaf through them. "How did he respond?"

"He said some mistakes weren't easily rectified."

Tommy's brow furrowed. Orville Luetz didn't admit making mistakes. "What else did he say?"

"Nothing. So I went about my business."

"Anything else out of character?"

Mary focused on her hands. "He left school early one afternoon, week before last. Rare for him. I assumed he visited Margaret."

"Most likely." Tommy flipped over several papers on the desktop. "Any angry parents threaten him recently?"

"Not that I know of."

"How about a teacher or student?"

Mary shook her head. "Nope. This school is as lifeless as they come, even worse than when I went here. We pushed back despite him. These kids don't even try. Afraid of being expelled, I guess."

Tommy agreed with Mary's assessment. After Ali's incident in 1976, the older students became reluctant to push back, deciding instead to endure the path of least resistance until they could walk out the door, diploma in hand. Orville Luetz won that battle and squashed all student initiative.

Tommy put the papers back and closed the drawer. Nothing of interest there. "When are the kids going home?"

"The bus drivers arrive at noon. I called several parents in PTA. They're spreading the word."

"Good. I'll question the teachers after the kids leave, then they can go too. Shouldn't take long." Tommy rose.

"Any idea who did it?"

"Not yet. Unless I find an eyewitness or the killer confesses, I'll have to wait for the evidence to be processed. Should be a day or two."

Mary trailed Tommy out of Luetz's office to her desk. "Anything I can do?"

"Keep your eyes and ears open. I can't imagine anyone wanting to kill Mr. Luetz. Many didn't like him, but not enough to beat him to death."

Mary's face grew pale again. Tommy put his arm around her.

"Sorry. I'm trained to handle these kinds of things, but you aren't. If you want to talk later, I'll listen." Mary patted his hand. He made sure she sat firmly in her chair before he left.

While he waited for dismissal, Tommy patrolled the length of School Street, stopping at each of the five houses to interview the occupants. The chilly night air had kept their windows closed. No one heard anything while they slept. He scanned the street for tire tracks, cigarette butts, and other marks or castoffs, but found nothing and ended up dawdling to avoid any student questions as they left school.

After the buses pulled away, he met the staff in the teacher's lounge, exchanging handshakes and receiving shoulder pats as he entered. Most had taught him, and he found their presence comforting despite the odd sensation of standing in their inner sanctum.

He outlined the future of his investigation, aware this information would spread. "I will patrol more often until I apprehend the killer, but I doubt we're in danger." Nods and polite smiles swept the room, prompting Tommy's opening question. "Have there been threats against Mr. Luetz? An unhappy parent or student, for instance?"

A few minor disturbances surfaced, but nothing out of the normal range of activity. Tommy let them talk it out. "Did Mr. Luetz act different lately? Was he worried or concerned?"

The teachers looked at Farmingham, standing next to Tommy. "I'd say more passionate than normal."

"Passionate? About what?"

Farmingham wore a hint of a smile. "I know few would describe Orville as passionate but..." He opened his arms to the teachers. "Remember last week's assembly before the homecoming dance?" Several teachers nodded. "Most of it was the same speech he gave every year since before Tommy was in high school, but at the end—"

Mrs. Schmidt, the high school math teacher, jumped in. "You're right. He really laid into the kids about not drinking. Told them students caught with liquor on school property would be expelled with no recourse. Delivered a short but vivid lecture about the evils of alcohol. Much more than his usual dry reading of the student hand-book rules. He didn't mention Margaret, but even the students know she's at a clinic sobering up. Surprised us all."

This story prompted other teachers to recall how Orville Luetz had surprised them with a few compliments. "He came into the band room and told my kids they sounded good after our first home game."

"When I told him we were performing *Annie* for our spring musical, I expected a warning not to use class time to rehearse the young ones, but he commended me on my choice and said it was good to have the entire school involved this year."

"I was stunned when he gushed over the pumpkin pictures my second graders drew, complimenting the children more than his usual grunt or nod."

Farmingham summed it up. "Not a complete reversal, but he did praise the students' work more."

"That's nice, but it doesn't change all the years Mr. Luetz was cold and gruff to us kids."

"No, in hindsight the change was too little and too late."

"He didn't deserve to die because he was strict, though. Chances are, we all know his killer, and it makes me sick to think—" Tommy put his hand over his mouth and took a moment to compose himself.

"You'll find Orville's killer, Tommy. We'll help any way we can. You will succeed," Mr. Farmingham said as he patted Tommy's shoulder.

"Thanks. If you remember anything, no matter how small, please call me."

Farmingham removed his hand. "Tommy. Uh... Is it true Ali Thorein's back?"

With all eyes focused on him, Tommy scanned the room. "Several have seen her. I'll talk to her later. Till then, please don't repeat unfounded conclusions."

"We won't. It's just... We didn't agree with the way Mr. Luetz handled her situation. Please tell Ali she's welcome at school anytime," Farmingham said.

"I'll do that. When you talk to the kids, make sure to tell them they aren't in danger. It's a good idea to leave your outside lights on, too, until we solve this thing."

After Tommy thanked them, he received encouragement along with handshakes as he left. Outside, he sat in his car and contemplated Luetz's change in attitude and its possible cause. Margaret's troubles? Maybe she made him see what he'd become. Unfortunately, the change came too late to undo a past grievance.

Tommy's next stop was Malkin's insurance agency on Main Street. Sandy Malkin waved through the front window as he approached.

"Suppose you heard the news," Tommy said as he entered.

Sandy's smile faded. "Can't believe it. Why?"

"At this point, I'm guessing. Is Doug around?"

"He's out selling. Can I help?"

"I want to know how much life insurance Orville carried. Margaret's the beneficiary, right?"

Sandy pushed back from the desk. "I'm pretty sure he had a simple term plan." She rummaged through the lateral file. "Orville wasn't over-insured. Several times Doug encouraged him to increase the policy. If you don't kick it up regularly, the insured fall behind the rate of inflation."

"Did he kick it up?"

"Not to my knowledge. If I remember right, we inherited the policy when we moved here."

Sandy pulled a file and sat at her desk to study it. "Margaret will inherit ten thousand dollars."

Tommy hooked his thumbs in his belt and shifted. "Not much."

"Orville has the same policy from the county all teachers have. Margaret will receive ten thousand dollars from that also."

"So she's not a rich widow."

"Not to my knowledge."

"In a way, I'm glad."

Sandy closed the folder. "You don't think Margaret did it, do you?"

"No. I have to check all the possibilities, but spouses are always suspects."

Tommy stepped to the door while Sandy returned the file and pushed the drawer shut. "Have you heard the other news?"

"You mean that Ali Thorein is back?"

"Yes. Already several have speculated she—"

Tommy cut her off as he opened the door to leave. "I doubt it, but I'll talk to her later. Thanks for your help. Tell Doug I said hi."

The Malkins had taken over the agency a few months before Ali left, so they knew her purely through gossip. Sandy was acting as a good citizen by passing along information, but accusing Ali of murder did nothing more than fuel Tommy's rage at Orville Luetz's past injustice.

7

While Tommy drove to Madison, he planned his interview with Margaret Luetz. Because she was already told the worst, she would have questions. How much to reveal? He didn't want to cause her to relapse.

Tommy met first with the rehab center's head counselor, taking a seat in his office while the counselor sat behind his desk. After inquiring about Margaret's progress, he opened his pocket notebook and asked the tough questions. "Could Margaret have sneaked out?"

"I watched the security camera tape after you called this morning. She never left her room."

"Was she angry with Orville? Ever threaten him?"

The counselor played with a paperclip before responding. "Every patient is resentful at first." He opened a desk drawer and tossed the paperclip inside. "Margaret was no exception. Didn't hear of any threats, though. She hasn't left the grounds during her stay."

"How often did Orville visit?"

"Most Saturdays and Sundays. No one reported arguing or fighting. I met him when she committed to our program and twice more when I had weekend duty. Seemed nice enough."

"Uh-huh." Tommy had noticed Orville treated adults better than his students. He never was a warm, friendly guy, but he wasn't the humorless dictator who ran the school either.

"Did he ever visit on a weekday?"

The counselor opened a file on his desk and flipped several sheets over before he answered. "No, nothing marked but Saturdays and Sundays."

"Did she have other visitors?"

He checked the file. "I see one other visitor. You. Apparently, Margaret has no family or children."

"No kids. Sister in Iowa. Decorah, I think."

The counselor noted that. "I'll ask if she wants to contact her sister."

Tommy returned his notebook to his shirt pocket. "I need to interview her and take fingerprints. It'll help speed the investigation."

The counselor tented his hands, bringing them to his chin. "Margaret's made good progress." He studied Tommy for a moment and opened his hands. "Try not to upset her."

"I'll be gentle. Is she able to make funeral arrangements?"

"When will that be?"

"Could be next week. The coroner will perform an autopsy before releasing the body."

The counselor shut Margaret's file. "She hasn't completed our program yet. If she gets drunk at the funeral, it'll ruin weeks of progress."

"I'll take her myself if her sister can't attend. Margaret has no close friends willing to drive that far."

The counselor smiled. "But she has you."

Tommy found Margaret in her room, gazing out the window. "Oh, Tommy," she cried with open arms.

Tommy held her while she sobbed, patting her shoulder until she stopped to dry her tears. When she plopped down on the bed, Tommy took the lone chair. "Margaret, I have a few questions. Are you up for it?"

She pinched the bridge of her nose and nodded.

"You stayed in this room all last night, correct?"

"Yes. The night nurse peeked in around three o'clock." She wiped her eyes. "We didn't have the warmest relationship, but I would never kill him."

Tommy laid his hand on hers. "The spouse is always a suspect in any murder investigation. You're not capable of consciously hurting another. I know I said your drinking might kill an innocent bystander when I threatened you with jail, but you're sober now."

"One day at a time."

Tommy remained silent to encourage Margaret to speak freely. "I want to return home sober. Few people in Rausburg remember me before my drinking got out of control."

She became quiet. After a long moment, Tommy pushed ahead. "How did Orville act on his visits? Was he different in any way?"

Margaret pulled a tissue off the nightstand to wipe her eyes before blowing her nose. "We talked about the future. He wanted to set things right."

"Did he say specifically what things he wanted to set right?"

She shook her head. "Just said he was wrong."

"About what?"

"Didn't say. He was a jackass to you kids, no need to hide it."

Tommy's head lowered. Margaret was right, but he saw no need to badmouth her dead husband. "Mr. Luetz ran a tight school."

Margaret smiled. "You're too forgiving. Orville treated all of you with little compassion, especially that poor Thorein girl. I told him not to prosecute her, but he wouldn't listen."

Tommy learned over the years that many had advised Orville to back off Ali, but he hadn't. As much as Tommy mourned the loss, Orville Luetz was often pigheaded. "Margaret, I need your finger-prints. I collected samples from the house. Yours will be all over the kitchen. It would help my investigation if you cooperate. I have no reason to suspect you."

Margaret sniffed. "Sure, Tommy. I'll help out."

Despite his relief at Margaret's solid alibi, her continued drunken-ness and occasional blackouts would have eased suspicion about Ali. By helping Margaret, he hurt the woman he loved.

8

After watching the noon news, Helga switched the TV off and both women finished their lunch without speaking. The silence continued as Ali helped her mother wash and dry the dishes. She sniffed once, prompting Helga to ask, "What's the matter honey? Something I said?"

"Nothing you said."

"Then why the sniffles?"

Ali leaned against the counter. "I feel cheated."

"In what way?"

Ali rubbed her forehead. "For years, I dreamed of waving my success in Mr. Luetz's face and showing him that I earn more in one year than he could in several. It's petty, but I wanted to. And the old coot dies before I have the chance, like Dad."

Helga handed Ali a plate and began scrubbing another one. "You have every right to those feelings, dear. Luetz was a vindictive man." She dreaded raising the one issue they had avoided so far. "Your father said the same thing. 'Someday Ali will show that old goat. He'll whistle a different tune after she has her say.'"

Ali laughed once, wiping her eye. "I can hear Dad saying that. I wish he could have shared my success, too."

Helga's head sank as the topic came out in the open. "I told him about your promotion to assistant manager and each time you finished another semester. He pretended not to be interested, but he was."

"He had a funny way of showing it. Pretended I no longer existed."

"He needed time to heal. Like you."

Helga rinsed the plate and gave it to Ali. "He figured you would pull yourself together, come home, and we'd go back to normal. Consoling wasn't his strong suit, even with me."

"I know, but he didn't understand. After my release, I needed him more than ever and he froze me out."

"Max thought he was doing the right thing, being tough."

Ali didn't respond.

"When he died, I agonized over what to do."

"I would have helped with his funeral." Ali jammed the plate in the cupboard.

Helga pulled the drain plug, letting the water swirl away. Three years of rehearsing the upcoming conversation didn't make it any easier to begin. She rinsed the sink while bracing for possible rejection. "You were right earlier. People here can be petty, with long memories. After you left, we cloistered at home to avoid the insincere smiles and judgmental stares. I didn't want that for you. Not while you were grieving over losing your father."

"I didn't want to hurt either of you, but Dad was so stubborn."

Helga wanted to tell Ali about the heated arguments she and her husband had whenever she suggested visiting Ali in San Francisco and mending fences. Max was stubborn to a fault. For most of Ali's childhood that presented no problem, but Ali made a terrible mistake that was made worse by their belief she would receive a fair, just punishment. After the justice system failed Ali, it became more a matter of pride. People look at you differently with a child in jail. Max didn't handle it well.

"I expected you to be upset with me for not writing until after the funeral. With a few weeks of college left, it reminded me of high school. Valedictorian expelled..." Tears streaked Helga's cheek.

Ali turned away. "I had saved enough to buy a plane ticket and planned on celebrating my diploma here at home. Your letter was devastating. I thought you were ashamed to have me around."

"Oh, no. Not at all. I wanted you back since the day you left."

"Didn't feel that way. Anyway, I buried myself in school and work. Corporate recruited me after graduation, and my job became my life. If Dad had lived a few months longer to see my success..."

Helga cuddled Ali the same way she did countless times when Ali was a child. "He expected you to prove him wrong. Maybe he sensed time was short. Near the end, he mentioned it several times. I didn't notice till later."

"Lost opportunities." Ali hugged Helga. "At least we have each other."

9

Tommy sat in his car, which was parked behind the Mineral Ridge Sheriff's Department, contemplating the situation. Margaret, normally the prime suspect, had an airtight alibi with little incentive to hire a killer. Ali remained the single workable suspect because others had already connected her to the murder. If anyone saw that note.... After a moment's hesitation, he stuffed the bagged note and the first roll of film under the seat.

Tommy took the other evidence bags with the second roll of film inside to Pat Leahy, the county's forensics expert. Leahy's immaculate lab sat in the back, away from the main offices. After Tommy entered the building unseen, Pat warmly greeted him, although they had met briefly once before. "Been expecting you. Sorry about the murder. How are you doing?"

Tommy intended to keep his visit as short as possible. "As well as expected. I've got evidence for you."

Leahy motioned to an empty table, Tommy laid the evidence bags on it while Leahy slipped his glasses on. "Anyone you want me to check out?" Pat asked.

"No one in particular. The widow's prints are there. She didn't do it, but you'll find her prints on the doorknobs and other places. I'm hoping the baseball bat will reveal the murderer. Start there if you're pressed for time."

Leahy lowered his head and peered at Tommy over his glasses, eyebrows raised.

"Sorry. It's my first murder investigation."

Leahy grinned. "No offense taken. I'll examine your evidence in the morning. I have tomorrow's court cases to prepare for. If that's not finished, Judge Lynch... Well, it better be done, and don't even consider working overtime."

Lynch's reputation for reprimanding deputies in open court was commonly known. "I've never testified before him. Rumor is it's not fun."

Leahy glanced at the door before lowering his voice. "Keep that to yourself, Peterson. Lynch doesn't take criticism well."

"I'm sure you'll get to my evidence as soon as you can."

"Having the spouse's prints will speed things along. By tomorrow night, we'll know what's on the bat."

"Baby Face," Sheriff Chuck Sinclair called out as Tommy tried to slip out the back door unnoticed. Tommy hated the nickname, and he didn't like Sinclair either. "I hear you had some excitement in Rausburg this morning."

Tommy faced him. Sinclair sat alone in the break area holding a soda. "Yeah, our school principal was killed by several blows to the head. Gruesome crime scene."

Sinclair frowned. "I've found a few grisly ones, too. Never leaves a guy." He opened the can and worked the pop top until it snapped off, and threw it in the trash. "A shrink's available if you need it."

"I'll see how it goes. I've seen murder victims before, but none I knew."

Chuck sipped. "Any suspects?"

"Not yet. I dropped off the evidence, hoping Pat can identify the killer's fingerprints. The widow has an ironclad alibi. She's in a rehab clinic in Madison, monitored with security cameras."

"Could have an accomplice."

"Frankly, I doubt it. She's under surveillance. No visitors. Won't profit by his death. Financially, she's worse off now."

"You find incriminating evidence at the crime scene?"

Tommy shifted. "Prints on the bat will lock it up, otherwise..."

Sinclair's eyes widened. "You found nothing else that would nail the killer?"

Tommy braced for potential ridicule. "No."

Sinclair gulped his soda. "Your first homicide, isn't it?"

"In Rausburg, yes."

Sinclair crumpled the empty soda can. "I could swing by and check it myself. I've been doing this longer than you have."

Tommy momentarily considered the offer. Sinclair's sympathetic tone was unexpected, but Tommy was wary. "Thanks. You have plenty to do here, I'm sure. Leahy will find stray prints. I've got people to question. If I get stuck, I'll call."

Sinclair rose and tossed the can in the trash. "Well, you know where to find me. Remember, we all work together keeping Kickapoo County safe."

Tommy thanked him, relieved Sinclair hadn't bullied his way into the investigation. On his way to the car, Tommy pictured Lynch chastising him on the witness stand after Sinclair testified Tommy held back a vital piece of evidence. *Find the killer. Everything works out if you find the killer.*

10

A few minutes past seven, Ali and Helga jumped at the sound of heavy footsteps on the front porch followed by a sharp knock. Helga switched off *TV Bloopers and Practical Jokes* before answering the door. "Why, Tommy, what a surprise. You've had a busy day, haven't you?"

Busy didn't begin to describe it. Tommy's answering machine was full by midafternoon. More people had stopped by his office that day than in a typical month. Others called whenever the phone sat idle. Even as he cooked hamburgers at home for supper, he continued taking calls.

"Yes, ma'am. I stopped by to welcome Ali home."

Helga stepped back. "Come in. I'm sure she'd enjoy seeing someone her own age."

Tommy stepped inside, shutting the front door. "Hi, Ali."

Ali sat on the couch, eyes widening as she smiled. "Tommy Peterson?"

He smiled. "Guilty."

She stood, laughing. "You've grown. What's with the costume? Practicing for Halloween?"

"Oh, I took over after Chief Hancock retired."

Ali offered her hand and he grasped it. "Good to see you. How's your mom?"

"She died about three years ago."

Ali's smile sagged. "I'm sorry. Bernice was always kind and considerate."

"Thanks. Sorry about your dad."

"Thanks."

"Max was a good man."

A pregnant pause underlined the momentary awkwardness. "Well, you have certainly grown. And you've become talkative, too. What gives?"

Tommy looked down. "Late bloomer, I guess. I'm not as shy anymore."

Ali studied him for a moment. "So what lucky lady snared you? Karen Johnson was sweet on you if I remember right."

"I'm single. Karen married a man from Copper Point. Has two kids now."

Ali nodded.

Tommy shifted. After years spent imagining a warm reunion with Ali, she wasn't responding as he had planned.

"Whatever you say can and will be used against you in a court of law."

Ali's eyes flared as her jaw dropped in surprise. "You're arresting me?"

Tommy raised his hands. "No, no. You don't have to say anything, but if you tell me where you spent last night, I can remove you from the list of suspects."

"Suspects?" Ali's voice rose.

He dropped his hands. "You've heard Orville Luetz was murdered, right?"

"Yes, but I never imagined I was a suspect."

"There are others," Tommy lied. "If I don't question you tonight, I'll get badgered about it tomorrow."

Ali crossed her arms. "I see attitudes about me haven't changed."

"I'm sure you're the same good person you always were." He smiled, hoping to ease the tension between them.

Didn't work. Ali kept her arms crossed. "Yet here you are."

Tommy was silent for a moment. This wasn't the direction he'd planned the conversation going. "Sorry. Arriving the same day as Mr. Luetz's murder... It's suspicious. I'd like to spread your confirmed alibi and stop any rumors."

Ali threw her hands up. "Fine. I have nothing to hide."

"Coffee?" Helga asked while motioning to the kitchen.

"Thanks, Mrs. Thorein. Coffee would be great."

Ali and Tommy faced each other, sitting at the table while Helga brewed coffee. Ali wrinkled her brow. "You think I'm capable of murder?"

Tommy wasn't sure if she was teasing or dead serious. He'd forgotten she could be like that. Helga rescued him. "Now, Ali, he's only being thorough. Tommy has done a great job taking over for Mr. Hancock. It's been a long time since we've had any serious crimes or accidents. Tommy relates well to the kids, too. Keeps them out of trouble."

"Too bad he wasn't our cop eight years ago," Ali said.

Tommy longed to tell Ali that he would have saved her, but those words sounded ridiculous considering where his interest in her lie tonight.

While Helga made coffee, Tommy wrote Ali's address and phone number in his pocket notebook. She told him that her visit was a complete surprise to Helga. "I heard knocking and expected the mailman, but there she stood," Helga added.

Tommy asked several more softball questions about her job, stalling before he asked the big one. "Where were you last night between midnight and eight a.m.?"

"At the Motor Lodge in Black River Falls, the one facing the interstate."

"What time did you arrive there?"

"A few minutes before ten."

Tommy wrote in his notebook. "When did you leave this morning?"

"Six."

"You have a receipt?"

"Yes."

Tommy waited a moment, hoping Ali would offer to show it to him. When she didn't, he asked, "May I see it?"

Ali went to her purse and returned with the receipt. "Their dial-up scanner wasn't working, so I paid in cash and requested a receipt for reimbursement."

Tommy studied it. The handwriting on the receipt matched the note. "The clerk wrote this?"

"The signature's his. I wrote the rest out myself."

"This is Robel's stationery, right?"

"Yes. I carry a pad in my briefcase."

Tommy read it again. At least the paper didn't match the note. "Who saw you leave this morning?"

"No one, to my knowledge. I left the key in the room and bypassed the office."

He handed the receipt back. "How long was the drive here?"

"Two and a half hours."

Helga poured coffee in Tommy's cup and sat at the table. "Ali got here a little after 8:30."

Tommy stirred sugar in his coffee. "Stop for breakfast this morning?"

"No. I didn't eat until after I arrived."

Tommy took a slow sip. "So you stayed at the Motor Lodge in Black River Falls last night, wrote your own receipt at check-in, didn't have contact with anyone this morning, and drove straight here."

"Correct."

Tommy took another sip. "That's a lousy alibi."

"What? You're convinced I killed that bastard?"

Tommy set his cup down. "No."

"I'm sure I wasn't the only one who despised Mr. Luetz."

"No, but you have a strong motive and you're here."

Ali exploded. "You think I've spent the last eight years in San Francisco plotting my revenge? I have better things to do than waste a minute of my time on that old fart or anyone else in stinking Rausburg."

"Ali, I'm sorry, I—"

"Save it, Tommy. I'm leaving." She stood and leaned over to put her hand on Helga's. "Mom, I'm sorry. We'll get together soon, I promise. I'll fly you to San Francisco where people don't accuse you of murder right off the bat."

Tommy straightened. "You need to stay through tomorrow at least."

Ali glared at him. "Fat chance, Tommy. Find another scapegoat."

"I can't let you leave."

"You can't detain me without evidence. I have rights."

Tommy knew she was correct, but she didn't know Sinclair's deputies had been hovering around the area all afternoon when they normally patrolled other areas in the county. If Fern Johnson or one of her friends saw the prime suspect leaving, Ali could end up in Mineral Ridge Jail. "I have evidence against you."

"Impossible."

"I found evidence in Luetz's house, but I held it back because it implicates you."

"How could evidence implicate me when I haven't seen or spoken to the man in eight years?"

Tommy raised his hands in self-defense. "I'll tell you what I know if you promise to keep it secret."

"You sure I can be trusted?"

Tommy dropped his hands to the table. "Yes. You wouldn't show up after eight years to kill Luetz. You're not that dumb."

"Not that dumb? Gee,thanks for giving me some credit."

"You could be in serious trouble if you're seen running away. A call to the sheriff's office could send you to Mineral Ridge Jail."

Ali leaned closer to Tommy. "You'd do that to me? After all the help I gave you in school?"

"Not me. Sinclair can investigate the murder whenever he wants. I told him I could handle it, but if he hears the prime suspect is running, he'll take over and I can't stop him."

"You told Sinclair I was the prime suspect?"

"No, but others might."

Ali glared at Tommy. After a long moment, she asked, "What is this incriminating evidence?"

Tommy lowered his head. "I found a note."

Eight years ago you lied,
I didn't forget, now you die.
Burn in hell.

Ali's eyes widened as she sat back. Apparently, she understood why he had connected her to the note. Her tone softened but remained frosty. "I didn't write that note. The last time I had contact with Luetz was at the Ranch House the night before I left."

Tommy relaxed. "What else happened eight years ago that might lead to Luetz's murder? My memories of 1976 keep coming back to you."

Ali's eyes narrowed. "But you're not arresting me."

"No. Once we pull fingerprints off the murder weapon, I'll check them against yours and you'll be off the hook. Until then, stay put. Please don't force me to detain you."

"You'd throw me in jail?"

"Half the village is scared to death, afraid they're next. You're a suspect in a murder investigation, and we have two empty jail cells. Better than going to Mineral Ridge."

"So I'm stuck here."

"As soon as I establish your alibi, you can leave."

Ali glanced at Helga. "I planned on spending a few days with Mom, so I guess it's no big deal. Okay, I'll stay." She pointed her finger at Tommy. "But only because we were friends. Otherwise, I'd call a wise-ass big city lawyer right now to take this village apart."

Tommy frowned.

Ali dropped her hand. "Sorry if I'm abrupt. You must expect push-back in your line of work."

"Mostly from people who hire wise-ass big city lawyers."

She forced a grin. "Okay, I deserve that. Anything else you want to ask me?"

Tommy wanted to ask her out to dinner, but after their confrontation, the timing might not be right. "No. It's been a long day." He rose from the table.

Ali led Tommy to the front door. "I'm glad you blossomed, but I don't like cops."

Tommy stepped outside. "I know. Don't leave. We'll talk once I know more."

"Good night, Tommy." Ali closed the door and cut off any further conversation.

After he left, Ali flopped in the straight-backed chair by the door. All vestiges of the confident young executive fell away as she raised her eyes to Helga. "Haven't I suffered enough for my mistake? Even little Tommy Peterson assumes I killed Mr. Luetz."

Helga knelt and patted Ali's hand. "I believe in you, and so does Tommy. He's being cautious, that's all. Saving you the embarrassment of dealing with that awful Sheriff Sinclair."

Ali tensed at the mention of Sinclair. He had visited her daily during her incarceration, always suggesting ways she could shorten her sentence and make her stay more pleasant. She rebuffed him but he kept the pressure on until shortly before her release. Tonight she leaned into Helga, nestling with her for a long moment before marching to the kitchen to take control of her life.

11

Ali opened her planner on the kitchen counter and stood by the wall phone. The chilly night air from the open window had cooled the oven's heat earlier, but now the cool air kept her alert.

Ali worked with Robel's San Francisco law firm often enough to have a good relationship with Charles Latimer, a senior partner. When she called his private office number, he answered on the third ring. They exchanged quick pleasantries before Ali mentioned she was calling from her mother's house in Wisconsin with a legal problem. "This isn't a company issue, it's personal. I need legal advice from an experienced lawyer. Can you help me?"

Charles was the only lawyer she knew, but he didn't handle small cases. As Ali twiddled the phone cord, relief came when he asked, "What's the problem?"

She told him that after the meeting in Minneapolis, she drove home and learned the school principal had been murdered early that morning. Her anger rose as she recounted Tommy's questioning her alibi.

Charles cut in. "I don't understand. Why ask for an alibi?"

Ali closed her eyes and steeled herself. She would have to confide the secret she had kept for over eight years, her reason for leaving

Wisconsin. "I called in a phony bomb threat as our senior prank. We all meant it as a joke, but my principal expelled me and had me prosecuted. I served four months in jail and missed college in the fall. After my release I fled to San Francisco and got a job at Robel's. You know the rest."

Ali heard Charles draw a sharp breath. "I see."

There it was. The silence preceding the same condescending tone people used after her incarceration, reminding her of her father's words of judgment and disapproval.

Her tone became more forceful as her anger rose. "He ruined my life here, and I hated him for it. The whole village wants me arrested for murder."

"Maybe you're overreacting."

Ali's voice rose. "I'm the prime suspect. I'm not overreacting."

Charles sounded cold. "Alicia, your anger gives people more reason to suspect you."

"For Christ's sake, our cop found a note at the scene that might as well be a signed confession!"

"Simmer down and listen!"

Charles had never raised his voice in her presence, even for an instant. His outburst shocked her. "Sorry."

"That's better. Alicia, I'm not familiar with Wisconsin statutes. You need a lawyer there. How far from Madison are you?"

"Forty-five minutes."

"Good. I attended law school with a colleague from Madison. If memory serves, he joined his family firm. I'll find him and get a recommendation for you."

"I'd appreciate it."

"Frankly, you don't need an attorney yet, and you may never need one. The local cop has doubts, otherwise you would be calling from jail."

"But the sheriff's department is examining the evidence and threatening to take over the investigation. What if they find more evidence implicating me?"

"Did you visit the crime scene?"

"I've never been in that house."

"And you haven't been in Wisconsin since..."

"1976."

"Then you have no reason for concern. You didn't write the incriminating note. Your alibi will check out. The sheriff's department won't find your fingerprints so they can't charge you. If you push back now, you might force your own arrest, which would force them to pin the murder on you to save face."

Not the answer Ali wanted to hear. "What if they arrest me anyway?"

Ali tapped her fingers on the phone receiver while she waited for Charles to answer. "Sit tight for now. I'll find my friend Justin, in Madison, and call you back in the morning. In the meantime, let people see these accusations don't affect you in the slightest. As soon as the forensics report comes back, you'll be off the hook."

"Darn. I was hoping I could sue the village and end up owning it."

"Now that's the Alicia you need to show them. You have nothing to fear. You're innocent, remember?"

Ali thanked him and ended the call. She shivered, but not from the brisk night air seeping through the open window. She had a much stronger motive for murdering Luetz than anyone suspected. If Tommy didn't solve the crime soon, she might be in even more trouble.

———

Tommy cursed himself during the short drive to his office. "Idiot. You wait eight years to show her you've changed and what do you do? Panic and recite Miranda rights. What is wrong with you?" He thumped the steering wheel. "Do you always want to be alone?"

Back in his office, he fell into his chair exhausted after a rough day spent investigating Rausburg's first murder in fifty years. He faced away from the glass front door and rested his head in his hands, allowing himself to grieve over Orville Luetz's murder and express his frustration for the lost opportunity with Ali.

Tommy did an extra patrol at ten thirty. Harv Middleton, village president and owner of the hardware store, flagged Tommy down as he walked his dog, Buddy, around the block. Tommy pulled over and leaned out his window.

"What's the latest?" Harv asked.

"Nothing new since this afternoon."

"Too bad. I was hoping you found the killer."

"Not yet. Tomorrow maybe."

Harv bent over by Tommy's window and lowered his voice. "You speak to Ali?"

"Yep. I'll check her alibi tomorrow. She spent last night in Black River Falls."

"Good. Personally, I can't see her killing Luetz, but some will disagree."

"They're wrong."

Harv straightened. "Any problems with Sinclair? I heard his deputies are camping out close by."

"Haven't spoken to him since early afternoon. I wouldn't be surprised if he swoops in and takes the case over tomorrow. Solving this murder will help him come election time."

Harv glanced around, making sure they were alone. "I don't care for that guy. It's better if you find the killer.

"I agree, but I have nothing so far."

"I don't mean to sound callous, but this could help justify a raise for you in next year's budget."

"I've got bigger things to focus on right now."

"I know. You're doing all you can. I'll sleep soundly tonight knowing you're out here."

"Didn't keep Orville Luetz safe."

Harv patted Tommy's arm, now hanging out the window. "Can't be everywhere all the time. Orville ticked off a lot of kids over the years. One of them must have snapped. Maybe lost a job or got a divorce and blamed it on Orville."

"But who?"

Harv shrugged. "I couldn't tell you." He cupped his hands and yelled, "Buddy, get back here." He chuckled. "Darn dog. Off chasing Mrs. Anderson's cat. I need to talk to her about keeping Mittens in after dark. Stupid cat riles everybody's dog in the middle of the night. Buddy! Get over here now!"

Harv laughed once. "Not too bright upstairs, but he always puts a smile on my face."

"Need help getting him back?"

"Nah, here he comes. Call me as soon as you crack the case."

"Can do."

Harv stepped back, allowing Tommy to pull away and continue his patrol.

By ten fifty-five Tommy sat at his kitchen table nursing a beer and thinking about Ali. Outwardly, she had changed little. Maybe five pounds heavier. Shorter, darker hair. The eyes, that's what he remembered most. Determined, inquiring eyes, eager to learn the world's secrets. She had been a school leader since her freshman year, at least for the younger grades. She badgered Luetz until he approved the Milwaukee Zoo field trip for the entire school. Later she organized an all-school fund-raiser for the baby seals, over Luetz's objections, and promoted many little projects no one else would have accomplished on their own.

When they were in school, Ali forced Tommy to talk to her every day, and he knew that wasn't easy. After Pa died, Tommy retreated inward, entering his own private world. His teachers helped, but Ali sought him out daily and encouraged him to talk. Ironically, her arrest at school became the tipping point that forced Tommy out of his shell. Standing by powerless to help the person he loved, second to his mother, made something inside him snap. Too bad Ali hadn't seen it.

He drifted back to analyze the case. Ali was the prime suspect, and motive was the main reason. Even though many disliked Luetz, she remained the leading candidate for a revenge killing. Her temper hadn't lessened. In school, Ali quickly forgave, but not after her release from jail, and who could blame her? After her arrest, everyone acted like she didn't exist until the news broke of her incarceration. People were shocked, but no one rushed to her defense. Ali must have felt abandoned. Even her own father stopped speaking to her.

She might have written the note to stick it to us. She wouldn't want to be caught. The crude rhyme, her attempt at throwing us off the track. Luetz was murdered like the baby seal poster, the one with the seal looking up at her killer before he clubbed her to death. But how did she drag Luetz to the table? Ali's not strong enough. He took another swig.

Maybe she hired a hit man to take care of Orville. That's ridiculous. No, she moved on. Made a new life in San Francisco. Ali hiring a hit man? Been watching too many cop shows.

Tommy drained the last of his beer and studied the can before crumpling it and slamming it into the wastebasket. *Why did she have to return today of all days? Years of waiting to show her what I've become. Now she hates me before I even ask her on a date.*

He passed by his mother's empty room. Bernice never went to bed until he came home, even at the end. He peeked in and imagined her lying there that last morning, peaceful, all worldly concerns lifted. "Guess you were right, Ma. I've wasted several years waiting on a relationship that will never happen."

He stripped off his uniform and laid it on the chair in case he needed to dress in a hurry. Checked his pager before placing it on the nightstand. Set his alarm. Climbed under the covers. Tommy no longer recited the child's prayer, "Now I lay me down to sleep..." for his mother's benefit. Tonight he had a simple request. *God, please don't let me find out Ali did it.*

12

Tuesday, October 16, 1984

Ali descended the stairs and stepped into the kitchen in more of a stupor than she wanted to admit. "Morning," she muttered.

Helga stood at the kitchen counter making breakfast. "Didn't mean to wake you."

Ali rubbed her eyes. "You didn't. I woke up on my own."

Helga twisted half around, holding a cereal box, to see Ali for the first time that morning.

"Like your robe."

Ali opened her eyes. Helga wore a robe identical to Ali's. "Oh. You buy yours at Robel's too?"

"Yep. Last summer. They had a sale on."

"Me too. Is taste in robes passed down genetically from mother to daughter?"

Helga laughed once. "More likely the taste for thrift. I can't see wasting money on a robe no one's ever going to see."

"Those were my thoughts too."

"Corn flakes?" Helga asked as Ali shuffled to the kitchen table.

"Please."

Helga wiped her nose with a crumpled tissue and threw it in the wastebasket while Ali filled her cereal bowl. "Sleep well?"

Ali ran her hands through her hair. "No. Bad memories kept surfacing all night."

Helga set two cups on the table, poured coffee and slid the sugar bowl closer to Ali. The sound of her padding feet emphasized the silence as she brought cereal bowls and milk to the table.

Ali ignored the sugar and milk and took a first sip. "How about you? You sleep well?"

Helga stirred a teaspoonful of sugar in her cup. "No."

"Can't be easy having a suspected killer in the house."

Helga rested her hand on Ali's. "We'll get through this."

Ali placed her other hand on top of Helga's and squeezed it once before releasing. "Yes. We will."

Helga poured her cereal and milk while Ali ate. Any joy they shared from mending fences yesterday was muted by the cloud of suspicion Tommy dumped on them last night. Ali was almost finished with her cereal before she broke the silence.

"Why did Luetz have to die now? It's as if he waited to maximize my suffering."

Helga swallowed. "Coincidence. He wronged another student but kept it quiet. There's your killer getting even."

Ali sipped her coffee before scooping the last corn flakes from her bowl. "Waving my paycheck in his face would have brought sweet revenge. I've already achieved more than he could ever dream of doing."

Helga frowned. "We didn't raise you to gloat."

"Just a delightful fantasy. I had planned to avoid him and everyone else. Val, my therapist says—"

Helga dropped her spoon in the bowl. The clank made Ali jump. "Oh, my God. You're in therapy?"

Ali grinned. People in Rausburg were stoic, wouldn't ever consider seeing a therapist. "It's not a requirement, Mom. Many people in California choose therapy. Val is in her late thirties. I talk to her without judgment, that's all."

"Is it helping?"

"I'm here, aren't I?"

Helga sipped her coffee. "I didn't realize you had so many problems."

"I don't. It's just... After I joined corporate, I imagined my life blossoming because I'd redeemed myself by finishing college despite the odds."

"You don't need to redeem yourself. I love you for who you are."

Ali rested her hand on Helga's. "Thanks, but the redemption is for me. I need to know in my heart I've made up for all the pain I brought by being so naïve. That's what compels me to work constantly."

"Can't you just stop working so hard? Take a day off once in a while?"

"I'm obsessed with my job. I work long hours, seven days a week, because I'm afraid my best is never good enough. It's helped earn raises and a promotion, but I have no personal life."

"If this Val convinced you to come home, it's a good thing," Helga said, taking another spoonful of cereal. "Maybe I should talk to a therapist. I sit here alone knitting much of the time. Even stopped attending Mass for a while. I have nightmares, too."

Without a doubt, Ali caused her mother's nightmares, but nothing could take that back now. "All I can say is therapy helps me, and Robel's insurance pays for it. Maybe your insurance does, too. We'll find a respected therapist in Madison. No one here ever needs to know."

Ali reached for the morning paper, ending the conversation.

Reagan and Mondale were in the headlines, and Orville Luetz blankly stared from his driver's license picture at the bottom of the front page.

Principal Bludgeoned to Death. Ali tensed as she read the opening paragraphs and flipped to page ten to continue. The paper failed to mention the note, but her relief was short-lived. Tucked in the last paragraph she read, *While police have not identified any suspects, sources close to the victim believe the killer to be a former student who threatened the principal.*

Attempts at conversation fizzled as Ali answered Helga with
grunts or shrugs. Helga pulled the paper down to lock eyes with Ali.

"We used to talk," she said in a testy tone.

"Sorry, Mom. I was preoccupied."

"You used to share with me. What's on your mind?"

Ali laid the paper on the table. "Last night Tommy told us the
killer's note read 'Eight years ago you lied.' So the killer accused
Luetz of lying back in '76, right?"

"Right."

"What did he lie about? He threatened to prosecute me to the full
extent of the law, and he did."

Helga stared into her cup while swirling the last bit of coffee. "He
said awful things at the trial, labeling you a troublemaker bound and
determined to cause mischief."

Ali remembered her shock when Luetz took the stand, ridiculed
her school accomplishments and twisted them to paint her as a
teenager with no respect for authority. "But he didn't lie. I did all
those things, lacking the malicious intent he emphasized."

Helga gasped. "You took the money?"

Ali's eyebrows furrowed. "What money?"

"Don't you remember? Luetz testified money was missing from
your class treasury. He suspected you took it or covered for a classmate who did."

Repressed memories of the trial stirred in Ali's mind. Panic had
set in when Judge Lynch denied her attorney the opportunity to
address Luetz's allegations before sentencing and the truth became
lost in the shuffle.

"I didn't take any money. He reversed the story. When it came
time to close the account, Ellen discovered the bank statement
differed from our records. As treasurer, she always filled out the
deposit slips. We double-checked every transaction together. Our
books balanced, but Luetz insisted we were wrong. Almost eighty
dollars was unaccounted for."

"What did your classmates say about it?"

Ali folded the paper and set it on the table. "They didn't care. We had two hundred dollars left over to spend on a gift to the school. More than enough to buy a bench or a small trophy case."

"Your class worked hard to earn that money. You raised more than most. We parents were all proud."

Ali turned away. A few weeks later her parents were anything but proud.

Helga cocked her head. "Who else knew about the discrepancy?"

"Mr. Luetz. Ellen had a dentist appointment, so I went in alone and informed him eighty dollars was missing. I had the receipts. They proved the money disappeared after it left our hands. That's when he lied and said he caught a student in his office taking the money."

"And you doubted him?"

Ali crossed her arms. "He claimed Tommy stole it."

Helga's eyes opened wide. "Tommy?"

"Luetz said small amounts of money had been disappearing for years. He had suspected him since junior high."

"Impossible. Tommy would never steal. Never."

"That's what I thought. I never accused Luetz of lying because I had no proof. After I was expelled, no one would have believed me anyway."

Helga wrinkled her brow. "Ellen knew about the missing money."

Ali caught Helga's inference. "Mom, it wasn't Ellen. I always counted it before I handed it over. The money was all there. She may have been an unfaithful friend, but she wasn't a thief."

"Then how does the killer know you were lied to? Luetz wouldn't have told anyone, would he?"

"Doubtful. If he had told a teacher or Mr. Hancock, they would have questioned me. No one ever did." Ali reconsidered the theft. "What if Tommy stole the money?"

"He didn't."

"Suppose, for the sake of argument."

Helga folded her arms. "Okay, but you're wrong."

Ali recognized Helga's mom-knows-best face. Apparently, her

own mother believed Ali capable of stealing, but not Tommy. No one said reconciliation was easy.

Ali closed her eyes before continuing. "It stands to reason Tommy wouldn't single out our class, so he would have stolen from other classes as well."

"But he didn't."

"No, he didn't, but the money disappeared and another student might have questioned Luetz about it."

"And Luetz fed them the same story." Helga stared in her cup. "That person could say Luetz lied."

"So could the thief. Two possibilities for the killer." Ali finished her coffee.

"And if the killer had a copy of your handwriting, he might have forged that note."

"I'd be in San Francisco with an alibi, Tommy wouldn't solve the case, and the killer would never be caught."

"But why kill Mr. Luetz now after all these years?"

Ali rose and took her cup and bowl to the sink. "Beats me."

Helga finished her coffee. "Suppose Mr. Luetz threatened to send the thief to jail like you and held it over his head all this time."

While she considered this, Ali took Helga's cup and bowl to the sink, washed them and set them in the dish rack to air dry.

"Who stands to lose the most now if petty thefts committed as a teenager came to light?"

"I suppose a person in a position of trust or authority." Helga put her hand to her mouth. "Tommy."

"One possibility," Ali took her seat at the table. "Anyone who's pushed far enough will snap. The question is, did Luetz push him too far?"

Helga's eyes grew moist. "No."

Ali didn't want to make her mother cry, so she added, "Could be someone who handles money, like a bank employee. If their stealing was discovered, it would constitute grounds for dismissal."

"I would hope."

"Anyone my age work at the bank?"

Rausburg's bank employed two tellers. Only one was the right age. "Melanie Schmid. She's Melanie Wharton now, with the cutest little girl."

Ali stared at the wall, remembering Melanie. "Graduated when I was a sophomore. Class treasurer, too."

"You're not accusing Melanie, are you? After all, she was away at college when you confronted Mr. Luetz."

"No. She couldn't steal, let alone commit murder." Ali grabbed the cereal box. "We used to be friends. Maybe she can confirm our theory. If money continually disappeared at school, she might know about it. If it stopped when Tommy graduated, maybe Mr. Luetz wasn't lying." Ali stood. "I'm running my own investigation. Let's go banking."

13
___

Tommy's two a.m. patrol achieved little except disturb his sleep pattern. Porch lights were on, and Rausburg was quiet.

At five a.m. Tommy rolled out of bed for his first Tuesday patrol. Groggy, he drove to Main, stopped at the intersection and looked in both directions. The flash of brake lights caught his attention as a dark sedan vanished around the curve by the river. He sped south, slowing through the early morning river fog. When he emerged, the car had vanished, and he pulled over to wait. Seconds later, taillights appeared a mile ahead on a visible stretch of the highway. Tommy began a silent, measured count. When he reached ten, the lights vanished behind trees. "Whoever it is, they're not speeding," he said before turning his car around.

As he drove past the Thorein house first, his entire body tensed. Ali's white Tempo sat in the driveway blocking Helga's Fairmont in the garage. "Whew." Tommy aimed his spotlight at the ground. No tire tracks in the heavy dew. "Good." He continued cruising the streets. Finding no suspicious activity, he parked by the diner a few minutes after six.

The inviting aroma of bacon and eggs greeted Tommy as he

stepped inside. Several heads swung his way, silently nodding support, maybe even sympathy.

He strolled past the usual conversations.

"Gonna be another warm one."

"George Olsen's finishing his beans today. Doin' mine tomorrow."

"Price is high, should do good this year."

"Harv's got those fancy snow shovels in. Wore mine out last year, better get one before he runs out."

Tommy took his regular seat at the counter. Bob, the owner, brought him coffee while the conversations faded away as the official interrogation began. "What's new?" Bob asked.

"Nothing. Should get the forensics report back today. Have more calls to make, checking on people's whereabouts. Mr. Luetz wasn't popular. Lots of potential suspects."

"The usual?"

"Three eggs and toast. No bacon, stomach's not right."

"Can do. You run into Ali Thorein last night?"

Tommy opened a sugar packet. "Yep, we talked. She has a great job. Helga's as happy as I've ever seen her."

"Quite the coincidence, Ali coming back the same day Luetz is murdered."

"She spent the night in a motel in Black River Falls. Some might believe she's involved. I don't."

Bob placed the carafe in the coffee maker. "Yeah, I've heard a few draw that conclusion. Can't see her that way myself. Bet you had a rough night."

"I could use more sleep."

"Your eggs will be right up."

As the conversations around him resumed, Tommy sipped his coffee, content, knowing his remarks would sweep the village.

A short nap in his chair at home and a hurried cleanup put Tommy in his office by nine. He faced tough decisions now. Margaret Luetz didn't kill her husband, but may have hired someone to do the job. A remote possibility, but he would check Orville's bank account later for questionable withdrawals.

Discounting Margaret, Ali became the prime suspect with a strong motive, a questionable alibi, and the note in her own hand. *Was she that spiteful?* Tommy thought not. *Who could have forged that note? Helga? She disliked Orville Luetz, the man who drove her daughter away. But Helga would never condone murder, let alone commit it herself.*

The forger must have a copy of Ali's handwriting from high school. *A teacher?* Tommy couldn't see any teacher committing murder to remove Orville Luetz. Even Mr. Farmingham, the teacher benefiting the most from Luetz's death, wasn't a likely suspect, although physically he could do the job.

One of our ex-classmates might have forged that note. Melanie, the bank teller, attended school with Ali and lives close by. *But she has no reason to kill Orville Luetz. The note is a dead end. Try a different direction first, call that motel, verify Ali's alibi.*

The motel's owner answered with an old phlegmy voice. Tommy explained he was checking on a woman who spent Sunday night there. The old man shuffled through the receipts and found two from Sunday night. Both males paid with credit cards. "She claims your card scanner wasn't working and paid cash," Tommy said.

"No cash here. You say Sunday night? What time?"

"She checked in around ten o'clock."

"That kid Darryl. He works Sunday afternoon 'cause that's a slow time. My night manager had car trouble. Didn't make it in until midnight. Not sure I trust Darryl. He could've pocketed the money. Seems the type."

Tommy wondered what type that might be and asked how to reach Darryl. The old man gave him Darryl's full name and phone number and added, "He's gone with his family on vacation. Two weeks. Family wedding out west."

"You have a contact number for him?"

"No."

"Is a neighbor watching the family's house? Feeding the livestock or taking in the mail?"

Another raspy breath. "Sorry."

"You have Darryl's address?"

The old man fumbled through some papers before reading the address while Tommy wrote it down. "The night manager. You say he came in at midnight?"

"That's what he told me."

"When did he go home?"

"Left at eight when I arrived."

The night manager must have seen Ali's car parked there during his shift. Tommy took his name and phone number.

The motel owner grunted. "He turns the phone off to sleep. Won't answer until midafternoon."

Tommy made a note to call later. "Is there another way to verify how many rooms were rented Sunday night?"

The owner cleared his throat. "Let me ask the maid. She's around somewhere." He set the phone down, shouting the maid's name as he shuffled away. Several minutes later he returned. "She cleaned three rooms yesterday morning, but I only have receipts for two. I pay maids by the room. They're always trying to get more money out of me. Darryl steals, and maids charge me for extra work. No surprise this place barely breaks even."

Tommy had one more idea. "Describe this kid Darryl for me. That might help."

Tommy recorded Darryl's description and left his office number before ending the call. Ali's alibi was slightly more believable now.

Tommy leaned back in his chair, enjoying a slight victory.

If Ali killed Luetz, she needed help. Who would help her? Helga's bad back rules her out. No one else has ever admitted contacting Ali. The other eight members of her class have moved away, but they might have rekindled Ali's friendship. A few have family in the area. They might have heard of Margaret's commitment, which left Orville alone and provided an opportune time for revenge.

Tommy called Myrna Lindquist and had a pleasant conversation that ended when she gave him the long distance number of her daughter Ellen. He sat silently, planning his conversation. Planning became stalling until he dialed. "Ellen, Tommy Peterson. From Rausburg."

Ellen panicked. "Oh, my God. What's wrong? Is it Mom? Did she fall?"

Not the response Tommy expected. "She's fine. I just got your number from her."

Ellen breathed a sigh of relief. An elementary school teacher taking a year-long sabbatical to care for her three-month-old baby, she lived ninety minutes away in Watertown. "You frightened me. Don't you realize what a call from the cop in your parents' hometown might mean?"

Tommy smiled. Ellen never minced words. "Sorry."

Ellen's tone softened. "Mom's hip worries me. She needs it replaced. I don't want her falling and suffering while Dad's at work."

"When I talked to your mom, I mentioned Delores Quinten got around better now after replacing hers. Unfortunately, your mom's hard to convince."

"She acts like it will go away by itself. I told her that I'd even come and stay while she recuperates. Since I took the year off, it'd be great timing, but I'm sure this isn't a courtesy call about Mom's hip. What's up?"

"You hear about Mr. Luetz?"

"Last night on the news. How awful. I didn't wish him dead, but if you're collecting for a memorial, you wasted a call. If Luetz hadn't been so pigheaded..."

Ellen's tone reminded Tommy how similar Ali and Ellen were. At school some called them the terrible twins. Not because of bad behavior. Both became volatile at perceived injustice. Both spoke their minds. "No, I'm not collecting for a memorial. Uh, have you talked to Ali recently?"

Ellen went quiet for a moment. "Ali? No. Why do you ask?"

"Well... someone wanted Orville Luetz dead. She came to mind."

"What? No. Absolutely not. Ali's no killer. I'm sure she was bitter, but Ali would never take another person's life. Anyway, isn't she in California?"

"Came home yesterday for a visit. First time since she left."

"Oh." Ellen's silence lingered, making Tommy uncomfortable.

"Well, it doesn't matter. Tommy, you of all people should know Ali isn't capable of murder. Have you forgotten how she helped you out of your shell?"

"I didn't forget, but I have a murder to solve."

He regretted snapping at Ellen, but she apologized first. "Sorry, that is your job. You must have found the body, right?"

"Mary Albright did. We were the only ones who saw him."

Ellen took a moment to digest that information. "Well, for the record, I haven't spoken to Ali since senior year. I doubt I'll ever get the chance. I sure wouldn't want me for a friend, not after the way I abandoned her."

"People do forgive."

Ellen huffed. "When pigs fly."

Tommy pictured Ellen as the kind of mother all the kids liked because she was funny, honest, and spoke her mind. "Look, Luetz threatened us with the same thing. We all let Ali down."

"I was her best friend. She deserved better." Ellen sniffed. "Anything else?"

"Do you have phone numbers for the rest of your class? I need to verify their whereabouts."

"Don't you mean you want to check their alibis?"

"You could call it that."

"Hang on. I'll get the list."

A minute later Ellen read off the other seven names with their phone numbers. "I haven't spoken to them in a while. We exchange Christmas cards now."

"My class is the same."

Ellen was silent. "Anything else you want to ask me?"

Tommy had planned to ask one more question but decided against it. "I'm sure you can account for your whereabouts at the time of the murder. You wouldn't risk losing your baby."

"For the record, I was here alone with Kristen. Mark left for Indiana Sunday afternoon. Calling on a big client."

"Did he call in yesterday morning?"

"Around eight. The TV said Luetz was killed before dawn. I suppose that doesn't establish an alibi for me."

"Where's your motive? Have you even seen him lately?"

"Not since I got married. You have a reason to focus on our class?"

"I'd better not say."

"The reason is obvious, Tommy. We are the most infamous class Rausburg ever produced. Not an honor I'm proud of."

"We were kids. None of us knew the way things worked yet."

"That's a polite way of putting it, but you always were polite to a fault. Anyway, I'm sure you'll find your man, although I don't have the slightest notion who it could be."

"Me either, unfortunately." Tommy had an idea. "I'll see Ali later today. Anything you want me to pass on?"

Ellen took a moment before answering. "Under the circumstances, no. If you're checking up on her, others must have suspicions, too. I'm sure she's having a tough enough time. Next time I see you, I'll get her address in California and send her a card."

"Okay, thanks for the help."

"Sure, Tommy. Good luck."

Tommy stared at the phone, stalling again. His conversation with Ellen brought back memories of the incident. Surprise became shame at their own inaction, while the adults applauded Luetz's get-tough policy. Did all that lead to murder?

———

Pat Leahy, forensics expert for the Kickapoo County Sheriff's Department, fretted over his report. He had double-checked the evidence from the Rausburg murder and found the fingerprints and stray hairs belonged to the victim or his wife. There weren't any bits of clothing left behind and no other bodily fluid stains.

What did Peterson miss? The killer always leaves evidence behind. Leahy studied the pictures again with a magnifying glass. Nothing. He dreaded telling District Attorney Dan Milenburg the news.

Normally the report went to Peterson first, but Milenburg issued warrants for the county. He already checked on Leahy's progress that morning, making sure Leahy understood that he expected to review the completed report first, before Peterson or anyone else.

Sheriff Chuck Sinclair was the one Leahy dreaded most. Once Milenburg found no justification for issuing an arrest warrant, Sinclair would run his own investigation, forcing Leahy's examination of the crime scene.

That wasn't the problem. Peterson did a good job collecting evidence. The immaculate crime scene suggested an experienced killer, not some local moron with a grudge. Leahy didn't like the implications, especially with Sinclair hovering over his shoulder. Sinclair sometimes found critical evidence others missed, evidence Leahy knew wasn't there during his examination.

————

Tommy called Ali's entire graduating class to check their alibis. All of them lived within a day's drive, but most restricted their visits to holidays. Three class members hadn't visited Rausburg in several years after their parents died or moved away, and no one had ever contacted Ali in California.

The conversations had been awkward, but everyone understood why Tommy called. Several spouses confirmed their partners were home in bed at the time of the murder. Tommy called two single classmates at work, verifying their whereabouts at eight a.m. with their supervisors, ruling them out.

After he made the last call, Tommy sat back, relieved Ali's classmates were in the clear. But now what? Who else disliked Orville so much they clobbered him with a bat?

His professional training pinpointed Ali as the killer. Years of festering hatred drove her to seek revenge. Any sane cop would come to that conclusion, but not Tommy. It had to be someone else. Just had to be.

14

"Too much paperwork," Department of Criminal Investigation Agent Dirk Malloy said, chucking another file in his outbox. "What a waste of time. I'm nothing more than a rubber stamp."

Betty Fowler, his DCI associate on the governor's task force, grabbed several files from his outbox. Although Malloy's blue blazer hung on the coat rack, his striped tie was knotted tight around his neck, a good indicator of Malloy's foul mood. "Cheer up. If the rumors are true, you'll soon be back on the interstate pinching speeders, increasing the state's revenue."

"Better than being stuck behind a desk like you."

Betty scowled at Malloy. His sterling reputation at solving cases had earned him respect within the law enforcement community, but working alongside him day after day was trying.

"Sorry." He rocked back in his chair and rubbed his forehead. "I'm a little testy today."

"Today?"

Malloy managed a slight grin. "More than normal. Abby didn't come home last night. Mary called at two a.m., crying."

"Is your ex drinking again?"

"Mary? No. Not sure about Abby. Waltzed in this morning like nothing happened." Malloy shook his head. "The divorce was tough on her."

"Abby will straighten out. I did, and look at me now. I'm a high-priced file clerk serving a high-priced rubber stamp. Years of dreaming big have finally paid off."

"I suppose." Malloy sat forward and opened the next file on his desk, cueing Betty's departure.

Malloy finished another report, tossed it in his outbox, and sipped the warm soda he'd nursed all morning. When his phone rang, Malloy answered and discovered the governor's chief of staff, Walter, on the line.

"Malloy, I've got a case for your task force. One of our sources mentioned a stalled murder investigation. In Rausburg, over in Kickapoo County."

Malloy couldn't refuse the assignment, but he could make Walter work for it. "You've been watching Martie Pepper on Channel 6 News again, right?"

Walter forced a laugh. "Yes, Governor Luce watched last night so I called—off the record. Martie says the local guy's in over his head. I called Sheriff Chuck Sinclair in Mineral Ridge this morning. He said the evidence is inconclusive, and he expects to take over the investigation soon."

"Let Sinclair have it. If he runs into trouble, he'll call the State Patrol. If they can't close it, I'll step in."

"The local cop is Tom Peterson. Word is he's better suited to writing speeding tickets in Mayberry than heading a murder investigation."

"Why does Luce want me involved this soon?"

Walter took a moment before answering. "Rumors. Attorneys refuse to defend clients in Kickapoo County because of Judge Lynch. The Judicial Commission is concerned. That's why the governor wants you on it."

"Since when did difficult judges concern the governor?" The Judicial Commission wouldn't involve Luce. "What's the real reason you called me?"

Malloy leaned back in his chair. Although he hated the politics surrounding police work, he was aware of it and knew Walter proposed cutting the high-salaried task force agents, lowering the budget to curry favor with voters. Making Walter squirm brought great pleasure to Malloy.

"Okay, Luce lost Kickapoo County in the election and wants this case solved expeditiously. Small town, people talk, and come re-election time..."

"They'll wonder why the governor cut his task force from the budget?"

"You know better than that. Besides, it's not a done deal. You could grab the spotlight this time. Wouldn't hurt."

Spoken like the politician you are. "Okay, give me the details. At least it'll get me out of the office for a while."

After Malloy dismissed Walter, he called Police Chief Tom Peterson in Rausburg. He got an answering machine and didn't like that at all.

15

After her shower, Ali fidgeted until ten thirty before calling Charles Latimer's office in San Francisco. His college friend, Justin Green, became a noted criminal attorney in Madison and had agreed to advise Ali. She immediately called Green's office for an appointment. Her insistent tone bothered Helga, who overheard the conversation. Soon Ali hung up, frowning. "Couldn't get past his secretary," she said. "Best I could do is ten a.m. tomorrow."

"Doesn't matter. You'll cancel later when Tommy gets his report and you're no longer a suspect."

"That would be the best outcome."

"We should wait here then."

"Better to be prepared. I can find the bank by myself."

Helga set her knitting aside. "Let's go."

Another beautiful fall day greeted them as they strolled downtown. The warm temperature, colorful foliage, and the occasional breeze from the west made the walk pleasant.

The bank decor hadn't changed since Ali opened a savings account with her birthday money in first grade. Melanie was on duty. She pushed a pile of receipts to the side and smiled. "Good morning."

Helga slid a withdrawal slip through the window and Melanie checked it before recognition set in. "Ali?"

Ali smiled. "Hi, Mel."

"It is you. I suppose I would have recognized you eventually, but ... you look great. I like your hair short. Whatever you're doing must agree with you."

Ali noticed Melanie carried the bedraggled appearance many young mothers wore. "Thanks, Mel. Good to see you, too. I'm glad you're the same friendly person I remember."

Melanie leaned forward and lowered her voice. "I don't believe the rumors for a minute. You're not the kind who holds a grudge. I don't care what others say."

Ali's eyes grew moist. *Stop it. Stay on task.*

"Mel, could we talk in private? It won't take long."

Melanie checked her watch. "I'm due for a break. We can meet in the park. I often eat lunch there. No one will bother us."

"Perfect."

Melanie counted out Helga's withdrawal. "I'll join you in a few minutes."

The two women sauntered another block to the park, found a bench, and waited. Helga had been quiet since leaving the bank. "Mom, I know this makes you uncomfortable, but I can't sit on the sidelines. I'm being framed for murder. I can't trust the situation to resolve itself."

Helga rested her hand on Ali's. "I want this over as much as you."

"But..."

"You were very pushy with that poor secretary this morning. You aren't going to treat Melanie like that, are you?"

"I'll be careful, but I need to find other people who hate Luetz enough to kill him. Cops have tunnel vision. Once they're convinced you're guilty, they make sure the whole world sees it that way too."

"Tommy's different."

"Maybe, but if push comes to shove, he'll go along with the rest."

"I guess you have changed."

Ali had no reply, and the two women sat in silence.

"Old woman," Helga said.

"Pardon?"

Helga pointed to a fluffy white cloud drifting by. "That cloud reminds me of an old woman."

Ali shaded her eyes with her hand and squinted. "I see."

"You remember how we used to watch the clouds and try to see objects hidden in them?"

"Yes, I remember. I was convinced you saw objects that weren't always there."

Helga smiled. "I did sometimes, to force you to use your imagination."

"Mmm. Young mother."

Helga scanned the sky for a moment until Ali waved at Melanie as she approached.

"I'm more a realist," Ali said, ending the cloud watching.

Mel joined them. Ali learned that Mel graduated business school in Milwaukee and married before returning home when her husband took a job in Madison.

Ali talked briefly about Robel's before steering the conversation to Mr. Luetz. Mel said, "Can't say I'll miss the way he watched me put his paycheck in my drawer, like I would steal it."

"So you've heard I'm the prime suspect?"

Mel's head drooped. "There are a few spreading that rumor, but I know you didn't do it. Somebody did, though, and that's upsetting everybody."

Ali forced a tight smile. "Tommy's asked me to stay around until he gets solid proof of my innocence. I'm taking the initiative to find other suspects."

"That's understandable. Tommy keeps everyone from speeding, but he might be in over his head with solving a murder. He could use help."

Tommy's inadequacies gave Ali a twinge of remorse. "I wanted to ask... Our class account came up short before graduation. I always double-checked before I gave it to Mr. Luetz, but our final bank statement was short almost eighty dollars."

Mel's eyes widened. "We had a similar problem. After prom, thirty dollars went missing. I knew I handed it all in. When I told Mr. Luetz, he confided he caught one of my classmates taking it."

"One of your classmates? You mean in your class, not the whole school?"

"Right. I didn't tell anyone, and the alleged thief moved away."

Ali became more animated. "He gave me the same story too, except the thief was in a younger class. Mr. Luetz said he caught him in the act and made the thief put that money back, but the remainder was gone. He picked an individual I pitied, so I never shared that information."

"That's what he told me. The thief's family wasn't as well off, and he didn't want to make matters worse, etc."

"Yes, when I pushed him, he blamed Tom—the other kid, I mean."

Mel caught the slip. "He actually told you that Tommy stole it?"

Ali and Helga both drew quick breaths. Ali said, "I knew he didn't do it."

"Of course not. Tommy would never do that. Luetz lied. He must've taken it himself."

"Do you suppose he was still taking money?" Helga asked.

Mel held her hands out. "No one else complained, but neither did we."

"So where did it go?" Ali asked. "That's not much of an embezzlement even if he stole from every class."

"Orville Luetz did not die rich, I can tell you that."

Ali had an idea. "Anyone with access to school funds could be the thief. Suppose Mr. Luetz blackmailed him."

Mel grinned. "Like a bank teller who stole once in the past and people never let her forget it?"

Ali winced, but Mel continued. "Don't you remember? When I was six, I borrowed a dollar from Dad's wallet for ice cream. He told everyone. At least once a week one of our senior citizens reminds me. 'Don't buy ice cream with this.'"

Ali let out a sigh of relief. She'd forgotten that story. "Sorry, it wasn't my intention to accuse you."

"Don't worry. I'll hear about ice cream until the day I die. We'll always be friends, that is, if you don't mind being seen with a known thief."

Ali grinned. "I never suspected you, but someone must have hated Mr. Luetz enough to have killed him. The sooner the killer's found, the sooner I get my life back."

Melanie checked her watch. "I'd better get back."

"Thanks for talking to me."

"No problem. If you're free one night, come over and I'll show off my cute daughter, Jackie."

"I'd better clear myself first. Two hardened criminals like us meeting after dark? That would terrify the old codgers."

Mel laughed. "Glad you kept your sense of humor. I'll keep my ears open. Are you staying a few days?"

"Till I'm cleared, then back to San Francisco."

Mel's smile sagged. "I don't blame you, but it would be good if this community welcomed you back. I remember Rausburg as a nice place to live when we were young, but now we have an unofficial committee of judgmental elders, criticizing people like me because I choose to work and supplement Jack's earnings. Doesn't matter that Mom loves to watch Jackie while I work or I might like a career of my own."

Ali put her hand on Mel's. "I'm glad you're here. Maybe we can get together the next time."

With a top-notch criminal attorney ready to take her case and confirmation that Luetz had lied about missing money, Ali felt optimistic for the first time since Tommy's visit. His investigation should exonerate her, but she was prepared to fight if necessary. Anyone expecting less would soon discover how wrong they were.

16

Tommy left his car by the office and went to the bank to withdraw a few dollars and view the Luetz account before lunch.

As he checked Orville Luetz's statement, Melanie surprised him. "Talked to Ali a few minutes ago. Almost didn't recognize her. She's still cute, though." Melanie liked to play matchmaker for the most eligible bachelor in Rausburg. Since there were slim pickings, Melanie teased Tommy more often than she offered workable options. "Your name came up."

Tommy frowned. "I blew it last night. Made her mad."

"Didn't act put out to me. Anyway, we discovered both our classes had money missing when we graduated. Could be a motive for killing Luetz." Melanie gave him the details, leaving out Tommy as the suspect in Ali's theft. He promised to investigate the matter even though he had quietly solved that issue over two years ago. He thanked Melanie as she slid her baby's latest picture in his direction.

"She's a cute one. Has your eyes," Tommy said and left for the diner.

After sharing his progress with the guys at the diner over a grilled cheese sandwich, Tommy reexamined the crime scene to make sure he didn't overlook anything yesterday. He tiptoed across the yard while scanning, squatting, and studying the ground for indentations or other signs of the killer's entrance or exit. Nothing. Inside, the dried bloodstains drew his attention.

Maybe the killer got blood on his clothes when he moved the body. I should inspect Ali's clothes. He rubbed the back of his neck. *No. If I don't identify the killer by tomorrow, I'll collect Helga's trash during patrol early Thursday morning before the garbage truck takes it and check if Ali discarded any clothes. Luminol will show traces of blood.*

Tommy spent another hour in Luetz's house but found nothing more and left. As he entered his office, the flashing answering machine light caught his eye. The first message was a reporter from the State Journal who had questions. Tommy stopped the machine, certain the other messages also came from the media, and took a moment to compose a short statement.

Over the next half hour, he repeated his simple statement to reporters from Madison, Janesville, Beloit, Dodgeville, and La Crosse. "It's an ongoing investigation. The evidence is being analyzed, and I'm waiting for our forensics expert to complete his report. In the meantime, I'm narrowing the suspect list."

The reporters pumped Tommy for more information, but over the phone he easily told them that he had no further comment and ended the call.

The sixth caller, Martie Pepper, was not so easy to dismiss.

"Thanks for returning my call, Chief Peterson. I have several questions."

Tommy read his statement, hoping that would suffice. It didn't.

"In talking to several of your constituents, many of them called you Tommy, but your answering machine message says Tom. Which do you prefer?"

No harm in answering that question. "Either. Many people in Rausburg remember me as a little boy and call me Tommy. I use Tom in more official settings."

"Do you find it difficult to serve people who picture you as a child?"

"Maybe I did at first, but not now. I've never felt any lack of respect if that's what you're asking."

"No one mentioned a lack of respect to me. Some were surprised Sheriff Sinclair wasn't there running the investigation, or the State Patrol."

"Other than using the county's forensics expert, I didn't find it necessary to involve other law enforcement at this point since I collected all the evidence. Once the forensics report comes back and I know who the killer is, I'll ask for backup in making the arrest."

"You have a person in mind as the killer?"

"No. I already answered that question."

"It's not your former classmate, Alicia Thorein?"

Tommy paused. Martie was good, he had to give her that. "As I said earlier, I'm eliminating suspects while I'm waiting for the evidence report."

"But you don't deny that many assume she's the killer."

He wanted to hang up, but that would indicate the truth in Martie's suspicion. "Chief Peterson?"

"I'm aware of the gossip, but as I said before, I'm waiting for the forensics report to identify the killer. Until that happens there is no prime suspect. Thank you for calling."

Tommy hung up, angry he let Martie Pepper indirectly confirm Ali was a suspect. He hadn't given Martie information she didn't already know, but Tommy hadn't discounted Ali as a suspect either. All he could do now was hope Martie had strong ethics and would refrain from reporting idle gossip. He took a soda from his refrigerator, opened it, and took a healthy swig as he calmed down.

One more message left to answer. He punched the button and heard Division of Criminal Investigations Agent Malloy's terse message informing Tommy he was taking over the investigation in the morning.

"Great. Now this."

Tommy knew Malloy by reputation. His name had been mentioned several times at the academy as an example of an officer who went above and beyond to solve cases. Initially, he built his reputation with the Wisconsin State Patrol before transferring to DCI.

Malloy's name surfaced again during the last few months of Tommy's tenure with the Madison Police Department. Newly elected Governor James Luce had inherited several police-related publicity nightmares across the state. He created his own task force from DCI personnel, giving them carte blanche to investigate any law enforcement agency in the state, which brought closure to several cases involving overlapping jurisdictions and questionable results.

Despite their success record, Governor Luce's current reelection strategy emphasized cutting government waste. Tommy's good friend Del, one of two state troopers patrolling closest to Rausburg, had recently mentioned the WSP and DCI were under scrutiny. Elite units like the task force were on the chopping block, and the state's highest paid investigators might be retiring early.

After another swig, Tommy took a minute to compose himself before replaying the message. He forced a smile and relied on the age-old advice that you can't be angry and smile at the same time as he dialed.

Malloy answered his own phone. "Tom Peterson from Rausburg returning your call, sir."

"Peterson, I left a message over two hours ago."

Already off to a bad start. "Yes, sir. I work alone. People page me for emergencies."

"Murder is an emergency."

"I know, sir. I was at the crime scene when you called."

"Have a suspect in custody yet?"

Tommy paused. "No, but I've eliminated a few."

"I see. I'll have my team in Rausburg at ten a.m. tomorrow. Clear your schedule. You'll take us where we need to go. Understood?"

"Yes, sir."

After Malloy hung up, Tommy froze with the phone in his hand. Now he had a problem. *What do I do with the note? Leahy should check it for fingerprints right away. Ali's won't be on it, but what if Leahy finds no prints at all? That little poem is a damning piece of evidence.*

The busy signal beeped in his ear, reminding him that he had another call to make which could solve his problem. He pulled his pocket notebook out to find the number and called the night manager from the motel in Black River Falls to verify Ali's alibi.

After the man answered, Tommy told him the situation and asked the question. "Sorry, officer, but I didn't notice any white rental cars. I don't stray from the desk at night. Took no calls. Far as I know, we had two truckers staying with us."

Not the answer Tommy wanted. "Did you check the room keys? How many were out?"

"Didn't notice. No reason unless I'm checking a guest in."

Tommy racked his brain and decided to come at it from a different angle. "Did the truckers turn in their keys at checkout?"

"One did. Had a phone call on his bill. We tell 'em to leave the keys in the room unless there are extra charges."

"Could an overnight guest have parked a car on motel property that you might have missed?"

The night manager paused. "I never went around back. Parked close that night since I was late and we weren't busy. A car could have been parked in the back and I didn't see it."

Tommy liked that answer. "Could you have missed seeing it drive away that morning?"

"Easily. Ever been here?"

"No."

"Our motel faces the interstate with the main entrance on the side. Guests can drive in and out without passing the office. The owner doesn't admit it, but local couples meet here discreetly all the time."

Tommy played dumb even though he knew what the man inferred. "Could you be specific?"

The manager laughed once. "We have couples who check in for two or three hours before they leave in separate cars."

"Gotcha. So the white rental car could have parked in the back and left without you seeing it?"

"Yes, it's possible."

Not the strong alibi he wanted but getting better. "One more question. How honest is the maid who worked Monday morning?"

"She's my sister. You accusing her of lying?"

"No, not at all. She told your boss she cleaned three rooms Monday morning, but he found receipts for two."

The man grunted. "You don't want my opinion of our boss. Few choice jobs here. Sis and I talk about moving on."

"I understand. Thanks for your time."

"Did I tell you what you wanted to hear? Didn't sound like it."

"You saw what you saw. I have enough to proceed." Tommy thanked him again and terminated the call. The manager couldn't confirm or deny Ali's presence, but Tommy remained convinced Ali told the truth. Would Agent Malloy agree?

Next Tommy dialed Pat Leahy in Mineral Ridge to ask if he had completed the report yet. "Checking it over now. Sorry, Peterson. The evidence you brought me belonged either to the victim or his wife. The blood on the bat is the victim's, and there were no fingerprints."

Tommy slumped in his chair. Thirty-two hours after the murder and he was no closer to solving it. "The evidence is useless?"

"As it stands, I have nothing for you. I could check the scene myself tomorrow."

Inviting Leahy meant inviting Sinclair as well. Since Agent Malloy was taking over the case, Tommy decided against it. "Let me sleep on it."

"Fair enough. You did a good job. Got all the right locations and measurements. I didn't mean to imply you weren't capable. Sometimes a new pair of eyes helps."

"No offense taken. I'll pick up the report later this afternoon. You stay till five?"

"Yep, anytime before five is fine."

Disappointed, Tommy lowered the phone. He needed to find a stronger suspect than Ali before the task force arrived, but now he had nothing.

17

After learning Mel's class had money stolen, Ali was convinced other classes had experienced the same. She wanted to continue her search for the thief, and possible killer, skipping lunch or eating it later, but Helga insisted on eating lunch at noon. Ali gave in to avoid an argument and helped set the table.

Channel 6 News ran the continuing story later in the newscast, rehashing yesterday's information. Ali's unreported suspect status relieved her and tempered her uneasiness that rumors would go public if Tommy failed to solve the case soon, but didn't mute her desire to find the embezzler.

"Did you keep my yearbooks?" Ali asked as she carried her plate to the sink.

"They're in the upstairs closet, boxed. After the first year, I knew you weren't coming home so I packed them away."

While the unspoken sadness of that moment lingered, Ali leaned into her mother. "I can do these few dishes," Helga said, and Ali ran upstairs.

Ali had seen the boxes labeled "High School" stacked in her closet. The topmost box contained award certificates for cheerleading, honor roll, perfect attendance, and several other clubs and events. Ali remembered her embarrassment on awards day because she was repeatedly called up for all those awards now stuffed in a box. Winning them was never the goal. She simply wanted to make her school better and more fun.

Her *Student Citizen of the Year* plaque lay on the bottom. She rubbed her hand over it, remembering. After Mr. Schaeffer, the bank president, handed her the plaque, he whispered, "The class of '76 did so much for the community. Most years the decision would have been tough, but the committee knew you were the spark plug behind it all. Congratulations."

That plaque represented the culmination of her young life in Rausburg. Her last accolade before her fall from grace. *If I hadn't taken it upon myself...*

But she had. Luetz threatened her classmates with prosecution if they continued associating with her, and every one of them caved. After twelve years of friendship, the camaraderie disappeared overnight. Adults gave her a wide berth as well, acting like she no longer existed.

Ali repacked the first box and pulled her yearbooks from the second box to take them downstairs.

As she opened her senior yearbook at the kitchen table, Helga grabbed her freshman yearbook. "Reliving happier times? You were in everything."

"No, Mom. I'm figuring out who embezzled money from both classes. If Luetz confronted the thief, that would be a terrific motive for revenge."

Ali studied the pictures as long-suppressed memories leaped off the page at her. Ali told her therapist, Val, she had forgotten most of her high school years. Val smiled and said the memories remained, but Ali chose to ignore them. That led to a good-natured argument, but Val was right. Ali hadn't forgotten. Didn't matter, though, because the hurt and shame never left her. Seeing all those smiling young faces didn't change a thing.

Both women remained silent while they searched for answers. After a time, Ali leaned back. "Wanda, the school secretary."

Helga shook her head. "Retired with Tommy's class. Living with her son in La Crosse."

"She had access to petty cash and was easily flustered. Could be simple carelessness, not theft."

Helga scowled at Ali. "No. We're not going down that road. Even if it's true, Wanda wouldn't remember. Tommy found her carrying a bag of groceries north of the school two winters ago, convinced she was headed home. Poor thing nearly froze to death."

"Alzheimer's?"

"Sad. She has to be watched constantly."

Ali shut the book. "I've reached a dead end."

"Doesn't matter. You didn't do it. The evidence will show the real killer."

"I hope."

When they moved to the living room, Helga took her knitting and set the TV to her favorite soap. Ali grabbed her junior yearbook and sat on the couch. While Helga knitted and watched *All My Children*, Ali scoured her yearbook for clues leading to the killer.

"I was in everything, wasn't I? Cheerleading, drama club, student council, class president, girls volleyball. My picture is everywhere."

"I didn't gloat to the other parents, but you were the heart of that school. Since you left, it never recovered. Some say the school should consolidate with Mineral Ridge."

"Has the enrollment dropped? I remember the elementary classes were smaller than ours."

Helga's needles stopped for a moment. "It hasn't grown, that's for sure. Hard to keep our graduates around. It's difficult for young families to support themselves farming like their parents did. Especially if they don't own the land. Fewer stores downtown too, and from what I hear our graduates no longer have fond memories that might keep them here."

"Too bad. I'm sure my experience didn't encourage the younger kids."

Helga shrugged. "Can't blame yourself. Others could make the school better if they wanted to."

"But they don't want to, do they? I used to get frustrated because so many kids were content to show up and go home at the end of the day. What good did any of it do?"

"You did a lot of good. Imagine what Tommy would be like if you and Ellen hadn't kept after him to come out of his shell."

"I suppose."

"And all the other things. You remember many of your classmates had never been to Milwaukee before you organized that zoo trip?"

Ali smiled. "Hard to believe after living on the West Coast. This area was provincial in many ways, probably still is."

"I hope you don't mean backward. There are many good people around here. Just because they aren't world travelers—"

"I meant they're content to stay close to home. I thought that way too until I realized I would always be shunned if I stayed."

"People change. I bet you wouldn't feel that way now if you had stayed."

Ali closed the yearbook. "Doesn't matter. What's done is done, and I have no idea who could have taken that money. I was hoping to hand Tommy the killer, but I've struck out. I'm no Jessica Fletcher, that's for sure."

Helga laughed. "You watch *Murder, She Wrote* too?"

"I don't watch much TV, but Sunday night I'm usually home or in a hotel with little to do, so I've seen it."

"I like that show. Tommy watches it with me."

"He does?"

Helga stopped knitting. "He comes over Sundays. It's nice to have someone to talk to."

"Really."

"Oh, it's nothing. He has no one his age to talk to."

"You mean he has no women his age to talk to."

"It's not like that." A commercial for a Betty Crocker cake mix came on TV. Helga put her needles down. "Crap, I was going to bake a cake for dessert tonight. You still like cake, don't you? Let's make one together."

"Changing the subject?"

"Ali, for heaven's sake." Helga put her knitting on the end table and rose. "Coming?"

Ali's brow furrowed. "Mom, you know my cooking stinks. Don't you remember the burned meatloaf and the half dozen other kitchen failures of mine when I tried to help out before?"

Helga rolled her eyes.

"Okay, I suppose I'm not too old to learn. Let's do this."

A few minutes later, a sharp rap at the front door caught their attention while they worked in the kitchen. Helga's hands were messy, so Ali answered and found Tommy standing there. "Am I free to leave yet?"

Tommy hooked his thumbs into his belt loops. "I called the motel. The kid who signed your receipt took off with his family for two weeks and didn't leave a contact number. You talked to a short kid with black hair and a scar on his cheek, didn't you?"

Ali studied him for a moment. "Why, yes. That's him—with a black eye patch over his left eye and a parrot on his shoulder. Said 'Arrr' a lot."

Tommy's head jerked back as his eyes widened. Ali glared at him. "What are you doing? I used to play that trick on you to make you talk."

He held his hands out. "I..."

"Look, the kid was eighteen or nineteen, six feet tall, blond hair, rosy cheeks, with no visible scars. That describes half the kids in this state."

Tommy tucked his thumbs back in his belt. "Sorry. I didn't get the hundred percent confirmation I expected."

"You talked to the motel manager, right?"

"Yes. He—"

Ali raised her hand to stop him. "Let me tell you everything I remember, and you'll see it fits."

Tommy nodded.

"I intended to leave Minneapolis after the wrap-up and drive straight to Madison, but several district managers buttonholed me at the afterglow so I didn't leave until after seven. By the time I reached the Black River Falls exit, fatigue had set in and I remembered there was a long stretch of interstate ahead with few signs of civilization.

"Frankly, the Motor Lodge wasn't appealing, but there were no other options. I circled the building once before I entered the office. Two semis were parked in front close to two lit rooms. I expected them to leave early, so I requested a room in the rear. Since it was late, I hoped to be undisturbed and get a decent night's sleep.

"I told you last night their scanner didn't work. I handed the kid two twenties and a ten. He ogled me like I was a high-priced hooker, and I caught him off guard when I asked for a receipt."

Tommy's eyes widened.

"Sorry. We have a wide variety of people in San Francisco. I forgot this is rural Wisconsin."

"You see hookers all the time in San Francisco?"

"No, of course not. I worked the night shift for several years. Sometimes, going home late I'd see nicely dressed ladies by themselves. Safe bet."

Tommy's cheeks grew red. She decided not to tell him that she had known a few of them by name since they were her neighbors.

"Anyway, the motel could be a rendezvous location for cheating spouses, that's all. I wrote the receipt myself and made him sign it. He handed me the key and told me that he was getting off work once the night manager arrived. I told him 'Good for you.' He slipped the money in his pants pocket. I was suspicious but didn't call him on it."

Now that Tommy was over his embarrassment, he grinned since Ali showed no sign of stopping. "I pulled around the back. My room was on the second floor, south end, by the outside staircase. I specifically asked for it because footsteps on the iron stairs would wake me. I parked my car by a room two doors away on the first floor, leading any criminal to assume I slept in the room right in front of it. If a thief broke in, they'd enter the wrong room, which would give me time to call for help. I chained the door, wedged a chair under the knob, and set my pepper spray on the nightstand next to me.

"The trucks drove past my room a few minutes after five and woke me anyway. I had no additional room charges so I left and drove here without stopping. In hindsight, I wish I'd returned my key. Whoever manned the desk might have remembered me."

"Maybe someone at the front desk saw you drive by on your way out."

Ali shook her head. "I didn't pass by the front office. The motel had an unconventional setup with two exits leading out to the highway. If I hadn't been so tired I would have kept driving and found a more secure motel."

"Anything else?"

Ali snapped her fingers. "I bought a soda from the machine before I left the motel and sipped it in the car. The empty can is sitting in the cup holder if you want to check."

Tommy smiled. "That's quite the detailed account."

"At Robel's we conduct safety seminars on shoplifting in our stores. We're taught to spot behavior that gives shoplifters away while remaining aware of our surroundings for our own personal safety. Usually I choose more secure hotels, but even then, I take precautions. Women traveling alone are often easy prey."

Tommy rubbed the back of his neck. "Anyone messing with you would have his hands full."

She smiled. "I also took self-defense classes a few years back. I'm cautious." Cautious enough to hide the fact that she taught the classes in spotting shoplifters, and the self-defense class was nothing more than a few dirty moves she learned from a bouncer in a strip club.

He held his hands out. "I believe you. Everything you've said fits with what I learned, but you lack incontestable proof. Tomorrow a DCI agent is bringing his team from Madison to take over the investigation. I wanted to tell them your alibi checks out, but I can't."

"A team from Madison? That means I'm stuck here for another day?"

"Sorry."

Ali was more forgiving today since she had an appointment with a lawyer and a possible revenge motive for the killer. "The person who left that note is the one I'm angry with. You're only the messenger. Hear from the crime lab yet?"

"Yes, a few minutes ago."

"And…"

"He found nothing conclusive."

Ali's jaw dropped.

"No stray fingerprints in the house, so the note is critical evidence. If I were certain the killer left prints on the note, I'd turn it in."

"But you're not."

"I'm keeping the note confidential for the time being because the lack of fingerprints would give the poem more importance and point to you instead of the killer."

"Great."

"The killer will slip up, and we'll use the note to verify his guilt."

Ali frowned. "I want this resolved so I can have fun tomorrow with Mom."

"What kind of fun?"

Ali clasped her hands together, chest high. "I get an employee's discount at Robel's. We'll shop there along with a few other stores by the mall."

Tommy stifled a grin. "Can you be back by late afternoon?"

"We could be."

Tommy stroked his chin. "I see no reason the two of you can't go. The DCI agent might want to talk to you later in the day, but I'm sure he'll work the crime scene first."

Ali wanted to know the agent's intentions before she spoke to her lawyer. "He's coming to examine the crime scene and not to interrogate me, right?"

"Right. He doesn't know about you yet, but he'll hear the rumors and want to talk."

She dropped her hands. "I'll consider it. I want to help the investigation but—"

"You don't have to say it. I know you're innocent, but after tonight

I won't be calling the shots." Tommy shrugged. "Look at the bright side."

"What's that?"

"We didn't find your fingerprints on the bat." Ali's nostrils flared. "I knew you never touched it, but now it's official."

She folded her arms. "Maybe it is good news then."

"Just make sure you're gone before he gets here."

"What time is he arriving?"

"Ten."

Ali suppressed a smile. Her appointment with Justin Green was at ten. "We'll be gone before that."

"Stop by my office before you leave."

"So certain people see me checking in with you?"

"Something like that."

"I could go ask Fern Johnson's permission myself."

Helga called out from the kitchen, breaking the sudden tension. "Tommy, why don't you join us for supper tonight? You can catch up with Ali."

Ali stood squarely in front of him, arms still folded across her chest. "Oh, I don't know, Mrs. Thorein."

Ali relaxed and let her arms fall. Beneath his police uniform, remnants of the shy little boy she used to help remained. "Why don't you?" she said. "Or will people hassle you if we're seen together?"

"That doesn't bother me. What time?"

"Six o'clock," Helga shouted from the kitchen.

"Six it is," Tommy said before he left.

18

———

Tommy listened as Helga directed the conversation through the meal. "Tell Tommy about your job." When Ali stalled, Helga steered the conversation to another of Ali's accomplishments.

While Helga cut the cake, Ali asked, "What would you like Tommy to know about me next?"

"Oh, you. Can't a mother be proud of her daughter's success?"

"You taught me that no one likes a braggart."

"You're not being a braggart if people ask and genuinely want to hear about your life. Right, Tommy?"

Tommy raised his hands in submission. "I stay out of domestic disputes unless they become violent."

"Are we violent, Mom?"

Helga looked up, clutching the cake knife.

"Let me tell you about Cal State," Ali said.

Tommy laughed first, and Helga and Ali joined him. Over cake, Ali talked about Cal State.

While Ali wiped the table off, Tommy joined Helga at the sink and offered his help with the dishes.

"Go for a walk," Helga mouthed.

"Oh, right."

Ali overheard the whispered transaction and took her jacket off the hook by the back door. "Might get chilly later," she said. "Coming?"

Tommy slipped his jacket on and followed her out.

Ali kicked a dried leaf off the sidewalk as they ambled along. "Enough about my grand accomplishments. What about yours? How did Tommy Peterson become the voice of authority for all of greater Rausburg?"

"Not much to tell."

"You aren't going to make me dig it out of you, like I did in school, are you?"

Tommy laughed. This was the Ali he fell in love with in high school.

"I didn't do too well last night on my own."

"About that... I shouldn't have taken out my frustration on you. I realized today how awful this experience must be for you."

"I could have handled it better. Seeing you after all these years made me forget my training. I knew you were innocent, but I didn't want you to say anything that could be used against you later."

"Thanks for your concern. Let's talk about other things. Like you. You didn't answer my question."

"I was a shy child," he said with mock seriousness.

She chuckled. "I remember that part. Skip ahead."

"After you left, I had a growth spurt. Karen Johnson dropped hints about the homecoming dance, and I asked her out. She helped me become more social. Never became the life of the party, but I got better around other people."

"Better late than never."

Tommy continued. "Ma didn't want me tossing feed sacks at the elevator like Pa. My grades were good enough for college, but I didn't enjoy school that much."

"College is different, less structured. You might like it."

"Thanks for telling me—now."

They both chuckled. Ali asked, "So what led you to become a cop?"

The timing wasn't right to tell Ali that her mistake led him into law enforcement. He shared the other version of his story. "I liked to shoot at targets."

Ali's hand went to her breastbone. "Whatever possessed you to do that?"

"Summer before ninth grade I helped Ma clean out her closet, and we found a pair of pistols. She told me that Pa was a sharp-shooter in the army during WWII. After the war, he entered several target shooting competitions. A few old folks remember him winning trophies and ribbons, but he put his guns away when I came along. Ma said he intended to show me when I was older, but he didn't live that long."

"His was the first funeral I attended. You too, I suppose," Ali said.

Tommy nodded. "She showed me how he taught her after I agreed not to hunt or shoot at anything but targets. Pa had built a range back in the woods at our old farm. I asked Mr. Olsen if I could use it, and he helped me repair it. I used the small pistol she learned on and enjoyed it. Did well, too. The money I made baling hay for farmers every summer went to buy ammo, and I practiced regularly."

Ali shook her head. "Seems out of character for you. At least the boy I remember."

He smiled. "I felt close to Pa, target shooting on the range. As I grew older, it also helped me release anger."

"Anger? You were angry?"

"I wanted to be outgoing like everyone else, but I wasn't, and I was angry with myself because of it."

"Never would have guessed."

Tommy shrugged. "I kept it in."

They took three steps in silence. "You were saying?"

"Right. People asked me what I was going to do with my life, and I didn't know what to tell them at first. 'Do what you're good at' everyone said, so one day I stopped by Chief Hancock's office and mentioned my shooting experience. I was thinking security guard, but he watched me shoot one day and called an instructor at the academy. When I tested well on the range, they wanted me despite the fact I wasn't going to college. Six months at Fort McCoy and the Madison Police Department recruited me. They were assembling personnel for a SWAT team. I was the best shooter they had and as a rookie, I was cheap."

Ali laughed. "I can see the ad now. Sharpshooter wanted at reasonable price."

Tommy laughed with her.

"I can't see you on a SWAT team. It doesn't fit the way I remember you."

"There wasn't an official team at that time. The MPD recruited qualified rookies for several years, putting the personnel in place. They didn't officially become the Emergency Response Team until after I left. As a rookie, I worked a regular beat in one of the tougher parts of town and saw enough injuries for a lifetime. Twice they called me during hostage situations. Fortunately, both situations were resolved before shots were fired."

"What led you back here?"

"Chief Hancock wanted to retire and recommended me as his replacement. Ma's health was declining, Harv and the village board members thought I was a good fit. Easy decision."

"Mom says you've done a great job. You're well-liked and respected."

Tommy's face grew red, but the waning daylight hid his embarrassment. "Most of the job is writing speeding tickets. I've never drawn my gun here."

"That's a good thing."

As they crossed Main Street in silence, Tommy waved at a passing car, and the driver waved back.

Ali said, "You must think I'm a terrible person."

"Why would I think that?"

"Because I've been such a horrible daughter. I didn't even attend

Dad's funeral. You changed careers to take care of your mom, and I ditched mine."

Sometimes Tommy had considered that, but seeing Ali and Helga together again reminded him that Helga and Max raised Ali to be independent. Ali didn't have the same relationship with her parents that Tommy had with his mother. "You did a brave thing. By leaving, you took the blame and let your parents continue with their lives. You sacrificed your own reputation to save theirs."

"Dad never got over it. We never spoke again."

"Max was a good man, but stubborn. We talked about you once."

"What did he say?"

"He said you were a lot alike. He expected to put things right the day you waved a diploma in his face."

"Should've come home sooner. I became obsessed about getting a college education without his help. After I missed his funeral, I was too ashamed to come back. What child misses their parent's funeral?"

They heard a door slam behind them and Tommy glanced over his shoulder. Bob was closing the diner for the evening. "Helga didn't tell you until after the funeral, did she?"

"No, she didn't. I was devastated."

"She was conflicted. Didn't want guilt forcing your return."

"Still..." Ali kicked at a fallen leaf on the sidewalk.

"Your mom had no warning. He keeled over at a job site. Coroner said he died before he hit the ground, so you couldn't have done anything. Helga made a tough decision. Others may assume you didn't care, but I know the truth. Helga made sure you finished your degree."

Ali changed the topic. "What's with you and Mom? You have a thing for older women?"

"No." Tommy smiled, relieved to be discussing something new. "Seriously, after Max died, she withdrew. No one saw her for several days, so I checked on her, which led to a long conversation about being alone. I take her to Mass with me, and she cooks me Sunday dinner. Most Tuesdays we eat together. If I don't see her around, I call. Like an aunt and nephew. I'm not taking over, in case you're worried."

"I'm not. I'm glad Mom has you in her life."

When they reached the park, Ali led Tommy to a bench close to the streetlight. They sat next to each other with Tommy's arm draped along the back, not quite touching Ali.

"Mind if I ask a personal question?" he asked.

"As a cop or a friend?"

"Friend. I'm off duty now."

"Ask, but I may decline to answer."

"After you left, everyone wondered where you went. By Thanksgiving we heard you made it to San Francisco. Sometimes I imagined what it was like. Probably rough, huh?"

Ali dipped her head. "Better than staying here."

"How did you get along out there? You didn't know anyone, did you?"

"No, not a soul. I found an inexpensive motel and hunted for a job. With no previous work experience, many places wouldn't hire me."

"But Robel's did?"

"Robel's was completing a major expansion phase in Northern California, opening several new stores simultaneously and hiring many workers. I went to a job fair and waited in line all morning to interview. The lady interviewing me came from Minnesota, and my Midwestern roots made all the difference to her. I started the next day."

"Wasn't it tough living by yourself? More expensive in California, isn't it?"

Ali tugged at her ear. "I found a generous roommate who carried me until my paychecks arrived. I worked every hour of overtime I could and managed to survive. After a year, I became a California resident, which meant reasonable in-state college tuition. I had enough money saved to attend Cal State part-time if I lived frugally. Within two years, I was promoted to assistant manager and received a substantial raise, enabling me to go full-time, summers included. I took classes or studied until midafternoon when I started my shift, worked several hours and studied more when I got home late that night. I worked as many hours as I could on the weekends. But it paid off. A month after graduation I joined corporate, and my financial situation improved considerably. Now I have a company car, generous expense account, and good perks on top of a fantastic salary."

"Not only pretty and charming, but rich too."

Ali laughed. "Sorry. I didn't mean to brag, but I am quite the catch."

Tommy's smile faded into awkward silence. Ali continued. "I didn't want to leave Wisconsin, but becoming a teacher was no longer an option for me. I didn't see much opportunity here."

"Things would've worked out if you had stayed."

A car rounded the corner at the other end of the park, sounding like the muffler had a hole in it. "Those four months locked away... changed my entire world. I came out a real mess. People I'd known my whole life avoided me, and I'd ruined my parents' lives. I forced Mom to drive me to the bus station, and I left with no idea of where to go. I became a new person in California and found my way again." Her eyes dropped. "Almost didn't stop here yesterday. In retrospect, I wish I'd driven on."

Tommy rested his hand on hers. "I'm glad you didn't. We'll get this mess straightened out. I promise."

The sinking sun put a noticeable chill in the air on the stroll home. Tommy's gentle persistence led the conversation to remembering the good times in Ali's childhood. At the door, she faced him. "Thanks for a wonderful evening. I've enjoyed this break from all the turmoil."

"My pleasure. I'd like to see you again tomorrow night."

Ali pursed her lips. "Let's see what tomorrow brings first. Despite this evening, I'm ready to leave. I want to make peace with my past, but it looks like I'll never get the chance. There's too much pain here. I'll fly Mom to San Francisco instead."

"I was hoping you'd visit more often."

Ali paused. "I might consider it once everyone knows I'm innocent. Anyway, thanks for an enjoyable evening." She stood on tiptoe and gave him a peck on the cheek. "Be safe, Tommy Peterson."

"You, too."

She watched from the door and waved as he pulled away. For Tommy, the wave was bittersweet. Despite his best efforts, Ali remained determined to put Rausburg behind her. His chance with her had passed with little to show except a pleasant evening together.

19

Wednesday, October 17, 1984

"So the stores in Rausburg aren't good enough for a girl from San Francisco, eh?" Tommy teased Ali after she opened his front office door and poked her head in a few minutes before nine.

She leaned in. "I'm not eighty and half blind. Besides, women always shop together. We connect with other members of our secret society to successfully dominate the world."

"Okay, I get it. I can take a joke."

Ali cocked her head. "What joke?"

He stood and motioned her inside.

She stepped in and straddled the threshold. "We're leaving now for the West Towne Mall."

Tommy came around his desk. "When will you be back?"

"Late afternoon. Is that a problem?"

"No. As long as you're home before dark." Tommy sat on his desk.

Ali's smile faded. "Wouldn't want Fern Johnson worrying about my safety."

Tommy crossed his arms. "Let's not give anyone a reason to call Sinclair. Bad enough a DCI agent is coming."

"We may be back earlier. We'll call when we get home."

"Thanks. Leave a message if I'm not here."

"No problem." Ali leaned into the door, pushing it open. "Don't worry, I will return. I wouldn't do that to you."

"I know."

Ali stepped aside and let the door close, unsure if Tommy really believed her.

————

At ten sharp, DCI Agent Malloy entered to find Tommy staring at the forensics report. "Chief Peterson?"

"Please call me Tommy. Agent Malloy?"

"Call me Malloy." Two more men and a woman entered. "My team. Fred, Betty, and Mike. We need a place where we can lay out the day's plans."

Tommy gestured to his tiny conference room. "Will that do?"

"For now. We want to get moving."

"Make yourselves at home."

After the task force members took seats around the single table, Tommy handed Malloy a copy of the report. Malloy scanned it in silence while Tommy leaned against the doorframe.

"I think—" Tommy started when Malloy looked up from the report.

"We'll study the crime scene first, Peterson. Give us your opinions later," Malloy said before reading the cause of death out loud and assigning his team members their jobs. "Questions?"

"If you don't mind me asking, why are you here? It's barely been two days," Tommy said.

"Do you have a suspect in custody?"

"No."

"There's your answer."

"Governor Luce heard it on the news and feared this situation had the potential to become another inter-agency embarrassment," Betty said, sugarcoating Malloy's blunt response.

Tommy nodded.

"Now show us the crime scene. If we want information from you, we'll ask. Otherwise, sit tight. We don't want you influencing our interpretations," Malloy said.

———

The sun was high overhead as the task force gathered around Tommy's car after they finished processing the crime scene. Malloy's pen was poised over his legal pad. "Have any suspects?"

Tommy rubbed the back of his neck. "Yes and no."

Malloy looked up. "What do you mean?"

"I eliminated the victim's wife because she's in a rehab center in Madison under surveillance. I checked. She won't profit by his death either, and I'm reasonably sure she didn't hire a hit man."

"Continue."

Tommy hesitated to mention Ali's connection, but Malloy would find out soon when his team interviewed the neighbors. Better for Ali if it came from Tommy's lips first. "A former resident who served jail time was visiting here the day of the murder."

Malloy cocked his head. "What was this resident convicted of?"

"She called in a bomb threat to the school eight years ago, right before graduation. Spent four months in Mineral Ridge Jail."

Malloy's face showed no emotion. "Stiff sentence for a minor. Was there a bomb?"

"No. We all knew it was a senior prank. You drove past our school. What would be gained by planting a bomb in it?"

Malloy's eyes narrowed. "The threat had to be taken seriously."

Tommy crossed his arms across his chest. "In context it was obviously a prank. Ali admitted it the next day, but Mr. Luetz made an example of her and had her arrested in front of the entire school. Two weeks later, she stood trial in Mineral Ridge as an adult because she turned eighteen the day after her arrest. Judge Lynch threw the book at her."

Malloy wrote on his legal pad. "And she was here on Monday?"

"Yes. She moved to San Francisco after serving her sentence. Earned a degree from Cal State and became an executive with Robel's department stores."

"I see. You've spoken to her?"

"I did. She has a weak alibi, but it mostly checked out."

Malloy wanted more definite answers. "What do you mean mostly? Does she or doesn't she have an alibi?"

Tommy swallowed hard. "Well, she was at a motel in Black River Falls when the murder took place. The kid who checked her in is on vacation with his family for two weeks and can't be reached."

"Isn't there a record of her checking in?"

"Their card scanner didn't work, and she paid in cash. The kid had never written a receipt before, so Ali did it and he signed it so she could get reimbursed."

"And the kid can't verify it because he's on vacation."

"Yes. The owner never found a receipt or extra cash, but he suspects the kid pocketed it. He found an extra set of sheets in the laundry that day and admitted they've had problems with their card scanner."

"Can anyone else verify her presence there?"

"No. She had no other contact all night, made no calls, and drove straight here the next morning. She didn't do it, but some will claim she killed him because of her past."

"You know this woman well?"

"We went to school together. I'm friends with her mother."

Malloy made a note. "Name?"

"Alicia Thorein."

Malloy wrote. "E-i-n?"

"Right. She's shopping in Madison with her mother. I expect them back this afternoon."

Malloy frowned. "Anyone else on the suspect list?"

Tommy grimaced. "No."

Malloy circled Ali's name.

"Many students didn't like Mr. Luetz. I expected our lab to find incriminating prints on the bat, but it was clean."

"We'll take over from here. Don't share our conversations with anyone. One of your friends probably killed Orville Luetz." Malloy tapped his pad for emphasis. "It could have been this woman."

Malloy walked away, shaking his head. "Shopping."

20

Ali's consultation with Justin Green left her satisfied and disappointed. Satisfied because she had retained a highly successful criminal attorney with a proven track record in court. Disappointed because his best advice was to say nothing more and wait them out.

Afterwards, in the car, Helga said, "I don't like it. Mr. Pinstripe Suit with his fancy oak furniture insisting you hand over a check for ten thousand dollars to retain him, and after he had your money his best advice was to sit back and wait?"

"You heard him, Mom. He doubts I'll need to use his services. I'll get the money back."

"Minus the two hundred and fifty dollars for an hour's worth of nothing." Helga threw her hand up. "Stay calm. I won't take action until you're arrested. What kind of advice is that?"

Ali wanted to point out Justin Green was a darn sight better than the attorney her parents hired for her trial. The novice who folded under the withering stare of Judge Lynch. Apparently, Helga remembered that too. "At least this one has experience. We made a big mistake in hiring someone fresh out of law school. If we'd known..."

Ali rested her hand on Helga's arm. "None of us knew. I wouldn't have placed the call if I had known it would be misconstrued and cause so much trouble."

Helga patted her daughter's hand. "That's in the past. This time we're better prepared."

They enjoyed shopping West Towne Mall and later used Ali's discount at Robel's. Afterwards, frustration and apprehension accompanied a silent ride home. As they crested the ridge into Rausburg, they found Tommy in his car parked in front of the school. Ali pulled alongside while Helga rolled down her window.

"What's new?" Ali yelled across the car.

"Task force is here talking to people."

"Don't suppose they've found the killer yet?"

"Not to my knowledge."

Ali frowned and checked her mirror.

"Any plans for supper?" Helga asked.

"Waiting to see if I'm needed."

"Call us later. Maybe we can eat together."

"Sounds fine."

Ali pulled away, disappointed at the lack of progress but ready to fight back. She might have to drain her bank account, but her accusers would regret messing with her.

———

At four p.m., the task force convened in Tommy's office.

"I'll be in my car by the school. Step outside and wave if you need me," Tommy said after Malloy dismissed him.

Fred reviewed the collected evidence. "I identified three distinct sets of prints. Two on numerous surfaces, safe bet they're the victim's and his wife's, plus a third set on the kitchen table and back door. No signs of forced entry, burglary, or vandalism. Peterson told me the victim never locked his back door.

"It appears the victim entered the kitchen around four a.m. and was struck from behind with a blunt object. He fell to the floor and was clubbed several more times before he was dragged to the table.

No usable footprints or tire tracks found outside. The killer left little evidence behind."

"Little?" Malloy asked.

"I discovered two wintergreen Lifesavers by the lilac bush at the far corner of the victim's yard, slightly dissolved but intact. They could belong to the killer. Trampled grass by the bush suggests someone loitered there, since the footprints left were size ten shoes or larger, possibly a man or a larger-than-average woman."

Malloy asked, "High school student hanging out?"

"Doubtful," Fred said. "Any student loitering there would have been noticed and reprimanded, according to the assistant principal."

Fred gestured to Mike. "I interviewed teachers. Several noticed a subtle personality change recently in the victim, most likely linked to his wife's stint in rehab, although the victim never mentioned it. Typical small town behavior. No one's supposed to know, but they all do. Peterson found her passed out alongside the road and convinced the victim to commit her."

"Interesting. He didn't mention that to us."

"Probably an oversight. Betty?"

"I talked to the neighbors. No one noticed any strange activity. One interesting development surfaced, though."

"What's that?" Malloy asked.

"Several people mentioned a note was found with the body. I couldn't pinpoint the origin of that information, but everyone knew Alicia Thorein wrote it."

"A note? Fred, is there a note in evidence?"

"No. After Betty told me about it, I called Leahy in Mineral Ridge. He didn't process any note."

"No one has seen it, but it's rumored Ms. Thorein left it by the body. Several older women insisted we arrest her immediately," Betty added.

"What have we learned about Ms. Thorein?"

Betty turned a page on her legal pad. "Here's what I've heard. All unsubstantiated hearsay. Alicia Thorein was a bright, precocious class leader. Tenacious, but also charitable. Well-behaved as a child, less so as a teenager. It's rumored she snuck out of the house without permission to attend a kegger with no ramifications from her parents.

"After her release from jail, her personality changed, which led her to a public shouting match with the victim at the Ranch House restaurant. She left the next day without warning. Several weeks later, people learned she was in San Francisco. Little has been said about her since until she unexpectedly returned this past Monday."

Betty lowered her pad. "Did everyone talk about her?" Malloy asked.

"Mostly the old biddies. They all claimed she was a bad seed waiting to sprout who didn't even attend her father's funeral three years ago. They're convinced she exacted revenge on Orville Luetz."

"That argument with the victim. When did it happen?" Malloy asked.

Betty checked her notes. "October 1976. Monday could have been the anniversary. No one remembered the exact date of the argument."

"Interesting that other people don't share Peterson's reluctance in naming her a suspect. Dig deeper into her background. Be sure to check aliases. Once she moved to San Francisco she might have changed her name. I doubt anyone has seen her ID so they wouldn't know. Anything else, Betty?"

"Alicia has kept to herself since she arrived, but talked to Melanie Wharton, a teller at the bank, yesterday. Ms. Wharton admitted they discussed stolen money from their respective class treasuries. Alicia's class of '76 lost eighty dollars. Melanie's class of '74 lost thirty dollars. When I asked her if she knew who stole the money, she said there were rumors but wouldn't elaborate. When I pushed her, she said the victim blamed two different students for the theft, but she didn't believe either one of them was involved."

"Think the teller's hiding something?"

"Doubtful. She and Peterson are the lone adults here who attended school with the suspect. I could press her for the names, but it sounded like a dead end to me."

"Could Alicia be threatening people to keep quiet about her past indiscretions?"

"No secrets here. Anything she tried to hide would become common knowledge. She left today to go shopping in Madison with her mother like Peterson said."

Malloy scoffed. "More likely she talked to Justin Green. One of his assistants called DCI yesterday afternoon, fishing. I'm sure Mr. Green welcomed her retainer. Anything else?"

Fred held up his legal pad. "I have more. Checked the local hardware store in case they sold the murder weapon. Harv's Hardware does sell bats identical to the one used, but it's not a unique bat. The killer could have bought the same bat in Mineral Ridge or Madison at many stores. Harv Middleton, the owner, remembered selling a bat last month to Helga Thorein, Alicia's mother. Harv also serves as village president."

Malloy perked up. "That's interesting. Baseball season is over. Why purchase a bat now? Did he offer an explanation?"

"He claimed it was for a gift. She doesn't play, and there are no children in her life. All speculation."

"Any other bats sold recently?"

"A couple bats were sold last spring to children. I got their names in case we decide to follow up."

Malloy considered this new information. *The suspect's mother buys the murder weapon, the village cop admits he's friendly with her and is downplaying the suspect's involvement. Might be more to this case than meets the eye.*

"Anything else?"

"No. The Luetz's were quiet, not neighborly, or at least the victim was quiet. His wife's a known drunk with little community involvement. I'll stop at the treatment center on my way home. But Peterson already told me she stayed in all night, and it was verified by the security cameras. I'll double-check and request phone records for the wife's room to see who she's been talking to."

Malloy nodded. "Any ideas at this point?" Silence.

"Other suspects?" More silence.

"Check the usual sources. I'll pay a visit to the sheriff's office to see what they have on Ms. Thorein. Send Peterson in here. I'll talk to him alone. Don't mention the note."

Malloy's staff exchanged knowing glances. Malloy didn't talk to the locals alone unless he intended to discipline them.

Fred hung behind as the others filed out. "What is it?" Malloy asked.

"Peterson did a better-than-average job of collecting evidence at the scene. When I asked, he gave me the right answers. He may not be as experienced as we are, but he worked the scene, ran crowd control, and talked to the media, all while assisting the coroner. We almost missed the Lifesavers ourselves, and they may be a dead end."

Malloy frowned. "But the note—"

"Could be hearsay. I don't expect any shocking new discoveries simply because Peterson did a good job collecting evidence. He's sharper than his position reveals, and the townspeople love him on top of it."

The townspeople's love for their cop meant nothing to Malloy if Peterson hampered his investigation. "Is that it?"

"That's all."

"Thanks, Fred. I'll use my best judgment."

"The village library has a copy machine. If you find a note, I'll take the original to analyze and leave a copy with you."

"Perfect," Malloy said as he leafed through Tommy's report.

———

Malloy stood and motioned Tommy to sit. Tommy barely got in the chair before Malloy said, "Tell me about the note."

Tommy froze. How could Malloy know about the note? Ali and Helga wouldn't share that secret. Only one possible conclusion. He smiled. "Congratulations. You solved the case. The killer gave himself away."

Malloy did not take the news well. "Several older women killed Orville Luetz? Maybe they belong to one of those rural geriatric gangs I hear so much about."

Tommy's jaw dropped. "Older women? How—"

Malloy raised his hand. "I don't want excuses. Several mentioned a note left at the scene, and it isn't in your report. Where is it?"

"Right here. Bagged."

Tommy opened his bottom desk drawer and handed the note over. Malloy studied it before glaring at Tommy. "That bomb threat was eight years ago, wasn't it? This ties Alicia Thorein to the crime, and you held it back?"

Tommy glared back as his anger swelled. "Ali didn't kill Luetz. This note must be a forgery. I knew someone like you would see it, jump to the wrong conclusion, and throw an innocent woman in jail."

Malloy leaned over the desk, resting on his fists. "Someone like me?"

Tommy rose out of his chair, his eyes never leaving Malloy's. "The papers say your task force will be cut from the budget. Looks to me you're taking advantage of this case to justify your existence."

Malloy stared back at Tommy. "Better be careful there, Peterson."

Tommy leaned in, invading Malloy's space. "You're not railroading anyone here to look good at their expense. If you use that note to justify arresting Ali, you'll have problems."

Malloy stiffened. "You better consider your position, young man, or you might find yourself in the cell next to hers. I'm your superior officer on this case."

Tommy's eyes remained locked with Malloy's. "The killer didn't know she was within driving distance Sunday night. He expected me to find her in San Francisco with a solid alibi. With no other suspects, the investigation would die." Neither man moved for a few seconds. "If you'd bothered to ask this morning instead of treating me like a chump, I would have told you why I didn't mention the note."

"We'll discuss withholding charges later, assuming you haven't already compromised the case. Is there anything else you want to tell me before I leave?" Malloy said with a cold hard edge to his voice.

"No. Are you taking Ali into custody?"

Malloy's focus had not wavered. "Will you keep her available for questioning?"

Tommy straightened. Malloy's stare conveyed his intent. If Tommy didn't back off, Ali would go to jail. He broke eye contact. "She stayed the last two days. If I ask, she'll stay a couple more."

"Then ask. I'll take her into custody if she runs or when I'm convinced she did it. I won't put an innocent woman in jail to save my job. You forget to mention anything else?"

"No."

"You have my number. Otherwise, I'll be in touch." Malloy straightened and chucked the note in his briefcase before leaving.

Tommy fell back in his chair. His anger had dictated his actions and put Ali closer to being charged with a crime she didn't commit.

21

Malloy drove south on State Highway 72, the scenic route to Mineral Ridge, familiarizing himself with the area while clearing his head after his confrontation with Peterson.

The Luetz murder puzzled him. Alicia Thorein had an undisputed motive, but only one piece of evidence linked her to the scene. Making matters worse, a young cop loved by his community hindered the investigation.

That's what troubled Malloy. Peterson cared for Alicia. Enough to cover her tracks? Peterson gathered all the pertinent evidence and sent it to the lab in Mineral Ridge. The clean murder weapon—coincidence? Like Alicia returning after eight years?

Several other things bothered Malloy. The killer struck Orville Luetz from behind as he entered the kitchen, and Orville never saw his attacker. If Alicia sought revenge, she wouldn't kill him outright. She would want him to see it coming and enjoy the terror in his eyes as he faced his own demise.

And why leave Luetz seated at the table? The coroner's report stated Luetz weighed two fifty-four. Unless Alicia was an Amazon, she would have a tough time lifting the inert body. Why go through that?

Alicia's alibi could have been faked. He was vaguely familiar with the motel. Not a place that catered to corporate executives. She could have checked in and slept for a couple hours before leaving in plenty of time to kill the victim at four. She could have paid off a dishonest clerk to say she spent the night when she didn't.

Many hastily labeled Alicia a suspect when, as a teenager, she was the village's rising star. Most people wouldn't change their opinion that fast. Did an unspoken act lead them to that conclusion?

Alicia's mother. Naïve enough to buy the murder weapon at the local hardware store where it would be remembered? *This case might not be solved so easily after all.*

He made a vivid first impression in Mineral Ridge when the desk deputy tried to call Sheriff Chuck Sinclair at home to tell him that Malloy was there. Malloy pushed the phone's cradle down while leaning over and repeating, "I said I'm here on the governor's orders. I'll talk to Sinclair in the morning. In the meantime, you'll do as I say and assist me in a timely fashion. Nod your head if you comprehend."

The deputy glared at him before nodding.

"Good. Call a secretary to pull several files for me. Is that understood?"

Marie, the secretary on duty, found no files for Orville Luetz but located Ali's old case file. Malloy flipped through it while Marie continued her search. A few seconds later she asked, "You have the forensics and coroner's reports, correct?"

"Yep."

"Then you have every file pertaining to Orville Luetz and Alicia Thorein."

Malloy left, grunting his displeasure.

He ate supper at the lone fast-food restaurant in town, Hardee's, before checking in at the Kickapoo Motor Inn. He hung his spare clothes and placed a short call to tell Betty where he was staying. His obligation met, he settled in the room's sole chair to study Alicia's file.

Justice moved fast in Kickapoo County. Two weeks after her arrest, she appeared in court. Her attorney entered a guilty plea and asked for probation, pointing out that she had an exemplary school record with no priors. Orville Luetz testified for the prosecution by labeling her a juvenile delinquent with a history of disobedience. Judge Lynch sentenced her to the maximum for her misdemeanor— a hundred twenty days in jail, remanding her into immediate custody.

Her attorney filed an appeal by midsummer, expressing Alicia's desire to enter college on schedule and citing a merit scholarship. Appeal denied. She was released in October.

The last document in the file was a photocopy of a handwritten letter Alicia sent to District Attorney Dan Milenburg.

> *Mr. Milenburg,*
>
> *While I don't agree with the severity of my sentence, I know you were doing your job, and I hold no grudge against you. I look forward to my release in a few days, at which time I will dedicate my efforts to getting back on track. I fully intend that you will never see me in the court system again.*
>
> *Sincerely,*
> *Ali Thorein*

She dated the letter two weeks before her release. He flipped through the file again. No record of trouble during her incarceration. No reason to seek favor with the DA.

He dug into his briefcase to pull out the copy of the crime scene note and compare it to the letter in the file. Same hand. Open-and-shut case. Malloy's momentary celebration was guarded, however. One piece of evidence linking everything was an easy challenge for a defense attorney. Several pieces would be better. And this was a copy. What happened to the original? She addressed it to Milenburg. Shouldn't the original be in the file?

22

"Yes, Tommy, that's fine. Six it is." Helga hung up and returned to the living room.

Ali looked up from the sofa. "Tommy coming over?"

"He's taking us to the Ranch House for supper tonight."

"The Ranch House? Mom, you remember my last visit there, don't you?"

Helga remembered, all right. She suggested supper out to stop Ali from moping around the house after her release from jail. The Thorein family kept to themselves and conducted a strained conversation over their meal when Orville and Margaret Luetz entered. Ali wanted to leave, but Helga suggested that Ali speak to her former principal. "People will see you together and realize any hard feelings are in the past."

Ali reluctantly agreed and went to Luetz's table. Their conversation was muted until Luetz exploded. "You tarnished my career and the entire village. Stay away from my school. No one wants an ex-con around."

She thrust her finger at him and yelled, "There's a special place in hell reserved for you. I hope you burn for all eternity."

Ali stormed out of the restaurant. Every diner had heard the exchange.

After a sleepless night, she withdrew her life savings from the bank, packed a suitcase, and told her mother, "Drive me to the bus station or I'm hitchhiking." Helga tried to reason with her, but Ali was having none of it. Helga took her, not suspecting Ali would stay away for eight long years.

Tonight, Helga was equally determined. Ali focused on Fern Johnson's judgmental friends, forgetting that Chet and Melanie welcomed her home. Helga knew others would welcome her back too, but Ali didn't give them a chance. "You're innocent. It's time people accepted it. You didn't become an executive by hiding at home, did you?"

Ali accepted her fate with a resigned, "Okay then."

———

Helga opened the door when Tommy arrived at six. "How was your day, dear?"

He shook his head. "Tough. Agent Malloy isn't the friendliest guy. Well, are we hungry?"

Ali rose from the couch. "Are you certain you want to eat at the Ranch House?"

Tommy patted his belly. "Yeah, I'm starved. Besides, since I became police chief, they always make sure my steaks are done to perfection."

The restaurant was located two miles south at the intersection of Highway 72 and County Road G. Despite her apprehension, Ali laughed when the giant plastic Holstein mounted on the Ranch House's roof came into view.

"Bet you don't have those in California," Tommy said.

"Not that I know of. That must be one sturdy cow to stand there year after year."

"This one's two years old. The last one cracked during a sub-zero cold spell. Head fell off. I'm surprised you didn't read about in San

Francisco. Made all the papers here. Had to use a high-lift crane to change them out."

"Somehow I missed it."

Tommy pulled in and parked in the half-full lot. The exterior of the Ranch House hadn't changed since Ali's last visit. The tall one-story wooden replica of a large fifties ranch-style house seated one hundred people in the front. The rustic brown restaurant was connected to a large banquet hall that hosted wedding receptions and other special occasions on the weekends.

As Tommy held the front door open, Helga stepped through first and Ali followed. Inside, the dark wood and Christmas lights strung year 'round lent a cozy warmth to the dining room. White hair and baldness ruled the room, but no one paid her any attention, and for the first time Ali thought dining out might not be the catastrophe she predicted.

A young waitress swung by, balancing a tray of drinks. "Open booths in the back. I'll be along in a minute."

Few paid attention to them as they made their way through the restaurant. A man called out, "Hey, Tommy," so Ali and Helga continued to the booth while Tommy hung back to talk.

The menu, like always, featured meat and potatoes. Walleye from Lake Superior fried in beer batter topped the seafood column along with other staples of fine Wisconsin dining. Their waitress dropped off the relish tray loaded with carrots, gherkins, and olives without fanfare and took their drink order.

Helga and Ali watched the waitress hustle, taking orders, bringing food out. Ali had anticipated waitressing the summer before college. She planned to work at Christmas and every summer until she finished her degree, but her incarceration ended that.

"Tough job," Helga said, nodding at the waitress.

"I suppose."

Tommy joined them. "Best prime rib in the county."

"That's a little heavy for me," Ali said.

Helga closed her menu. "I'm getting the Chicken Kiev. You used to like that, didn't you?"

"Haven't had it since I left. Sounds good to me."

Their waitress apologized for making them wait. "Darlene called in sick, and we're short-handed. What can I get you?"

They ordered and afterward munched carrots off the relish tray while Helga relived their afternoon shopping trip. "You should have seen the way the Robel's manager fawned over us after Ali introduced herself."

"I did that to reassure him I was shopping with my mother, not secretly spying on his store. We weren't introduced last week at the sales meeting, but he would have recognized me from my presentation, especially after the service desk rang up my discount."

"Didn't hurt. He offered to accompany us while we shopped."

"And I declined. He has more important things to do with his time."

"Maybe I should have gone with you," Tommy said. "I'm about due for my annual shopping spree. Sure would have been an improvement over my day."

Ali swallowed a bite of carrot. "Did you make progress in the investigation?"

"No, and it's out of my hands now. Agent Malloy and his task force are in charge. On top of it, I overheard several radio conversations between Sinclair and his deputies. They all think I bungled the investigation and aren't happy with me."

"I'm sorry to hear that. I don't mean to be blunt, but what does that mean for me?"

"Facts don't change. Malloy's team will find the killer."

Their salads arrived, providing a natural excuse to end the conversation. "Farmers grow a lot of lettuce in California, don't they?" Tommy asked.

Ali stabbed her salad. "I guess. I've driven past large lettuce fields around Monterey, but no one discusses crops or milk prices where I work."

"Must be hard to strike up a conversation," Tommy said.

Ali had forgotten a Wisconsin meal covered everything but the edges of the plate. Tommy's steak was enormous, but he showed no signs of being overwhelmed by its size.

"Tommy's still growing," Helga said as he cut into his steak.

"Obvious why he filled out," Ali said. An outburst of laughter from a nearby table forced her to raise her voice. "Be sure to chew your food so you don't choke. I don't want your death on my hands."

The laughter subsided as abruptly as it started and left a sudden lull in the restaurant. During the lull, Ali's raised voice covered the room, "...your death on my hands."

"Well at least we'd know where to look," a man's voice wisecracked, followed by silence.

Tommy stopped cutting his steak mid-stroke. The vein on his temple stuck out.

Nervous laughter rose in the room. Ali patted his arm. "Never mind them." But she was too late.

Tommy threw his napkin down, bolted out of the booth, and strode to the room's center.

"Listen up, people," he commanded. The entire room fell silent, focusing on the enraged young cop in their midst. Tommy opened his mouth. Helga caught his eye, waving her finger back and forth mouthing *No, no, no.*

He closed his mouth for a moment and saw many friendly faces staring back at him in astonishment. These were good people, but they were hasty to point an accusing finger without evidence. "Orville's murder has us all scared. I can't believe there might be a killer among us. You must feel the same way."

All eyes focused on him and all activity stopped. "Let's face facts. Many of you supported Mr. Luetz's 'do what's required and nothing more' way he ran the school. He always denied us field trips and extracurricular activities beyond basic sports. Even homecoming and prom were barebones affairs that most schools would be ashamed of. Every student resented him because of it, and we all can be considered suspects."

He rested his gaze on Ali.

"Few were brave enough to challenge him, and the one who

succeeded most suffered for it. You all complain the young people move away year after year yet you let him run our school like a prison. We were all glad to leave that gym for the last time after graduation, knowing he was out of our lives. If my job had not required it, I would have never set foot in that building as long as he remained. It's time you faced the truth. Orville Luetz had many enemies.

"Even though he angered us, we all were taught to respect the sanctity of life. As much as we disliked the man, I can't think of anyone capable of killing him. Anyone.

"When I collected evidence at the scene, I felt confident it would identify the killer, but it didn't. Agent Malloy has examined everything with a fine-tooth comb, and by the end of the day, his team of experts couldn't name Orville's killer either.

"Keep in mind that we're all innocent until proven guilty in this country. The best investigative team in the state is assisting me, and we will find the killer. In the meantime, keep your ill-informed opinions to yourself."

Tommy raised his hand in a dismissive way. "That's all I have to say." He took two steps before stopping. "And if you don't approve of the company you're dining with tonight, leave your check at the register. I'll take care of it."

Hurrying back to the table, the rustling of Tommy's uniform remained the lone sound until Carl Dolph said. "Edna's been yappin' at me all night, Tommy. You mind picking mine up? She can handle hers on her own."

Edna gave her husband of forty-six years a swat on the shoulder. A gentle wave of laughter swept the room as people continued their meals. Words failed Ali. Helga leaned over the table and whispered, "Well put. Your mother would be proud of you."

Tommy cut his steak, wolfing two silent bites before Helga remarked the weather was warmer than normal.

"Storm front's headed our way. Probably hit tomorrow night," Tommy said between bites.

Polite conversation resumed at their table. A more subdued atmosphere filled the room, but no one rushed over to apologize.

By the time they left, the restaurant was nearly empty. No one left without paying, but as Tommy paid the bill, he told the waitress, "I meant what I said. If anyone leaves their check, I'll pay for it."

The waitress smiled. "Don't worry. If anyone tries, I'll guilt them into taking care of it. Sorry I didn't introduce myself before, Ali. Debbie Lundgren is my mom. She was several years ahead of you in school."

Ali studied the girl, and now she noticed the resemblance to the long-forgotten classmate. "I remember her. She showed the girls in our class how to double Dutch with our jump ropes."

"She taught me and my friends too. We live in the same house if you want to stop by. Grandpa and Grandma moved to Florida."

"Maybe next time. Tell your mother I said hello and her daughter does her proud."

———

After a quiet ride home, they climbed the front porch steps. Helga suggested it might be nice to sit outside and enjoy the sunset. Tommy agreed, and Helga went inside to grab her jacket, leaving Ali and Tommy alone on the porch swing, gently rocking back and forth.

"I appreciate you defending my honor at the restaurant, but I'm not sure it changed anything."

Tommy shrugged. "They needed to hear it. Things change slowly around here. Too many are stuck in 1950. Most of our graduates leave and rarely return, except for holidays."

Ali glanced away. "I didn't even do that."

"My point is if Fern Johnson and her crowd don't learn to be less judgmental, no one will want to live here. The village will die."

"Well, Tommy Peterson, I appreciate what you said. It was amazing. The kid who rarely met anyone's eyes, lecturing a roomful of people on their bad behavior."

Tommy laughed once. "There was another benefit to not looking you in the eye, all the other girls, too."

Ali stopped swinging. "Were you checking us all out?" She gave his shoulder a playful slap.

Tommy rubbed his shoulder, grimacing in mock pain, bringing a grin from Ali as they resumed swinging. "So, tell me what you did in Madison today."

"We shopped at Robel's and a few stores at the mall like Mom said."

He shook his head. "Besides shopping. I assumed you met with an attorney, but you came back deflated. I figured an attorney would pump you up."

Ali planted her feet, stopping the swing. Tommy opened his hands. "I'm not dumb. Who did you see in Madison?"

"I'm sticking with my story." Ali crossed her arms. "You dodged my question earlier. How did your day go with the hotshot detective?"

"Could have gone better. He's a sharp guy. I'll give him that. A real stickler for detail."

"Did he discover anything new?"

"Didn't say. His team spent the day going over Orville's house and interviewing potential witnesses."

Ali crossed her arms. "Does he consider me the prime suspect?"

Tommy half-heartedly tried to swing again, but Ali dragged her feet, thwarting his efforts. "Oh, all right. Agent Malloy's not a talker. He might question you tomorrow, but he's interviewing several people. I wouldn't read anything into it yet."

"What if I refuse to speak with him?"

"I wouldn't recommend that."

"Okay then." Ali started swinging, and Tommy gratefully joined her. "For your information, I retained an expert defense attorney today who assured me after a wrongful arrest, I could end up owning the village. You can help me choose a new name for it. I was partial to Aliville."

Tommy furrowed his brow, exaggerating a thoughtful nod while looking her in the eye. "Maybe Aliciasburg or Thorein's Folly. That has a nice ring to it."

"Nice to see you can look me in the face now, pervert."

"I could have then. Why give up a good thing?"

"Ha," Ali laughed once.

The chilly night air made Ali shiver, and she snuggled closer to Tommy. He put his arm around her while they rocked back and forth, watching the sun dip behind the trees. All talk of murders, jail, and the rest were temporarily forgotten as they enjoyed the peace and quiet.

Behind them, Helga snuck over to the window. Seeing Ali and Tommy snuggled together, she whispered, "Thank you," before continuing with her knitting.

23

Thursday, October 17, 1984

The task force had worked late into the night, analyzing evidence and digging deeper into Alicia's background. Sunrise found Fred back at his desk, tired but ready for Malloy's call. As expected, the phone rang a few minutes before eight a.m.

"What'd you find out?" Malloy asked.

"Margaret Luetz's alibi checked out. The fingerprints we lifted came from the victim or his wife with a few strays from Peterson not included in his evidence. The bat was clean of prints with traces of fiber residue on the handle. The killer wore common work gloves. Once we find the gloves, we can match them. Otherwise, it's a dead end."

"What about the note Peterson hid?"

"Found a partial print there. Alicia's prints were in the database. Not hers, and not Luetz's either."

"Damn."

"We'll keep searching. Except for Alicia's misdemeanor eight years ago, her record is clean. We pulled several newspaper accounts of her conviction too."

"Anything there?"

"Nothing we didn't already know. Reporters highlighted the fact that Alicia received the new maximum sentence enacted by legislature a month prior. Luetz wasn't mentioned."

"I read the court transcript. Luetz's testimony justified the severe sentence."

Malloy had dimly remembered reading a newspaper account of the trial. His recollection was that the reporter painted Alicia's sentence to be an overreaction to typical teenage hijinks. At the time he scoffed at the reporter's bias. Now, after spending time in Rausburg, he was less sure.

"What else did you find?" Malloy asked.

"Alicia has worked for Robel's since November 1976. Her secretary told Betty that Alicia is on vacation for the first time in three years. She scheduled a week off but said nothing about visiting relatives."

"So her arrival might have been a surprise to everyone."

"She booked a room at the Saint Paul Hotel last Thursday through Saturday, lending credence to her Sunday night stay at the Motor Lodge in Black River Falls. I called that motel and confirmed Peterson's explanation of her flimsy alibi. They have no record of her stay, but she could have paid in cash and spent the night in a room in the back. The assistant manager suggested that bookkeeping is not the owner's strong suit."

"Ask around DCI. Another agent might have information on the Motor Lodge that we could use to sharpen their memory. Anything else?"

"Betty got lucky looking for aliases and found an Alice Thorn who materialized March 1978 in San Francisco. We're waiting for a picture from the California DMV. Might be her."

"Any record on Alice Thorn?"

"No information before 1978. No birth certificate or Social Security number."

"How did she get a driver's license?"

"Fake documents? California's a big state. Easier to slip through the system there. Alice Thorn is connected to addresses in Denver,

Las Vegas, and Los Angeles for short periods, each time returning to San Francisco."

"Interesting. Any ideas?"

"How about one far-fetched theory?"

"Let's hear it."

Fred hesitated. "Entirely speculation."

"Your speculations usually bear fruit, but I won't take it to trial yet."

Fred took a moment to gather his thoughts. "The clean crime scene raises the possibility that Alice Thorn is a professional hit woman. Alicia probably had little money when she ran away, and San Francisco is an expensive place to live. Desperation may have led her to commit crimes for money."

"Didn't you say she worked for Robel's the entire time?"

"Yes, but she started at minimum wage. I doubt she paid her bills with her paycheck alone, much less financed a college education. Maybe she moonlighted as a stripper or a hooker and became connected to the underworld. Her bank account was much larger than I expected, given what she earned at Robel's."

"Good point."

"I'm searching for a less dramatic explanation, but no one mentioned Alicia moving around. Her father's funeral took place while Alice Thorn was in Denver."

"Keep checking until you find something or it becomes a dead end. I'll either be at the sheriff's department or the courthouse this morning. They might help us fill in the blanks."

Malloy hung up, shaking his head. *Professional hit woman? Fred needs some time off.*

———

Sheriff Chuck Sinclair didn't bother to hide his resentment at the way Malloy commandeered the case. Malloy stood in Sinclair's office doorway, skipping all pretense at amiable small talk. "What can you tell me about Rausburg?"

"Sleepy little village. Peterson is a nice kid for a ticket writer. I offered my help, but he wanted to do it on his own, so I let him flounder. I should have stepped in and saved you a trip here."

Malloy showed Sinclair the victim's picture. "Recognize him?"

Sinclair scowled as he gave it a fleeting glance. "Saw his picture in the paper. It's possible our paths crossed. Small county, ya know."

"You've met before. Eight years ago, he testified at a trial here. A bomb threat at Rausburg School. You worked in court that day and escorted the convict, Alicia Thorein, to jail. I read it in her file."

Sinclair checked the photo again. "I've seen many people like that. Do you remember everyone you've ever met?"

"No, of course not. I assumed the picture might jog your memory, that's all."

"What was the case again?"

"A young girl named Alicia Thorein called in a fake bomb threat. Her principal, Luetz, testified for the prosecution. Judge Lynch sentenced her to four months in your jail."

Sinclair stroked his chin. "I remember her now. Caused no problems as I recall. You interested in her?"

"Showed up Monday in Rausburg." Malloy paused. "Incredible coincidence."

"She killed him?"

Malloy handed his card to Sinclair. "Too early to say. I'll be around if you remember anything else."

"I'll let you know."

"One more thing," Malloy said, turning back on his way out. "Peterson found a note at the scene. Didn't get delivered here."

Sinclair tossed Malloy's card on his desk. "Is Peterson withholding evidence?"

"He claims he held it back until he found other evidence to convict the killer."

Sinclair leaned back and folded his hands across his belly. "Good thing he doesn't work here. I'd chew his ass out good before I showed him the door."

Malloy left. *Interesting choice of words. Withholding evidence. Not screwed up, not forgot. Why does this guy say Peterson's soft and assume he withheld? Why not incompetent or forgetful? And he never asked about the contents of the note, did he?*

———

District Attorney Dan Milenburg shuffled papers on his desk while Malloy talked. "Here's the homicide victim from Rausburg. No one's in custody yet," Malloy said, watching Milenburg's reaction as he displayed Luetz's picture.

Milenburg glanced at the photo and turned back to his paperwork. "I reviewed the crime scene photos before Peterson claimed them. Victim looked familiar, but I couldn't place him."

"He was a witness in the Rausburg bomb threat case you prosecuted eight years ago."

Milenburg studied the photo as he grabbed a pen. "Oh, yeah, right. I'd forgotten. I've tried numerous cases since then."

"Have you seen or spoken to Orville Luetz recently?"

"No reason to."

"Do you remember anything else about the case?"

Milenburg leaned back in his chair. "I believe she pleaded guilty, and Judge Lynch sentenced her to maximum jail time as a deterrent to others. That's standard for him."

"Does it work?"

Milenburg clicked his pen. "Depends on who you ask."

"Your opinion?"

Milenburg went back to a file on his desk. "My job is to push for maximum sentencing."

"You remember Luetz's testimony?"

"Vaguely. I believe he testified Alicia was destined to break the law."

"Didn't Alicia's attorney produce witnesses to speak for her?"

"No. He was fresh out of law school, and he never tried another case here if I recall correctly." Milenburg opened another file on his desk. "If that's all..."

"For now. Thanks for your time."

Milenburg ignored the sarcasm as Malloy left, certain both men knew Orville Luetz better than they let on. *Why hide it? How could they forget Alicia's case? It made papers across the state. Didn't they talk to reporters?*

24

A somber mood presided at Helga's kitchen table Thursday morning. Both women slept fitfully throughout the night, caught in nightmares, worrying about the DCI agent and any conclusions he might arrive at today.

"How could the killer forge my handwriting? I haven't written to anyone but you." Ali lightly blew on her coffee and took a sip. "Did you keep my letters?"

"For a while. I threw the oldest ones away."

"Any disappear? Maybe you left one out and the killer stole it."

Helga shook her head. "No one's been in this house in ages, except for Tommy. I showed him a couple postcards, but they didn't leave the room."

"The forger had to be holding a serious grudge against Luetz."

Helga sipped her coffee. "Maybe we should talk to Mr. Farmingham. He was close to Mr. Luetz. He always asks about you. He regretted what happened and told me several times he wished he'd been... What did he say? Proactive—that's it. He wished he had been more proactive instead of assuming it would all work out."

Ali shook her head. "Farmingham was a good teacher, but visiting him at school? The only student ever expelled and sent to jail? I doubt he wants me there now, especially after the murder."

Helga slapped the table. "I'll ask Mary Albright. She used to be Mary Schaefer. She's the secretary now."

Ali's eyebrows furrowed. "Name doesn't register."

"Doesn't matter. I'll call and see what she thinks."

———

Malloy spent almost two hours at the Mineral Ridge News Leader, researching Alicia Thorein, working backward from the trial four years. She won Rausburg's Young Citizen of the Year, whatever that was, had a supporting role in the school musical, and made the honor roll. Pictures of her on the cheerleading squad ran in the paper as well.

"Any big stories in Rausburg during the last few years?" Malloy asked the editor as he prepared to leave.

"Nope. Guess they made up for it this week, huh?"

"I didn't read much negative from there either. A few sheriff's department reports but little else. I found that odd."

"I report the occasional fires and accidents, but most of these villages don't want their secrets broadcast."

"You're selective on what you print?"

"I'm saying I can't report it if I don't hear about it. We're a small operation. Most of our news comes from Mineral Ridge unless I get a call or hear it on the scanner."

Malloy thanked him and left for a light lunch at Bob's Diner in Rausburg. Coffee and pie were alluring, but he had another motive. Diners were a great place to learn a village's secrets and overhear something helpful to the case.

———

All eyes fell on Malloy as he entered the diner and acknowledged a few polite smiles before sitting at the counter. Marked as an intruder, he left two stools open between him and the next patron.

Bob, the owner, came over. "Coffee?"

"Please."

Bob placed a cup on the counter and poured. "How's the investigation going?"

"Making progress."

Bob set the carafe down before sliding the sugar and cream over.

"How's the apple pie today?"

"Baked fresh this morning." Bob stepped away to get it, which is what Malloy wanted.

Several Rausburg Shopper Gazettes lay on the end of the counter. Malloy grabbed one.

Bob noticed as he dished out a slice of pie. "That came out yesterday."

"I suppose the bargains are already gone."

"Most likely."

Malloy laid the paper out as he sipped his coffee. When Bob brought his pie, Malloy thanked him and scanned the paper, allowing the other patrons to relax. Conversations around him increased while Malloy eavesdropped. Behind him, an older gentleman complained about his corn yield. "That dry spell at the end of July—that's what did it." Another man lamented the high cost of a truck muffler. His table mate scoffed and told him where he could have gotten it cheaper. Malloy listened to several conversations taking place across the room. Two bites into his pie, he got his first bit of useful information.

"You hear about Tommy giving everyone what for last night at the Ranch House?" an older man said.

"Yeah, Carl Dolph was there, said Tommy read everybody the riot act," the guy's booth companion responded.

"Heard a comment he didn't like and told them to lay off Ali. Surprised he had it in him."

"You think she did it?"

"Nah, she's no killer."

Out of the corner of his eye, Malloy watched Bob grab the carafe before hustling to that booth. He poured coffee and talked about the Packer game Monday night. The two guys discussed the Packer's abysmal record and forgot the previous conversation.

Malloy lingered, but the conversations drifted to politics and the weather. After he settled his bill, he walked to the pay phone outside the drugstore across the street.

"You're getting Alicia's phone records from San Francisco, aren't you?" Malloy asked.

"Be here early next week," Fred said.

"Get them for Peterson, too. Home and office."

"Really? Why?"

"When he's the prime suspect, everything fits. He could have killed Luetz and forged the note. If he knew Alicia was coming, it gave him leverage to force her to stay. If she was in San Francisco, it gave him a reason to call her, and as he admitted, it makes the crime unsolvable. Maybe he wanted to impress her by eliminating her enemy. Either way, the evidence wouldn't convict him so he didn't worry about handing it over to Sinclair. His phone records might confirm a connection much quicker too."

"You think he's involved in this? I don't."

"Talk to Margaret Luetz again this afternoon. Ask her what she remembers about the day Peterson made the victim commit her. Peterson grew up here. Maybe the victim threatened him with past indiscretions."

"You're barking up the wrong tree on this one."

"Humor me. Anyway, I'll be with Betty at the school if you find any important evidence."

Small towns don't always divulge their secrets. Malloy had yet to learn the vent three feet over the open-air pay phone provided a perfect conduit for overhearing phone conversations from inside the drugstore.

Salesmen had blown deals by not knowing that secret, bragging how they unloaded inferior equipment on an unsuspecting farmer. A best man hiring a stripper for his friend's bachelor party hung up mid-call when the bride's mother burst out of the drugstore and fixed him with a glare that still gave him nightmares.

And eight years ago, a young girl's life was upended because she assumed the drugstore was closed and empty when she placed an early morning call. In fact, a loyal customer sat inside, waiting while the pharmacist filled her heart medication, listening through the vent with great interest.

Today that same customer sat in that same chair, eager to go home and phone her friends. "Is my prescription ready yet?"

"Another moment, Fern. I'm almost done."

"Well, snap to it. I'm not getting any younger."

———

Trudging up the school sidewalk, Ali was on edge. Despite twelve carefree years attending school there, the memory of leaving in hand-cuffs while the entire student body watched lingered in her mind. Even though Mary said Farmingham would love to meet with her after fourth period, Ali wasn't sure she wanted to see him. As they approached the front door, Helga said, "This is my first time back, too."

"You haven't been back since..."

"Never. Not with that bastard around."

"Better curb your tongue. Don't forget where we are."

"I haven't forgotten."

Ali took Helga's hand before pulling the door open.

Little had changed in the foyer. A case full of now-meaningless trophies lined the wall across from the office. The most recent gradu-ating class picture hung over the case. Ali's photo would be around the corner by now, assuming Luetz left it hanging.

They entered the office and Mary smiled at them. "You're glowing today, Helga."

Helga smiled back. "You remember my daughter, Ali?"

"Of course. Last time we talked, you were in elementary school. You resemble your mother."

"Thanks. I remember you now. You had Beatles pictures all over your notebook, right?"

Mary laughed. "That was a long time ago. Mr. Farmingham was glad you called, Helga. He'll be here shortly. He had to teach fourth period. Take a seat. Let's catch up."

Several minutes later, Ali had shared all she intended when Farmingham breezed in, wearing a smile. "Good to see both of you. Thanks for stopping by. Please, come inside."

Ali tensed as she entered the room where she had confessed and left in handcuffs. Farmingham noticed. "We can go somewhere else if you like. I'm uncomfortable in here myself. As anxious as I've been for Mr. Luetz to retire, I never expected to get the job this way."

"It's okay," Ali said. "This room brings back unpleasant memories, that's all."

Farmingham motioned for them to sit in the wooden chairs facing the desk. "Ali, I'm glad you came by." He sat behind the desk and took a moment to find the right words. "I'm sorry I didn't help more. We teachers all agreed you didn't need to stand trial. I told Mr. Luetz he'd made his point, and I insisted he drop the charges. We had a heated discussion, and I left for summer vacation convinced he withdrew the complaint. I didn't realize he lied until I read about your conviction in the paper. I'm sorry, I failed you."

Luetz lied to Farmingham eight years ago? Helga and Ali both straightened.

"I placed the call," Ali said. "It was immature and childish, but I did it. There was nothing you could have done once the situation spiraled out of control."

"You will always be one of my best students. We all have impetuous teenage mishaps." He shook his head. "I perpetrated several ill-advised actions in high school. Luckily, I never got caught."

Ali formed a tight grin. "I wish you had been the principal back then. The whole school would have benefited."

Farmingham shifted. "Thanks. I'll be the interim principal for the rest of the year. If I'm lucky, the school board will ask me to continue and hire a new science teacher. So, you're an executive with Robel's. How do you like it?"

Ali had forgotten how much kids liked and respected Mr. Farmingham. He was always an inspiring teacher, always interested in the students. He asked Ali about her job and personal life and lifted her spirits with his praise.

"How can I help you today?"

"You've heard I'm suspected of killing Mr. Luetz."

Farmingham shook his head. "I don't believe it. None of the teachers do. The Ali we taught couldn't take another person's life."

"Thanks, but this cop from Madison believes I could."

Farmingham sat back. "I spoke with Agent Malloy yesterday. He's blunt but fair."

"Did he ask about me?"

Farmingham shifted in his seat. "Yes. I told him Mr. Luetz exaggerated an incident that would have been better handled internally, and I mentioned the positive things you did too."

"Thanks. I appreciate it."

"I showed Agent Malloy the senior pictures hanging in the hall and told him, 'None of them cared much for Mr. Luetz when they left, but no one was vengeful enough to commit murder, Ali included.'"

"If no one here had a reason to kill Mr. Luetz, the killer must be an outsider."

Farmingham smiled. "Applying the Socratic method?"

Ali smiled back. "Yes, I guess so. Did Mr. Luetz mention anything that could be a possible motive for murder or revenge?"

Farmingham tented his hands and rested his index fingers against his lips. "I mostly talked about school matters with Mr. Luetz."

Ali often used silence as a powerful motivator. She didn't want Farmingham holding back so she remained quiet. "Recently he spoke about righting wrongs and wishing he'd done things differently. The bomb threat, for one."

"He mentioned that specifically?"

"Yes, it surprised me. It was the first time he ever admitted he was wrong to pursue it, and he wanted a second chance to do the right thing."

"But he didn't say what that was?" Ali crossed her fingers.

"No. I changed the subject because I didn't want to dwell on our past differences."

Ali hid her relief that her secret remained safe for the time being. "Did he mention any other incidents outside school?"

"No. Since Monday I've wondered what would drive a person to commit such a heinous crime. I wanted answers to ease the children's concerns, but nothing came to mind. Sorry."

"If you think of anything, tell Tommy. He'll be glad to pass it on."

"I'll be happy to. Speaking of Tommy, I'm sure you were just as surprised as the rest of us to see how he turned out."

"I'll say. The village cop?"

"Another success story, like you. The extra time you and Ellen spent with him helped him immensely."

"All the students did their part."

"True, but the two of you went above and beyond. I hope when this is resolved, you'll visit us and share your success stories with our students."

Ali tilted her head. "Perhaps."

"Helga, I haven't forgotten how you volunteered with the young ones. If you're interested, we could use help in the elementary grades."

"Oh, I don't know. I'm much older now."

"Even better. The students will respond to you like a beloved grandparent. It'd be good practice for your own... someday."

Helga beamed. Ali rolled her eyes, making Farmingham laugh. "Seriously, if I can help..."

Ali's eyes flew open.

Farmingham blushed. "I meant help in your current situation. If either of you need assistance, you merely have to ask."

"Thanks." Ali rose and offered her hand. "I appreciate your support. I'm glad you're principal."

"Again, I'm sorry I didn't help more. If I had known he lied about dropping the charges…"

"It wasn't your fault."

Ali led Helga out and concealed her inner disappointment by smiling at Mary as they passed her.

What have I become? Can't believe I'd consider ruining Mr. Farmingham's career to save myself. No, I won't point suspicion at him unless there's no other way.

Despite her noble intentions, Ali knew she would stop at nothing to avoid murder charges. Ruining Farmingham's career might make her sad, but it beat destroying her own.

25

Tommy's squad car sat in front of the police station as Malloy drove to the school. After last night's heated exchange, Malloy didn't find it necessary to keep him in the loop, but the more Peterson talked, the more likely he would pass useful information.

Tommy rose as Malloy entered. "Agent Malloy, glad you came in. Please have a seat. Something needs to be said."

"What is it?" Malloy remained standing.

"I want to apologize. I overreacted yesterday."

"Yes, you did."

"When you took over my investigation, I ranked you the same as another individual who I believe would arrest Ali based exclusively on the note and be done with it. I didn't give you credit for being fair or thorough. I will cooperate with the investigation in every possible way, but I do have one request, sir."

Here it comes, I've been soft-soaped. He wants all charges against him dropped.

"And what's that?"

"I believe you'd be wrong to arrest Ali. But if you do, please detain her in my cell. I'll make arrangements to watch her twenty-four hours a day."

"And your reasoning?"

"Mineral Ridge Jail has had a bad reputation for years. I know Ali will have to transfer there if she's arraigned, but until then she would be better served in my cell."

Malloy glared at Tommy while holding his tongue, forcing Tommy to elaborate.

Tommy continued, his voice calm and measured. "We could use the seventy-two hours before her initial appearance to make certain we're doing the right thing. My opinion hasn't changed. Ali's innocent, and I want her to receive a fair chance."

"And I won't be fair?"

Tommy shifted. "It's not a question of your fairness, sir. Seventy-two additional hours will help build a stronger case against her or prove her innocence."

"I'm listening."

"After her initial appearance, Lynch will order her jailed without bond. With legal maneuvering, it might take several months to win a not guilty verdict. Chances are, it would destroy her career. I doubt you want that on your conscience, and I don't want it on mine."

Malloy broke eye contact. "All you want is to jail her here until we file formal charges?"

"Yes. I'm still convinced you'd be making a mistake, but she'd be safer here."

Malloy remained suspicious of Peterson's motives, but the young man sounded sincere.

"When you said another person would arrest Alicia because of the note, were you talking about Sheriff Sinclair?"

"I don't want to speak out of turn, sir."

"Understood. Answer off the record."

"Rumors have circulated about Sinclair and his deputies mistreating prisoners for years. My predecessor pushed the village board to build those two cells in the back to avoid taking temporary prisoners to Mineral Ridge. I work hard to keep Sinclair out of Rausburg. Sorry I lumped you into the same category."

Malloy remained surprised, suspecting a ploy to get the withholding charge dropped. He softened his voice. "Alicia can stay here until the initial appearance. That much I can promise."

"Thank you, sir."

"I met Sinclair this morning. I can assure you that we're not alike. Just be honest with me. I want to ferret out the truth. If that leads to Alicia, you have to be prepared."

"I understand. If you find it necessary, I will arrest her even though I believe she's innocent."

"The evidence isn't all in yet. Right now, she is the prime suspect, but I'll interview her before I make an arrest."

Malloy headed for the door. "Oh, one more question."

"Yes?"

"My staff got the impression since she left here, Alicia has lived in San Francisco the entire time. Is that true?"

Peterson mulled over his answer. "As far as I know. Helga showed me several letters over the years postmarked from San Francisco. Ali told me she arrived in San Francisco several days after leaving here, and she's worked for Robel's ever since."

"Okay, just curious. I'll interview Alicia later today."

"I'm going out on patrol in a few minutes. Won't be far away. Use the radio if you need me."

Malloy headed out the door.

———

Ali and Helga crossed Main at the crosswalk to head down Washington Street on their way home from school. Two blocks along, Helga stopped short.

"Oh, darn. I planned to grab a few things at Chet's grocery. You've been eating me out of house and home this week."

Ali protested. "I don't eat that much, do I?"

"Guess not. I forgot how much food we used to eat. Living alone now, a whole package of cookies lasts a week."

"At most, I ate half a dozen yesterday."

"And the day before, and—"

"Okay, I get the message. Let's cut over to Chet's."

Despite Chet's friendly manner, Ali received a chilly response at the grocery store. The tight-lipped smiles and the polite, but insincere, greetings from the other customers strengthened her resolve to leave as soon as possible.

"Hard to fight everyone," Ali said to Helga as they ambled home. "They're all convinced I killed Luetz. Once this cop from Madison hears, he'll go along regardless of what the evidence says. I wish I could point him in another direction."

"Mr. Farmingham might be a good suspect."

"I thought you liked him."

"I do, but he's obviously excited to be principal now, and he admitted Luetz lied to him eight years ago. If you put him on the stand with Perry Mason, he'd crumble in a heartbeat."

Helga shifted her grocery bag, freeing a hand to wag her finger at Ali. "If that nincompoop detective the governor sent makes false accusations, I'll give him something else to think about."

"But Mom—"

Helga put her hand on Ali's shoulder and forced her to stop. "Mr. Farmingham isn't any guiltier than you, but if I have to raise a ruckus, I will. I paid a heavy price eight years ago by not camping out on Luetz's doorstep and making his life miserable until he dropped the charges."

Helga took her hand off Ali. "I've changed too." She hugged the grocery bag and continued on.

Ali followed, speechless. She had noticed the change in her mother too, and it worried her more than she wanted to admit.

———

As Malloy parked, he noticed two women strolling the side street across the highway from the school's visitor parking. Mother and daughter, except the daughter was too old to attend school. The mother threw her hands in the air and stopped. They argued for a moment, the younger one lowered her head in defeat before both cut diagonally across the street, heading downtown. He watched them amble out of sight, neither looking in his direction. Malloy opened his briefcase and studied Alicia Thorein's mug shot. Could be her.

———

"Agent Malloy, what can I do for you today?" Mary, the school secretary, asked.

"I'm here to conduct a thorough search of the principal's office. His files may contain relevant information."

"I helped Tommy search Monday. We didn't find anything useful."

"I can get a warrant, but I assumed you'd cooperate."

Mary stiffened. "Mr. Farmingham will decide. Wait here." She knocked on the office door before peeking inside. "Agent Malloy's back. He wants to search this office."

Mary pulled back as Farmingham stepped out and offered his hand. "Good afternoon, sir. Any news?"

Malloy shook hands. "Nothing solid yet, but we're working on several strong leads. I need to search the principal's office."

"Do you have a warrant?"

"Not yet. I expected your cooperation to solve the murder."

"Of course, students' right to privacy is my concern."

"Unless a student made recorded threats, I won't harass them because they got detention. I'll get the warrant."

Farmingham's brow wrinkled and he pursed his lips for a moment before he stepped aside. "You may proceed. If you find anything of interest in a student file, please ask me first before pursuing the matter. The school board might be more comfortable if you had a warrant in case of liability issues, but you'll get one anyway, and we want this solved quickly."

"My associate Betty will join me soon. Send her in when she arrives."

"Of course," Mary said.

"I have budget decisions to make soon and need to take a few papers with me. Would you care to examine them first?" Mr. Farmington asked.

"Yes, I would."

Malloy sorted through the papers on the desk and gave Farmingham permission to remove them. Farmingham grabbed his work and started to leave.

"Oh, I do have a question for you," Malloy said. "The two women who left a few minutes ago. The Thoreins?"

Farmingham rested his free hand on the doorknob. "Most likely. They just left."

"What did they want?"

His hand dropped as he faced Malloy. "Renewing friendships. Helga knows how sorry I was about Ali's fall from grace. We were all convinced Ali would get a slap on the wrist. The whole affair became a dark stain on the school. When Helga called this morning, I invited them over for a friendly conversation and I apologized. Ali is welcome in my school anytime."

"She's a suspect in this case."

Farmingham gripped the doorknob. "She's not the killer. I will assist you in solving this murder, but I'm also welcoming one of our best former students whenever she visits."

Malloy pulled a file drawer open as Farmingham left and shut the door behind him. *Farmingham's benefiting from the principal's death. He already considers it his school. Is he being conscientious? Or has he planned this all along? Well, if there's incriminating evidence here, Betty will find it.*

———

After Malloy left his office, Tommy called Helga, but the phone went unanswered. He sat for a minute, fingers drumming the desk before trying again. The phone rang ten times before he hung up. He paced around the room several times and called again to no avail, so he locked up. The last thing he wanted was for Ali to run after he promised Malloy she would stay.

No one answered the door at Helga's, but Ali's car sat in the driveway. She hadn't fled. Tommy scanned Colfax in both directions. They were nowhere to be seen, so he climbed in his car and cruised the neighborhood.

As he turned on Jefferson, two streets north of Colfax, Ali and Helga disappeared around the next block carrying groceries. Neither woman noticed him playing hide-and-seek behind them. He composed a snappy opening line. "Hey, need directions to the Miss America pageant? Our year to host it." He grinned and tapped the gas, closing the gap while undetected.

Ali's head jerked in his direction as he coasted close by and rolled his window down. The pickup line never left his lips. "Keeping an eye on me? Afraid I might run?" Ali snapped.

"No, I'm on patrol. Part of my job."

Her frosty glare softened. "Sorry. I got the cold shoulder at Chet's. I shouldn't have taken it out on you."

Tommy waved her off. "Sorry I startled you."

"Anything new to report?"

"No."

"Too bad."

"I haven't given up. By the way, Agent Malloy wants to interview you later today."

"Thanks for the warning."

Tommy nodded in the silence. "Want a lift?"

"No, I need the exercise. Mom thinks I overdo it on the cookies."

"I never said that," Helga said.

"Truth is, I suspected you were both contestants in a Miss America pageant who got lost."

Ali laughed. "That line might work on the unsophisticated local talent, but I live in the big city. You need to do better if you want to impress me."

"I'll come up with another one while I watch for speeders."

Ali shooed him away. "Go write some tickets."

"See you later," Tommy said, pulling away.

Tommy was out of sight before Helga asked, "What kind of lines do big city girls respond to?"

"Don't know. Truth is, Tommy's line was the first one I've heard in a long time."

"Then why weren't you honest with him?"

Ali took her time answering. "We have no future. After this is over, I doubt I'll ever return. I'll fly you to San Francisco instead. We can vacation together somewhere else. I don't want our time together ruined because of my past."

"You could find a similar job in Madison. Other companies could use your talents."

"Possibly, but Robel's has treated me well. I'll go much further in my career with them. I want to climb the corporate ladder to the top."

"Don't you want a family?"

"Not especially. I wrecked ours, and I couldn't stand wrecking another one. Single is safer."

Helga frowned but let the subject drop.

26

Betty and Malloy spent an unproductive afternoon in Orville Luetz's office. Alicia Thorein's permanent record confirmed she was an excellent student with no disciplinary action noted until the expulsion. A letter from the Wisconsin State Board of Education stated Alicia satisfied the GED graduation requirements. Nothing else proved useful except the May 1968 Playboy magazine Betty found stuffed in the back of a filing cabinet.

"I doubt Farmingham will miss it. Must be lonely at the motel," Betty said.

Malloy shook his head.

"I hear the jokes are funny," she said as she slipped it in his briefcase unnoticed.

School had been dismissed, and the children were long gone when Malloy and Betty stepped out of the principal's office. Mary Albright sat at her desk with her purse on top, waiting to lock up. She glared at Malloy. "Are you finished?"

Malloy stopped and stared blankly at Mary for a moment. "Did Chief Peterson confer with Mr. Luetz regularly?"

"What do you mean by regularly? In what way?"

Something was wrong. He guessed Mary stayed late because he and Betty were there, but she appeared too huffy for that little inconvenience.

"Say a student acted up. Did Luetz call Peterson in to scare the kid?"

"No. Tommy comes in the school whenever he pleases. He gives presentations to the high school kids about drugs and safe driving and reminds the young ones to use the crosswalks. If a teacher wants Tommy to visit, they call him. He loves the kids. Does everything in his power to keep us all safe. Nothing wrong with that."

"So, he never chewed the fat with Luetz."

Mary stood. "No one chewed the fat with Mr. Luetz. He wasn't that type of guy. I was in elementary school when he first arrived. Rumor was the school board hired him because they wanted a hard-nosed disciplinarian. Newspapers reported trouble at a rock-and-roll concert in Madison, and the village fathers were determined to keep that kind of behavior out. They feared Elvis's wicked ways."

"And Luetz succeeded?"

She pushed her chair under the desk. "Without a doubt. It felt like we'd been sentenced to boot camp when he first came here. He was never friendly with students or teachers. So, no, Tommy didn't chew the fat with him. Neither did his predecessor, Chief Hancock."

"Any bad blood between them from Peterson's student days?"

Mary turned off the lights. "Not that I know of. I didn't live here when Tommy was a teenager, but he was quiet as a small child. Wouldn't hurt a fly. Ask around, everyone will tell you the same. He may have come out of his shell, but he's incapable of hurting anyone."

"We're done now," Malloy said and left.

Betty stopped in the doorway. "Nuts. I left my pen in the office. Go ahead Malloy, I'll be along in a minute."

Betty pulled the office door shut and faced Mary. "All right. Woman to woman. What's wrong?" Betty asked.

When Mary averted her eyes, Betty gently touched Mary's arm.

"Malloy can be a royal pain, but we need to find out who killed Orville Luetz. Tell me what's wrong."

Mary locked eyes with Betty. "Tommy did not kill Mr. Luetz, and neither did Ali. I understand why you suspect her, but Tommy? Really?"

Betty's head jerked back. "We don't suspect Chief Peterson of murder."

Mary gestured to the door. "Tell that to your boss. He was overheard ordering one of your friends to interrogate poor Margaret Luetz again because he thinks she's covering for Tommy. Ridiculous."

Mary's sudden change of attitude made sense.

Betty preceded Mary into the foyer. "Who else knows?"

"The whole village by now."

Betty shook her head. "Look, if others ask, tell them it's routine. Since Chief Peterson's the sole law enforcement officer here, we have to investigate him."

Mary locked the office door. "He deserves better treatment."

"I agree. I'm sure Malloy never expected anyone would find out. We don't want to tarnish Peterson's reputation."

"Too late for that now. All I can say is when Tommy and Ali are found innocent, they'd better hear a great big apology from your boss."

Betty frowned. Malloy rarely apologized. "I'll see what I can do. We're not out to ruin a good cop."

Mary's keys jingled in her hand as she pointed at Betty. "Once accused, forever tarnished. That's what my mother always said. Push the front door shut tight on your way out. I'm parked in back."

Mary turned and left, ending the conversation.

Betty approached Malloy's car, parked in front of the school. "What did she say?" he asked through his open window.

"Thanks to your big mouth, the whole village knows you suspect Peterson too."

He held his hands up. "I didn't tell any locals, and I used an outside phone to call Fred."

"You were overheard, that's all I know."

Malloy shrugged and started his car. Betty continued shaking her head on the way to her car. Malloy carried an impressive law enforcement record but had a lot to learn about dealing with people. Alicia would bear the brunt of his insensitivity next, and if she wasn't careful, her world would collapse again. Guilty or not may be decided in court, but to those who were accused, it was a life sentence.

27

It was midafternoon when Sheriff Chuck Sinclair lightly knocked on Judge Lynch's chamber door. "Come in."

"Got those papers you asked for," Chuck said, waving a folder in the air.

"What? Oh, right. Close the door behind you."

Chuck strode to Lynch's desk and laid the file folder on it. "Here's the DUI for your friend. Far as I'm concerned, it never happened."

"Good. He promised to be more careful. No need to pursue the matter further."

"We've got a real problem with this Malloy character. Not your average cop."

Lynch sat back. "A real pain in the ass. Thank that wimp of a governor for sending him."

"Listen, if we don't get rid of this guy soon, he'll make big trouble for all of us."

Lynch leaned over his desk. "We'll make him go away."

"How are we going to do that?"

"By solving the murder ourselves. And this is how we're going to do it."

A minute later, Chuck let out a low whistle. "You better be right about this."

Lynch smiled. "Trust me, the voters in this county want justice. Many people in her own hometown believe she's the killer, and it won't take much to convince them that she is seeking revenge on those courageous public servants who gave her the punishment she deserved eight years ago. In the end, they'll wish I could have given her an even harsher sentence."

Chuck's eyebrows furrowed. "Okay. I guess you know what you're doing."

Lynch pointed his finger at Sinclair. "And make sure Malloy stays out of the way."

"I'll do my best."

"See that you do."

After Chuck left, Lynch looked through his friend's file before putting it in his briefcase. "This should be worth a sizeable campaign donation," he muttered to himself. "Not that I'll need it."

28

The bright fall weather turned blustery by late afternoon with dark clouds rolling in, confirming the forecast of heavy rain overnight. "Let's enjoy the fall colors one last time before we eat," Helga suggested. "The trees will be bare by morning."

The women stepped out on the porch to catch a final glimpse of the radiant red and yellow leaves. After spending another day facing murder charges, Ali identified with the trees. Her full bloom soon might be ripped off, leaving her defenseless. A shiver ran through her.

"Better get your jacket," Helga said.

"I'm fine." Ali crossed her arms as she hid the real reason for the shiver.

———

A few minutes before six, Malloy entered Tommy's office. "Is Alicia at home now?"

"Yes, she is."

"I need to place a private phone call."

Tommy grabbed his coat. "I'll wait outside."

Malloy sat behind Tommy's desk, legal pad out, and called his office. Fred updated him. "I talked to Margaret Luetz."

"And?"

"Keep in mind she was legally drunk at the time."

"And her testimony is not admissible in court. I get it. I want to know if my theory about Peterson is credible, that's all."

"Okay, but I think you're barking up the wrong tree."

"My theory makes sense, doesn't it? Everything fits when he's the suspect."

Fred took his time before answering. "Yes, it does. Margaret Luetz remembers shopping at the liquor store in Mineral Ridge. She opened a bottle of brandy and took a few swallows in the parking lot but doesn't remember driving. Later she learned Peterson found her passed out on the roadside in her car and brought her home. Peterson carried her inside and brewed coffee before calling the victim at school.

"Margaret remembers the two men arguing. She told me that her husband sulked when things didn't go his way, but that day he yelled at Peterson. Told him to butt out of their affairs. It'd been years since she'd seen him so livid."

"And what about Peterson?"

"Never heard him utter a harsh word until that day. She confirms his painful shyness as a child and called him a man of few words. But the day he found her passed out, she had never seen him so angry. Peterson was emphatic. 'Check her into the clinic or she'll go to jail.' The victim kept insisting he'd handle it, but Peterson wouldn't let it go. Margaret chose rehab over jail, which ended the argument."

Malloy stood and went to the front glass door, stretching the phone cord out as far as it would go. He saw Peterson talking to an old farmer sitting in his idling truck on the other side of the street. "Did the victim threaten Peterson?"

"No. Peterson threatened him. Margaret confessed she snuck money out of her husband's wallet occasionally, not knowing if it was the school's money or not. It didn't sound like much, but Peterson already knew about it and threatened to tell the school board."

Malloy sat on the desk, keeping his eye on Peterson and the farmer. "Did she ever witness Peterson with the victim after that day?"

"Both men visited her but not at the same time. Margaret asked the victim if he apologized to Peterson. He said not yet. She doubts he ever did. When Peterson visited, he never mentioned her husband."

"So Luetz riled Peterson and called him a few names he didn't like."

"Peterson doesn't seem the type to commit murder over an argument. He could have told the school board about the missing money and gotten rid of Luetz that way."

Malloy watched Peterson look both ways before waving a car around the truck. "Perhaps. Maybe firing wasn't enough."

"I still say it's far-fetched."

"No more than a professional hit woman."

Fred laughed once. "Better tread lightly on Peterson. My gut says he's not the guy. Might be Alicia, but maybe it's neither of them."

After the farmer pulled away, Peterson waved once and ambled down the far sidewalk, moving farther away from the office. "I found another suspect with a motive. Obtain phone records for John Franklin Farmingham, the new principal. He's eager to take over at the school. Maybe he grew tired of waiting for Luetz's retirement."

"Another long shot."

Malloy moved back to the chair and pulled out his pen, ready to take notes. "If we eliminate enough people, the killer will stand out. Any new information on Alice Thorn?"

"Alice Thorn has a credit card. I'm waiting for the statements."

"Keep at it. And the note?"

"No luck on the stray print yet."

Malloy tossed his pen on the pad and sat back. "Okay. Time to interrogate Alicia. I'll hold off on the Alice Thorn thing until we know more."

"Sorry."

"Not your fault. Professional hit women are hard to track."

"I knew I should have kept my mouth shut."

————

Alone in Peterson's office, Malloy took a minute to prepare for a confession before the night was through. He expected to rattle Alicia, and once she erred, he would make the arrest. Mentally, he went over his checklist. He was ready.

He opened the front door and saw Tommy sauntering back. Malloy waved and Tommy picked up his pace. When he came through the door Malloy asked, "How do I contact you when I arrest Alicia?"

Tommy shook his head but went to his desk and handed him a card with his pager, home, and office phone numbers. Malloy slipped it in his shirt pocket. "Do you have a spare key?"

Tommy opened his desk drawer and fished around to find a key. "You'll bring her here if you make an arrest, right?"

Malloy took the key. "You have my word."

29

Tommy phoned Ali. "Agent Malloy is on his way."

"Are you coming over, too?"

"I offered, but no."

"Crap. I hoped for a friendly face on the other side of the table."

"Sorry. Not my choice."

"Well, I have nothing to fear. If this hotshot's any good, he'll realize I didn't do it after a few questions. I'll call you after he leaves."

Despite her outward bravado, this interrogation worried Ali. Disillusioned by the treatment she received after her conviction, she mistrusted cops.

"He's coming, Mom," Ali said as she stepped into the living room.

"I'll answer the door," Helga said while rising from her chair. "I want to check him out before I let him into my home." Ali had forgotten how protective Helga could be. She didn't know what her mom would do, but Helga's feelings about the justice system had changed in the last eight years.

After a car door slammed outside, determined steps on the porch preceded several sharp raps on the door. Even though Helga stood on the other side, she waited to open it.

He flashed his badge. "Agent Dirk Malloy, Wisconsin Department of Criminal Investigation, Jurisdictional Task Force, here to interview Alicia Thorein."

"Pleased to meet you, Mr. Malloy. I'm Ali's mother, Helga."

She offered her hand, forcing Malloy to set his briefcase down. "May I come in?"

Helga studied him. He wore a blue blazer, gray pants, and a blue-striped tie. His auburn hair was moderately short, and everything about him was perfectly in place. She opened the door wide. "Please."

Malloy stepped in.

Helga shut the door. "Ali's in the kitchen. Follow me."

Ali stood by the sink pretending to shelve the last dish. "Alicia Thorein?"

"Yes?" She wiped her hands on a dishtowel.

"Agent Dirk Malloy, Wisconsin Department of Criminal Investigation, Jurisdictional Task Force."

"I've been waiting for you... Dirk." Ali barely hid the contempt in her voice.

"I'm here to question you regarding the murder of Orville Luetz."

"State Journal said the murder took place before I arrived. I'll only be repeating what I read or watched on TV."

They stared at each other for a moment. "We could conduct the interview at the police station."

Ali gestured at the table. "Have a seat."

Helga sat at the head of the table after Malloy took a seat and Ali sat facing him. "I'll interview Alicia alone," Malloy said while opening his briefcase.

Helga crossed her arms. "It's my house. I won't bother you."

He hesitated before taking out a yellow legal pad and pen. "Your full legal name, Alicia."

"Alicia P. Thorein."

"The P stands for what?"

"Priscilla. I always use the initial."

Next came her address, phone, place of employment, all common knowledge and information he had accessed already.

"You grew up in Rausburg?"

Ali's patience wore thin. "You tell me. Two days is more than enough time to perform a background check. Cut to the chase."

Malloy flipped over a new sheet on his legal pad. "Did you kill Orville Luetz?"

Malloy was poised to write. Ali remained silent, forcing him to make eye contact. "No, absolutely not."

"Where were you Sunday night?"

She repeated her alibi in response to his questions, giving brief answers. Malloy didn't lead her to elaborate but asked to see the motel receipt. She fished it out of her purse and handed it to him. "May I keep it?"

"Not without a warrant. I need the original for my expense report. I'll leave a copy at Tommy's office in the morning."

Malloy scribbled on his pad. "Don't bother. I'll take it when I bring the warrant."

Ali remained stoic as he made an obvious check mark on the pad.

"When were you in the Luetz house?"

Ali cocked her head, pretending to think, forcing him to look at her again. "Never."

"When was the last time you saw or spoke to Orville Luetz?"

"Eight years ago, before I moved to San Francisco."

Malloy scribbled on the pad. "You quarreled with Orville Luetz before you left, didn't you?"

"Yes."

"Tell me what happened."

Ali clasped her hands. "Not much to tell."

"Humor me."

Ali had prepared for this moment. Three people heard the entire conversation that night: a dead man, his drunken wife, and Ali. She wouldn't lie, but her version wouldn't give Agent Malloy more reason to suspect her.

"After my release, I avoided people as much as possible. Dad offered to take Mom to supper at the Ranch House, and she persuaded me to tag along against my better judgment. We were nearly finished with our meal when Mr. and Mrs. Luetz were seated. I went over to tell him that I was sorry for my actions. Mr. Luetz exploded, pointing his finger at me and yelling, 'You tarnished my career and this village. Stay away from my school. No one wants you corrupting the other students.'"

Ali paused to force Malloy's next question. "How did you respond?"

"His reaction stunned me at first. I stood dumbfounded before calling him a poor excuse for a human being with a special place in hell reserved for him. I stormed out after that. The next morning, I boarded a bus. I haven't been back until this week."

"Did you ever contact him afterwards?"

"No."

"Did he ever contact you?"

"No."

Malloy turned to Helga. "You must have run into him from time to time."

Helga's head snapped back, and she sat silent for a moment. "I avoided him."

"In a village this size?"

"I've never forgiven him for the terrible things he said at the trial. He never mentioned that Ali had problems at school before. Ali was a good student. A few times she was less than perfect, but no one ever told us she had problems. Everybody expected her to become a successful young woman, but after that business—"

Helga pulled a tissue from her pocket and wiped her eyes. Ali glared at Malloy. "Aren't you here to question me?"

Malloy said nothing.

"I'm sorry, Mr. Malloy. It was horrible watching Ali go through that. We didn't realize Luetz felt that way, and afterwards it appeared many agreed with him. I didn't want her to leave, but she wasn't going to get much of a chance here."

Malloy focused on Ali. "I read the transcript of your trial. The victim made several damaging remarks that contradict your permanent school records. What prompted him to lie?"

Ali knew where this question led.

"Luetz didn't lie."

Malloy straightened.

"He told a different version than I would have, but he didn't commit perjury. His testimony caught us all by surprise. My lawyer asked for a brief recess to confer with me, but Lynch wouldn't allow it, so Luetz's testimony stood unchallenged."

Malloy cocked his head. "You don't think he lied about you?"

"No. Hearing his testimony hurt, but I had little respect for him before the incident. Like everyone else, I tried to get along. That's the one constant in Rausburg."

"What's that?"

"You'll deal with your enemies as often as your friends. That's why I prefer the big city now. I can ignore my enemies there."

Malloy studied his pad. "Describe your relationship with Chief Peterson."

"Tommy? We went to school together. He was a grade behind me."

"Did you ever date or encourage him—"

"What?" Her voice rose. "Listen… Dirk. Tommy was a shy, small boy in school. He's smart, but his shyness made school difficult for him. All his teachers and most of the students helped him any way they could. I befriended him like everyone else, but I never dated him."

"How about now?"

"Make no mistake, I'm flying back to San Francisco as soon as this mess is resolved. I doubt I'll ever see Tommy Peterson again."

As Ali crossed her arms, Malloy's eyebrows furrowed.

"Perhaps a neighbor mentioned Tommy visits me," Helga said.

"Yes, several did."

"Tommy's mother died shortly after my husband. We started spending Sundays together after her funeral. He takes me to Mass, and I make him lunch, and we spend the afternoon talking or watching the Pack. Sometimes he does odd jobs around the house for me. Ali didn't know."

"I see." Malloy fiddled with his pen. "I'll take an example of your handwriting now, Alicia."

"Why?"

"We have a handwriting expert who can determine if a person is truthful by examining their penmanship. Not admissible in court, but often it's helped me determine when I'm on the right track."

He's lying. Time to end this charade. "Since I'm innocent, I don't see any significance in your request. My attorney will need to be present if you insist."

Malloy lay his pen down and gazed straight at her. "Call Justin Green if you like. I have no objection to having your attorney present, but you need to understand I conduct interviews with attorneys under my conditions which means I take you into custody first."

Ali scowled. "What makes you think Justin Green's my attorney?"

"Mr. Green defends the most heinous criminals. Word gets around."

Malloy pulled a pair of handcuffs out of his briefcase and dropped them on the table. "You are within your legal rights to have an attorney present just as I am within mine to detain you for twenty-four hours. If you wish to involve Mr. Green, it's my duty to inform you that I have enough evidence to detain you."

"What? But I didn't do it. I've never even been in Luetz's house."

"Evidence exists linking you to the murder. With a strong motive and an unsubstantiated alibi, I have probable cause. You reside in another state and confessed your desire to leave Wisconsin as soon as possible."

Ali wanted to lash out but held her anger in check. "You're willing to do this over a silly handwriting analysis?"

"You can call Mr. Green after you're processed. It'll be late when you reach his service, but they'll tell him first thing in the morning. He'll arrive at the jail sometime tomorrow afternoon and demand to take you in front of Judge Lynch. District Attorney Dan Milenburg will charge you. Green will demand that bail is set. When I tell Lynch you present a tremendous flight risk, the judge will deny bail or set an exorbitant amount, while restricting you to remain in the county until the preliminary hearing several weeks from now."

"Hold on there, mister," Helga snapped. "You have no solid proof. Arrest her now and you'll suffer the consequences when you find out she has no connection to the murder."

Malloy appeared cool and levelheaded. "I'm asking for a handwriting sample. If Alicia's as innocent as she claims, why not do it and move on?"

Both women glared at Malloy in silence, making him shift in his seat. They knew what he was after but couldn't call his deception without surrendering their own secret.

"Give me the sample and I'll let you stay with your mother while I continue my investigation. Peterson will watch you and if you flee, you'll be taken into custody. It's the best I can do. All you need do is write a few words on a sheet of paper."

Ali drummed her fingers on the table while studying Malloy, but his eyes never left hers. "I'll humor your request over spending a night in jail to prove my innocence."

Malloy pulled out a pen with a fresh legal pad and slid them across the table. "Write the alphabet in your normal hand."

Ali wrote the alphabet before he dictated a few words containing letter combinations common to the words in the note. He took the pad back and studied it for a moment before putting it in his briefcase along with his own legal pad.

Malloy pulled a roll of wintergreen Lifesavers from his shirt pocket, opened it, and popped one in his mouth. "These candies are addictive," he said, attempting to be friendly. "Care for one?" he asked Ali.

"No."

He offered the roll to Helga. She stared at it. "Sure."

He gave her the roll and let her take one before returning it to his pocket. "Can you think of anything pertinent that might help the investigation, Mrs. Thorein?"

Helga blinked in surprise. "I slept through the murder if the papers have the correct time of death."

"Maybe you're an early riser."

"Not since my husband died. I usually wake at seven. The day Ali arrived, I had just finished my morning chores."

"I see. Earlier you mentioned you had little to do with Orville Luetz these last eight years, correct?"

"I tried to have nothing to do with him, but we sometimes bumped into each other at community events."

Malloy stroked his chin. "Is there a women's softball team here?"

"What?"

"Don't you play in a recreational league?"

"No. Why do you ask?"

"You bought a bat at the hardware store not too long ago. Do you use it for protection?"

"No. I donated it to Toys for Tots. I buy several toys in the fall and drop them off when I'm in Madison shopping."

"Did you get a receipt?"

"Why would I want the receipt?"

"Tax purposes. It's a deduction."

"That isn't right. A person gives from the heart, not for the IRS."

"Wait a minute," Ali cut in. "Why this sudden interest in a bat?" As the words tumbled out, the realization struck her. Luetz died from bludgeoning. She gasped. "Murder weapon?"

Malloy grimaced. "Do you remember which bin you put it in?"

"The one in their office along the beltway." Helga's face showed her indignation.

Malloy asked Ali. "What size shoe do you wear?"

"What size shoe?" Ali paused. No harm in sharing what he would find out anyway. "Nine."

He turned to Helga. "And you?"

She glared at him. "Nine."

"That'll be it for now," Malloy said as he rose out of the chair.

"That's it? No apology for suspecting an innocent woman?" Ali stood, glaring at Malloy.

"Enjoy your mother's company tonight. Next time might be through plexiglass."

"That's enough," Helga said, pushing her chair back. "Ali's innocent and you know it, Numbnuts. It's time you left." She headed for the door.

Malloy locked eyes with Ali. "One other thing, Alicia. I learned you've been conducting your own little investigation. If you get in my way, I'll have you in jail in a heartbeat. Obstruction of justice is a difficult charge to beat. If I were you, I'd back off asking questions at the bank, school, or anywhere else."

"Out," Helga snapped, opening the door for him. Malloy slid out with no further comment.

30

While Malloy interrogated Ali, Tommy went home. When the phone first rang a few minutes after he arrived, he answered with a shaky hand.

It wasn't Malloy but Mary Albright. "How are you doing, Tommy?"

"Fine." Maybe Mary wanted to talk about finding Orville Luetz's body. She didn't mention that, but she said Malloy spent the afternoon in Luetz's office and found nothing pertinent.

"Yes. Agent Malloy told me."

"Oh, well, I guess I'll just say you're doing a superb job as police chief. I support you one hundred percent."

Tommy thanked her and said goodbye.

Chet called a few minutes later. After a minute of small talk, Chet said, "I'm behind you all the way. It's been a rough week for everyone. You do a great job, and many others agree."

Tommy thanked Chet. Mary and Chet must have noticed his concern for Ali. Just being neighborly.

Six more times the phone rang that night, and each time sent Tommy's heart to his throat before he learned another neighbor supported him. Nice to know, but he wasn't the one who needed support.

Ali called close to nine. To Tommy's relief, Malloy left her at home. She didn't mention anyone calling her in support. He didn't want to broach the subject and tell her several had called him. People remained guarded toward Ali, and he didn't want to draw attention to it. He reassured her that Malloy would soon admit her innocence and move on to find the real killer.

"Good. As soon as I'm in the clear, I'm hitting the road. No point in tempting fate."

"Could you call before you leave? I'd hate to miss you."

Ali was silent for a moment. "Sure, but don't expect a teary farewell. You may be happy here, but I'm not."

After Tommy said good night, he settled in to catch a late nap before his ten o'clock patrol, wondering how he could persuade her to stay longer.

31

Back at the Kickapoo Motor Inn, Malloy kicked his shoes off and reclined on the bed while dialing a number in Madison. A sultry voiced woman answered. "Hello, big boy. Lonely?"

"Betty?"

"Betty's gone. Foxy Roxy's here now."

"All right, Foxy Roxy, let me talk to Betty."

"Oh, you never want to have fun," Betty said.

Malloy laughed once. "You shouldn't answer the phone that way. What if the governor called?"

"Foxy Roxy just got off the phone with him. He usually calls this time every week."

Malloy let his breath out.

"Relax, our new caller ID system works like a charm. It's early so I assumed you needed consoling because you didn't arrest Alicia. What did you conclude? Is she guilty?"

"Good question." Malloy paused and carefully chose his words. "She is assertive, took charge immediately, and threatened to lawyer up. She forced me to play the take-you-into-custody card."

"Wow, she must be tough. On the first meeting, no less."

"Not sure I could make her arrest stick, but she gave me a handwriting sample. There are similarities. I'll send it to Mike in the morning. Alicia didn't go for the Lifesavers, but her mother did. Helga claims she dropped the bat in a bin at Toys for Tots' west side office. Look for it. It's a long shot, but maybe it'll be there."

"Okay, can do. Anything else?"

"That's it for now. What's new on your end?"

"Nothing. Fred's in Jefferson tomorrow, testifying at that homicide trial, remember?"

"Thanks for the reminder. Unless we find concrete evidence tomorrow, I'll be forced to let Alicia leave."

"What happens if we can't nail her?"

"She may not have whacked him with the bat, but she's involved."

"Okay. Do you want to speak with Foxy Roxy?"

"No, I found the Playboy in my briefcase."

"Sweet dreams, then."

"Thanks, Betty."

Malloy hung up, confident his team would find incriminating evidence. Within twenty-four hours, he planned to put Alicia Thorein behind bars and sleep in his own bed.

32

Ali experienced another miserable night's sleep, her mind racing until after midnight before drifting off. A few minutes before two she awoke, startled by a heavy rain gust pummeling the roof. With her heart thumping and no chance of sleep soon, she rose from her bed.

As a child, she often climbed out of bed to gaze at stars through the front window. The first few times awakened Helga, who came to fuss over Ali, but Ali preferred being the solitary human awake in Rausburg. Soon she figured out where to step so the floorboards didn't squeak. Mom didn't wake, and Ali had her late-night independence. Tonight she placed her feet carefully on the wooden floor as she had for the last three nights, tiptoeing to the front room without Helga's knowledge.

Ali eased into the rocking chair facing the window and rested her feet on an old ottoman. Mom used to sit in this chair while rocking baby Ali at night when she refused to sleep. When Ali grew older, Mom and Dad moved downstairs and left the rocker behind. It was a place to stargaze or sit wrapped in a blanket and watch the snow paint the village white, a place to dream of possibilities.

Clouds obscured the stars tonight, and man-made light shone through while leaves blanketed the pavement under the street light half a block away. Ali let her mind drift, accompanied by the steady rain and gusty winds.

As lights moved on the street, Tommy's car crept into view. The beam from his spotlight pierced the darkness, flashing on her rental car as he made sure she didn't sneak out.

While his mistrust disappointed her, he was doing his job.

When Tommy pulled away, Ali gazed off in the distance and let her mind drift until lights flashed on Knutsen's overlook, drawing her attention. The overlook was a local Lover's Lane before a young couple almost drove over the edge. After that, Mr. Knutsen put a gate across the entrance. You could view the whole village from up there, but not without his permission.

Kids must still sneak up there, but what parent would let their kid stay out this late on a school night? Ali pondered that until another set of lights on the street below caught her eye. A dark car appeared under the streetlight. An unmarked cop car. Agent Malloy.

He slowed to a crawl and lingered by the driveway. She gripped the chair arms. *Damn, he's here to arrest me.*

Malloy's car accelerated slightly before speeding away. She released her grip a minute later when his taillights dissolved into the mist on Highway 72 South, but she sat motionless staring through the window, fearful her slightest movement might bring Malloy back. After many minutes, her pulse slowed and drowsiness took over. She tiptoed back to bed and eventually fell asleep.

33

Friday, October 18, 1984

Malloy awoke in yesterday's clothes after a rough night at the Kickapoo Motor Inn. Alicia Thorein's file lay strewn across the bed while her eight-year-old mug shot rested on his chest. He last remembered staring at it and comparing the young executive he met to the frightened convict in the picture.

He sat up to grab the TV remote. A folksy coffee commercial burst on the screen. "Best part of waking up, my ass," Malloy grumbled as he scooted to the edge of the bed. A short promo for *Magnum, P.I.* gave him time to stretch before Channel 6's morning newscast began.

"Good morning. We're going live to Mineral Ridge where Martie Pepper is at the scene of another brutal murder. Martie."

Martie stood outside a house encircled with yellow crime tape. "The victim has been identified as Kickapoo County District Attorney Daniel Milenburg. Authorities say an anonymous caller alerted them to suspicious activity. When the sheriff's department arrived, they found Mr. Milenburg dead."

Malloy stared at the TV in disbelief as Martie asked Chuck Sinclair, "Sheriff, what can you tell us about this shocking crime?"

"We know Mr. Milenburg was bludgeoned and stabbed to death in his kitchen early this morning, similar to the murder in Rausburg on Monday."

"Have you made an arrest?"

"No, but we'll be interrogating a suspect soon. The same person committed both crimes. We're waiting until the evidence comes back from our lab to be sure."

"How long will that take?"

"Not long. Serial killings are always top priority."

Malloy grabbed the phone from the nightstand and furiously punched the numbers. Walter, the governor's chief of staff, answered.

"You watching the news?"

"Yes, I—"

"I want authorization to head this murder investigation. I need it now before the locals compromise the scene." Walter remained silent for a long few seconds, weighing the political consequences. "It's already been labeled a serial killing."

"Okay, you got it. Who do I call?"

Malloy read him Sinclair's number and hung up. Next he punched in his own office number.

Betty had anticipated Malloy's call. "Saw it on the news. I already have the address. Mike and I will hit the road within five minutes."

Malloy jumped in and out of the shower and threw on his clean suit before grabbing the phone again. This time he punched in Tommy's office number. Fortunately, Tommy answered.

"Peterson?"

"Yes. Agent Malloy?"

"No time for chitchat. Dan Milenburg was murdered early this morning, and Alicia's the prime suspect. Don't let her leave today. Got that?"

"Yes, sir. If it helps, her car was parked in the driveway when I did my patrols at two and five."

Malloy was silent. "Did you check the hood? Warm to the touch either time?"

"Didn't check."

"Then keep her there until I interrogate her. Got it?"

"Yes, but—" Malloy hung up, ending the conversation.

———

Tommy put the receiver down, stunned. *Has Ali been fooling me? Is she getting revenge on everyone who sent her to jail?* He couldn't deny she carried anger towards her former neighbors, but Tommy remembered the moments when she joked about renaming the town and kidded about her accomplishments. Good had always prevailed in Ali, even in this trying week. *No, she's being framed. But by who?*

Before long, he realized Milenburg's murder created a new possibility. Yes, he knew someone with a plausible reason to want Ali convicted of both murders. He grabbed the phone to dial Helga's number and warn them.

34

Morning's bright light lifted Ali's spirits.

Right is on my side. Malloy won't find more evidence to jail me. He's lazy like the rest. Thought he'd badger a confession out of me and be done with it. In twenty-four hours, I'll be out of here. She wrapped herself in her robe before opening her suitcase on the bed. *I'll pack now so I can leave once he admits defeat. Drive south to Illinois. I'll be beyond his reach in thirty minutes. I can fly home from O'Hare as easily as Madison. Easier even.*

Staring at the open suitcase, guilt kicked in. *Mom deserves a day where we can be ourselves without the threat of an arrest hanging over me. We could drive to Milwaukee this afternoon, shop that new mall, and stay at a motel. I could drop her off Sunday, catch the evening flight from Chicago, and be back at my desk Monday morning with no one the wiser. Perfect.*

Ali raised that possibility over breakfast while waiting for the morning weather. Channel 6 reporter Martie Pepper led the morning newsbreak. "I'm here in Mineral Ridge where a shocking brutal murder occurred overnight. Daniel Milenburg, Kickapoo County District Attorney was found bludgeoned to death in his home early this morning. Sources say this murder resembles the grisly murder of Orville Luetz in Rausburg four days ago. Channel 6 News will have more for you as this case develops, but for now the sheriff's department is urging residents to be vigilant. Kickapoo County may have its first serial killer. I'm Martie Pepper reporting live from Mineral Ridge."

Both women remained silent as the TV blared an orange juice commercial. Helga switched it off. "Milenburg prosecuted you."

"Yep." She had spent a precious few minutes with Milenburg in the courtroom when he played his part in her sham of a trial and led Luetz through his slanted testimony. But that's what lawyers did. She had accepted that fact long ago. No reason to settle that score. No remorse over his death either. "Maybe this is the break I need. Milenburg's murder might convince Agent Malloy of my innocence. Even he should see how ridiculous the idea of me committing two murders is."

Despite her attempt to be positive, the unspoken, unrecognized thoughts won, and Ali's stomach tightened. *This is too big a coincidence. The killer wants me to pay. But why? And how did he know I'm here? I didn't tell anyone my plans.*

"You didn't kill either man, dear. That's a fact. Agent Malloy will come to that same conclusion. I guess hiring Justin Green wasn't such a bad idea."

As Ali wiped off the table, the phone rang, and she answered.

"Are you sitting?" Tommy asked. "You won't believe this."

"Let me guess. I'm the prime suspect in Dan Milenburg's murder."

"How—"

"We had Channel 6 on. I'm a serial killer now?"

"No. Malloy called."

"Let me guess the rest. He suspects I'm the killer."

"He didn't say that, but he wants you available for questioning later today."

"So much for gaining my freedom."

Ali rolled her eyes at Helga, who was listening while wiping the counter.

"Something smells on this one, Ali. Better be careful around Malloy," Tommy said.

"Why, don't you trust him? Cops always cover for each other, don't they?"

Tommy didn't answer immediately. Ali regretted her flip remark and was about to apologize when he continued.

"The Luetz case is growing colder each day. Malloy won't find new evidence implicating you. We know the note is forged, and he can't win a conviction without evidence. Now a second copycat murder occurs and revitalizes the first one."

He makes sense. "Didn't like the guy, but I didn't get the impression Malloy would kill to send me to prison."

"Does sound like a stretch. I hate to admit it, but many cops do back each other no matter what. He might not like Sinclair or his deputies, but they're already convinced you're Milenburg's killer. It'd be easy for Malloy to arrive at the same conclusion. That would solve both murders."

Ali's knees weakened, and she sank in the chair nearest the phone. "You think that's what he's planning?"

"Malloy has the governor's ear. Who's going to question his actions? If he finds something of yours at the Milenburg crime scene, a hair, or a print on a light switch, he'll have all he needs. Sinclair won't object because he's running for reelection next year, and he needs to make an arrest for Milenburg's murder, too."

"But I've never been there. I don't even know where Milenburg lives."

"I don't doubt that, but Malloy entered your house last night, didn't he?"

"Yes, but—"

"Wouldn't take much for him to collect evidence from you and deposit it elsewhere."

Ali gasped. "Oh, God. I wrote a few words on a piece of paper with a pen he gave me. He has my fingerprints. Mom's, too."

176   G. F. HUNN

Tommy's momentary silence underscored the severity of the situation. He continued in a softer tone. "Ali, you didn't do it, but please be careful. I'm not sure he's above putting you in jail to grab headlines for his team and blame the judicial system later when you're acquitted."

"What am I going to do? Once my boss finds out I'm arrested for murder—"

"I'll do everything I can to prevent your arrest. Maybe you should give me the name of your attorney. If Malloy arrests you, it won't be like TV. Might be several hours before you're allowed to use a phone. I could notify your attorney immediately."

"So could Mom."

"If she's not arrested as well. If Malloy believes you killed Milenburg, he might suspect Helga was involved too."

This was too much. Could she trust Tommy? He might help Malloy make his case. What if Tommy didn't have any intention of calling Justin Green? Or maybe he wanted to feed him erroneous information? "Wouldn't contacting my lawyer jeopardize your job? Isn't that aiding and abetting the enemy?"

"I want justice. You didn't kill either man. If that costs me my job, so be it."

Ali's eyes met her mother's. Helga had sat alongside her and had taken her hand.

"You have to trust someone," Helga whispered.

"Okay, my lawyer's name is Justin Green. Hang on. I've got his private number in my purse."

While Ali ran upstairs, Helga picked up the phone. "How serious is this?"

"Too much of a coincidence. The one connection Luetz had with the DA was Ali's trial."

"I was afraid of that."

"Promise me that you'll call if something bad happens. I'll do everything I can to protect Ali. Malloy agreed to put her in my cell until she's arraigned. That will buy us more time to prove her innocence."

Helga handed the phone back to Ali as she sat at the table and read Tommy the number. He promised to keep her informed about Milenburg's murder investigation. Reassuring words ended his side of the conversation. Ali thanked him, but her heart wasn't in it.

Ali held the phone even after the conversation had ended as Helga stood over her and massaged the tension out of Ali's neck.

"I don't get it, Mom. Who would kill two men to put me in prison?"

"There has to be another connection. No more talk of prison. You can't go to prison for a crime you didn't commit."

The phone beeped busy so Ali put it back in the cradle, leaned back into her mother's soothing hands and shut her eyes. Even with planted evidence, Justin Green would unravel the state's case against her. She had been asleep three hours away during Luetz's murder, and she had never been in Luetz's or Milenburg's house. Without absolute proof, that should be enough doubt to convince a jury. But a verdict of not guilty would ruin her career and her life. Murder trials garnered a lot of publicity, forcing her termination from Robel's. She would be lucky to stock shelves for a lower-priced competitor after that.

Ali enjoyed the massage, but it did little to quell her conflicting emotions. As she stood, once again terror and anger fought for attention. "I'm going to lie down upstairs." Helga hugged her before stepping back to let her pass.

Further incarceration in Mineral Ridge Jail terrified Ali. Sinclair and his staff treated her badly when she was a teenager convicted of a prank gone wrong. They would be much worse if she were suspected of murdering one of their own. And if Justin Green failed, she would have to spend years, maybe a lifetime in prison. She climbed the stairs, lost in painful memories of the past, projecting atrocities yet to come. But the overwhelming emotion swelling inside her was anger. Pure, unadulterated anger seeking a target. Who should the target be? Tommy and Malloy for failing to solve the case? Luetz and Milenburg for their behavior at her trial?

No, Ali's anger was self-directed. Her instincts were correct eight years ago. She no longer belonged in Rausburg. Independence was her destiny. Some people went through life alone, and she already had several years' experience at it. It hadn't been that bad. Ali would never set foot in Rausburg again. If Helga wouldn't visit her in San Francisco, a phone and letter relationship would suffice. It was best for all concerned.

35

Malloy felt a chill the instant he arrived at the crime scene. The deputy working crowd control gave him an icy stare, nodding at the house after Malloy asked for Sheriff Sinclair.

Sinclair was even less hospitable as he emerged from the house with forensics specialist Pat Leahy trailing behind. "What's the matter? Aren't we solving it fast enough for ya? Christ, it's barely been a few hours, and we both know who did it."

Malloy glared back. "What do you expect? You went on TV alarming everyone that a serial killer is loose in Kickapoo County, and I got a wake-up call from the governor. Now I'm stuck here with a hostile sheriff's department."

"This ain't Rausburg. We don't need your help. We can solve our own crimes. Stay out of it, and let us do our job."

"You'll get to do your job. When it's over, take all the credit you want. But I'm calling the shots. Accept it. Now what have you got?"

Sinclair cursed under his breath. "The killer clubbed Milenburg with a baseball bat and stabbed him with a knife from the kitchen counter. We found another note by the body, and the caller described someone 5'7" running from the house to a white car, but they didn't get a plate number."

"Too bad. Was the caller male or female?"

"Male, I guess."

"You guess?"

"Our system malfunctioned. The call wasn't recorded."

Malloy looked skyward and huffed. "Did the runner mention why he was out at such an early hour?"

Sinclair shrugged. "Out for a morning run?"

Malloy's brows furrowed. "In the rain? Must be dedicated."

Sinclair made no attempt at hiding his disgust. Malloy addressed Leahy. "No offense, but I work with the best forensics expert in the state. You are dismissed." Leahy left without objection.

The deputies were a different matter. They objected when Malloy called them together and dismissed all except two for crowd control. Sinclair added his objection, forcing Malloy to pull rank. "I work for the governor. Defy me and you defy the highest elected official in the state." Malloy pointed at the closest deputy. "The last cop who crossed me advanced to night watchman at a retirement home in Rockford. I want two out front and the rest to resume your normal routine." The grumbling tapered off as deputies stomped away in disgust.

Sinclair took out a cigarette and put it in the corner of his mouth. "I'll bring the girl in for questioning."

"No you won't. Still too many unanswered questions. What about Milenburg's wife, for instance? Where is she?"

"They're separated. She's in Madison."

"Have an address?"

"I can find it easy enough."

"Good. Interview her. Establish her whereabouts last night. Any other suspects?"

Sinclair flicked his lighter open and lit the cigarette. "The Thorein girl. She's the link between the two murders. The note cinches it. She had a score to settle."

"I questioned her. Alicia feels she got a raw deal the last time—"

"She got what she deserved."

"Shut up, and let me finish." Sinclair removed the cigarette and blew out a puff of smoke, never taking his eyes off Malloy. Malloy didn't blink. "Alicia has the sharpest defense attorney in Madison on retainer. We need to cross every t and dot every i or there'll be no conviction, leaving us with egg on our face. Now go interview the widow. If she has a rock-solid alibi, I'll consider making an arrest."

Sinclair inhaled, grunted, and headed for his car while Malloy stepped inside the house to examine the crime scene alone. After a few minutes he concluded that while the murders were similar, significant differences existed. Different floor plan with Milenburg facing his killer for one, leading Malloy to wonder if he was stabbed first to avoid a struggle.

Malloy tried the back door. Unlocked. It was unlikely a lawyer would leave his house unlocked. Would he have let Alicia in at four in the morning, or did she pick the lock? Answers would come from his team. Better to let them process the house. On his way out, he reminded the deputies to seal the house until his partners arrived.

Malloy continued his investigation at Milenburg's office in the courthouse. Assistant DA Wendell Ferguson had taken over by the time Malloy arrived. Ferguson had white hair and the red nose of a serious drinker.

"Isn't court canceled for the day?" Malloy asked.

Wendell leafed through several files on his desk without looking at him. "Phil doesn't like inconveniencing anyone. People miss work to be here."

"Any important cases being tried today?"

"The usual. Several DUI's, two disorderly conducts, and a child support case head the list. After that, minor traffic violations. See for yourself, but court convenes in ten minutes. Phil's punctual."

Ferguson slid the pile across the desk. Malloy thumbed through the files. "Nothing worth killing over in there. I'd better grab Lynch."

"He plans on speaking to you later after he's done for the day."

"Oh, he does, does he?" Malloy wouldn't force a judge to halt court. But given the situation, most would take a few minutes from their schedule to accommodate his investigation.

Ferguson straightened the files Malloy handed him and put them in his briefcase. "He doesn't like being disturbed before a session. I barely caught a few minutes with him. He can't add anything other than offering his condolences. None of us know who would murder Dan. I mean, other than that young woman from Rausburg who held a grudge against the two dead men."

"Did Sinclair tell you that?"

"We spoke briefly when I arrived. He says she's the one. Told me to prepare a warrant."

"Not yet, Wendell. I'm in charge now. Don't issue a warrant until I tell you."

"But—"

"No buts. I'll tell you what I told Sinclair. One of the best criminal attorneys in the state is anticipating our next move. If you value what's left of your career, you best exercise patience."

"Your show."

"The room will be secured until I'm finished with it. I'll interview the staff while court's in session. Do not issue any warrants in this case without my knowledge, understand?"

"Phil—"

"No warrants without my authorization. Conduct your regular business, but I'm in charge of this investigation. Not Lynch, not Sinclair. Got it?"

"Yes, sir." Wendell closed his briefcase and left without further comment. Malloy noticed a sweet alcoholic aroma, probably whiskey, as Ferguson passed by.

Malloy interviewed the entire courthouse staff within an hour. Shaken and saddened, the staff boiled their reaction to the same observation. Dan Milenburg was a responsible attorney who served his county well. How unusual the same words came out of everyone's mouth. Malloy expected emotional moments and tearful reminisces and at least one employee with a negative opinion of Milenburg but found neither.

And they were all certain *that woman* from Rausburg was the killer.

With Fred testifying at a trial in Jefferson, Betty and Mike were busy working the crime scene when Malloy returned. Malloy saw Betty on a neighbor's front porch as he parked so he opened Milenburg's front door and yelled at Mike. "Safe to enter?"

"Might as well. Everyone and his brother has already been in here."

Malloy followed the sound of Mike's voice to the kitchen. "So the crime scene is compromised. Deliberately?"

"Hard to say. Judging by the footprints, my guess is the deputies all came in to see for themselves."

"Any sign of a woman's presence?" Malloy asked.

"Can't be certain. If the picture in the hall is recent, Milenburg's wife has long blonde hair. That might help me sort through this mess. I've collected several sets of fingerprints to run back at the office this afternoon. Was Milenburg well-liked?"

"He was a responsible attorney who did a good job serving his county. Everyone said so."

"Everyone?"

"Smells funny, doesn't it? DAs always rub at least one co-worker the wrong way, but we apparently have one big happy family at the courthouse."

Mike grimaced. "After I'm finished, you want help with the interviews?"

"No. Help Betty knock on doors. I'll search Milenburg's office myself. Stop by when you're finished, but the sooner you get the evidence back to our lab, the better. I'll interrogate Alicia Thorein this evening. If you find her fingerprints, the interrogation will take less time."

"We'll have answers late this afternoon." Malloy clapped Mike on the shoulder. "One other thing…"

"What's that?" Malloy asked.

"Photographing the crime scene this morning, I remembered the Luetz note didn't appear in Peterson's pictures."

Malloy cocked his head and gave Mike a nod. *Peterson could have culled the blurry or underexposed pictures before he handed them over. Or maybe the note wasn't there to begin with.*

Betty was heading up the walk when Malloy came through the front door. "What did you find out?" he asked.

"I've talked to three neighbors. At four a.m. they were all buried under the covers, furnaces not on yet. Milenburg was friendly but wasn't close to anyone. No one knew who the mystery runner or caller might be. I'll finish out the block and call two neighbors already at work."

"If there's anything to be found, you'll find it. Keep in touch."

Going into the house earlier, Malloy had brushed off the Channel 6 news team camped out across the street with the promise he would talk to them on his way out. Martie Pepper waited next to the crime scene tape, talking to the deputies as Malloy left Betty. The deputies pulled away to distance themselves from Malloy as he approached.

"Your charming personality has won you several friends here today," Martie said under her breath.

"I clipped Sinclair's wings hard this morning. I'll give you a short statement. No new information yet."

She guided him to the van. "Sticking with the serial killer theory?"

"More like two similar murders that might have been committed by the same person. Doesn't appear to be a psycho running loose."

"I thought Sinclair jumped to that conclusion too fast this morning."

"He's hot to arrest the suspect in the Rausburg case."

"The Thorein woman?"

Malloy rolled his eyes.

"I won't broadcast her name until the arrest. I'm not a rookie."

"Tread lightly with that information. Problems exist, but I can't say any more."

When Martie hopped in the van to freshen her makeup, Malloy asked the cameraman, "When did you first hear about this?"

"An informant called the tip line around five."

"What time did you arrive here?"

His eyes darted left. "Six forty-five."

"Was it raining?"

"Was it ever. I got soaked when we pulled up." He tilted his head at Martie. "The ponchos were all the way in the back where the talent left them last time. I couldn't get to them from the inside."

Martie stepped out, ready to go. They lined up the shot, and Martie flashed the okay sign to her cameraman.

"Agent Malloy, what's the latest?"

"At the governor's request, the task force is taking jurisdiction on this case. We are focusing on likely suspects, but it's presumptuous to label this a serial killing. This may be connected to the murder in Rausburg, but until we compare the evidence, we won't know with any certainty."

"Have you found a motive for the killing?"

"We're in the early stages of investigation, and it's too soon to say. The entire local law enforcement community is working hard to catch the killer. We take the brazen murder of a member of the justice system seriously. The killer will pay for his actions in court."

As Malloy stepped back, Martie signed off. While the cameraman set his equipment inside the van, Martie followed Malloy to his car. Malloy lowered his voice. "This one is bound to be big. Make yourself available for the next two or three days."

Martie brushed Malloy's lapels, pretending to remove lint. "You'd better call me first. I know you called the governor, he didn't call you. You owe me."

She stopped brushing, and Malloy flashed a tight-lipped grin. Martie always worked the system. "Unless something breaks, I won't have a statement at five. If I make an arrest, it'll be later. Keep the scanner on tonight. I'll signal where we're going."

"Do it before ten."

"No guarantees, but I'll try."

"You have my number," Martie said before sauntering away.

After he slipped behind the wheel, Malloy slammed his car door hard. Sinclair's irresponsible statements had forced Malloy to stick his neck out on this one. If he couldn't solve the case after stealing it from the sheriff's department, his career, along with the task force, might be finished.

36

After a fruitless two-hour attempt to shut the world out by taking a morning nap, Ali went downstairs to watch TV with her mother. She tried to read the paper while Helga watched game shows and knitted. Any effort at conversation fizzled, and both women retreated into their private worlds.

With two murders hanging over her head, Ali obsessed over the worst outcome. Her innocence might prevail, but she would experience collateral damage before arriving at that point. Unless Malloy found the real killer soon, people would say she'd beaten the system. Any future awards or recognition would be tainted with the fear that the whole village waited to tell the world she had gotten away with killing two men.

Recognition? Who am I kidding? I'll be unemployed once I'm charged with two counts of murder. Robel's isn't that forgiving. Even if I'm later vindicated, the damage will be done.

Helga put her knitting down when the *Price is Right* finished. "I need groceries. We'll walk to Chet's. The fresh air will do us both good."

Ali sat on the couch, morning paper in her lap. "What do you need now?"

Helga shuffled to the TV and switched it off. "Enough to feed us over the weekend, plus I cook for Tommy on Sunday. With you around, my staples are low."

"That's what you said yesterday."

"And you ate last night, didn't you?"

"You go ahead. I'm tired of being stared at by the old biddies."

Helga came over to the couch and gave Ali a playful shove on the shoulder. "Oh, come on. The fresh air will do you good."

"Leave me alone," Ali yelled. "Go alone or not at all. I don't care."

Helga drew back, eyes wide, mouth open.

Once again, Ali had stuck a knife in her mother's heart. Instant regret swept Ali, and she jumped up to seek the comfort of her mother's arms. "I'm so sorry, Mom. I didn't mean to snap at you."

Helga stroked the back of Ali's head. "It's okay, dear. I understand."

Ali sniffed. "Why, Mom? Why me? I loved it here. I wanted to teach and raise my children here. Why do I have to go through this? Haven't I suffered enough?"

Helga patted Ali. "You're destined for bigger things. This mess is a reminder to stick to the life you created in San Francisco."

Ali pulled back and wiped her eyes. "I won't desert you again, Mom. Come join me. We'll find a small town close by where you can be happy. You'll make new friends, and we'll see each other whenever we want."

"Maybe you're right, dear."

Ali wrapped her arms tight around her mother. They consoled each other, rocking back and forth.

"I still need groceries. Sure you don't want to tag along?" Helga asked.

Guilt proved a powerful motivator, and Ali released Helga. "Let me splash water on my face. You're right, the fresh air will do me good. But let's not waste time there, okay?"

"I'll make it quick. In and out."

"Thanks."

———

All morning Tommy monitored the deputy's radio conversations while sitting at his desk. Sinclair had pumped up his deputies to arrest Ali as soon as the ink dried on the warrant, but now they were upset because Malloy pulled rank and ordered them to stand down.

He stared out the door, lost in thought, considering Milenburg's murder, when Ali streaked by in her white Tempo, alone. Tommy sprung from his chair and ran out the back to pursue her in his squad car.

Ali was already out of sight when he turned on Main, and Tommy didn't want to broadcast his pursuit, so he drove faster than the limit, but not fast enough to attract attention.

As soon as he crested the north ridge, he accelerated, hoping to catch Ali on the open road. A swift two miles brought him to the first crossroad, Seidel, where he could see ahead several miles.

Gone. No sign of Ali's car ahead. She wouldn't head west toward Mineral Ridge knowing deputies would arrest her on sight. Seidel also went east, winding toward Madison or branching off south at several locations. Ali wouldn't drive by his office to head south for the state line. *She must be making a run for Madison the back way.*

Two hurried miles later, Tommy pulled over and terminated the chase. She had vanished. *Helga will know where Ali's headed, and I'll arrange for her pickup without telling Malloy. No need to sound the alarm yet.*

———

On the way to Chet's grocery, Ali and Helga cut through on side streets to avoid Main. Neither wanted to run into law enforcement at that moment, even Tommy.

When they arrived at Chet's, Ali sat and waited on the bench outside. "You can shop by yourself, can't you? I don't want to face anyone if I don't have to."

"I'll be quick."

"Stick your head out the door when you check out, and I'll help with the bags."

Ali sat less than a minute before a white Tempo, same year and model as her rental, accelerated on the hill, heading north. The woman driver had short hair and wore sunglasses. Soon after, Tommy sped off in the same direction.

Helga poked her head out the door. "Chet's alone in here. Why don't you join us?"

"Sure, Mom." *Chet's all right. Easy to talk to.*

———

On the drive back, Tommy remembered Helga shopped on Friday morning. He pulled into Chet's empty parking lot and entered the store.

Chet was behind the checkout counter. "Tommy, what brings you in today?"

"Has Helga been in this morning? Ali drove away, alone in her car, and I'm worried she might be running."

"You are, are you?" Ali asked as she stepped out from the canned food aisle, burning holes through Tommy with her eyes.

"I... I... uh... I thought I..."

"You were chasing a fugitive? I watched a white Tempo like mine drive by while I was sitting on Chet's bench. Guess you missed the Wisconsin Power logo on the side."

Those logos are painted in pale colors. I must have overlooked it. "Sorry, I was sitting at my desk when you drove by alone."

"It wasn't me."

"Looked like you. Sorry."

"And you assumed I ran away because I'm guilty."

Tommy was speechless. *I can't say anything right around her.*

Chet came to his rescue. "The three of us were discussing the murder in Mineral Ridge. Sounds like the same killer."

"Yes, it does, but it's not Ali," Tommy said.

Ali stepped closer to Tommy. "Then why did you chase after that car?"

"I told you earlier. As far as Sinclair's concerned, you should already be behind bars. You're not planning on driving anywhere, are you?"

"No," Helga said, avoiding eye contact with Tommy while she unloaded her shopping cart on the counter. Tommy watched in silence as Chet bagged Helga's groceries and she paid him.

"If you use your car today, better call me first," Tommy said.

Ali grabbed a grocery bag and headed for the door. "Nice talking to you, Chet. Have a good weekend," she said without turning around.

Helga took the other bag. "See you Monday," she said to Chet, ignoring Tommy.

Tommy hurried to the door and held it open for them. "Need a lift?"

"No, we can take care of ourselves," Helga said, glaring at him.

Tommy watched them leave. Once the door closed, Chet said, "They're both walking on eggshells. If you want my advice, I'd suggest you tread lightly around those two."

"You're right. I panicked and assumed she was running away again."

"Wouldn't blame her if she did, but Ali's just as innocent as you. Don't know what this Malloy fellow thinks he's doing, but frankly I hope we've seen the last of him around here."

Chet's anger surprised Tommy. "Don't mention my blunder either. If folks know I suspected Ali was running—"

"My lips are sealed. Can I get you anything?"

"I'll take a soda, please." After Chet rung it up, Tommy took one from the cooler, opened it, and took a sip on the way out, relieved the excitement was over.

———

Tommy cautiously knocked on Helga's door a few minutes past three. When Ali opened it, he braced for a tirade.

"Are you okay?" she asked. "You look exhausted."

Tommy welcomed Ali's concern after another rough day. "The night patrols are wearing me out. Not getting enough sleep. Everyone wants this solved yesterday."

"They want my arrest, don't they?"

"Nobody's said that. People want their lives back to normal. Friends avoid me. Nobody's kidded around with me today."

Tommy's sadness touched Ali.

"Where are my manners? Come in. Please." Once Tommy was inside, Ali hung her head. "Sorry I snapped at you this morning. You were simply trying to protect me."

"I should apologize to you. Should have known you wouldn't run."

"We're all on edge. Let's just forget about it," Helga added from her chair, knitting.

"Works for me," Ali said.

"Me, too."

Ali turned off the TV and patted the cushion next to her so Tommy would sit on the couch with her. "What's new?"

"This is all I know. Sinclair's office received an anonymous phone tip someone 5'7" drove off in a white car around the time Milenburg was killed. White cars are rare around here, except for government vehicles. You're 5'7", driving a white Tempo, and that makes you the prime suspect."

"But I have an alibi. Mom can vouch I never left this house last night."

"I know. I saw your car. Malloy thinks you drove to Mineral Ridge between my rounds, but I don't. I think the killer struck again, certain you'd take the blame."

"But why?"

"Beats me. I can't imagine any connection between the two victims other than your trial. I've never seen Milenburg in Rausburg, and Luetz didn't shop in Mineral Ridge anymore. He went to Madison if he couldn't buy it here. Has to be another answer."

For a moment, Ali considered sharing her secret with Tommy but decided against it. She folded her leg underneath her and faced him. "Malloy doesn't see it that way, does he?"

Tommy sat on the edge of the couch. "He stepped on everyone's toes today. Doesn't want Sinclair's deputies handling the evidence. Doesn't share information about the case. You need to be careful with him."

Ali swallowed hard. "Maybe he'll back off if I assert myself. I stuck with the nice approach last night."

"Possible, but I'm betting he's more likely to throw you in jail now. He could take his time solving Luetz's murder because I'm no threat to him. Sinclair is waiting for a misstep then he'll be all over Malloy."

"Agent Malloy was brutish, but I think he's a fair man. Ali stayed here with me last night. She couldn't have killed that DA. When Malloy finds out, he'll change his tune," Helga said.

Ali looked over her shoulder to Helga. "Don't count on it, Mom."

"He must know by now you're honest." Helga leaned over and waved a knitting needle at Ali and Tommy. "Both of you forget Ali confessed eight years ago and took full responsibility for her class's bad idea. She was painfully honest, and everyone knows it." She waved the needle once more before she sat back and resumed her knitting.

Tommy pointed his finger at Ali. "Be careful around Malloy. I'm cooperating with him so he doesn't take you into custody. If that changes, I won't worry about ruffling his feathers."

"Thanks, Tommy. I appreciate your help. Agent Malloy will acknowledge my innocence before this gets out of hand."

Tommy rose from the couch. "Relax and be friendly when he gets here. Don't provoke him."

Helga smiled at Tommy. "Don't worry. I'll be here, too. I'm good at calming people."

37

Malloy sequestered himself in Milenburg's office. Sinclair found him there and informed Malloy that Mrs. Milenburg had been staying with her sister and brother-in-law for several weeks. Both swore she spent the entire night with them. "I've met her a few times. Her grief was real. Who do you want me to interview next?"

Malloy focused his attention on a pile of papers from Milenburg's desk drawer. "My people took care of the interviews. You can conduct your usual business. I'll call if I need you."

Sinclair lingered for a moment, staring at Malloy. Malloy continued to ignore him until he left. Malloy had met many sheriffs during his career. Most accepted help willingly if it involved solving a difficult case. A few were territorial and challenging to deal with, but none of them had been as openly hostile as Sinclair. Malloy was ready to solve the case and say goodbye to Sinclair.

A few minutes past three he discovered something of interest. In the back of the bottom drawer of a file cabinet, he found an unmarked folder containing several papers. He opened it to discover Milenburg had solicited support in his upcoming campaign for county judge.

Milenburg was ambitious and secretive. So what? Politics as

usual. The next few handwritten pages outlined instances where Judge Lynch overstepped the bounds of his office. Malloy read each page. When he flipped the last one over, a scribbled line caught his interest. *Call Luetz + Thorein.*

The last page was dated one month ago, indicating Milenburg revisited his old case recently. *Why did he lie to me? Did he place those calls?*

Malloy found nothing else of value in the DA's office that afternoon. After he finished searching, he sat in Dan Milenburg's chair to clear his mind. He enjoyed a few minutes of peace before his pager vibrated. Fred.

"Sorry to take so long getting back. The defense attorney fancied himself another Perry Mason. Cross-exam took longer than expected. I jumped on the new evidence as soon as I got here."

"Find anything useful?"

"Mike didn't find prints on the bat or the knife. Gloves again."

Malloy pounded the desk with his fist. "Damn."

"But the killer didn't use the same gloves."

"How can you be sure?"

"On Luetz's bat, the residue came from conventional work gloves. On Milenburg's, the killer used latex, like women use to wash dishes or clean toilets."

Malloy sat back in the chair. "Like Alicia."

"Exactly. In Luetz's murder, the evidence suggests a male killer. Except for the note, nothing else points to feminine involvement. In Milenburg's murder, several things suggest a female killer, like using a knife to finish him and leaving the body on the floor."

Malloy mulled over Fred's observations. "So Alicia killed Milenburg, confident she got away with Luetz's murder."

"But why was she careless this time? If she made it appear that a man killed Luetz, why not do the same for Milenburg?"

"Maybe Peterson killed Luetz and Alicia showed up coincidentally like she claims. But now she's presented with a great opportunity to kill Milenburg and stick Peterson with that, too."

"I don't see Peterson capable of murdering anyone. None of us witnessed him at the restaurant. I bet he wasn't as irate as the rumors implied."

Malloy had considered that but didn't admit it. "Maybe Helga's involved. She admitted she couldn't stand Luetz. She can be forceful too. Wasn't afraid of me."

"We dusted a bat found at the Toys for Tots pickup center. A print matches the one Mike lifted off the Lifesavers tube from Helga. Sorry."

Malloy let out a silent breath. At least she didn't willingly purchase the Luetz murder weapon. "She might be an accomplice, though."

"It's possible. Betty pushed the Milenburg note through, and we got a preliminary report. The same person wrote both notes. Based on the sample you obtained, there's less than a fifty percent chance it was Alicia, and no prints were found on the Milenburg note."

"Less than fifty?"

"The more samples we get, the better chance we have of pinpointing, but it'll take days for her driver's license signature or bank records to come back."

Malloy sat up. He didn't have days. If Alicia was the killer and he let her leave the state, he was certain she would disappear. "We need more. Has Betty found anything Alicia might be hiding?"

"No. We didn't find any unexplained deaths or missing persons reported in Kickapoo County. We're checking on former classmates of Alicia's, but it's slow going."

How could Alicia be so involved, yet not leave any evidence other than the note? "What did you find on Alice Thorn?"

"A DMV picture. Alice Thorn is definitely Alicia Thorein."

This is the first good news you've given me. "What else?"

"When she spent time away from San Francisco, she used a credit card to charge flights, rental cars, decent motels, and average meals. You remember I tracked her to Denver when her father died?"

"Yes, I remember."

"She used the credit card in San Francisco the day after he died. Purchased an airline ticket at the Denver airport two days before.

Maybe she knew and didn't want to attend. Could have missed the call, too. We don't know if she had an answering machine."

"But we know she visited those other cities."

"Yes, and her heavy credit card usage coincides with the address changes we got from the DMV. Clusters of activity in LA, Denver, and Las Vegas followed by weeks of inactivity."

How could she be gone for days at a time and keep her job? "Was she working in corporate by then?"

"Las Vegas fits in that timeline. For the others she was assistant manager and paid by the hour. Consider this. Assistant store managers might have computer access to change information for the employees under them. Maybe it was easy for Alicia to falsify her own work records after the fact."

"If she wanted to hide her absence."

"I checked her vacation records, too. She has over three months accrued. Rarely took days off, and she never used vacation time during her out of town trips."

Malloy stood. Time to get moving. "Stay on it. Find everything you can."

"What's next?"

Time was running out. New information would take days, even weeks to obtain, much less confirm. "I'll pay Alicia another visit tonight. With luck, she'll slip and we'll have what we need for an arrest."

He thanked Fred and promised to check in later, dooming him to spend another Friday night at the office. Malloy regretted keeping Fred in the dark about his alternate plans if Alicia didn't slip up tonight. Better he take the risk alone than tarnish his team members' reputations if things went wrong.

———

Malloy had one more visitor as he straightened Milenburg's office before leaving. Judge Lynch tapped on the door and opened it without waiting to be asked. "Good. You're here. I couldn't speak to you earlier. Busy day."

Malloy continued putting files away. "What can I do for you?"

"Sinclair told me you were in charge. The suddenness surprised me."

"Me, too. But the governor panicked at the words *serial killer*, and couldn't wait."

"He suspects Alicia Thorein too?"

"He didn't say that. I told him she's a possibility, that's all."

"Chuck says it's an open-and-shut case."

Malloy made eye contact with Lynch. "Are they ever?"

Lynch's jaw clenched and loosened. "This is Kickapoo County. We're tough on crime here. We have a high conviction rate."

Malloy continued straightening as if ignoring the judge. "So I've heard."

"Then why aren't you arresting Ms. Thorein?"

Malloy locked eyes with Lynch. "I don't have enough evidence to make a homicide charge stick. Many things point to her involvement, but it's hardly an airtight case. Unless you want this to become a farce, we need more."

Lynch clenched his fists as his face reddened. "We should arrest her and get her off the streets before she kills again. I don't grant bail in homicide cases."

Malloy focused his attention on the desktop, refusing to acknowledge Lynch's growing anger. "Keep in mind that Justin Green is representing Alicia. He will dump a ton of trouble in our laps if we arrest her now. We're better off mounting a tighter case first."

Lynch raised his index finger, waving it to make his point clear. "I warn you, if she runs, I will make sure everyone knows we were ready to bring her in, but you stopped us."

"I'm willing to chance it." Malloy stopped and met the judge's glare. "And I should warn you, whoever this killer is, you might be the next victim. The lone connection I can find between these murders is Ms. Thorein's trial. You were involved in the trial, too. It'd be a good idea to station a deputy outside your house until we bring the killer in."

Lynch huffed. "I'll be safe enough. Besides, what would the voters think if I show fear over a young disturbed woman?"

Malloy stood. "It's your funeral if you're wrong."

"I can take care of myself. Call me when you need the warrant signed."

"If I need one, I'll call."

"Suit yourself," Lynch said and stormed out.

When Malloy left, he considered the eagerness in Mineral Ridge to arrest Alicia. Even this morning while Milenburg's body was warm, Sinclair wanted to cuff her.

Are they always this quick? Must be the fastest-acting sheriff's department in the state.

The judge's safety concerned Malloy, too. Since Alicia's trial linked the two murders, Malloy expected the judge to demand a squad car parked in front of his house. That was the prudent thing to do. Was Lynch that foolhardy to dismiss his advice?

38

At seven thirty Agent Malloy gave a crisp hard knock at Helga's front door. She cracked it enough to show her face and greeted him without the cordial tone of the previous evening.

"I'm here to speak with Alicia," he said.

She turned to Ali, who was sitting on the couch, and Ali nodded once. "You may enter," Helga said.

Malloy stepped inside, and Helga shut the door. "Alicia, I trust you know why I'm back."

Doesn't waste any time. She rose from the couch. "Tommy told us about the DA's murder this morning. I burned another vacation day waiting around for you."

The trio approached the kitchen table in silence and took the same seats as before. Malloy opened his briefcase and pulled out a legal pad.

"Alicia, where were you last night?"

"Right here. Mom and I stayed in after you left. We went to bed after the ten o'clock news, and I came downstairs about eight this morning."

"I see. The two of you spent last night sleeping here, correct?"

"Correct."

Malloy made a note on his pad. "Can anyone else verify that?"

"It's doubtful. Even nosy Mrs. Olson sleeps sometimes."

"I see."

Ali recognized the pessimistic tone of a cop who never trusts anything he hears. It made her furious, but she bit her tongue and stayed in control of her emotions.

"Why did you kill Dan Milenburg?"

"I didn't kill Milenburg or Mr. Luetz. I told you, I stayed here with Mom last night."

Malloy was weary of this. "So you say."

"I'm her alibi," Helga snapped. "We were both here last night. She didn't kill that DA."

"Were you in the same room with Alicia?" Malloy shot back. "Did you stay awake all night watching her? How do you know she didn't slip out while you slept?"

Helga spoke through clenched teeth. "She was here the whole night."

"No mother ever admitted her child committed murder. Any jury will assume you are lying."

"What?" Helga threw her hands in the air. "I invite you into my home and you accuse my baby of murder and call me a liar?" She pointed her finger at him. "Because of bastards like you, my baby spent four months in a hell hole. And for what? For a stupid prank call any idiot, even Orville Luetz, knew was a joke. Ali has an ironclad alibi, and you're saying you can't trust me?"

Malloy faced her and answered in an icy tone. "Your precious Alicia slipped out of the house, drove to Mineral Ridge, killed the DA, and slipped back in again while you slept. Evidence at the scene implicates her."

Ali held her hands out, palms up. "But I've never been there. I don't even know where Milenburg lives."

Malloy's eyes locked with Ali's. "We'll continue to dig until we produce a stack of evidence that says you're lying. Make it easy on yourself. Confess to your crime."

"But I didn't do it."

Helga poked him in the shoulder. "Enough. You have the gall to treat us like lying criminals when you have as much of an ax to grind with that DA as Ali does. You've been here for two days and have gotten no further than Tommy and it's killing you, isn't it? You terrorize innocent women when in fact you have no better alibi than we do. Weren't you in Mineral Ridge last night?"

Helga's outburst left Malloy speechless.

She poked him again. "Well, weren't you?"

"Yes, but—"

She poked him a third time. "What were you doing at the time of Dan Milenburg's death? Answer me."

"I was asleep in my room."

"Alone?"

"Mom?"

Helga's head snapped toward Ali. "Hush." She waved her finger at Malloy. "Who can place you in your room when the murder took place?"

"No one."

"I thought as much." Helga straightened to her full height and lowered her hand. "We've told you nothing but the truth. Ali didn't leave the house last night, and I'll swear it under oath."

Helga kept her gaze fixed on Malloy, forcing him to study his pen. "The problem is... reliable sources will testify Ali snuck out of the house at least once before without you catching her. Despite your claims, she could have left without you knowing."

Helga cracked a smile. "What she did at sixteen has no bearing on today. Did she sneak out last night? No, she didn't. I'm not lying, and I can prove it."

Malloy locked eyes with Helga. "Show me the proof."

Helga's eyes flared. Ali remembered that look and how it preceded her mom's occasional tirades. She put her hand on Helga's. "Mom, this is my future we're discussing here."

For a long second Helga didn't move. She let her breath out before shifting her attention to Ali. "I know. You didn't sneak out like before."

Ali's brow furrowed. "You knew about that?"

"Yes, dear. You snuck out to go to Nancy Schmidt's party because I said you couldn't go. Her mother told me that they were going away for the weekend, and I suspected the worst. I heard you leave and chose not to catch you in the act, figuring you'd be hung over the next morning and I would make your life miserable then. But you weren't, and you never disobeyed me again, so I made the right decision that night." She pointed at Malloy. "And she certainly didn't leave last night."

"You'd best proceed with caution. If you're mistaken, I will arrest Alicia. I have enough evidence this time." Malloy pulled a pair of handcuffs out of his briefcase and dropped them on the table.

"Hogwash. You cops are all alike. You claim to have all the answers, but you don't know crap about Ali or me. I'll prove Ali didn't sneak out last night, and you will leave us alone. Or would you prefer to be embarrassed in court when it comes out that you overlooked something even a child could see?"

Malloy pointed to the handcuffs. "It's her funeral."

"Follow me upstairs," Helga said, rising and leading the way.

The upstairs of the old house was made up of two bedrooms and an attic with the stairs opening right into Ali's room. "Max and I slept in the front bedroom until she wanted her privacy and we moved downstairs. Shortly after her sixteenth birthday, she snuck out. Max slept through anything, and I never told him. You're smart. How did she do it?"

Malloy pulled the curtain back and smiled. "Easy. Slipped out the window onto the flat porch roof and used that overhanging limb to climb down the tree."

"Ali, is that how you did it?"

"Yes, Mom. Sorry."

"That's all right, dear. It was a long time ago."

Helga turned back to Malloy. "See another way to exit this room besides the stairs?"

"The front bedroom has a window, doesn't it?"

"See for yourself."

After they went into the front room, Malloy opened the window with ease to reveal an old wooden storm window. He gave it a light push. It didn't budge.

"I'll save you time. This window locks on the outside. She would need a ladder. I loaned our ladder to Carl Liecht. It's sitting in his garage three blocks away."

Malloy gave no reaction.

Helga stepped over to open a half-size door and pointed inside. "There's a small window in the attic."

Malloy peered in. "She could squeeze through that."

"Straight drop from there, and she would need a ladder to climb back in. The window is covered in dust. And here's a cobweb, too."

Malloy stepped back. "Nobody's touched it recently."

Helga shut the half door. "Take another look in Ali's room. Since she snuck out the window once before, you assume she did it again last night, right?"

"She got away with it once. You're older now, and your hearing's not as good."

Helga's eyes flared. "If it's so darn easy, why don't you try it? Open the window and show us how Ali snuck out last night."

"I don't have to do it myself to see—"

"Do it," Helga snapped, pointing to the window. He eyed her for a moment before flipping the old lock off and pushing against the frame. It didn't move, so he pushed harder.

"Spend too much time behind a desk?"

Malloy pushed again, straining every muscle. He pounded the window frame and tried wiggling it before giving one more big push. Nothing budged.

"Told you. There's no way Ali used that window because I painted it shut two years ago. Carl promised to pry it open from the outside when he puts a new roof on the porch next spring."

Malloy flicked his wrist at the stairs. "She could have slipped out in a more conventional way."

Helga smiled. "Ali, stay here. When I yell, tiptoe down the stairs."

Helga led Malloy to her bedroom directly under Ali's room.

"Okay," Helga yelled.

The old staircase creaked and groaned under Ali's descending steps. "The carpeting muffles the stair noise on top, but not in here. I always knew when she came home."

Malloy threw his hands in the air. "Okay. Alicia couldn't have snuck out of here without you knowing it."

Helga led Malloy back to the kitchen. "So, Ali's no longer a suspect, right?"

Malloy paused, his hand on the back of the kitchen chair. "No. An eyewitness reported a white car leaving the scene the same time as the murder. Ali's rental is white, and she fits the description of the person who drove away. You could have gone with her and stayed in the car or just stayed here."

Ali pulled her chair out and leaned on it with one knee, ready to sit. "But we didn't drive anywhere last night or today."

"Have you moved your rental for any reason today?"

"No."

Malloy glanced at Helga frowning and shaking her head, confirming Ali's answer.

He looked back and forth between Ali and Helga. "You're sure? Didn't drive to the diner for lunch or anywhere else?"

Ali shook her head. "Nope."

Helga continued shaking her head.

Malloy jerked his thumb toward the front door. "Move your rental car for me then."

Ali stood. "Why?"

"If you refuse, I'll arrest you."

Ali crossed her arms. "Traveling the same road as last night? Call your lawyer and I'll arrest you?"

Malloy glared at her. "I'm not bluffing this time. Move the car or face arrest. The choice is yours."

Ali stared at him, unsure of what infuriated her more—finding out Malloy bluffed last night or gambling that he was tonight.

"You want me to move it? Then what?"

"I'll take several pictures with the camera in my car. Evidence for the trial."

Ali leaned in. "Trial? Aren't we getting ahead of ourselves?"

"No."

Malloy knew something she didn't. What could it be? If she insisted on calling Justin Green, would he arrest her? She straightened. "I need a minute."

Malloy held his arm out and checked his watch. "One minute."

Ali drew a glass of water from the sink, stalling for time. She gazed out the window and noticed the yard blanketed with dead leaves. One stray leaf spiraled down from the Sycamore closest to the house. Ali faced him, smiling. "Okay, I'll move the car."

Malloy opened the door and followed her out.

———

Malloy grabbed his camera while Ali started her car. Helga stayed on the porch with her arms crossed and glared at Malloy.

Ali waited until Malloy signaled her before backing the rental. A car length back, Malloy frowned and signaled Ali to stop. She ran around the front of the car to learn her suspicions were correct.

"It was raining with heavy wind gusts when the murder occurred. If you drove this car, you would have parked on fallen leaves," Malloy said.

"Clean to the gravel, isn't it?"

Malloy took several pictures. "Pull it ahead. We'll finish inside."

They settled at the kitchen table. Ali smiled. *So I lied, huh? Big eyewitness, but it wasn't my car.*

"Are we finished now?" Ali crossed her arms.

Malloy ignored her question and took out his pen. "Why do you maintain a second identity as Alice Thorn?"

Ali's smile vanished before her head dropped into her hands.

Malloy sat back to wait her out. Ali muffled her cries as her body shuddered. Helga's eyes widened, and she touched Ali's arm.

Ali lifted her head, her eyes teary from suppressed laughter.

"Sorry. I never even considered that." She wiped her eyes, fanning her face with her hand.

"What time is it?" she asked, regaining her composure.

"Eight fifteen."

"Perfect. Malloy, since you aren't convinced I'm telling the truth, I'll make a call and let someone else explain who Alice Thorn is."

"I want to hear it from you."

Ali's jovial mood vanished as she grabbed her purse off the counter and dropped it on the table. "Fine."

She dug inside, pulled out a small wallet and waved it at Malloy. "My fake Alice Thorn ID provided by Robel's for my protection." She handed it over.

Malloy put his pen down and took the card. "Why do you need a fake ID?"

"I've worked undercover several times to catch dishonest security guards in our stores."

He handed the ID back. "I'm listening."

Ali stuffed the wallet back in her purse. "I shoplift items in the troubled store and when I get caught, I bribe the suspected security guard. If he accepts, I claim my uncle will come for me with the money and give him a number to call. If he refuses the bribe, I ask him to notify my parents to meet me at the jail and give him a different number. Are you an honest cop or a thief?"

Malloy glared at her.

Ali rolled her eyes. "For the phone call, I'll dial the number and the gentleman on the other end will verify what I've told you."

"Honest cop, of course."

Ali rose and dialed. She listened for the ring before handing it over.

Malloy took it, and an instant later a man answered.

"This is Agent Dirk Malloy with the Wisconsin DCI. I apprehended a woman shoplifting. Name is Alice Thorn. She gave me this number to call."

Malloy listened, occasionally grunting an "Uh-huh." He made a sour face. "Thanks for the explanation." He handed the phone to Ali.

"Henry, you still there?" Ali turned away from Malloy.

"Yes."

"Sorry about the misunderstanding. I was conducting an impromptu sting for a friend when Agent Malloy spotted me and exercised his civic duty."

"I wondered why you didn't alert me first," Henry said.

"Thanks for straightening him out. Say hello to the guys for me, okay?"

"Sure thing."

Ali said goodbye and eyed Malloy while she returned the phone to its cradle.

"Satisfied?"

Malloy picked up his pen and clicked it. "And if I had taken the bribe?"

Ali sat. "Henry would have asked you to detain me. When the local police arrived, you would have been surprised when they cuffed you instead."

Malloy's eyebrows raised. "I see. You've worked with police before."

"Several times. Henry is head of West Coast security. Right now, he's wondering why I'm running a sting in Wisconsin. I haven't gone undercover for over a year and a half."

Malloy wrote on his pad. "Uh-huh."

"I keep the Alice Thorn ID so I can work secretly in my troubled stores if need be. I have a credit card in that name too. I suppose you discovered that."

Malloy stopped writing and looked up. "We found out-of-state charges."

"I spent two weeks in Denver right before Dad died. The Vegas trip involved a major takedown. The former head of security for our Nevada stores is in jail now."

For the first time since Malloy became involved, Ali sensed her ordeal was ending. "You won't find anything on Alice Thorn that has relevance to these murders, and I've established an alibi for last night. Isn't it time to end this so you can pursue the real killer?"

Malloy tapped his pen against the pad, stalling to catch his second wind. "I can't ignore the evidence placing you at both crime scenes. A jury will believe that over what you've shown me this evening."

"The killer is framing me."

Malloy dropped the pen on the pad and sat back. "Okay. The killer is framing you."

"Darn right, they are."

He opened his hands, palms up on the table. "He must have a reason to implicate you. When I catch him, there's no telling the story he'll give. Might tell me you encouraged him or tricked him into committing the murders."

"But it'll be a lie because I didn't."

Malloy crossed his arms and leaned against the tabletop. "His word against yours. You have a criminal record, and your undercover works suggests you're good at deception. If your accomplice is... say, a police officer, the jury will believe him over you."

"A police officer? Why would you consider—" Ali's eyes widened. Her hand rose to her mouth. "Tommy? You're accusing him of murdering two men?"

"He had heated words with Orville Luetz. That establishes motive, and he withheld evidence found at the Luetz murder scene to protect you."

Ali didn't want to admit she knew about the note. She kept quiet and feigned concern.

Malloy smiled. His alternate plan was working. She knew more than she let on. "All I need to prove in court is that you were aware of this and failed to acknowledge it to me. That alone makes you an accomplice, eligible for jail time, maybe even prison."

Malloy sat back, confident his interrogation was back on track.

39

Ali was reluctant to split legal hairs with someone more knowledge-able about Wisconsin law, and she didn't want to make matters worse by admitting she knew about the note the entire time.

"You have no incontestable proof you were at that motel during Luetz's murder. Last night, Peterson could easily have driven you to Mineral Ridge. His exceptional friendliness with your mother ties you into this."

Ali locked eyes with Malloy. "I didn't kill either man, and Tommy Peterson isn't capable of doing the things you're implying."

"The call placing you at the scene this morning might have been him. Peterson's obviously smitten with you. He kills Milenburg and makes the call, forcing you to stay."

Ali stroked her lower lip and kept silent.

Helga's eyes darted back and forth between Ali and Malloy.

Malloy kept his focus on Ali. "I've subpoenaed your phone records. If he's the killer and the two of you have spoken—"

Ali crossed her arms. "I haven't spoken to Tommy in over eight years."

Malloy smiled. "Ever answer the phone and the caller hung up?

How about your answering machine? Have you ever played back a dropped call?"

Everyone got dropped calls. There was no way to know who called or prove she hadn't briefly spoken to the caller.

"Wouldn't take much to convince a jury you two planned this together. Once I see those phone records...."

Ali ran her fingers through her hair and remained silent.

"You're not buying this, are you, Ali? You don't believe Tommy would commit murder, do you?" Helga asked.

Ali took her time before she answered. "Tommy hated Luetz. His flare-up at the Ranch House the other night caught me by surprise."

Helga's forehead wrinkled. "No."

Ali lowered her voice. "I told you, I've changed."

"Tommy wouldn't hurt a fly, much less kill someone."

Ali shook her head. "It's a rough world out there. I've seen guys like Tommy before. There's even a term for it. Hero syndrome. Like a fireman setting fires he can extinguish to play the hero."

"No."

Ali tapped the table with her index finger as she spoke. "Any man who waits eight years to speak to someone he's... he's... smitten with has to have issues."

Helga crossed her arms and assumed her mother's voice. "I'll not have talk like that in my house, young lady. Tommy's been like a son to me. I never doubted your innocence, and you reward me by turning against him?"

Malloy remained silent, observing their confrontation.

Ali addressed Malloy in a soft, well-modulated tone. "Excuse us for a minute? Mom and I need to talk."

The request caught Malloy by surprise. Helga sat with her arms crossed, fuming. She could order Ali to leave her home, which would force him to take immediate action and kill his momentum.

"I'll wait here," he said.

Ali smiled. "It might be better if you waited on the front porch. The neighbors might overhear us."

Malloy glanced at Helga, who looked ready to explode. He stood.

"Call me when you're finished."

The two women sat in stony silence until they heard the front door slam shut. Helga pointed her finger at Ali and opened her mouth. Ali jumped in first, whispering, "Watch Malloy through the front window. Make sure he stays on the porch."

"What?"

"Step back and pretend you're scolding me while I search his briefcase."

Helga's eyes widened. "But that's—"

"Illegal. Malloy knows something he's not telling us. He's bluffing. He's on shaky legal ground with that accomplice crap."

"So you don't think Tommy—"

Ali opened her purse and took out a handkerchief. "Not at all. Tommy couldn't hurt anyone except in self-defense."

Helga stood in plain view of the front window while Ali examined Malloy's legal pad.

"Don't lecture me, Mom," Ali yelled, waving at Helga to make noise.

"I'll do what I darn well please in my own home. Who are you to tell me what I can and can't do? You... you waltz back into my life after ignoring me for all these years and expect me to devote all my attention to you again? Wake up, missy. You aren't a child anymore and haven't been for some time now."

Helga's words stung, but Ali was on a mission as she scanned Malloy's legal pad. Nothing more there than what they had discussed. The open side of his briefcase was empty except for the handcuffs, so she fanned through the file compartments in the lid using the handkerchief. She pulled out a plastic bag marked *Luetz Note*. Inside was the note implicating her as the prime suspect. A glance told her what she needed to know. She motioned Helga over and held the note up for Helga to see.

"Your handwriting, all right."

"Look again."

Helga moved closer and studied it. "You don't write like that anymore, do you?"

"Not since high school. I don't use little circles instead of dots, and I don't put long tails on words. I print certain letters now like that capital E. The killer copied this from an old letter or paper I wrote."

"But does Malloy know that's how you used to write? Maybe that's why he suspects Tommy."

"Could be. Everyone gets phone hang ups. He's sweating me by claiming he can connect us and ruin my life over it."

Ali motioned Helga back. She didn't want Malloy to poke his head in while she rifled through his briefcase.

"Are you sure?"

"I've sat across from desperate men before. He's covering it well, but he's desperate too. Malloy's no closer to finding the killer than when he started."

"What's he going to do? Sounds like he's ready to arrest you as an accomplice."

Ali searched the remaining file compartments. Empty. *Odd he doesn't carry more in his briefcase.* She froze. *Could he be setting me up to discover the note? He's smart enough to take his briefcase with him. Well, two can play that game.* "I doubt that. He knows I'll clam up and won't offer to help him unless he proves Tommy is the killer."

"You learn all this legal stuff in college?"

"No. Before I worked undercover, I got extensive training from Henry, our head of security, and legal advice from our company attorney, Charles Latimer. My boss wasn't comfortable using me because of my age and inexperience so Henry and Charles role-played with me until they were satisfied I could make clean busts."

"And you didn't tell Agent Malloy—"

"More reason to suspect me." She put the evidence bag containing the note back, careful to avoid touching anything bare-handed.

"Should we call Justin Green?"

Ali folded the handkerchief and put it in her pocket. "No. That would force Malloy to walk away or arrest me. I doubt he'll walk away. My picture will be on tomorrow's front page, and I'll lose my job."

Ali stared at the briefcase, thinking. "I'll have to play along to get Agent Malloy off my back."

"And try to convict Tommy?"

"He didn't do it. No way."

Helga hugged her daughter. "I knew you hadn't changed."

Ali wasn't so sure, but she returned the hug. "Tommy's innocent, and now it's time to prove it before Malloy sees the phone records. Truth is, I get many hang ups, but whether it's Tommy or a telemarketer, I'm not sure. Once it's clear Tommy's innocent, the records won't matter. Malloy can't link me to the killer."

Helga squeezed Ali tighter. "What do you want from me?"

"Act huffy. Convince Malloy I'll turn against Tommy to save my own skin."

"What if you're wrong and Malloy arrests Tommy?"

Ali paused. "I'll gain my own freedom at Tommy's expense."

Helga pulled away and caressed Ali's cheek with the back of her hand. "He's innocent. You can bet on it."

"Call Agent Malloy. Let's hear him out."

———

Malloy paced back and forth on the porch, frustrated that the key elements of his case, Ali sneaking out unnoticed and the placement of the white rental car at the scene were all explained. Even the notes were questionable. Could Peterson be responsible? He had to admit his far-fetched theory now sounded like the logical answer.

He peeked in through the window. Helga was lecturing Alicia and doing a fine job of it. He wondered if Alicia was buying time to search his briefcase. Didn't matter. *If she finds the copy of the Luetz note, she'll see why I think she's an accomplice. Her forced cooperation will help move the investigation forward.*

I underestimated Helga. There's a lot more fire in her than I imagined. I thought her presence would work to my advantage, but it did the opposite. How could I be so stupid to let her sit in during an interrogation?

40

Malloy followed an incensed Helga to the kitchen in silence. As she took her seat, Ali confronted him.

"For the record, I answered your questions truthfully. I've played no part in either murder. Mom is the only person in this area I've spoken to in eight years. Be forewarned. If you're planning on arresting me, I will spare no expense in making your life miserable. Justin Green can build a summer home with what I'll pay him to seek legal revenge."

Malloy took his seat at the table. "You're in no position to make idle threats, young lady."

Ali admired his style. Bluffed like a pro. With her career on the line, it was time to take it down a notch. She leaned forward, elbows on the table, and laced her fingers together.

"Sorry. It's been a frustrating week. I understand why I'm a suspect for Mr. Luetz. But Milenburg? I barely remember the man. No matter how perturbed I was at the time, I've moved on." Ali opened her hands, palms up. "Why jeopardize my future success by murdering two men who mean so little to me now?"

Malloy clicked his pen and studied it before he responded. "Because the evidence places you at both scenes, Peterson is the obvious choice to have planted it. If you are as innocent as you claim, it's in your best interest to assist us in discovering the truth. Peterson will clam up if I interrogate him, and you'll be on the hook."

Ali sat back. "You're asking for my help?"

"You could say that. I want you to get Peterson talking."

"And how am I supposed to work his confession into casual conversation?"

"Simple. I'll bug his jail cell and lock you in. I'll tell him that I've placed you under arrest and leave, but I'll be listening outside in my car while you lead him to confess. Play on his sympathy. If he is guilty, he will confess."

"What if he doesn't?"

"Better make sure he does. Juries will question an ex-con's statements. A respected officer of the law, though...."

Ali crossed her arms and looked away. "Yeah, right."

Malloy stayed silent to let Ali think. When she glanced back at him, he said, "Call him now, and convince him I'm closing in on you. Can you manage that?"

Ali sat forward, resting her elbows on the table. "I'll do my part." She waved her finger at him. "But if you think for a moment you're pinning the murders on me—"

"I know. Justin Green gets a new summer home."

"Bingo."

Malloy coached her before she placed the deceptive call. Knowing Tommy wanted more than her friendship made it difficult, but it didn't stop her.

"Hey, Tommy. I'm home."

"Ali, thank God."

"It's not over yet. Malloy left annoyed, that's for sure. He said as soon as the lab reports are finished, I'll be changing my tune."

"He's bluffing. If incriminating evidence comes back from the lab, it was planted. Want me to sit with you until we're sure he's not returning?"

Ali gave an audible sigh. "No, I'm beat. No one is working on

Malloy's evidence this late on a Friday night. Nothing will happen until tomorrow."

"You're right."

"Thanks for the offer."

"Once this mess is resolved, I hope you'll stay another day or two. Let me show you what's good here."

"We'll see." Ali moved away from the counter and prepared to end the call. "For now, promise me that you'll make sure I'm taken to your cell if Agent Malloy arrives with a warrant. I'll call Justin Green, and he'll give Malloy his comeuppance. Don't worry, I won't sue the village."

Tommy laughed once. "I knew you were kidding the other night. You're not that petty."

Ali turned to avoid Malloy. "Look, Agent Malloy isn't the type to admit he's wrong. He'll probably contact you and tell you I'm free to go. When he does, come over and we'll celebrate over breakfast at the diner."

"Okay. Call if you need me. Helga knows my pager number for emergencies. I'll be on patrol at ten, two, and five."

"Thanks," Ali said, hanging up and facing Malloy. "Is that what you wanted?"

"You sold me. Remember, none of the allegations against you are off the table until I'm convinced you're an innocent bystander. If you warn Peterson, I will bring charges against you."

"I won't. I'm innocent, and by the time we're through tonight, I expect you to acknowledge it."

"Do your job right. If you're telling the truth, it'll be over for you."

Ali looked away, hoping to end the conversation. No such luck.

"Remember, the charge of accessory to murder carries the same sentence as the actual crime. I expect your full cooperation on this. Warn him, tip him off in any way—"

"Don't worry. I want complete absolution of these murders. I won't hold back. Are we finished?"

Malloy closed his briefcase and stood. "Be ready to leave at one. I'll call then."

"I'll be ready."

Helga led him to the door in silence and returned to find Ali sitting at the table with her face buried in her hands.

"Please don't let it be Tommy."

"It isn't," Helga said, rubbing Ali's shoulders. "It can't be. Just can't be."

But Malloy sowed powerful seeds of doubt in Ali's mind. She was no longer one hundred percent sure of Tommy's innocence.

———

The Kickapoo Motor Inn bed beckoned Malloy at the end of one disappointing day. A couple hours of sleep before he drove back to Rausburg would help, but first he had a call to make.

"Mike. Draw the short straw tonight?" Malloy asked, faking good humor.

"Volunteered. Fred had a rough day on the stand, and Betty's been here late every night this week."

"I'm sure you're as tired as I am. Sorry for the long hours."

"We knew what we were getting into. I have new information for you, that's why I waited."

Malloy untied his shoes and kicked them off. "Make it good news. I need it."

"Depends. Peterson's phone records arrived late this afternoon. No out-of-state calls at either home or office."

"Any unusual calls?"

"Not that I can see. Most are to Rausburg phones. Many to Helga Thorein, but they fit the pattern we discovered during the interviews."

Malloy pulled his tie off. "What pattern?"

"They have dinner together on Tuesday and Sunday. He must call before he goes over. Calls her other times too, but nothing suspicious. The rest are to businesses and other village citizens."

Malloy lay back on the bed. "It's possible he could have called Alicia from a pay phone."

"Someone would have overheard and blabbed about it, like they did to you. You made one call and the whole village knew you suspected Peterson for Luetz's murder."

"Still haven't figured that one out. I talked softly and no one was around."

"Well, Peterson never contacted Alicia. Her phone records might indicate something different, but we won't get them until next week. You find out anything tonight?"

Normally Malloy would've shared, but tonight he stayed noncommittal. "Nothing of great importance. Didn't make an arrest."

"Too bad. I hoped we could all enjoy the weekend."

"You, maybe. I'll be here tomorrow. I'll call if I need anything."

"Okay. Get some sleep. I'm going home and hit the sack."

Malloy set the alarm before reclining on the bed. He considered calling Alicia to cancel their charade and tell her she was free to go. Certainly safer for his career, but Malloy didn't become head of the task force by playing it safe. No, stick to the plan. Besides, Alicia couldn't fly home until morning. Might as well take advantage of the situation and see what shakes loose.

41

Malloy called Ali shortly after one a.m. from Tommy's office. "I'm in place. Enter through the back."

Ali hugged her mom before slipping out of the house. The swishing of her pajamas broke the silence as she hustled to Tommy's office in the chilly moonlight, bundled in her robe with her coat thrown over her shoulders to fight the night chill. Malloy hadn't wanted to risk the slam of car doors prompting Mrs. Olson next door to peep through her windows and see Ali leaving with Malloy. After years of big city noise, the dead calm made Ali uneasy.

Malloy greeted Ali at the back door of Tommy's office as she entered unnoticed. "Might want to use the facilities before I lock you in. I'll give Peterson strict orders not to let you out."

"I'm fine." She regarded the new addition behind Tommy's office. Two cells on one side, a bathroom and small closet on the other, one folding chair next to the cells. "This wasn't here before."

"Peterson said his predecessor convinced the village council to build it after your arrest."

Ali eyed the cells. "I'm surprised there isn't a plaque with my name on it."

"Let's lock you in and make everything look official."

Ali stopped outside the jail cell, her hands trembling. "I have your word, correct?"

"I will return you to your mother's tonight and discuss your future in the morning after my team interrogates Peterson."

"Make it early tomorrow. I want to leave as soon as possible."

Malloy stepped into Tommy's office without answering.

Ali remained outside the cell. Her eyes darted over every square inch and she had trouble catching a full breath.

Malloy returned with a pair of shackles. Ali's eyes widened, she swallowed hard and covered her mouth with her hand.

He looked at the shackles and back at Ali. "What's wrong?"

She swallowed again. "I puked when they did this before and I feel like I'm going to again."

Malloy stepped back and dropped the shackles on the floor of Tommy's office, out of Ali's sight. "Ginger ale will soothe your stomach. Peterson has a couple in the fridge."

He hurried back with the soda, not wanting to clean up vomit tonight. He opened it, she snatched it with trembling hands and took two big swigs.

"Stomach better now?"

She burped. "A little."

She took another swig. "It's the cell and the shackles. I went to court expecting probation and community service. Sinclair shackled me instead and took me directly to jail. I got sick and stayed covered in my own mess for over an hour while they took their sweet time processing me."

Malloy opened the cell door wide. "I planned on leaving the shackles out to show Peterson I was serious. I wasn't going to use them."

"I can do this. Give me a minute to calm down."

"You can pull yourself together while I activate the bug." Malloy left her alone to sip the ginger ale while he retrieved a small wireless microphone and transmitter from his car.

A minute later he knelt on the floor, flipped the folding chair on its side, and taped the bug in place. "Unfortunately, there's no better place to hide this. Keep Peterson on his feet. If he sits and squirms, I might miss something."

"Are you recording?"

"Wouldn't be admissible. Once he admits his guilt, I'll arrest him and obtain a warrant to search his house. We'll find convicting evidence there, I'm sure. I searched his office earlier."

"You didn't find anything, did you?"

Malloy set the chair upright and checked to make sure the bug remained hidden. "Concentrate on getting him to confide in you. He's hiding something."

"Impossible, Tommy would never—"

Malloy held his hand up. "He'll either confess or convince me of his innocence. Anything else won't be good for you."

Taping completed, Malloy stood. "Talk to yourself while I listen in the car. Let's make sure the mic works."

Ali recited the alphabet several times before Malloy returned. "Came through loud and clear. I'm ready. Are you?"

Ali took a final swig of ginger ale before tossing the can in the trash and entering the cell. Malloy swung the cell door shut. She plopped down on the bench and leaned back against the cold concrete wall.

"You're not going to be sick, are you?"

She closed her eyes and took a deep breath. "Call him."

Malloy awakened Tommy at home. "Peterson, Alicia's in custody. I found additional evidence linking her to Milenburg's murder. I need you here to guard her while I get the truth from Helga." Tommy didn't respond. "Peterson?"

"Be right there."

Malloy returned to Ali's cell. "If you shed a few tears, he'll crumble and talk. I'll park a block away. If he goes the other direction and his anger escalates, I'll be here within seconds."

"Tommy's not that kind of man."

42

Ali sat alone in the cell, wondering if she could signal Tommy about the mic while convincing Malloy that she had no connection to the murders. She didn't want to send Tommy to prison, but the stakes were too high. Unlike the other times when she led men into taking a bribe, this time her own innocence required verification. Any mistake could ruin her life. When she heard Tommy's car screech to a halt out front, she was afraid anything less than her best effort would doom them both.

"Where's Ali?" Tommy asked as he burst in his office, breathless and frantic. "You brought her here, didn't you?"

"She's in your one of your cells."

"What? Why?"

Malloy raised his hand. "We'll talk later. Watch her now. She'll be charged with two counts of murder one and face Judge Lynch tomorrow. He'll deny bail, so she'll spend the rest of her life behind bars."

Tommy shuddered. Lynch was tough on repeat offenders. She would get two life sentences with no chance of parole if she were convicted.

"I patted her down. She's in her pajamas and robe. I hung her coat up. She doesn't need it in here. Make sure she doesn't hang herself while I interrogate Helga. Now that she knows Alicia's guilty, I'm betting Helga will turn on her to save her own skin."

"Helga, too? You've got to be kidding."

"You told me Alicia couldn't have put Orville Luetz in that chair without help."

"But—"

Malloy waved him off. "No matter what, don't enter that cell. Alicia's a desperate killer who will lure you in, grab your gun, and kill you too. We'll make the transfer to Mineral Ridge in the morning. This time she'll get her wish. She won't come back to Rausburg. Ever."

Malloy glared at Ali as he strode past the cell and headed for the back door. With one hand on the doorknob, Malloy admonished Tommy. "Remember, don't go in the cell. Don't let her fool you. She's a caged animal who'll stop at nothing to get free." Malloy left, and the door fell shut behind him.

———

Tommy cradled his face in his hands. "God, I've messed this up." He pulled himself together before stepping into the back room.

Ali's face was wet with tears. Easy to conjure them knowing she might lure sweet, shy little Tommy Peterson to prison. She hated doing it, but if the truth didn't come out, everything she sacrificed for would be lost and she would always live under a cloud of suspicion.

Tommy moved closer to her cell and hung his head. "Sorry. Never thought Malloy would arrest you."

Ali sniffed and wiped her eyes. "I didn't do it, but Malloy claims he can prove otherwise. I'll be locked up. Forever." She shuffled to the cell bars, clutching and shaking them to no avail. "Please, please let me out of here. I'll do anything if you release me."

"This is all my fault. I'm responsible for this mess."

Ali rattled the bars harder, seething now. "Your fault? Are you the one framing me? Did you kill Luetz and the DA? Is that why I'm here now?"

Tommy took a step back, startled at her sudden hostility. "What? No, but I'm responsible."

"What do you mean you're responsible? How could you be responsible if you didn't kill them?"

Tommy crossed his arms. "Right away Fern Johnson told me that you were here and already pronounced you guilty. The note made things worse so I held on to it. Should have burned the darn thing since nothing else pointed to you."

"But you weren't sure, were you? You suspected I killed Luetz out of spite, didn't you?"

"Luetz's killer dragged him across the floor and set him in a kitchen chair. You're not capable of lifting him alone. He was much heavier than you remember. The coroner and I struggled to get his body on the gurney."

"And no one else noticed that?"

Tommy shook his head. "Sinclair sees what he wants to see. That's why I hid the note. I was certain you couldn't have killed Luetz even though the note is in your handwriting. When Malloy found out about it, I had to show it to him."

Ali grimaced. Malloy now knew she was aware of the note when he demanded a handwriting sample. He never asked about the note, so she hadn't lied, but he might file an obstruction charge or worse. Now it was imperative Malloy accepted she didn't write either note. One question had troubled her ever since Malloy forced her to write on the tablet. "If you didn't tell anyone, how did Malloy discover the note?"

"Malloy's partners heard rumors while conducting interviews. Fern Johnson, Irma Koepke, Harriet Rowe, and Opal Olson all talked to them at length. Could've started there."

Ali plopped down on the bench. "Crap, must have been me."

"You told them? After I—"

"Didn't mean to. After you left Monday night, I called an attorney in San Francisco and yelled at him. Mom had opened the window by the phone earlier. I'll bet Mrs. Olson overheard next door."

"That explains it."

Yes, and Tommy had unknowingly implicated her as an accomplice to his cover-up. "I don't get it. Malloy took a sample of my handwriting. It couldn't have matched because I never wrote the note."

"Ali, the note looks like your handwriting."

"How can you tell? I never wrote you or gave you a sample."

Tommy's head sunk. "The sixteenth birthday card you sent me in high school. I've read it hundreds of times over the years. You wrote inside I could be anything I wanted to be."

Ali brought her hand to her mouth. "I'd forgotten."

He raised his head and held his hands out, palms up. "That's how I recognized your penmanship. The receipt from the motel looked a little different, but the note resembled that birthday card. I figured you hurried with the receipt."

"You kept a birthday card from me all this time?"

He leaned against the bars and avoided her eyes. "I... I've been in love with you ever since high school. You were pretty, smart, and funny, and I wanted to date you. But you were already dating someone, and I never found the courage to ask you out."

"I never knew."

"After your release from jail, I hoped for a chance, but I didn't know what to say before you left."

Ali remained silent.

He straightened and tapped his fist against the bars once before sitting down. "I became the kind of man that would stand a chance with you, and you picked the second worst day of my life to return."

"Second worst day? What topped Luetz's murder?"

"The day Chief Hancock walked you to his car in cuffs in front of us."

"Oh."

Ali closed her eyes and remembered that day, the first of many worst days of her life. Chief Hancock reluctantly cuffed her in Luetz's office, begging Luetz to reconsider. "You don't need to do this. You've made your point. Let's work something out."

"It's your duty as police chief, or should I call the sheriff's department and inform the village council that you refused to uphold the law?"

Hancock caved and Luetz used the intercom to instruct the teachers to bring their students to the front classroom windows immediately. A minute later Hancock led Ali to his patrol car in handcuffs while the entire school watched. She glanced back as Hancock opened his car door and saw the astonished faces of every kid in school. Reliving that moment, she remembered Tommy wore the same expression he had at his father's funeral. Blank, like his whole world collapsed. She opened her eyes and saw that face again.

Ali stepped to the cell door and clung to the bars. "That was a bad day for both of us."

He rose from the chair, shaking his head as if trying to shake away a bad memory. He covered her hands with his. "In my heart, I knew you didn't kill Luetz, but others assumed you did, and I couldn't let you leave without proving your innocence. Now, I wish you had stayed in San Francisco and never come back."

"That makes two of us."

Ali pulled her hands away to wipe her eyes. Tommy reached through the bars to caress Ali's hair. Ali jerked back before he touched her and furrowed her eyebrows.

"Don't lie, Tommy. Malloy let it slip that you didn't submit any pictures of the note. You wanted to keep me here indefinitely, didn't you? How can I believe you didn't invent this whole note thing after you learned I was here?"

Tommy stepped back from the cell. "The note pictures are on a separate roll of film in my desk. I never submitted it."

"You claim."

"I didn't plan it that way. When I turned in the evidence, I knew Sinclair would see the note and obtain an arrest warrant, so I left the note and the film in the car and hid them in my desk drawer when I got back. When Malloy took over, he didn't want to hear what I had to say, and I wanted him to focus on gathering other evidence leading to the real killer so I kept it a secret. After Malloy found out about the note, I had to surrender it to him. Figured I'd get the pictures developed after we found the killer and suffer the consequences then."

Ali's shoulders drooped. "You risked your job for me?"

"Wasn't a risk while I was in charge. Once Malloy took over, I tried to steer him away from you so you'd be free to go." He hung his head. "Wasn't successful at that, either."

Ali mulled over this new information. If Tommy wanted to frame her, he could have submitted the first film roll along with the note, giving Malloy more evidence to detain her as the prime suspect. Tommy wouldn't kill Milenburg when it would have been easier to turn in the film.

"I bungled everything this week. I couldn't find Luetz's killer, and I let the woman I love get arrested for a crime she didn't commit."

Ali rattled the cell bars. "Fix it now. Let me out before Malloy gets back. Drive us into Illinois. I'll rent another car, and we'll disappear."

Tommy shook his head. "I have to prove you didn't kill Mr. Luetz. Once that's resolved, Malloy's case against you for Milenburg will fall apart."

"And how will you do that?"

Tommy rubbed his chin. "I'll start with that Darryl kid from the motel. I'll drive to Black River Falls in the morning and ask around. Someone must know where to reach him."

"Why didn't you do that already?"

"That won't tell me who the real killer is, only that you didn't do it, and I knew that. That kid will verify your alibi."

He snapped his fingers. "The two truckers. I'll get their names and track them down, too. They might remember seeing your car when they left. You said they woke you up at five. You couldn't have been in Rausburg killing Luetz at four and make it back to Black River Falls by five."

Tommy crossed the room. "Security cameras at the rest stops along the interstate. It's possible your car was caught on film with a time stamp. Long shot, but worth pursuing."

"Why didn't you check that before?"

Tommy stopped. "Because you're innocent. Why waste time

chasing information that won't find the actual killer? That's where Malloy went wrong. He's wasting time making a case against you, but he can't because you didn't do it."

He waved his index finger as he continued brainstorming. "I'll hire an independent forensic research team before I leave in the morning. They'll scour Luetz's house, maybe find new evidence the task force missed."

"But what about the evidence Malloy found at Milenburg's?"

He lowered his hand. "If he found evidence placing you there, it was planted."

"By you?"

Tommy froze, staring at her in disbelief.

"You withheld the note, didn't you?"

He put his hands on his hips. "Because it didn't serve the law. Making a case against you with a forged document stole time away from solving the crime. Killing Milenburg to force you to stay? I can't believe you would even consider that a possibility."

Ali rattled the cell door. "Then let me out. I'll hide while you figure this out. Don't send me to Mineral Ridge. Please, Tommy. If you love me, don't let Malloy take me there."

Tommy studied her face, now wet with tears. "Sorry, I can't do that. I took an oath. I'll stay by your side and help you fight this, but we need to convince Malloy you didn't do it. Releasing you now will make things worse."

Ali rattled the bars once and turned away. "Worse than life in prison?"

"We'll figure out the truth. I'll work with Justin Green to prove your innocence. Helga, too. There's no possible way she's involved in this. Malloy's case against her will fall apart when he discovers your mom doesn't lift anything heavy because of her sciatica."

Ali spun around. "Mom's got back problems?"

"Pinched a nerve last year while moving the couch. Now she calls me to move anything heavy. If she lifted Luetz's body, she couldn't have moved for days. When Malloy returns, I'll talk sense into him. His case against you will fall apart."

Ali pursed her lips and reviewed everything Tommy had told her. It didn't appear that he killed either man, and he didn't have any flashes of anger, only disappointment because she assumed he was the killer.

He explained his sound reasons for hiding the Luetz murder note and had a solid plan to remove her as a suspect in either murder. Any handwriting specialist would find the Milenburg note was not in Ali's hand. *That should prove my innocence along with Tommy's.*

Exhausted from the stress of the last twenty-four hours, she plopped down on the bench. "Guess it's time to confess."

"Confess? But you didn't kill those men."

"No, I didn't, and Malloy is leaning that way too. I've been lying to you. The second note is the only evidence linking me to Milenburg's murder, and I'm confident any analysis of it will prove I didn't write it or the Luetz note. We were checking on you."

Tommy's jaw dropped. "Checking on me?"

"Sorry, but somebody is framing me. You were the most likely suspect. We staged this whole event tonight to find out if you were the killer."

He perched on the folding chair. "You believed I framed you for killing two men? Why?"

Ali avoided Tommy's gaze. "Malloy told me that you argued with Mr. Luetz the day Margaret was committed to the clinic. After seeing your outburst at the Ranch House..." Ali sniffed. "I assumed you killed Mr. Luetz, panicked, and forged a note in my handwriting to cover your tracks. You controlled the evidence, so you could get away with it. You'd have an excuse to call me, but I would have an alibi. Except I came home unannounced, and you were forced to hide the note to protect me."

Tommy leaned over and put his head in his hands. "Luetz threatened me, all right. I let him rant before I yelled back that I knew Margaret took school money from his wallet." Tommy sat up. "Took the wind out of his sails. He had blamed it on several students over the years, including me, and squelched any further inquiries."

"How did you find out?"

Tommy grinned. "Couple years back, a concerned senior came to me saying she was afraid because money from their class treasury was missing and she didn't know how that could happen. I had my suspicions so I marked a twenty before making an anonymous donation to the senior class and told Chet to watch for the bill. It surfaced when Margaret used it a few days later to buy booze."

Ali crossed her legs. "Why didn't you act then?"

Tommy intertwined his fingers. "I told Orville I knew money was disappearing and I was happy to conduct a full investigation. That solved the problem until Margaret got thirsty and drove to Mineral Ridge. I spent the afternoon waiting for her and eventually found her passed out on County Road G with the car half on, half off the road."

"And you confronted him."

Tommy nodded. "Poor Mr. Luetz. His wife was a hopeless drunk, and little Tommy Peterson could destroy his career if I told the school board she stole money from their children and he covered it up."

"Wow. I'm sure that was a bitter pill to swallow."

Tommy met Ali's eyes. "All those years of despising that man for what he did to you and in that moment, I felt sorry for him. The school was his whole life, and right or wrong I was about to take it from him."

He stood. "I gave him a choice. If he committed Margaret, I'd forget about the rest as long as it never happened again."

"And he agreed?"

"Ironic, isn't it? He got a second chance with the person he loved most but his death ruined my chance with you."

Tommy's brow wrinkled. "How could you even consider me the killer?"

Ali couldn't meet his eyes. "Sorry, Tommy. Someone's trying to send me away for life. You've never served time, but I have. I'd do anything to stay out of prison, even betray a friend. Malloy placed a microphone and transmitter under the chair to listen in on our conversation."

Tommy stared at the chair.

"You've grown into an outstanding young man, Tommy. I wish I deserved to be your girlfriend, but I don't. You deserve better."

———

Malloy punched the steering wheel in frustration. He never dismissed any suspect until he made an arrest, so he always had a backup plan prepared. Now was the time to launch it. He parked behind Tommy's office.

When Malloy strode through the back door, Tommy wore a frown.

"Sorry I ruined your investigation."

"Wait in the conference room while I unlock Alicia."

Tommy left and Malloy opened Ali's cell. She scurried out and took a deep breath before whispering, "Tommy's innocent. What are you going to do about it?"

Malloy pushed the cell door shut. "Questionable call on the note. Speaking of which—"

She pointed her finger at him. "You never mentioned a note, and I saw no reason to volunteer that I heard about it. Do I need to call Justin Green?"

The corners of Malloy's mouth turned up. "No, I heard he already has a summer home up north anyway."

She laughed once and let her hand fall.

"I'm curious, though. Do you know Peterson's reason for discussing the note with you and no one else?"

"I threatened to leave after he questioned me, and he knew a sheriff's deputy would take me in. He was protecting me while trying to solve the murder, which I might add you haven't solved yourself, have you?"

Malloy rubbed the back of his neck. "I'm getting closer."

They stared at each other for a moment.

"You're welcome," Ali said.

Malloy laughed once.

"Am I free to go now?"

"I've got a plan. Stay, and help my investigation."

"Why should I? You've made my life miserable these past few days. I've had enough of that, thank you."

"I'm not the one making your life miserable, and I think you know that too. The real killer is waiting for you to take the fall. When he learns you've gone back to San Francisco, he'll place an anonymous tip and your DMV picture will be plastered all over the media. When I tell them that Alicia Thorein is not a suspect they'll still report what they learned so far about you, including the bomb hoax and your incarceration."

"So I'm not free to go. Justin may still get his gazebo."

Malloy gestured towards the conference room. "If that's the way you feel when I'm finished, so be it. But it's in your best interest to help me."

"I'll be the judge of what's best for me."

———

Tommy's badge lay on the table when Malloy and Ali entered the conference room.

"I'll make this easy," Tommy said. "I hampered your investigation, and you know why. My personal feelings got in the way of good judgment. I'm ready to pay whatever price the justice system asks."

For the first time since they met, Malloy envied Tommy. The ability to believe a person was innocent despite the evidence left Malloy long ago. "You told Alicia you didn't plant the Luetz note. I found the roll of film earlier in your desk drawer. I assume it's time stamped."

"Should be."

"I have another area of concern. You left no fingerprints at the scene, correct?"

Tommy's brow furrowed. "I used a hanky when I first went in, and later I wore latex gloves."

"And you touched nothing in there with your bare hands."

Tommy remained silent, reliving the events in his mind. "Crap,

crap, crap," he said, shaking his head. "Oh, Jeez what a dumb thing. I'm sorry, I forgot all about it."

"What did you forget?" Malloy said as he narrowed his eyes.

"I used my hanky to enter. All the blood... Luetz had been beaten with the bat. I grabbed the table to steady myself before I ran outside and puked. The back door stood partially open. I may have touched the door frame or the knob on the way out. I leaned over the rail and puked into the bushes off the side of the porch."

"We found your prints in the house. Coupled with your secrecy regarding the note led me to suspect you either killed Luetz or conspired with Alicia."

"Do you believe us now?" Tommy asked.

Malloy stared at the wall before answering Tommy. "You should have shown me the note without qualification and let me decide how to proceed. After hearing the unsubstantiated accusations against Alicia, I can see why you suspected I might jump to that conclusion."

Malloy tossed Tommy's badge back to him. "If I wanted it, I would have demanded it. Despite your blunder, cops need to use their instincts, too. If it weren't for you, Alicia would be in jail while I wasted valuable time on a case that couldn't be won. I'll keep any charges to the absolute minimum, but I need continued cooperation from both of you."

Tommy spoke without hesitation. "Ali's innocent. I'll do anything to prove it."

"Good." Malloy gestured for Ali to take a seat.

Ali sat and crossed her ankles. "How long do I have to stay?"

Malloy leaned over the table, resting on his knuckles. "Over the weekend. I want everyone convinced I'm building my case against you while I comb Milenburg's files. Peterson, perform your normal duties as needed, but monitor Alicia to make sure no one discovers our deception before I'm ready."

Ali hugged herself. "I'll be at risk from the person framing me. The real killer might come after me."

"Another good reason for Peterson to watch you. Consider this: Until I make an arrest, public opinion says you're guilty, but I haven't proved it yet. In two days, I'll have the killer, and everyone will know you were framed."

Tommy arched his eyebrows, his eyes pleading with her to stay. Her head sagged as she nodded. "Goes against my better judgment, but I'll stay. Keep me out of the papers. I don't want to be famous."

Malloy straightened. "I'll do my best. Peterson, spend the weekend at their house, if that's acceptable to Alicia and Helga. Alicia's right, the killer might become impatient. As of this moment, report directly to me or my team. No one else. Got that?"

Tommy nodded. "Yes, sir."

Malloy thumped the table. "We're done. Go home."

"There's one problem we haven't discussed yet, Malloy," Tommy said.

"What's that?"

"Come tomorrow morning, people will see my car parked at Helga's and wonder why I'm there."

Malloy frowned. "Stay at your house."

"Then people will wonder where Ali is."

Ali stood. "He's right, Malloy. Mrs. Olson's always been a big gossip. By noon, the whole village will have questions."

Malloy rubbed the back of his neck. "Can't tell the truth, that could cripple my investigation. I may never solve this thing."

Ali raised her index finger. "Here's a solution. Spread the rumor I demanded to leave and you threatened to lock me up. My attorney got involved and threatened a big lawsuit. After a heated discussion, we compromised. I stayed, and you ordered Tommy to watch me. Mom invited him inside so he wouldn't have to sit alone in his car."

"Okay with you, Peterson?"

"I can live with it. You'd better call our village president, Harv Middleton, in the morning. Tell him you've ordered me to watch Ali, but I'll be on call. That way, it won't cost the village a lack of service. He won't have a problem with it, but if I tell him, he'll get suspicious, and I'm not that good at deception."

Tommy's implication that Malloy had no problem with deception bothered him, but he let it pass. "I'll call tomorrow morning and tell Harv you answer to me on this investigation."

Ali waited in Tommy's car while he walked Malloy out. After Tommy slid behind the wheel and shut the door, they sat in silence for a moment.

Tommy glanced at Ali. "You were wrong."

Ali looked away. "I know. Can you ever forgive me for accusing you?"

"Already have. Malloy cornered you. You had no choice except to save yourself. If our positions were reversed..."

Tommy put the keys in the ignition and started his car, but he didn't move it.

"You were wrong when you said you didn't deserve to be my girl-friend. You were wrong there."

Ali met his gaze. Tommy had the sincerest face she had ever seen. Even though his heart must be broken, his eyes carried a longing she never expected to see in anyone. "Girlfriends don't accuse their boyfriends of framing them for murder. I might do right by Mom, but I doubt any man is interested in taking me and my baggage."

He put the car in gear. "You've been looking in the wrong places. I've been waiting for you and all your baggage."

"Well, you're a darn fool then."

"Been called worse."

After they drove home in silence, they were greeted with warm hugs from a relieved mother.

———

"What's my move now?" Malloy said aloud while driving to the motel.

I need to move the investigation in a different direction come sunup, but where exactly? If Milenburg were running for judge, why would he contact Luetz and Alicia? How could Alicia contribute to Milenburg's success from San Francisco?

He missed something, and it bothered him. "Must be losing my edge."

What he needed was sleep and a mind uncluttered by failure to make a case against Alicia and Peterson. Highway 72 was deserted, with long stretches of road safe for high-speed driving. Malloy made record time to Mineral Ridge.

Dead tired, he climbed into bed. A minute later, as he passed between the conscious and unconscious dissecting his investigation, he had a revelation. He fumbled for the light and jotted "Margaret Luetz" on the motel stationery before sinking back and smiling as exhaustion overcame him.

43

Saturday, October 20, 1984

Ali awoke when the delicious aroma of brewing coffee tickled her nostrils. She indulged in one full-bodied stretch as her blinking eyes opened to her childhood bedroom after a night devoid of nightmares. Malloy no longer considered her a suspect, and soon she would resume her normal life. *Be patient over the weekend, and fly home Monday.* She could live with that.

Most likely the day would turn warm, but now the house held October's frosty chill. Socks insulated her feet from the cold wood floor. After pulling on her robe, she used a comb to smooth her hair and make it presentable before descending the squeaky old staircase.

———

Tommy sat on the couch with his arms stretched high and his face bright red as his body shook off sleep.

Ali stepped off the last stair. "Mom, there's a bum in the living room."

Tommy dropped his arms and exhaled. "Sorry ma'am. Thought you knew."

"Knew what?"

"This ain't the big city. Our bums sleep inside on chilly nights."

"As long as you're here, I guess you can stay. If you're good, Mom will feed you too. Like gruel?"

"Love it. Your family eat like that every day?"

Ali laughed, waving him away. Tommy rose from the couch in yesterday's rumpled uniform. "Sleep well?"

"For the first time since I arrived. You?"

"Woke up once. The welcome sign bangs against the siding when the wind's just right."

Helga appeared holding the coffee pot. "Sorry. Guess I've gotten used to it. Have a seat while I scramble eggs. Toast will be ready in a minute." She set the coffee pot on the table.

Ali checked the kitchen clock. "Nine o'clock, almost a record for me."

Tommy filled Ali's cup before his own. "That early, huh? I figured big city life made you soft. Out all night on the town, sleep late, linger over a fancy brunch, half the day gone before your eyes open."

"Hardly. I'm at my desk by seven thirty. When I'm on the road I'm up even earlier. I accomplish more before nine than you do all day."

Helga glowered at Ali. "It isn't a contest."

Tommy's smile faded as he reached for the sugar bowl.

"Of course, I don't save lives in my work. I merely entice people to purchase the many high-quality, low-priced, name brand products Robel's offers," Ali said with a wink.

Tommy's smile returned. "Selling soap is important, too. Imagine the chaos if children couldn't wash behind their ears." Ali made a mental note to be more careful with her sarcastic remarks. A few moments later, she snickered.

"What's so funny?" Tommy asked.

"You, me, seeing each other in the worst possible light. All week long you were afraid I killed Luetz. I snapped at you the whole time. Last night I suspected you were the killer framing me, and on top of that, we both look our absolute worst ever."

Tommy rubbed his cheek. "Sorry. Haven't shaved yet, but you're beautiful as ever. You have nothing to worry about."

Ali blushed a light pink. "Good thing you feel that way. In some cultures, once the man sees a woman in her sleepwear, they have to marry."

Tommy stirred his coffee. "Okay by me. I'll call Father Raschke. By noon you can make lunch for me like a good wife should."

"Where did you learn that? *Leave It to Beaver*?"

He set his spoon on the saucer and took his cup. "Common knowledge. That's why those shows were popular. They're truthful. People identify with them."

As Tommy sipped his coffee, he received blank stares from Helga and Ali. He lowered his cup. "Maybe the right woman could correct my faulty thinking. Know anyone up for the job?"

Ali rolled her eyes and exaggerated a sigh. "You'd need a team of women working night and day for several months."

"You think he's bad now? You should have seen him before I started," Helga said as she shoveled eggs on their plates.

"Hey." Tommy winked at Ali as he grabbed his fork. She smiled back.

While Helga and Ali showered and dressed, Tommy dialed Harv's Hardware. Malloy had called, all right. "I don't like him ordering you around, especially after he accused you of killing Orville," Harv said.

"He told you that he suspected me?"

"Heard it Thursday. Didn't anyone mention it?"

"No, but everyone acted funny. No kidding around."

"Well, Malloy admitted he was wrong about you. I've made a few calls already. The whole village will know soon enough."

Tommy glanced out the open kitchen window to see Mrs. Olson turn away while raking leaves between their houses. "Thanks. I'm surprised Malloy told you."

"I threatened to call reporters and put him in the hot seat. That got his attention."

"Did he tell you about Ali?"

Harv laughed. "Sicced her lawyer on him, did she? Can't blame her for defending herself. Malloy's still investigating Orville's murder, right?"

"Right."

"Look, Tommy, most of us know she didn't do it. It's terrible for her, I'm sure, but we all want Orville's killer found. When Agent Malloy arrests him, Ali will have the last laugh. Tell her that she's all right in my book. You're both welcome in my store and my home. I figured she would spend as much time with Helga as possible."

When the bathroom door clicked, Tommy thanked Harv before abruptly hanging up.

"Who'd you call?" Ali asked.

"Checked in with Harv. Malloy gave him the story. I assured Harv that you won't keep me from doing my job."

Ali's smile faded. "I hope Malloy solves this soon. I want to go home."

"This is your home," Tommy said quietly.

"Was my home. Now I live in San Francisco."

Tommy wanted to wrap his arms around Ali and reassure her that everything would work out. Even though Malloy had directed his investigation away from Ali, the court of public opinion still found her guilty. If the real killer remained at large, Ali would never find peace in Rausburg and Tommy would never stand a chance with her.

———

Ali visited Tommy's house a few times back in elementary school. Sitting with Helga in his living room while he showered, she noticed that little had changed. The furniture was old, but clean, with few signs of a young bachelor living by himself.

Someone knocked on the front door. "We'll get it," Helga yelled.

"Be there in a second," Tommy called out from the bathroom.

Ali and Helga opened the door to find two young blonde girls.

"Hi! We're selling cookies for the Girls club," the older one said.

The younger opened a paper sack filled with cookie boxes. "Would you help support us by buying our cookies?"

Who could resist such charming young saleswomen? "Let me see what you have." Helga picked a box of peanut butter and a box of chocolate chip.

The older girl opened her bag to Ali. "Hmm. I'll take chocolate chip. Mom, what does Tommy like?"

"Can't go wrong with chocolate chip."

"Then I'll take two boxes of chocolate chip."

The girls totaled the purchases while Ali brought her mom's purse and her own wallet. Cash changed hands, cementing the deal with a cute little girl duet. "Thank you."

The older girl started to leave when the younger one asked, "Are you the lady who killed Mr. Luetz?"

Ali stared at the girl. Cuteness and innocence saved her. "No, honey. I didn't kill Mr. Luetz. We argued a long time ago, but that's all."

"I didn't think you did."

The older girl grabbed her sister's hand. "Cindy, that's enough. You're being rude."

"No, she's being honest. She overheard people saying I killed Mr. Luetz. That's their opinion. I didn't do it. Tommy will find the person responsible, and everyone will know the truth soon."

"Sorry." The little girl's head dropped in shame.

Ali knelt to force eye contact. "That's all right. Good luck with your sale. What's the money for?"

"We're going to the Madison zoo next spring to see monkeys, and tigers, and lions."

"Oh, that sounds like fun. I went to the zoo in Milwaukee once. I liked the seals."

"Me, too! I like seals."

Ali stood. "Then you'll enjoy yourselves. Good luck on your cookie sale."

"Thank you," Cindy said before hurrying away.

As Ali shut the door, Tommy emerged behind her, buttoning his sleeves. "You were good with her."

"For a while this morning, I forgot. Guess I'll always be the one suspected of any crime here."

Tommy stretched his arms and adjusted his sleeves. "People will change their minds once they learn the truth."

Ali shook her head. "If Agent Malloy ever solves the case. Are you finished here? I'd like to go back to Mom's."

"Give me another minute."

———

"Why don't you two rake leaves? "It's a beautiful day. Don't waste it. You can work while I read the paper on the porch," Helga said as they entered her house.

"Sure," Tommy said. "Coming, Ali?"

"Right behind you."

When Ali found the rakes in the garage, she handed one to Tommy and they started. At first, neither spoke, with Ali sneaking a few glances at him while they raked. Seeing Tommy dressed in jeans and a plaid flannel shirt helped lighten Ali's mood. Tommy's uniform served as a constant reminder that he could arrest her whenever he wanted. Without it, he was little Tommy Peterson who had grown into a handsome young man.

He became more confident than she imagined all those years ago, telling him that he could be whatever he wanted and a wonderful young man hid behind his shyness. She didn't know he fell in love with her. Would she have treated him differently if she had known? She wasn't sure.

Tommy snuck a few glances at Ali, too. She was all he remembered and more, but she wasn't as positive as before, and her emotions were more intense. Yet, every time he looked at her, his heart quickened, hoping they might be together soon.

Most of the week he saw her forceful side, the determined side that got things done or became enraged, while glimpses of the friendly, helpful side peeked through occasionally. With Malloy convinced of her innocence, Tommy hoped to see more of her positive side.

They raked the leaves into piles, drifting closer together until both reached for the last little square of fallen leaves.

Ali playfully attacked his rake with hers. "My leaves, get away."

"If you love them so much, maybe you should be in the pile with them," Tommy said as he dropped his rake and scooped her into his arms. She squirmed in protest when he laid her in the big pile. Ali threw a handful of leaves at him and he threw a handful back, laughing as they made a mess.

Gazing at Ali, surrounded by the yellowed leaves, he smiled at his good fortune.

Ali sat up. "What are you grinning about?"

"Just glad I'm here doing this with you, that's all."

She smiled back while idly running her hand along his arm. "You know there's one thing I've neglected to tell you all week."

"Only one? What would that be?"

He expected her to tease back, but she grew quiet before continuing. "I've been fluctuating emotionally since I got here, and I want to say... thank you. Thank you for believing in my innocence. Thank you for protecting me from whoever wants me convicted."

"That's my job."

"There's more to it than that." Her smile sagged. "I'm not the easiest person to be around. But after this charade is over, if you're still interested, you may get a chance."

Tommy smiled. "You've made my day."

44

Malloy slept until eight a.m., which meant he hustled to start his day. He faced several hours of tedious file searching and the weekend offered the perfect time to do it. Barring an emergency, the courthouse in Mineral Ridge would be vacant, and he'd have the place to himself. Free to roam, free to snoop.

When he arrived, he followed the lone sheriff's department secretary straight to the file room. "I'll pull the files myself," he said, dismissing her at the door.

He located the L drawers and found the spot where any file on Orville Luetz would reside. Nothing there but the file before it, Margaret's file, drew his attention. He opened it and discovered a missing piece of the puzzle.

He pulled several files corresponding to the names found in Milenburg's hidden file yesterday. Not what he expected. He locked the file room behind him before taking his prizes to Milenburg's office. A few minutes spent studying each folder prepared Malloy to call the first candidate.

The first man owned a roofing company in the next county and agreed to talk.

"I'm investigating the murder of Dan Milenburg. I came across a list of people he spoke with concerning his run for the judgeship next election. Several on that list appeared in court before Judge Lynch, including you."

"Don't know about a list. But yes, Dan Milenburg called me."

Malloy sensed the man was already second-guessing his decision. "I pulled your file. Last year you paid a speeding ticket after a court appearance. Since that's not a case he would reopen, I figured there must be more involved. It'd be best if you told me now."

No response.

"I'm only interested in the reason Milenburg singled a few people out to call. I'd prefer to take your voluntary statement but I could bring you in for questioning."

"Okay, okay. I had business in Mineral Ridge. When I came into town, I got a ticket for speeding. Forty-five in a thirty-five. The deputy was abusive, which ticked me off. I've received nothing more than a warning in twenty years. Never had an accident, either. Anyway, I buttoned my lip and let the deputy rant. On the way home, I checked the area where I got nailed and found the sign leaning over, covered by tree limbs. The county road crew must have caught it with a mower. Impossible to see if you weren't looking right at it.

"I had a disposable camera with me so I snapped a picture of the sign and contested the ticket. Jeez, Lynch made it sound like I'd assassinated Reagan, treating me with no respect or common courtesy when I stood before him. I'm sure everyone who appears in court says they're innocent, but I was ready to pay the fine. It's not right, expecting a visitor to know the sign was hidden behind the limbs. When I offered to show him the picture I took, he threatened me with contempt of court. I apologized, paid the ticket and got the hell out of there. The other defendants I saw that day got treated the same way."

"Did you provoke the judge?"

"I respected his authority and never made any accusations. I wanted to point out that the county needed to fix the sign. Does that seem fair to you? Ticketing people when the sign's hidden?"

"No, not at all." Malloy remembered a time when he welcomed opportunities like hidden signs.

"Because of that, I changed suppliers and ended all my business dealings in Mineral Ridge. That ticket offset any savings I ever got from going to Mineral Ridge. That's probably how Milenburg found me. One of my suppliers must have mentioned the judge cost him business."

"So Milenburg contacted you?"

"Twice. The first time, he told me that Lynch was way too harsh on most people. He asked me to speak with a few supporters at a fund-raiser. I told him as long as it wasn't in Mineral Ridge, I would speak to them. He said it wouldn't be, so I said yes."

"And the second call?"

"About a month after that, he called back to touch base. Said he organized a quiet little party at the Copper Point Village Hall. Potential campaign contributors were attending with a few guests like me. Said it was an informal affair. I could circulate, talk to prospective donors, and if I wanted to contribute, he wouldn't reject it. That's the last I heard until the report on the radio yesterday."

Malloy's suspicions came closer to being confirmed. "Did you ever meet Orville Luetz?"

"Who?"

"The murdered principal from Rausburg."

"No. Read about it in the paper. I forgot the name. Don't you suspect the same guy did them both?"

"That's a possibility."

"Pity about Milenburg. He sounded like a nice guy."

All politicians sound like nice guys when they want your money. Malloy thanked the man and hung up.

Malloy's second call didn't go as planned. The man wouldn't talk over the phone, but he invited Malloy out to his farm a few miles west of Mineral Ridge. Malloy took directions and left right away.

Twenty minutes later, Malloy knocked on the front door and waited a minute until the door opened to reveal a white-haired gentleman in bib overalls. "Are you the guy from Madison I talked to?"

"Yes. Agent Malloy from the DCI."

The old man shouted behind him. "A man's here. Wants to rent the pasture. Be right back."

Malloy followed the farmer around the back of his barn. "Sorry to walk so far, but if my Millie knew what you're here about, she would get upset. I should let it drop, but I lived my whole life in this county. Always paid my taxes and been a law-abiding citizen. We don't have too many more years left. Most people treat us nice, but that asshole judge in Mineral Ridge still makes my blood boil."

"What did he do to you?"

The farmer leaned against the barn wall and looked out over his pasture. "Well, me and Millie don't drive anymore, a neighbor takes us out for groceries. He took us to pay our taxes last year, and when we got there, a car blocked the handicapped ramp. Millie can't climb stairs so that ramp is the only way in for her. I took down the plate number and reported it to a deputy inside. He found the car and came back to tell me it belonged to the judge's wife. 'Didn't realize she had trouble getting around,' I said. 'She doesn't. Gets to park close. Live with it.'"

The man turned to Malloy. "Our tax dollars built that ramp. Why should an able-bodied citizen block it? When we got home, I called a number in Madison to complain. A nice lady said she would check into it."

"Did she?"

"About a week later, a deputy came out and told us to let the matter drop. He said county inspectors might find code violations here, old wiring, plumbing, that kind of thing. 'Sometimes we even find stolen merchandise. You got receipts for everything?'"

"What did you do?"

He looked away, and his body deflated. "Told him I'd let the matter drop. Heard no more since."

Malloy remained silent to let the man regain his composure. "And Dan Milenburg contacted you?"

He straightened and stood away from the barn. "Yes, sir. Not sure how he found out about our little incident. But he came out one day, and I told him my story same as you. He said he was running against the judge in the next election and asked if I would mind talking with some contributors. He'd bring them out, and I'd tell my story before he asked them to finance his campaign."

"And you agreed?"

"Eventually. He was persuasive."

"Did he say anything else? Was he afraid Lynch might find out?"

"He asked me not to broadcast it around. Believe he said, 'I want the money and support before I make a formal announcement.' He reassured me that he would never use my story in public. 'I have others for that.'"

Malloy extended his hand and thanked him for his time.

They shook. "Was Milenburg killed because he spoke to me? Are we in danger?"

"I'm still investigating Milenburg's death, so I can't say why he was killed. I doubt you're in any danger, but I would keep that story to yourself for now."

Malloy walked the farmer back to his house and left.

He stopped at a pay phone in Mineral Ridge to call Fred and tell him that he wanted a meeting at his office at one o'clock. "It's important. I'll fill you all in when I get there. Better warn Betty and Mike, it's a working weekend." Malloy hung up, glad he didn't hear what Fred said to the dial tone.

45

Tommy wiped a lunch plate dry. "Been to the lake yet?"

Ali handed him another plate. "No. Has it changed at all? Still water in a hole?"

"Last I looked. Shouldn't be crowded today."

Ali pulled the drain plug. "Are you asking me to go there with you?"

He arched his eyebrows.

"Out loud," Helga said, sitting at the table.

"Will you go to the lake with me?"

Ali smiled. "Thought you'd never ask."

"Helga, you want to come along, too?"

She stood. "No, I have things to do."

"We'll pitch in and get them done so you can join us."

Helga rolled her eyes at Ali as Ali stifled a laugh. "It's a woman thing, Tommy. Would you just take her?"

"Oh, sure, right."

When Tommy offered his arm, Ali took it, and they left.

As Tommy drove, Ali remembered a different natural beauty in Wisconsin after the leaves fell. Now the naked trees were gray, some with a light shade of brown, broken by isolated evergreens. Not as vibrant as fall or spring, but solid and respectable. Ali enjoyed seeing it again.

They had the lake to themselves. Now that the leaves had fallen, no one came to admire them. Hunting season was a few weeks away, and the fishermen were gone by noon. She buried her hands in her jacket pockets after she got out, eliminating the possibility of hand-holding.

They meandered for a minute before Tommy asked, "Will you ever come back here to live?"

"I hadn't planned on it. How about you? Ever consider leaving?"

Tommy kicked a pine cone several feet ahead. "Sometimes. I like my job but... If I didn't own my home, I'd be hard pressed to support a family on my salary. Hasn't been an issue yet, but someday..."

"More young wives are working now. Melanie seems happy."

"She is."

"Besides, people here like you. They respect you. There's a lot to be said for that."

Tommy kicked the pine cone again. "Caught more than enough criticism from Fern Johnson and her friends this week."

Ali sighed. "Some people never change. Fern acted the same way when we were kids."

"Her friends control the village board. Drives Harv nuts. Every time he suggests something new or different, they torpedo it."

The pine cone proved a tempting target for Ali, and she kicked it before Tommy could. "Rausburg isn't as alive as I remember."

"Fewer young people, less activity. Since you left, none of the graduates have stayed around. Few people our age live here. Hate to say it, but seeing you led out of school in handcuffs that day changed us."

Ali shook her head. "I failed the entire school."

"I don't see it that way. We did nothing in your hour of need. We should have defended you, but we didn't. Talked to Ellen the other day. She's still ashamed."

Ellen. Whenever a co-worker mentioned a best friend, Ali remembered. They had been inseparable since childhood, but Ellen vanished after Ali's arrest. The one person Ali always expected to be there never offered her support. "I don't blame her anymore. I lost all my friends when Luetz threatened to expel anyone who supported me."

"If we had stood by you, he would have caved." Tommy shook his head. "But we didn't. Luetz got his way. The rest of us started our adult lives under a dark cloud of shame and guilt. Not because of you, but because of us. We didn't do the right thing."

Ali kicked the pine cone several feet off to the side. "Your life turned out the way you wanted."

"I was lucky. Mr. Hancock set a good example of what a village cop should be. I took his advice and added my own touches. I've received criticism. Some want me to be tougher and make more arrests."

"How do you get past that?"

Tommy veered off the path to scoop up an empty potato chip bag and cram it in his pocket. "I caught a carload of seniors driving drunk one night so I brought them in and called their parents. I gave them the option of facing Lynch or working with me. After a serious discussion, the teenagers went home with no arrests, and their parents sang my praises. All around, a happy ending."

"That was nice of you." Ali saw the other half of the bag on her side and picked it up.

Tommy held his hand out and took the bag. "It was a fair trade. I warned them of the consequences if they did it a second time. The offenders worked around the village for a month of Saturdays with no further incidents. Most people thought it was a good idea."

"What about drunken adults?"

"I make sure they have a designated driver when they leave the bars. I've even driven a few home myself."

"No wonder so many like having you for police chief."

"I work at it."

After strolling the entire lakeshore, Tommy opened the car door with a flourish. "Your chariot awaits, madam."

Ali entered, laughing and using a stuffy British accent. "Thank you, my good man. Proceed to the queen's castle posthaste."

Tommy pulled his door shut. "Anyone you want to see? I'd be glad to escort you."

Ali thought. "No."

Tommy frowned. "Once people learn the truth, their attitudes will change."

"Guess we'll see, won't we? If Malloy does his job, the real killer will be caught soon and I won't be a prisoner in my own hometown."

Tommy grinned.

"What?" Ali asked.

"At least you called Rausburg your hometown. That's progress."

Ali turned away, not yet ready for that much progress yet.

As Tommy started his car, Ali asked, "Your squad car is old. Won't the village board spring for a new one?"

Tommy patted the steering wheel. "Plenty of life left in her. Don't put many miles on. The few times I go shopping in Madison, Helga usually tags along and we take her car. I rarely drive more than five miles in any direction."

"But still... I remember state troopers driving cars like this when I lived here."

"The village bought her used before Hancock retired. Low mileage. Got a good deal on her."

"Her? Does she have a name?"

Tommy looked away. "Bernice."

Ali's eyes widened. "You named the car after your mom?"

"I know. Sounds childish, but I spend a lot of hours in this car. It's like she's still here."

To his relief, Ali nodded. "You miss her, don't you?"

"Yes. Helga has helped me the last few years. I had more growing up to do, and she's reminded me what needed to be done. I hope you don't find that weird. After Pa died, I retreated inward. Ma understood. You were another one who helped me, too."

"I was just being friendly."

"You made an effort above and beyond the others. For as long as I can remember I've been attracted to you."

"And you waited this whole time to tell me? Why didn't you write or call?"

Tommy held his hand out, palm up. "If I had gone to you, I would have been the little boy who tagged along. You wouldn't have given me a second glance. Besides, you needed to come to grips with Helga first. I figured if you couldn't manage that, I wouldn't stand a chance."

"Good point, but you shouldn't have avoided dating on the chance we might meet again."

Tommy shrugged. "I've dated, but not recently. Most women aren't strong enough. I don't want a wife sitting at home, crying her eyes out whenever I go on a call. There's always a chance I could have an accident or get shot by a drunken hunter. I need a strong woman."

Ali turned in her seat to face him. "You realize I have issues to work out, don't you? To most people here, I'm damaged goods. Just because Malloy no longer considers me the killer, others have no reason to change their opinion."

Tommy smiled at her. "Well, they're wrong."

"At any rate, it may be difficult for you to include me in your life."

"I'm willing to take that risk. Didn't wait eight years to say, 'Oh, gee, this might be tough.'"

"God help us both then," Ali smiled. "And I think Bernice is an appropriate name for your car."

A moment later she added, "Could we pick up a bag of curds on the way home? At Simonson's? My treat."

"Sounds fine to me."

Fred, Betty, and Mike greeted Malloy at the office with all the fake enthusiasm they could muster.

"Sorry to ruin your weekend," Malloy said, "but the investigation is going in a new direction now. If I'm right, we have a narrow window of opportunity available to us. Let's move to the conference room, and I'll fill you in."

Malloy stood at the head of the table as he recapped last night's interrogation of Alicia followed by the setup he used to dispel Peterson's involvement in both murders. "His mistake was withholding the first note from evidence, but last night when he was convinced I had locked Alicia away forever, he chose the right path."

"How so?" Fred asked.

"She begged him to release her, even tried to bribe him. He refused without hesitation. Promised her that he'd find that kid from the motel to verify Alicia spent the night there. He explained that his focus was on catching the killer because when he did, her ordeal would be over."

"Given his limited resources, that was a smart move," Fred said.

Malloy leaned over the table slightly, resting on his hands. "He even offered to hire an independent forensics specialist to find anything we missed. I feel safe in saying he's in the clear."

Malloy thumped the table and straightened. "However, if push comes to shove, there's enough coincidental evidence to arrest Alicia. If Lynch or Sinclair pops off to the press, Governor Luce might fold. The notes are the only hard evidence linking her to the murders, and a less than fifty percent chance she wrote them is not convincing."

"And you've got another suspect in mind?" Fred asked.

"Here's my new theory. One or more people in the Mineral Ridge Sheriff's Department is the killer, with Lynch pulling the strings."

Malloy froze and let his statement sink in. "This morning I confirmed Dan Milenburg secretly launched a campaign for the judge's seat in the next election. He knew things that would embarrass Lynch, Sinclair, and maybe others. For instance, it appears Orville Luetz made a deal eight years ago to skewer Alicia in return for dropping DUI charges against his wife, Margaret. I think he came forward, ready to admit Lynch pressured him into giving prejudicial testimony during Alicia's trial. The Luetz murder was a message for Milenburg."

"Makes sense," Fred said.

"That's plausible," Betty said.

"I need to hear more," Mike added.

Malloy locked his hands behind his back and rocked back and forth on his heels. "When the killer planted the first note, he was certain Alicia was in California with an unbreakable alibi. He blackmailed Milenburg, claiming the DA forged the note from a letter she wrote to him eight years ago. That stray print on the Luetz note might be from Milenburg."

"I didn't check his prints," Mike said.

"They told Milenburg they would use it against him and arrest him for the murder if he didn't remain loyal."

"Why the second note for Milenburg?" Mike asked.

"The killer saw a better solution. Pin both murders on Alicia. Don't worry about Milenburg spilling his guts," Betty said.

Malloy pointed at Betty. "Exactly. With the evidence in their lab, they could plant her fingerprints on the murder weapon or place a stray hair at the scene after they arrested her. With Lynch allowing the evidence, Justin Green would agree to plea bargain to a lesser charge."

"That would tie things up," Betty said.

Malloy let his hands drop to the table. "You bet it would. But right now, it's a theory with little evidence. Lynch will never issue search warrants for his own men."

"What's our next step?" Betty asked.

"I'll search for cases that suggest judicial misconduct, such as unwarranted sentences, like Alicia's and other chicanery. The few I've already stumbled across are petty annoyances, not enough to prompt a judicial review. If Luetz had lived, documentation exists that confirms his story. It's not readily apparent, but it's there. If Lynch has another documented discrepancy, perhaps more recent, buried in his files, his career would be over."

"With all of us pitching in, we should find incriminating evidence soon enough."

"That would expedite things, but I'm afraid that would also spook the guilty parties into destroying evidence. We don't know where the skeletons are hidden, but they do. Better I find one or two verifiable cases of misconduct and interview the involved parties on Monday to see what will stand. When we have something concrete, I'll see the attorney general for warrants to commandeer the evidence we need.

"If we're lucky, we'll identify the killer and lean on him while the rest plays out with the appropriate agencies. If our true purpose is discovered prematurely, I'm afraid we may have to seize the entire Kickapoo County justice system to prevent the destruction of incriminating evidence."

Mike let out a low whistle. "Can we do that?"

"Theoretically it falls within DCI guidelines, although I've never heard of it being done."

"Damn," Fred said.

Malloy continued, quieter now. "I need you to line up temporary replacements to staff the entire department in case that happens. Our replacements must have three qualifications. They must be available to mobilize on a few hours' notice, be honest as the day is long, and have an unblemished work history. Get them on board today."

"That's a tall order," Fred said. "We'll need personnel lists."

Malloy raised his hand. "One more thing. You know I prefer we stay in the background. You've heard the rumors about our necks being on the budgetary chopping block."

Yes, they had. All three had updated their resume in anticipation of transferring to another department within DCI.

"Our success will give Governor Luce a good reason to spare us. I won't take over the department unless it's needed, but if we go ahead, we must perform this act fast and beyond reproach. We'll pay the consequences with our careers if we fail. I've assembled the best of the best here. Don't let me down."

"We won't," Fred said.

47

Two hours later, Fred and Mike presented a preliminary list of replacements to Malloy for his approval.

"Great. You know what I'm after. Get as many of these people nailed down as you can. Make sure they live close enough to arrive promptly if we need them."

"Can do," Mike said.

"If we choose to go this route, we can't dawdle. We have to be swift and precise. If the right person gets the opportunity to destroy evidence, we may end up with egg on our face."

"Don't worry, we'll be ready," Fred said.

"I have every confidence in both of you. Use my pager if you need me. I plan on spending tonight and tomorrow in the lion's den. Secrecy is critical for our success."

On his way out he stopped by Betty's desk as she hung up the phone. "No luck finding large real estate purchases for any Mineral Ridge deputy. The DMV is next on my list, searching for expensive cars, boats, or other motorized toys."

"Your tenacity has paid off before. Find the right person to squeeze and our investigation will end faster. I know it's boring, tedious work."

"No argument there, but I'll stay on it until I find a smoking gun and the fun starts."

Malloy rapped his knuckles on her desk. "Like a bloodhound on the scent. That's why I brought you on the team."

"Not because I make good coffee?"

Malloy laughed. "That too. Page me if you find anything."

"Same for you. I'll be here late."

The crisp, clean air and bare trees gray against the dried brown grass went unnoticed as Malloy drove the interstate to Mineral Ridge and considered all the possible suspects in the two cases.

Who beat two men to death? A deputy? No one I've seen so far has acted that aggressive. Could the killer have come from outside the department? A convict they struck a deal with, a relative or friend with a score to settle? Two different killers? Was the second killer given enough information to make Milenburg's murder look like a copycat? A pro, maybe. But why hire a pro when you already have a whole department of pros at your disposal? No, it was kept internal. Find a deputy with the most to lose and convince him to turn state's evidence.

A minivan beeped twice as it passed. Malloy had drifted out of his lane, scaring a woman hauling several kids. He waved and mouthed *Sorry* as she sped past him. Fifteen years ago, he would have pulled her over for speeding. Today he wished her a trip safe from meandering drivers.

Malloy hadn't planned on stopping in Rausburg. A phone call would have sufficed to check on Peterson and Alicia, but Peterson was wary of the sheriff's department. He might be privy to inside information about the potential killer. Malloy exited at Highway 72 to head for Rausburg.

Tommy's Dodge cruiser wasn't parked at his office, so Malloy followed Colfax to the Thorein house and found the car parked face out in Helga's driveway. Malloy parked on the street before climbing the front porch and knocking. No answer. He was tempted to peek in the window, but before he could, he heard noise coming from the backyard.

He rounded the house to see Helga pulling her charcoal grill out of the garage. The grill rattled across the gravel, covering Malloy's footsteps. She was faced away from him as she removed the grill's lid, muttering, "Nuts. Needs more charcoal."

Malloy cleared his throat. Helga whirled around wide-eyed, clutching her heart. "Oh, Agent Malloy. You startled me."

Malloy grinned. "Sorry. Saw Peterson's cruiser out front."

"He took Ali to his house for a bottle of ketchup. I forgot to buy some this week with all the excitement."

"Why do I get the feeling you weren't telling them the truth?"

Helga smiled. "Just helping things along. Any news today? Case solved?"

"We found other possibilities. My team is working through the weekend. Unfortunately, the known evidence doesn't change and still points to Alicia. Finding the person or persons involved in the frame might take time, but I won't quit until I find the killer."

"I'm sure you will. They'll be back soon if you care to wait. I'll start the coals. Tommy will be hungry when he gets back."

"What can I help you with?"

She pointed to a bag of charcoal leaning against the garage wall. "If you don't mind bringing that over, I'll light the fire."

Malloy grabbed the bag while Helga took the grate out and leveled the old coals. He hoisted the full bag one-handed, intending to cradle it with the other as he poured. The bag ripped in midair, flipping over as it fell and throwing charcoal dust all over Helga's jeans.

"Eek!" she shrieked.

"I'm so sorry," he said while scooping the spillage.

Helga laughed. "You scared me, that's all. I've been dirty before."

"My apologies."

"You've had me on edge the last two nights. Didn't realize how uptight I was. Really, I can brush it off. I have another pair of jeans."

After they gathered the briquettes bare-handed and tossed them in the grill, Helga led Malloy to the spigot to rinse his hands. Water spurted out, soaking Malloy's pant leg, making him jump and provoking more laughter.

"Guess we're even," he said.

"We're both on edge."

"You have good reason. I'm sorry I brought all this unpleasantness into your home."

"Two men have been murdered, and even though I know Ali didn't do it, I can see why you had to interrogate her."

They strolled back to the grill. "I've had some tough cases in my career. This one deceptively so. Whoever is framing your daughter did a good job of it."

"You will find the real killer, won't you?"

"Count on it. Criminals always overlook something. We'll find it and arrest the killer."

"Good." Helga grabbed the electric charcoal starter hanging in the garage. "So what do you do when you're not investigating murders?"

"Lots of things. I investigate fraud and kidnappings too."

Helga snickered, and the corners of his mouth tightened. "I have no personal life to speak of. That's what drove my ex-wife to drink and ultimately file for divorce."

"That's a shame. When you're not investigating, you're actually charming."

Malloy laughed once. "You know, that's the first time I've ever been called charming."

"Well, some of the time."

Malloy's smile widened. "Honesty is the best policy."

Helga plugged in the electric starter, and they engaged in small talk for a few more minutes until Ali and Tommy arrived.

"What happened to you?" Ali asked Helga.

"I had an accident with the charcoal. Excuse me, Agent Malloy, I have things to do in the kitchen. Ali?"

"I'll help."

Tommy moved the electric starter to ignite more coals while the women went inside.

"Any trouble today?" Malloy asked Tommy as Ali shut the back door.

"No." Tommy put his finger to his lips and discreetly pointed next door to Opal Olson's house.

"Did you know Milenburg was running against Lynch in the next election?" Malloy whispered.

Tommy's jaw dropped. "No. Why would he do that?"

Malloy kept his voice low. "I assumed Lynch was leaving the bench, but that's not the case. Sounds like a foolhardy move unless Milenburg had damning information about the good judge. Any idea what it might be?"

"Not a clue. Lynch has strong support from the law-and-order crowd because he gives stiff sentences. Many voters in Kickapoo County like that."

"Do you?" Malloy asked.

Tommy rubbed his chin. "It's warranted sometimes. Repeat offenders, violent crimes."

"But not senior pranks."

Tommy shifted his weight. He didn't know if Malloy was trying to prod him, but he wasn't going to let his anger show. "You didn't know her before. Ali didn't deserve the maximum sentence. Probation and community service would have been enough."

Malloy watched the coals whiten as they ignited. "Did Orville Luetz ever give a reason for testifying against Ali at her trial?"

"Not that I know of. I suspected he was angry with her because she brought unwanted attention to his school. Some thought the State Journal implied an overreaction to a senior prank."

"How long has Margaret Luetz been a drunk?"

Tommy cocked his head and rubbed the back of his neck. "She got worse over the years. By the time I entered high school, everyone knew she drank too much."

"Was she ever arrested for DUI here?"

"No. Chief Hancock kept his eye out for her. I believe he drove her home a few times but never cited her. She was the principal's wife. No one wanted a scandal."

"Do you know if she was ever caught in Mineral Ridge?"

"Not to my knowledge."

"Would you have heard about it?"

"It would have been in the paper if she was ticketed. Everyone would know. Do you think Margaret is involved in the murders?"

"I have a theory, and your answers confirmed it." Malloy checked to make sure Mrs. Olson was nowhere around. "Margaret was picked up in Mineral Ridge two days after Alicia's arrest."

"Funny we didn't hear about it." Tommy's eyes widened. "Wait, are you saying that Orville testified against Ali to get Margaret's charges dropped?"

"That's my theory."

Tommy stroked his chin. "That would explain why he got so upset when I threatened to run Margaret through the system. He knew I'd find out and tell the school board, and they would demand his resignation."

"I suspect Orville Luetz planned on spinning his story so he appeared to be the victim along with his wife. Lynch was going to send his wife away because she had a little too much to drink. Ali was going to jail anyway, so what would another month or two matter to her? She already admitted her guilt."

Tommy raked the coals with the starter, causing the hot charcoals to flare. "The bastard."

Malloy crossed his arms. "I'm not defending Luetz, but that's a tough position to be in. On the other hand, Lynch used the situation to further his own personal interests. He got a lot of favorable publicity over Ali's case."

"So Lynch killed Mr. Luetz?"

Malloy shook his head. "I doubt he would soil his own hands. Must have ordered an underling to do it. Milenburg too. With Ali here, he found the perfect scapegoat."

"If your theory is correct, that would solve his problem."

Malloy's eyes darted toward the house. "I don't have the proof yet. Don't tell Alicia. Keep this confidential."

"I will. Enough rumors are flying around. I know we had our differences this week, Malloy, but I appreciate your help. Without it, Ali could be in serious trouble right now."

"It's a baffling case. You're a good cop. Inexperienced in expecting the worst from people, but that's not such a bad thing. I'm sure tired of thinking that way."

Tommy wasn't sure how to answer while he unplugged the electric starter. "Let's put the lid on. By the time we throw on the brats, the coals will be ready."

Helga met them at the door, wearing a new pair of jeans. "Have you had supper yet, Agent Malloy? I made plenty." She held an inviting plate full of hamburgers and brats. Malloy's eyes widened, but he caught his tongue before he licked his lips.

"Thanks, but I'll grab a bite in Mineral Ridge."

"Are you sure? Won't take long. I've got steak fries in the oven and potato salad. More than enough for us."

"I wouldn't want to impose."

"It's no problem. Tommy, grill these, please. We'll eat in the kitchen. I'll set an extra place."

A few minutes later, the men entered with a plate of grilled meat and hungry eyes.

"Mom says you're not here to arrest me tonight. That's different." Ali softened her tone after receiving a stern look from her mother. "Have you identified the killer yet?"

"I'm researching Milenburg's cases. Got a few leads. Can't say any more, sorry."

Ali placed the bowl of potato salad on the table. "As long as you're not researching me."

"I'm pursuing other areas of interest."

Ali pointed to the chair Malloy used for his interrogation. "I believe you've established your favorite place at the table."

Despite Ali's formality, the conversation flowed as they passed the food. Malloy listened while Ali and Tommy relived old school experiences. Helga beamed, watching them together. Malloy's eyes met Helga's for an instant, and she smiled at him. As they ate, Helga led a gentle interrogation, discovering Malloy had two daughters around Ali's age. When Tommy asked about his career, Malloy glossed over his early days as a state trooper.

Malloy sat back when he finished.

"Could I interest you in a beer, Agent Malloy? I've got Leinie's," Helga asked.

"No, I have to get going, but thanks for the fine meal and the fine company. Much better than I had planned."

"Our pleasure," Helga said.

Malloy stood. "If you'll excuse me, I have a lot of reading to do tonight. Peterson, follow me to the car."

Outside, Malloy lowered his voice. "If I need something from either of you, I'll call myself or have my staff do it. They speak for me. Let everyone believe I'm building the case against Alicia. I'm sure it's tough on you both, but it's for her good as much as mine. For now, it's better if everybody thinks Alicia is suspected of committing both murders."

"Okay."

Malloy opened his car door. "Remember, your main duty now is to provide Alicia with an irrefutable alibi if the killer strikes again."

"You expect him to strike again?"

"One important member of the team that convicted Alicia is still alive."

"Lynch?"

"I advised him to station a deputy at his house. He refused. I want Alicia to have an ironclad alibi just in case. Otherwise, I may be forced to charge her."

"I won't let her out of my sight."

Malloy put his hand on Tommy's shoulder. "See that you don't."

48

After supper, Helga sat in her chair knitting while Ali and Tommy sat on opposite ends of the couch facing each other, playing cards while they half watched *The Love Boat*. When the news came on, he told Ali she had to ride with him on patrol once the weather forecast was finished. "I cruise around until the bars close. More precautionary than anything."

"Sounds like fun," she said.

"Sorry, trying to balance work and pleasure."

"And which am I? Work or pleasure?"

"Tonight? Both."

After she rolled her eyes, he winked at her.

―――――

Ali found patrolling dull, driving around, watching vacant buildings and parked cars in the moonlight.

Around eleven thirty, Tommy parked in front of his office. "I sit here for a while before my last round."

Ali checked up and down the empty street. "You lead such an exciting life."

Tommy swiveled in his seat to face her. "All right, it's dull for you. How do you usually spend your Saturday nights?"

She tilted her head, twisting her neck to catch his eye. "You really want to know? Think you can handle it?"

"Try me."

She gazed out the windshield. "I quit early on Saturday night and leave my office around six if I'm not on the road. After eating dinner alone out of take-out boxes, I read business magazines. Later, I watch the news. If I've been a good girl all week, I treat myself to the first hour of Saturday Night Live. If it's boring, I fall asleep in the chair."

Tommy was silent.

Her head sagged. "That's it. Pathetic, huh?"

"More unnecessary than pathetic. How does an attractive, smart lady like you end up alone all the time?"

"I scare men away, that's why. Since work comes first with me, they disappear."

Ali's hand rested on the seat. Tommy covered it with his, experiencing an awkward moment until she flipped her hand over and laced her fingers in his. When he smiled at her, she smiled back.

"Bet you can't tell me who's driving that car headed this way," Ali said.

Tommy glanced. "Ryan Kranutz. His mother's Camaro."

"Lucky guess. How about the next one?"

They held hands while playing the car game, neither acknowledging the physical contact again.

"You spot anything unusual on patrol this week?" Ali asked as they drove the last round. Tommy turned on Jefferson and didn't answer.

"You saw something, didn't you?"

He shifted in his seat. "Tuesday morning, a dark sedan headed south around five. I didn't recognize it."

"Dark sedan? Like an unmarked police car?"

"You jumped to that conclusion awfully fast." The dim light from the dashboard outlined her face as he studied her. "What do you know?"

She gazed out her window. "I haven't slept well since I got here. Every night I got up and slipped into the front bedroom to stare out the window until I settled down."

"And what did you see?"

"We have an excellent view south, especially with the moon almost full this week. I was up and saw a dark sedan crawl past our house before dawn, possibly an unmarked police car. The night before last, a similar car stopped in front of the house around two."

Tommy stroked his chin. "Odd. I didn't see it."

"You passed by a little earlier, checking on me."

He let his hand drop. "Sorry. You didn't notice where the car came from, did you?"

She swiveled in her seat to face him. "Lights flashed on Knutsen's hill, and the car drove by a few minutes later."

"You can see the whole village from up there."

"I remember."

He stopped as they approached Main. "The Knutsen's don't hear well anymore, and their gate's unlocked so it's easy enough to open it without them knowing. Kids know better."

"I couldn't imagine any parent allowing their child out at two a.m. on a school night. Wouldn't they have called you in a panic?"

He twisted toward her while they remained stopped. "True. Maybe the mystery car watched me on my rounds."

"Who would do that?"

He shrugged. "Malloy, checking on me, or Milenburg's killer making sure you were still here. Or maybe it was nothing."

After a final inspection along Main they went home and found Helga's bedroom door shut. Ali and Tommy tiptoed to the kitchen to split a Leinie's and a few curds while sitting in the dark, whispering. When Ali finished drinking, she gave Tommy a light kiss on the forehead and wished him sweet dreams before going upstairs.

Tommy moved to the couch and made himself comfortable under the blanket. By one thirty the Thorein house was quiet, the women asleep while Tommy lay awake considering that dark unmarked car. It could have been Malloy on Thursday, but not Tuesday. If it was the same car, Tommy could think of one other possibility. He shivered despite the blanket.

His hand dropped to the floor to check on his gun, lying within reach and pointed to the door. He practiced gauging the distance and grabbing it several times in the dark before he let sleep overtake him.

49

Exhausted after six hours of reading file after file in the dank court-house basement, Malloy leaned over an old desk concealed in the back to rest his eyes. Success had eluded him in his search for corruption. Malloy had read through four major trials and found Lynch was abrupt with defense attorneys, as well as with Dan Milenburg, but not corrupt.

The file room door creaked open, and an intruder entered. Soft-soled shoes produce little noise, but in the dead calm of the deserted building, even a tiny squeak announced their approach. The intruder rounded the cabinets to find files open on the desk. Cursing under her breath, something moved in the shadow cast by a full-sized cabinet, and she jumped in fright.

Malloy stepped out of the shadows, holstering his gun.

Eyes as big as saucers, she clutched her chest. "Jesus. Lucky I have a strong heart."

"What are you doing here?"

"Making sure you locked the door. It's after two. I thought you'd left by now."

"Well, I haven't." Malloy sat at the desk and leaned over the open file.

She stepped closer to the desk and peered over his shoulder. "Searching for dirt on Sinclair or Lynch, right?"

"Why would you assume that?"

She studied him for a long moment. "Because they're dirty, and a big-time DCI agent wouldn't waste his Saturday night in this tomb unless he thought so too."

He sat back. "Do you have an ax to grind with your superiors?"

"I didn't volunteer to work the weekend graveyard shift because it's fun. I used to work days until Lynch was elected. He prefers secretaries who don't ask so many questions."

"I see." Malloy was curious now. He acted nonchalant to keep her talking.

"They wanted me to quit, but I need the job. My husband's got Parkinson's and can't work so here I am."

He closed the file. Another wasted effort. "If you know of any prosecutable offenses committed by the staff, it's your duty to inform me."

"Like I said, I need this job. Who's gonna stick up for me after you go back to Madison and Lynch fires me for helping you?" Malloy's mouth opened, but she cut him off. "He's careful with the big trials, knows they'll be appealed in a higher court. Stay there. I'll pull a file."

She went to a nearby cabinet and pulled a thick file, handing it to Malloy. "I'll find a few more."

He leafed through the file. By the time she plopped several more on the desk, he knew she had steered him in the right direction.

"Gotta get back." She pointed at the open file. "Is that what you're after?"

"Appears to be."

"This is about Milenburg, isn't it? You think they killed him."

"Who's they?"

She took a step back. "Read those files and figure it out, but not here and not now. The deputies already wonder what you're doing here on the weekend."

Malloy yawned. "I'm beat. One question, though. Do the other staff feel the same way as you?"

"We've learned to keep our mouths shut. If Lynch and Sinclair are removed, you may find more people willing to help."

He stood and grabbed the stack of files. "Better tell the deputies you checked and found I already left."

"Can't. They spotted your car here. I'll say you fell asleep and I scared you. Makes you look bad, but I doubt you care."

Malloy smiled. "I care, but I can live with it. Thanks. Didn't catch your name."

"Marie. Please forget we ever spoke."

"No problem. I'll wait a few minutes before I leave. Thanks again."

"Make sure you nail them. I'm taking a big risk for you."

After Marie left, Malloy checked that he left nothing lying around before he locked the door and snuck his treasures out. Back at the motel, he skimmed through several files before falling asleep, satisfied he found the right track.

50

Sunday, October 21, 1984

After Ali's travel alarm rang at eight, she threw on her robe and tiptoed downstairs to find her protector, Tommy, sleeping on the couch.

Maybe waking him for Mass isn't such a good idea. Tommy hasn't slept well all week. He must be exhausted.

Helga's bedroom door clicked as it opened. Tommy woke with a start and grabbed his gun.

"Don't shoot. We're not armed," Ali said.

Tommy scanned the room, blinking.

"Sorry. If we're going to Mass, we'd better get ready."

"I wasn't going to make you go, dear," Helga said.

"You attend every week, don't you?"

"Well, yes. You don't, do you?"

"I haven't since I left. Tommy's friends will say I'm a bad influence on him if we don't go."

Tommy stretched. "I'm awake. We might as well go."

Helga scurried to the kitchen. "Okay, I'll scramble eggs. We can make it if we hurry."

They arrived at St. Joe's with Ali in the lead as the service began and slipped in a back pew, positioned for an easy exit. Once seated, Ali zoned out and worked on a mental to-do list for her stores in California.

When the service ended, Ali's plans for a quick getaway fell apart when Ben Silas engaged Tommy in conversation. George Olsen joined Ben, which made a center exit impossible.

Ali sidled to the outside, but several parishioners squeezed past Tommy's friends to head out. Ali needed to hustle to beat them out the door, but that would be too obvious. Melanie approached from the side aisle holding her baby, solving the dilemma. Never a big fan of babies, Ali could fake enough interest to get by. As expected, Mel offered the baby to Ali. They sat and formed their own group, oblivious to the others.

Little Jackie flashed a winning smile, making Ali's job easier, and Mel introduced her husband Jack as they chatted while the congregation ambled past Tommy, many shaking his hand, asking the latest. Ali faced the outer wall and focused her attention on the baby to avoid Fern Johnson's disparaging gaze as she shuffled out.

As the last few people exited, Tommy, Ali, and Helga sauntered out with Mel and Jack. To Ali's relief, no one had lingered outside. No awkward moments, no forced congeniality. Ali left Mel with a hug and the promise to visit her during Ali's next trip home, even though she never planned on returning to Rausburg.

At lunch, Tommy and Helga shoveled their food in their mouths. "What's the rush?" Ali asked.

"Packers play the Seahawks today," Helga said. No further explanation was necessary, and they cleared the table in record time. Tommy switched Helga's old TV on, allowing it to warm up while Ali and Helga rushed to finish washing and drying the dishes.

They watched an exciting first half, with the Pack leading, and Helga made popcorn at halftime. Seattle played a good third quarter, shooting ahead with Green Bay staging a comeback in the fourth that ultimately stalled to give the Seahawks a victory.

With the game over, Ali carried the popcorn bowls to the kitchen. On the way back, she overheard Helga tell Tommy that a walk might be nice. Ali decided not to fight the conspiracy so she yelled from the kitchen, "Let's go to the park, Tommy. It's comfortable out, and you need to work up your appetite for supper anyway."

"Sure," he said, rising from the couch. "Grab my jacket?"

With the temperature hovering around fifty, they stuffed their hands in their pockets and strolled along Colfax in silence. When Ali sniffed, Tommy put his arm around her. "It'll be over soon," he said.

She leaned into him. "That's not it."

"Then what is it?"

Ali sighed. "Going to Mass and watching the Packers reminded me of many Sundays when I lived here. Mom even made popcorn then too. I didn't realize how much I missed it."

Tommy gave her a comforting squeeze. "I felt the same way when I lost Ma. Someday I want to create those kinds of memories for my own family."

Ali chuckled. "I can picture you giving pony-back rides and reading your children stories at bedtime. You'll be a wonderful father."

"You'd make a wonderful mother, too."

Alarms rang in Ali's head. *I don't want children.*

"Hey, I've got an idea. Let's find a secluded spot and make a baby." *That should scare him off.*

"Do you know how? I've always wanted to learn."

Ali stopped and leaned away from him, furrowing her brows. His growing smile betrayed him.

"You devil," she said, giving him a playful slap. "Who taught you to talk like that?"

Tommy laughed. "Oh, being a cop, you pick things up."

Ali laughed too, but she refrained from making smart remarks about parenthood, babies, or tomorrow as they continued to the park.

They played on the swings, teeter-totters, and merry-go-round, pretending to be kids again. No cares in the world, laughing and enjoying life, the events of the past week put on hold. When the afternoon shadows grew long, they sauntered home holding hands.

———

The phone rang about six p.m. and Helga answered. "Agent Malloy?" She stiffened before remembering the polite man who ate with them last night. That man acted different from the detective who accused her daughter of murder. The nice version of Malloy asked how her day went and Helga relaxed. "Oh, we had a wonderful time," she said. "The Pack played great today. Can you believe that?"

"They didn't fold in the second half?"

"Nope. Played a good game almost to the end. Seahawks won, but we looked better than any time this season."

"Maybe next week. Is Peterson there?"

Helga waved Tommy over. "I hope you have a better day tomorrow. Here's Tommy."

"Any news to report?" Tommy asked.

"Making progress, but nothing definite yet."

"What can I do to help?"

"Since you mentioned it, I may insist that Alicia stay beyond tomorrow. Anything you can do to win her cooperation would be appreciated."

"I'll do what I can."

"Make sure she stays with you. That's all I ask. I'll call tomorrow afternoon with an update."

After Tommy said goodbye, he faced the eavesdropping women.

Ali folded her arms. "He's no closer to the truth, is he?"

"Conducting an investigation on the weekend is harder, you know."

"Ha. I'll give him another day. I don't want to drag this back to San Francisco with me."

Tommy slapped his belly and exaggerated a sniff. "Supper sure smells good. Is that the casserole from lunch yesterday?"

Ali laughed as Helga waved her finger at him. "Is food always on your mind?"

Tommy cocked his head. "Yep."

Helga raised her eyes and opened her arms as if asking for divine assistance.

"Just being honest. Can I help you set the table?"

———

Later, while preparing for bed, Tommy accompanied Ali to the kitchen for a glass of water. He leaned against the kitchen counter and sipped from his glass. "I really enjoyed spending the weekend with you."

He expected a smart remark.

"It was much nicer than I expected." She took a swig of water, dumped the rest out and put her glass in the sink. "But there's no point in chasing false hope. I don't fit in here." She smiled at him. "You can visit me in San Francisco, and I'll show you the sights. You know, with your wife and family. I'll tell them how shy you were, and they'll laugh."

Tommy wanted to take her in his arms, but she stepped away, and he lost the moment. She smiled before rounding the corner to the stairs and waving good night.

Sleep eluded him on the sofa as he lay awake wondering what to tell Ali tomorrow night if Malloy needed to stall for more time. "Please need more time."

51

Sunday night, Malloy enjoyed a leisurely burger at Hardee's and took a short walk before returning to the courthouse. He was surprised to find the new DA, Wendell Ferguson, working in his temporary office. Stepping softly on the granite floor, Malloy materialized in Wendell's open doorway.

Wendell jerked and took in a sharp breath. "Oh, hi. You work Sundays too, huh? I figured you were in Madison today."

"Wish I was, but I need to work on Milenburg's murder so I can hand you a winnable case."

"I appreciate the effort, but—"

Malloy crossed his arms. "We can't afford to take Ms. Thorein lightly. She's a tough cookie, and the evidence is circumstantial at best. I'm making sure Justin Green doesn't find someone with a better motive to establish reasonable doubt. I don't like losing."

"Judge Lynch can handle him. We've got enough to bring her in."

Malloy shook his head. "Sorry, I don't agree. My gut says she's the one, but there are too many loose ends. I'm still searching for more solid connections to ensure her prosecution will stick." Malloy shifted, shoving his hands in his back pockets and widening his stance. "So, what brings you here on Sunday? New case?"

"What? Oh, no. I was watching the game and remembered some paperwork I forgot to do for tomorrow. I need to be caught up by mid-week. Crime won't stop because we lost a good DA."

"I hear you on that. I didn't see the game. Who won?"

"Shut it off at halftime. Wasn't much of a contest, and I'm tired of seeing them lose."

Malloy shifted again, bringing his right hand to his chin, grabbing his forearm with his left. "Too bad. Well, I'll be in Dan's office. I figure I'm less in the way at night. After tomorrow, I'll be out of your hair, so you boys can do your work without my constant disturbance."

"The important thing is convicting Ms. Thorein. I'm sure that will be resolved soon."

Malloy tipped his finger at him before he left.

Wendell didn't watch the game. Helga said the Pack played a close game right into the fourth quarter. He's lying. What's he doing here tonight?

As he lowered himself in Milenburg's chair, Malloy caught his pager on the chair arm, ripping it from his belt for the third time that day.

"Damn this thing," he said, setting the pager on top of a filing cabinet behind him. "If it goes off there, it'll make noise. Just remember to grab it before you leave."

Shortly after ten, Malloy went to the courthouse lounge to buy a candy bar. To his surprise, a deputy sat there reading a paperback.

"Taking a break?" Malloy squinted to read the name tag. "Larry."

"Yes sir. It's been a quiet night."

Malloy dropped his change in the machine.

"I heard you used to be a trooper."

Malloy chose a Milky Way and punched the button. "Yes, I was. Part of me misses being out on the road, at least when the weather's nice."

"I'm sorry summer's over. All those cold snowy nights ahead."

The Milky Way dropped with a loud thump. "Make sure you grab a car with a good heater."

"We've got new ones coming soon. If you don't mind my asking, you must have worked on some important cases to get where you are now."

Malloy sat at the lone table. "They were all important. We had a lot of leeway. Fewer regulations, more creative thinking in the field."

"You remember your first big case?"

Malloy cocked his head. "I saved a divorced mother's life in Beaver Falls and received my first commendation."

He tore the candy bar wrapper and took a bite.

"But you had more big cases than just that one."

He chewed and swallowed. "One led to another. I was wounded while working a hijacking. That helped me advance, but I wouldn't recommend it."

Larry's partner sauntered into the break area and tapped his watch. "Sorry, but we need to get out there. Bars are clearing out. The die-hard drunks will be on the road soon."

Larry rose. "Pleasure talking to you, sir."

Malloy shook hands with Larry. "Stay safe. We've had enough deaths around here this week."

Malloy finished his candy bar and went back to work. Time was his enemy now. When Lynch discovered the task force was interviewing people involved in his "special" cases, there could be a showdown. He'd call the governor and insist on arresting Alicia, and he would make it sound like Malloy created a mess instead of solving the case.

52

Tommy awoke with a start when his pager vibrated around two a.m. He recognized the Mineral Ridge dispatch number and ran to the phone. The dispatcher reported an accident with possible fatalities several miles north of Rausburg. "Ambulance is on the way. You're the closest responder. The night team is stuck in Copper Point and can't leave the scene."

"I'm on it."

When Tommy's heavy footsteps awakened Helga, she jumped out of bed and caught the tail end of the conversation. After the commotion awakened Ali, she threw her robe on before hurrying downstairs.

"Bad accident by the interstate. Get dressed. You have to stay with me," Tommy said while tucking his shirt into his pants.

"We'll be safe here," Ali said.

"Might be gone for a couple of hours. Better get dressed."

"We'll be fine. We'll lock the doors and leave the lights on."

Tommy cinched his belt. "Ali, please. Remember what Malloy said. I'm guarding you, but I've got to go. You have to ride with me."

"You'd better go, honey," Helga said.

"No one will bother me tonight with Mom around, and the sheriff's office won't serve warrants when they're responding to an accident. I'll be here when you're finished."

Even though she had a good point, Tommy urged Ali to come with him again, but she was strong-willed and independent. No time left to argue. People could be dying, but he couldn't force Ali to go.

"Lock this," he said as he pulled the front door shut behind him.

He ran to Bernice, brought her to life, and tore out onto Colfax. On accident calls, he seldom knew what he'd find. To a person lying in agony, a minute felt like an eternity. As he sped north, he grabbed the mic to call the ambulance driver. Although closer to the scene, the ambulance driver had no more information than Tommy.

State Highway 72 was a wide two-lane road, north of Rausburg, with several slight curves where it wound around hills. At this late hour the biggest threat on the deserted highway would come from deer. Hitting one might create another fatal accident, so he gripped the steering wheel tighter as he watched the speedometer go to eighty miles an hour.

———

Helga locked the front door after Tommy left. "You should have gone, dear. Tommy's only doing his job."

Ali folded her arms. "I didn't want to waste the night sitting in his car while he investigates some blood-and-guts accident. And I don't want to watch him handcuff a drunk teenager."

"Please don't tell Malloy. Tommy's already in enough trouble from hiding that note to protect you."

"I won't."

Ali went to the kitchen and Helga started for her bedroom when three sharp knocks echoed through the house.

"See? False alarm. I'll get it," Ali said. She ran to the door and opened it to two uniformed men.

"What the—"

"Alicia Thorein, you are under arrest." Sheriff Chuck Sinclair grabbed her right wrist in one swift move before handcuffing it.

"Where's Malloy?" Ali shrieked as he spun her around.

"Couldn't make it. Sent us instead," Sinclair said, securing both hands behind her back.

Helga watched helplessly as Ali struggled. Courtroom memories flashed in her head, springing her into action.

"Hold on there," she yelled. "Agent Malloy said he'd make the arrest. Ali will surrender to him. I'll keep her with me until he arrives. Go wait in the car."

Sinclair grimaced. "Doesn't matter. Either way, she'll be in jail. We have the necessary evidence, and he's tied up. We're making sure she doesn't run."

"Where are you taking her?"

"Mineral Ridge Jail. You can visit her tomorrow. Come on, let's go," he said while pulling Ali outside.

Helga followed through the door. "You wait right there. I'm coming, too."

Sinclair spun around on the steps and aimed his finger at Helga. "Lady, if you come along with us, we'll put you in cuffs for interfering with an officer. Now stand back."

Ali's eyes met Helga's while the deputy dragged her to the car. "Stay here, Mom. You know what to do."

Helga watched, horrified, as they shoved Ali in the squad car before speeding away.

As she ran to the phone, her resolve rose. She wouldn't blindly trust the justice system tonight. If Malloy didn't give her the right answers, she would wake Justin Green and light a fire under him. No one was going to falsely arrest her daughter for murder.

———

Five miles outside Rausburg, cruising at eighty, Tommy's pager buzzed. Not a good sign. When he read the number, a cold fear gripped his insides. "Helga."

Harold and Sarah Schaeffer's farm was a quarter mile ahead. Tommy switched his siren and lights full-on and raced up their driveway while laying on the horn. An upstairs window lit as he approached, and a downstairs light came on as he bolted from his car. He climbed the porch steps in two strides before pounding on the door. Harold opened the door. "Tommy—"

Tommy ran for the kitchen. "Sorry. Emergency. Need to use your phone."

The older rotary dial phone took forever to dial, but Helga answered on the first ring.

"What's wrong, Helga?"

"Sheriff Sinclair showed up with two deputies right after you left and arrested Ali. She's headed to jail right now. They claimed Malloy sent them. I called the number Malloy gave us, but he hasn't called back. I paged you instead."

"Damn." Tommy saw the Schaeffers' worried expression. "Listen, keep trying Malloy, and alert him to the arrest. I'll chase after Sinclair and stay with Ali. Don't worry. She'll be fine. I promise." He hung up, trusting he hadn't made a promise he couldn't keep.

"Sorry, folks. You can go back to sleep now," Tommy yelled over his shoulder while running back to his car.

As he sped out the driveway, he grabbed the mic to call the ambulance driver. "You there yet?"

"Yep, you have the exact location? I can't find the accident."

Sinclair tricked me. Bet he's listening in.

Tommy took a deep breath. "Keep searching. I'll be there soon to help you find it."

———

After Deputy Dave Stram shoved Ali into the back of Sinclair's cruiser, he slammed the door shut.

"Welcome back," a woman said with a smile. Ali recognized Leslie Moore, the deputy in charge of the women's side of the jail.

Ali grunted, the only civil response she could muster.

Sinclair hopped in the driver's seat and sped away. Once he passed the village limits, Sinclair maintained normal highway speed. Ali fumed inside, furious with Sinclair, Malloy, but mostly herself.

This is my fault. Should have listened to Tommy. Focus, damn it! Watch and listen. Turn this thing around.

She studied Sinclair.

Sinclair appeared much older now that he was in his mid-fifties. He lit a cigarette as he drove, and his paunch told Ali he still enjoyed more than a few rounds at the bar with his buddies.

Tommy boomed over the police radio, telling the ambulance driver he would be at the accident scene in a few minutes.

"Baby Face is gonna be disappointed when he finds out there's no accident," Sinclair said. He glanced in the rearview mirror at Ali. "By the time he figures it out, we'll have solved two murder cases."

"I'm innocent," Ali said.

"Funny thing, all criminals say that when they sit back there. None of them are ever guilty."

"Malloy knows I'm innocent. Did you speak with him?"

"I've had enough of that big shot this week. We can prove you killed two men. Why waste time?" He laughed. "Too bad we can't fry you like they do down south. If this were Florida or Georgia, you'd be sittin' in Old Sparky. We're civilized up here, so we'll lock you away and let you rot."

Sinclair started the unofficial round of interrogation as they drove through the night. "Still can't see why you did it. Your principal maybe, but Milenburg? Sounds like you're begging to be caught."

"I told you, I didn't kill either of them."

He exaggerated a shake of his head. "That's not what the evidence says. Those notes you left are proof you're a hard-hearted killer. That's premeditated murder. Maximum sentence. Besides, we'll have a signed confession before the night's over."

"I won't sign a confession for a crime I didn't commit."

"Don't have to sign it. I planned ahead and did it for you."

Ali's throat tightened. Sinclair was responsible for the two murders. "You? But why?"

"Not important now. Let's just say if you had stayed away, Milenburg would be alive, so that puts his death on your hands. That idiot principal, too. If you weren't such a smart-ass eight years ago, he'd be alive. Someone's got to pay the price. Might as well be you."

"You won't get away with this."

"The signature on the confession matches both notes. I've got two witnesses who watched you sign it. You'll never get out."

Ali's shoulders went slack. Would anyone believe her over them? "Malloy knows I'm innocent."

"By the time he gets his chance to prove it, you won't be a problem. Amazing how despondent people become when facing a life in prison. Some choose an easier way out."

"You'll never pull this off. Your best bet is to dump us and get as far away as you can. You're a cop, you know how to get lost. Live out your life on a beach in South America."

Sinclair grinned. "You've learned how the world works, I'll give you that. But I'll stay right here, thanks. This is my town, Sweetmeat."

Sweetmeat. His disgusting nickname for her that forecast his intentions. Ali's anger grew, but she held her tongue. Sinclair's phony confession combined with Lynch's refusal of bail guaranteed jail time. Malloy would fall in line. Justin Green would prepare for a trial that would never happen.

Sinclair was a lost cause, and Dave was nothing more than a toady. She had one last choice.

"Are you still the women's matron?" Ali asked Leslie.

"Yep."

"I'm surprised you haven't been promoted by now."

She gave a slight nod toward Sinclair.

"Too bad. It's the same in my company. Men feel threatened by a strong woman. You've dealt with some tough customers. What was that old drunk's name, the loud, mouthy one?"

Leslie looked up. "Brenda?"

"Yeah, you had your hands full with her. She still around?"

"Yep. In and out several times."

"Not surprised." Ali sighed loud enough for Leslie to hear. "When we met before, I hadn't been out in the world yet. I've experienced a lot since then, and it's changed me."

When Leslie looked over, Ali smiled. "I've been on my own these past eight years, and, well, I understand."

Did she register a connection?

Ali met Leslie's eye. "It's tough for us, isn't it?"

Sinclair turned to the back seat. "Save it for the next quilting bee. We've got a job to do."

Leslie ignored Ali, choosing to gaze out the car window at the moonlit countryside.

Would she defy Sinclair if push came to shove?

53

Tommy's squad car, Bernice, was one of the last gas hogs the local law enforcement officers drove. She was powered by a massive engine, with heavy-duty shocks, tires, and brakes, built for sustained high-speed driving. The Mineral Ridge team drove newer, more fuel-efficient cars that did the job, but they were slower. Even though he trailed Sinclair by at least ten miles, Tommy expected to catch them before they arrived in Mineral Ridge. As Bernice's engine morphed from the usual low rumble to a throaty roar, he glanced at the speedometer as he flew along a straightaway to see it wavering near one hundred twenty.

Tommy knew Highway 72 like the back of his hand and knew where he had to slow down. In less than two minutes, he zoomed past the village limit sign and tapped the brakes. Mrs. Anderson's cat ambled across the highway when Tommy crested the hill at one hundred. Wide-eyed Mittens scurried to safety, the solitary witness to Tommy's high-speed pursuit as he streaked through Rausburg with his lights flashing and his siren off.

Tommy braked hard for the south curve before flooring Bernice and flying along a highway built for vehicles going no faster than sixty.

The call was a fake. Sinclair grabbed her a couple minutes later, so he knew I had been there. Does he suspect I'm protecting Ali instead of detaining her? What if she had come with me? Would he have pulled me over? He must know I wouldn't surrender her.

Tommy tapped his brakes, slowing to eighty, negotiating a slight zig-zag in the road. *What if this arrest is legit? What if he was watching me to make sure I'm doing what I'm supposed to? No, Sinclair would have taken the accident call. He's operating off the books on this one.*

Tommy focused in the distance, aiming down the center on a wavy section of highway. *Small movements.* A reminder from his high-speed pursuit training years ago. Bernice held the road as Tommy pushed her, swaying through the slight curves, closing the gap to Sinclair.

Back on a straightaway, his misgivings resurfaced. *Interfering in a legitimate arrest won't help Ali in court. I need better reasons to support my theory.*

Two orange dots reflected on the highway ahead. Tommy hit his brakes hard and honked his horn. The deer stared at him for a moment and bounded off, averting his own death. Tommy continued to slow, wary of driving through a herd of deer, but there were no more and he floored it.

"Saved the village some money there," he muttered.

Saving money. Of course. Overtime. The county board always complains when anyone presents a bill for overtime. Why would Sinclair rack up the extra expense when Ali's arrest could be carried out during the regular shift? He would have to answer for that.

Sinclair won't surrender Ali voluntarily. Having her in custody gives him the advantage and I'll be outnumbered. How will he respond when I pull him over?

Tommy was the youngest law enforcement officer in the county and still smarted at the razzing Sinclair's deputies gave him when he became chief at twenty-one. It didn't matter that he had graduated from the academy in the top ten percent or spent two years in Madison on the force. They called him Baby Face. In this case, it was a term of derision, not endearment. *Sinclair doesn't take me seriously.*

And why should he? Most of the time, I issue speeding tickets and warnings to people passing through Rausburg.

While Tommy stewed, an even worse scenario came to mind. Sinclair was approaching the most desolate part of the highway with two miles of nothing but farmland or forest on either side.

No witnesses.

How far ahead are they?

Grabbing his CB mic, he pitched his voice low to sound relaxed as he hurtled along the highway.

"Hey, y'all. Any bears on 72 'round Mineral Ridge tonight?"

A voice answered after a few seconds. "We're here. What's up?"

Must be the deputy.

"Drunk nearly ran me off the road south of Rausburg. You seen him?"

"Nope."

"Where you at?"

"Tyler Road area."

"Must have turned off."

"Got lucky then."

He set the mic in its cradle. Tyler Road lay two miles ahead. At one hundred miles per hour, he would arrive in little more than a minute.

What will Sinclair do when he sees my headlights barreling down on him?

Tommy was out of his jurisdiction now, the aggressor if push came to shove.

The full moon shone in a cloudless sky.

Can I drive without lights? 72's mostly straight, and I know where the curves are. No other cars. Once I'm close enough, I'll follow their taillights.

Tommy eased Bernice over the center stripe and slowed to eighty while switching to his parking lights. The state road crew had repainted the white fog lines and yellow centerline last summer. After his eyes adjusted and with the full moon shining, he followed them easily on the straightaway.

When he flicked his parking lights off, the lines grew faint but visible. With Sinclair's taillights guiding him, and his accumulated knowledge of hundreds of trips along this highway, he could follow in the dark without their knowledge, but it could prove fatal. Hitting a deer at that excessive speed would send him careening out of control. Despite the danger, he switched his headlights on and floored Bernice.

A half minute later, he squealed around the last curve before Tyler Road. As the road straightened, a pair of taillights loomed in the distance. He flicked Bernice's lights off. With no approaching traffic and a straight and level road ahead, he centered her and mashed her accelerator to the floor. If one hundred twenty miles an hour felt fast before, the inky darkness made it terrifying. He focused on Sinclair's growing taillights as he closed the gap. Two miles ahead, a sharp curve dropped to the valley floor. He was less than a mile behind him when Sinclair's taillights vanished around it. He flicked his parking lights on and kept Bernice floored, easing right to hug the inside of the curve.

His foot slid to the brake pedal when the fog lines veered right too soon. He slammed on the brake, locking the rear wheels, forcing a slide as he fought to keep the front end on the pavement. The rear wheels hit grass on the berm and threatened to spin out of control as Tommy jerked the wheel hard left to steer into the slide. For an agonizing second, Bernice slid sideways, threatening an uncontrolled spin. When he let up on the brake, the rear wheels gained enough traction to throw the rear end onto the pavement again. He spun the steering wheel hard right, arresting the skid ending with straight fog lines on either side, the speedometer reading seventy.

With Sinclair's taillights visible a mile ahead, Tommy punched the light switch off and stomped on the gas pedal. Seconds later, the taillights vanished again with a half mile separating them.

He squealed his way around the next curve with his parking lights on, relieved he hadn't lost ground when the road straightened. Running completely dark, he closed the gap to a quarter mile before settling back to follow.

Five miles outside Mineral Ridge, Tommy's heart pounded as he relaxed for the first time since talking to Helga. His plan was to follow Sinclair in, have a rational discussion at the jail, and take Ali back after calling Malloy. Ali could spend a few hours in his jail until cooler heads arrived in the morning.

Without warning, Sinclair's taillights careened back and forth across the road, and his brake lights flashed when he abruptly pulled off the pavement and stopped. Tommy hit his own brakes, creating a wall of red light behind him. His foot flew off the brake pedal as he gently stepped on the parking brake and shifted into neutral. He pulled off the road, lights extinguished, and came to rest less than a quarter mile behind Sinclair. He switched Bernice off.

Now what?

54

Ali slammed into the rear door and bounced back into Leslie when Sinclair fishtailed the car. He stomped hard on the brake, which plastered Ali's face against the front seat because no one had bothered to fasten her seatbelt.

Once the car stopped, Ali shouted, "Hey! What was that for?"

"Hit a nail. Had a blowout. All part of the plan. Flat tire's already in the trunk."

Sinclair unfastened his seat belt. "While we change the tire, you'll see your chance to escape and grab Dave's gun. There'll be a scuffle, and I'll shoot you in self-defense. You won't make it."

Sinclair put his hand on Dave's shoulder. "Poor Dave will get a reprimand."

When Sinclair opened his door, the overhead light came on, temporarily blinding everyone. Sinclair used his hand like a visor as he grimaced at Ali. "I'll be off the hook for those two idiots. That's how Lynch wants this ended. Case closed. No need for a trial."

———

Tommy sat undetected and watched from behind. When Sinclair's door opened, the inside lights came on and Ali's head became visible in the backseat along with deputy Leslie's. Tommy switched his dome light off and gently opened his door. He drew his sidearm as he silently tiptoed in the direction of the voices while keeping a watchful eye on Sinclair's car.

Ali bounced around in the back seat, yelling at Leslie. "Don't let him do this. He'll own you. He killed Milenburg, and he'll kill you, too. You know he's a psycho."

Sinclair opened the back door and reached to pull Ali out, but she stiffened her body and hooked her feet under the front seat until Sinclair kidney-punched her. He dragged her out as she gasped for air and dumped her on the cold ground. While Sinclair and his deputies surrounded her, Tommy closed the gap unseen.

Ali coughed and rolled around on the ground. Sinclair grabbed her robe by the shoulders and hoisted her. "I don't care about your damn town or what goes on here," she screamed. "I've got money. I'll give you each ten grand if you take me home."

Sinclair shoved her against his car. "That's a laugh. After all I said, you expect to go free? Make it easy on yourself. Haul your sorry ass out in the field and shut your eyes. I'm a good shot. You'll never feel a thing. The more you struggle, the more it's gonna hurt."

Tommy swallowed hard. Sinclair faced him and would see him if he moved, so he stood still. Ali crumpled and fell to the ground, drawing Sinclair's attention away from Tommy. If Tommy called out to Sinclair now, Ali would become his human shield. She needed to move away or he'd be forced to shoot them in the back without warning. Back shots? Never a good idea for a cop.

"Drag her in front so she's lit up when I shoot," Sinclair barked at the deputies.

Dave and Leslie grabbed Ali's arms. Under Sinclair's direction, they dragged her a few feet off the side of the road in front of his car and dumped her.

Ali flipped on her side and curled into the fetal position as Sinclair stood over her.

"If I shoot you while you're on the ground like this, I'll have to pump two or three rounds into you, and it will hurt more. Stand and one will do the trick. Either way, it's over. You see any white knight coming to rescue you?"

Tommy had mirrored their movements, keeping close enough to see and hear what was going on. While Sinclair spoke, Tommy sidled to the opposite edge of the road, staying behind and to the left of the death squad. Ali glanced in his direction causing Tommy to step back before Sinclair's headlights outlined his form. He froze, but Sinclair and his deputies remained focused on Ali and didn't notice him.

Ali rolled on her back and pounded her bare feet on the ground, momentarily throwing a child's tantrum. "All right, twenty grand apiece. Leslie can take me to a bank. I'll give her the money and disappear. I'll throw in twenty for Lynch, too. Call him, and see what he says."

"You expect me to believe you have eighty grand sitting in the bank? I'm not stupid. You'll blab that I killed those two idiots. You won't keep your mouth shut."

"I won't tell. Promise. Take me to jail. Make sure I get bail and the money's yours. I've got it."

Sinclair considered the offer before shaking his head. "Lynch has already decided. Stand, and make it easy on yourself."

Tommy inched closer as Ali grew more belligerent. "Forget making it easy for you."

Sinclair undid his holster flap and pulled his sidearm. "Suit yourself."

Tommy trained his gun on Sinclair. "Freeze! Drop the weapon." Sinclair froze.

"Agent Malloy placed Ali in my custody, pending arraignment. Holster your sidearm and stand down. She stays with me until he says otherwise."

Sinclair glanced over his left shoulder. "Baby Face? Where did you come from?"

"Followed you in the dark. Now stand down."

Sinclair raised his hand to calm Tommy. "Hold on there. We have a warrant for her arrest, and you're not in Rausburg."

Tommy kept his focus on Sinclair, watching for signs of aggression. "Malloy's in charge, and he swore he would personally call me if Ali was to be brought in. You're insubordinate. Until he says otherwise, she stays with me. Your phony accident call didn't work."

Sinclair slowly pivoted with his hand resting on his weapon. "That was you on the CB, wasn't it? You figured out our plan. Good work."

"I said drop the weapon."

Sinclair calmly faced Tommy. "Think this through. You're pulling your gun on three experienced officers outside your jurisdiction. If you persist, you'll be in big trouble."

"You're the one in trouble. I overheard you threatening to kill Ali. No way will I back off."

Sinclair opened his free hand towards Tommy. "Now, son, I've been sheriff for a long time. I'll forget about this little stunt if you come work with us. You don't make much money in Rausburg. Better money with us, and that innocent face will buy votes. In a few years you might even take over for me as sheriff. Put the gun down, and we'll discuss your future."

Tommy knew how the situation would play out now. As much as he wanted to, he couldn't shoot Sinclair first without provocation. After the confrontation, the deputies would claim Tommy was the aggressor, and he'd be the one going to jail. Once Sinclair posed a clear threat, Tommy could get three rounds off and disable them so Ali could escape. Malloy would exonerate her. Tommy would take at least one bullet. Might be fatal since they would aim for his heart. None of Sinclair's deputies had shot anyone in recent years, and he knew Sinclair and Dave weren't as accurate as he was. Leslie qualified at the range, but he doubted she was little more than competent. Sinclair was the lead dog, the one to take down first.

"Nope," Tommy shook his head. "Got to be my way."

Sinclair drew his arm back. "You're bluffing. I know what it takes to kill a man. You don't have it in you. Three against one. We'll be heroes, saving a killer from her crazed boyfriend. She'll die in the crossfire, and it'll be a big human-interest story for all the papers. I'll tell you one more time, holster your weapon. We could use a smart cop like you. You'll keep Kickapoo County safe with extra money in your pocket while doing it. Work with Lynch like we do."

"Stand down now."

Four cops stood silent, frozen in the moonlight. Sinclair made the slightest movement of his head and his shoulder rose.

55

"Don't!" Tommy yelled as Sinclair's gun cleared his holster.

Tommy's first round caught Sinclair high in his right shoulder, temporarily immobilizing him. Tommy swiveled, training on Dave and firing his second round. Dave's muzzle flashed simultaneously as he jerked back clutching his shoulder.

Tommy swung toward Leslie. Her gun was out, but she had not yet aimed it. Time stopped as they faced each other.

"Drop it," Tommy yelled. She froze, but Sinclair was fumbling the transfer of his gun to his good hand. Tommy intensified his focus on Leslie. Another few seconds and Sinclair would fire. She softened before dropping her weapon, allowing Tommy to swing back to Sinclair.

Tommy stepped closer to Sinclair. "It's over." Sinclair's eyes burned holes in Tommy before he let his gun dangle from his finger.

"Slowly put your weapons on the ground," Tommy said.

Dave and Sinclair hesitated before bending over and placing their guns on the ground. "Ali, can you walk?"

"Yes."

"Walk wide around us."

Ali came around, skirting her abductors. Tommy nodded to his far right, and Ali stopped there.

"Take three slow steps back," Tommy ordered Sinclair and the deputies.

After they stepped back, Tommy kicked their pistols under the car. "Sinclair. Dave. On your stomachs. Both of you." Dave and Sinclair took their time, dropping first to their knees before lying face down on the ground.

Tommy glanced at Leslie. "Key for Ali's cuffs. Throw it carefully."

Leslie took the key off her belt and tossed it to Tommy. Ali backed up to him and Tommy jiggled the key to unlock her cuffs one-handed while aiming his gun at Leslie.

Leslie put her hands behind her head. "I won't cause you any trouble."

He kept his gun raised as Ali wiggled her hands against the cuffs. "You can trust her. She's not like the other two."

Tommy slid his gun back in the holster, keeping his eyes on Leslie while he used both hands to free Ali. He raised his gun as Ali backed away.

"Where do you keep the other cuffs?" Tommy asked Leslie.

"Glove compartment."

"Ali, open the glove compartment and bring me two pair."

Sinclair caught his second wind as Ali retrieved the cuffs. "Now, Peterson, I don't think you're the type to hold a grudge. I know we've teased you over the years, but you've kept your village safe. Let's work this out for the good of everyone. We don't have to pin the murders on your girlfriend. We'll figure something out."

"Like what?"

"Could be several solutions. Milenburg can be blamed for killing your principal. That solves your crime, makes you look good to your people. I'll sit on the Milenburg investigation until someone surfaces to pin it on. Your girlfriend can go back to California a free woman."

"What about Malloy?"

"Not much he can do about it if we all agree. Milenburg's murder is obviously the result of some wacko reading about Luetz's murder in the paper and copying. Milenburg prosecuted plenty of real criminals to blame it on. We'd be doing society a favor by pinning it on one of them."

Ali handed the cuffs to Tommy. "You're not accepting his offer, are you?"

Tommy frowned. "You heard everything?"

"I couldn't help overhearing. Tommy, you can't go down this road. It isn't right."

Tommy's frown became a grin. "Don't worry. I just wanted to see what other lies he was willing to tell. Go stand behind their car until everyone's cuffed."

He tossed a pair of cuffs to Leslie and signaled her to move closer to Sinclair. "Cuff him first. If you try any funny business, I'll put a round in each of you."

Sinclair begrudgingly put his arms behind his head. "Now's the time to figure this out, Peterson. We can still walk away with our jobs. Malloy told me you withheld evidence. You think he's not going after you when this is over?"

Sinclair had a point. Malloy already said he would file charges.

"I'll make my appearance in Lynch's court. He won't let the county sheriff rot in jail. Before long you'll be the one in the hot seat."

"Cuff him, Leslie."

When Leslie pulled his arms together and fastened the cuffs, Sinclair groaned. "At least call an ambulance. I need medical attention."

"We've got a doctor in Rausburg. I'll call him when we get back. Now cuff Dave." Tommy tossed Leslie another pair of handcuffs.

Dave remained quiet as Leslie cuffed him. Tommy ordered Leslie back, tossing her Ali's cuffs. "Put one on, and place your arms in back." She put the first cuff on and held her hands in back. Tommy fastened the other side one-handed while pressing his gun against her back.

After Tommy backed away, he opened his arm to Ali. When she ran over to hug him, she discovered his shoulder was damp. "You're bleeding."

"I am?" He brought his hand to his ear. "Ow."

Ali pulled him closer to the bright headlight beam to examine him. "A bullet grazed your ear."

"Jeez, it stings," he said as he lightly stroked the side of his face.

"We should get you to a hospital."

"Not yet. I can't call this in. Sinclair's other deputies won't let me arrest him. Last I heard, Helga couldn't reach Malloy. We have to return to Rausburg. We can defend my office until help arrives."

"Tell me what to do."

"Stay here while I load these three." Tommy opened the back door of Sinclair's car. "All right, get in."

Sinclair hesitated. "Not enough room."

"You'll survive. In."

Sinclair slid across the back seat, cursing under his breath. Dave and Leslie remained sullen as they joined him.

Tommy slammed the door, locking them inside, and led Ali farther away from the car.

"You saved us both. Sinclair was wrong. You are my white knight." She caressed his cheek.

Tommy met her gaze. *I wish I could take you in my arms right now, but we're both in danger and I need to stay focused. One thing at a time.*

"This isn't over yet. We need to get back. Out here, we're sitting ducks."

"Can't you leave them here?"

Tommy shook his head. "Have to see it through and arrest them."

"Then we'll all go back together."

"I'm not putting you in the same car with them. You'll have to follow in Bernice." Tommy pointed down the highway. "She's parked a quarter mile back."

"Anything special I should know?"

"No, the regular controls are like any car. Leave the rest alone. Keys are in the ignition. Push lightly on the gas. She has a bigger engine than anything you've ever driven."

"I'll go get her. Wait here." Ali sprinted away.

Tommy moved Sinclair's car and retrieved their guns. In the

distance, Bernice started, and a few seconds later her headlights were lit. He heard Ali shoot gravel while taking off, and he flattened against Sinclair's car as she screeched to a stop in front of him.

"Whoa, you were right. I barely touched the pedal," she said through the open window. "Did I scare you?"

"You always scare me."

Tommy opened Bernice's back door and laid Sinclair and Dave's guns on the floor.

"Ever handle a gun?" he asked Ali before he shut the door.

"No," she answered when he leaned in the front window.

"Let me show you the basics in case something goes wrong."

Tommy held up Leslie's sidearm. "It's loaded with one in the chamber." He showed her how to put the safety off and on before handing it to her.

"Leave the safety on, and tuck it under your leg. If you need to shoot it, use both hands, aim it at the target, and squeeze the trigger."

"Sounds simple enough."

"The hard part is hitting the target. Since you've never fired a gun before, you'll probably miss with the first one." He put his hand on her shoulder. "I doubt we'll have any more trouble on the trip back, but whatever happens, save yourself."

She put her hand on his. "I'll be all right. You're the one taking all the risks. Please be careful. Sinclair doesn't give up."

"I know. If you see any funny business happening in our car, pass me, lock yourself in my office with the gun and wait for Malloy. He's the only one we can trust."

As Tommy stepped back, Ali put Bernice in gear and feathered the gas pedal. The big car took the entire road and shoulder to turn around, and Ali was grateful she didn't shoot gravel this time, although it was fun before. Once she straightened Bernice out, Ali caressed the brake pedal with her bare foot and managed to stop without screeching.

Tommy had stayed well back.

"You going to be okay?" he yelled.

She gave him a thumbs-up.

"Don't answer the radio, no matter what. If you need to get my attention, flash the headlights. I'll drive faster than the limit where I can."

Tommy sprinted back to Sinclair's car, jumped in, and led the way home.

To Tommy's relief, Highway 72 remained deserted. The two-car caravan sped through the night and arrived unseen behind his office.

As Tommy stepped out of Sinclair's car and approached, Ali rolled down her front window. He leaned in and lowered his voice. "You okay?"

"No problems. Bernice was watching out for me."

"Good. Park in front while I unload the prisoners. Leave the motor running until I give you the all clear. If anything looks suspicious, head toward Madison on the interstate. If you're pulled over, contact Malloy's team through the DCI switchboard."

"Shouldn't you wait for backup?"

"Malloy hasn't responded. Anyone else I can trust is too far away. I can't leave them squeezed in there all night."

"Can't you deputize a private citizen? Harv, maybe?"

"Too dangerous. It'll be safer if I do it alone. They're unarmed. I'll be careful."

Ali pulled Leslie's gun out from underneath her leg. "I could help."

"Out of the question. You'd be putting us both in danger."

Ali's head sank. Tommy put his hand under her chin and made her look at him. "What I mean is if things go wrong and you get hurt, I couldn't live with myself."

She smiled.

Tommy stepped back. "I'll be fine. Park across the street. I'll see you in a few minutes."

"Be careful," she said before putting Bernice in reverse.

Tommy unlocked the building's back door, flipped on the lights, and made sure the inner door to his office remained locked while both cell doors stood wide open. He escorted Leslie in by herself, locking her away before returning for Sinclair and Dave. Tommy opened the rear car door and backed away, keeping his gun trained on both men. "Don't try anything funny. Dave, you first."

Dave slid out and stood motionless by the car as Sinclair slid out, saying, "Listen Baby Face, you've got this all wrong. Back there on the highway, I lied to scare your girlfriend. I wasn't confessing. I was working her so she would admit her crimes, that's all. If you're convinced she's innocent, I'll go along with you. We can work together on this."

"Why the change of heart?"

"We were both caught up in the heat of the moment. Uncuff us and call the ambulance. I'll testify that your shot was a mistake. You won't have to go to jail."

Tommy relaxed noticeably and lowered his weapon, taking his aim off Sinclair and Dave. "Okay. We'll talk this through once you're in my cell. I'll holster my gun, and we will figure out how to proceed."

"It'd be easier to uncuff us now."

Tommy shook his head. "I'm all pumped up. Might accidentally shoot again. Safer for all of us if you wait in the cell until the ambulance arrives."

Dave and Sinclair reluctantly entered the cell. Tommy slammed the cell door shut behind them and motioned Dave to put his hands through the bars. A few seconds later, Dave's hands were free. and Tommy handed him the key for the cuffs.

"Take Sinclair's off."

Once he was free, Sinclair rubbed his wrists while Dave handed the cuffs out along with the key. "Okay, Peterson, let's talk about this."

Tommy smiled. "I'm not much of a talker. How about we let Agent Malloy decide?"

Sinclair's eyes flared. "Offer's between us. If that asshole gets involved, you'll be charged with two counts of attempted murder along with obstructing justice, theft of public property, and any other charges that fit."

"I'll take my chances."

Tommy slammed the inner door to his office shut behind him, ending the conversation along with Sinclair's cursing.

With his prisoners safely locked in, Tommy leaned out the front door and motioned Ali inside. He propped himself against the door-frame and shut his eyes.

Ali shut Bernice off before running and grabbing Tommy around his middle, steadying him while she led him to his chair. After he plopped down, she grabbed a soda from the refrigerator and opened it for him.

"This will help. Relax. We're safe now."

He took a sip. "Sorry. All of a sudden I felt weak."

She patted his hand. "All the excitement. You keep any food here?"

Tommy pointed to an overhead cabinet by the refrigerator. "Potato chips."

She found the bag of potato chips and opened it. "Here. Eat these while I call Mom. She must be worried sick."

Helga answered on the first ring. "We're both safe in Tommy's office."

"Thank God."

"Grab my jeans and sweatshirt and bring them here. Shoes and socks too, my feet are freezing."

"I can come get you."

"I can't leave. Tommy got shot, but it's not serious."

"What?"

Tommy had eaten several chips, one after the other. He nodded at Ali. "He's all right. Did you reach Malloy?"

"He's not answering."

"We'll try from here. Enter through the front. Sinclair and his deputies are locked in the back."

"Oh my, I'll be right there."

Ali wetted several paper towels and patted the dried blood off Tommy's cheek and neck. "Color's returning to your face."

Tommy sat up and reached for the phone. "I have to call Malloy."

"I'll do it if you give me the number."

"The soda helped. I'm fine."

He took the telephone and dialed the Kickapoo Motor Inn. The desk clerk sounded groggy but connected to Malloy's room. No answer. Tommy paged him before calling Rausburg's lone doctor.

"Doc, Tommy Peterson here. Sorry to wake you, but I need a favor. Come to my office. I have two wounded prisoners."

"What?"

Tommy repeated his request, adding, "Do not call the ambulance yet. I'll explain when you get here."

"It'll be a few minutes. I have to stop at my office first."

A minute later, Helga ran in with Ali's clothes.

After one look at Tommy, she exclaimed, "Good Lord. What happened to you?"

"He got shot saving me, Mom. I messed up again, and this time it almost cost our lives. I should have gone with him."

Tommy rested his elbows on his desk. "You didn't mess up. Sinclair would have killed us both if you had gone with me. Worked better this way. I caught him by surprise."

"The next time I'll do what you tell me. No questions."

Tommy managed a smile. "Willing to put that in writing?"

"See, Mom? He's not hurt that bad."

Helga fussed over Tommy's injury while Ali changed clothes in the conference room.

By the time she came out, Doc was examining Tommy's ear. "Part of the lobe is gone, that's for sure. You suffered a nasty powder burn, but it'll heal. I'll have to stitch the earlobe. You could have cosmetic surgery done later if you don't like the way it looks. I'd say you're mighty lucky. Another inch and the bullet would have entered your skull."

"Save my ear for later. I've got more pressing matters right now. Two of my prisoners are shot and need medical attention. You can't enter the cell. If either are in danger, I'll pull them out, but you need to sedate them first."

Tommy leaned against his desk to steady himself as he rose. He took shuffling steps at first, his strength and stability returning as he ushered Doc to the back room cells.

Doc's mouth fell open when he recognized the prisoners. "My God, you put our sheriff in custody? What happened?"

Sinclair jumped up from the bunk. "Talk sense to Baby Face here. We arrested his girlfriend, and he went nuts and shot us. If you help him now, you'll be an accessory. Reason with him. He'll listen to you."

Doc raised an eyebrow. "Tommy, did you shoot them?"

Tommy leaned against the wall. "Yes, sir. They were going to kill Ali. I called Agent Malloy. Once he responds, we'll transport them to the hospital so they can receive the attention they need."

Sinclair gripped the metal bars. "I'm telling you, Doc, it's not like that. If you don't release us, both of you will face serious charges."

Doc studied the prisoners for a moment.

"C'mon, Doc, use common sense," Sinclair said.

"You're right. I've known Tommy since he was a baby, and he's never behaved like this before. On the other hand, I've heard some nasty rumors about you. I'll let Agent Malloy decide. In the meantime, let's examine your wounds."

"Start with Sinclair," Tommy said. "Stick your good arm through the bars, Chuck."

Sinclair reached his arm through, Tommy cuffed Sinclair's wrist to a bar, stepped back and drew his gun from his holster. "Do I need to remind you what I'll do if you try anything? Lean against the bars and let Doc look at your wound."

Making sure he stayed out of Tommy's line of fire, Doc opened Sinclair's shirt and examined the wound. "The bleeding has stopped. Lift your arm to the side and try to rotate it."

Sinclair grimaced as he raised his arm and made a tight circle.

"Still works," Doc said. "Once the bullet's out you should get your full range of motion back. I'll clean it and slap a bandage on it for now."

After Doc finished, Tommy opened the handcuffs. Sinclair glowered at Tommy for a moment before backing away.

Dave looked weak, but after his examination Doc reassured Dave that his wound was not lethal. When Doc was through cleaning and bandaging Dave's shoulder, he handed Dave two pills while Tommy brought soda for all three prisoners. "One pill for you, one for the sheriff. They'll minimize the pain until you get to the hospital. I doubt either of you will have long-term damage, but the surgeon will give you a more accurate appraisal."

Tommy opened the back door. Doc took the hint and stepped outside, Tommy following.

"How serious are their wounds?" Tommy asked.

"The bullets should be taken out, but they don't appear to have damaged any vital organs or arteries. You shot them in a relatively safe location."

"It all happened so fast."

Doc put his hand on Tommy's arm. "You inflicted minimal damage."

"Good. These men are dangerous, Doc. As long as their wounds aren't fatal, they'll have to suffer."

"The pills I gave them will relieve their pain and relax them for about four hours. Should help with the transfer."

"Thanks for the help. Mind staying with us? I'm waiting for Malloy to call back. He'll tell us what to do."

"Be happy to. Don't forget I can handle a gun, too. Learned in Korea."

"Thanks, Doc. I appreciate your help."

"Let's work on your ear now."

"It'll have to wait until I reach Malloy. No telling who might come looking for Sinclair."

Doc shook his head and followed Tommy back to the office.

———

Tommy leaned back in his chair. "I hope they didn't get Malloy. He hasn't answered his pager, and he's not at the motel. I would call dispatch but they'll recognize me. No telling who's in on this. I might put him in danger."

Ali picked up the phone receiver. "I'll call. They don't know my voice. What do you want me to say?"

"Anything to get him to the phone. Otherwise, ask where he can be reached. If we can't locate him, we'll have to locate another member of his team."

Tommy dialed Kickapoo County dispatch.

"This is Alice Thorn from the governor's office. We need to reach Agent Dirk Malloy, but he's not answering his pager. It's imperative I speak to him."

All eyes watched Ali as her face hardened and her eyes narrowed. "Listen up, Numbnuts. I'm Alice Thorn from the governor's office. You want to keep your fat ass in that cushy civil service job, you'd better locate Malloy pronto. Now move it." Ali covered the mouthpiece, whispering, "He's gone to find Malloy."

Two long minutes later, Malloy squawked over the phone. "Who is this?"

"Alice Thorn."

"Who?"

"Alice Thorn," Ali spat out. "Remember? We talked earlier."

Tense silence preceded Malloy's genial response. "Oh, Alice. Sorry. I didn't recognize your voice. What's up?"

"Tommy will explain. We've had an interesting night here."

Tommy took the phone. "Our situation has changed, and if you react, you may be in danger. Stay calm for your own safety."

The phone's slight hum emphasized Malloy's ominous silence. "Sorry to hear that. You surprised me. I didn't expect your call."

"Great. Here's what's happened."

While Malloy kept his composure, Tommy told him about Ali's abduction, the subsequent gunfire, and incarcerating Sinclair and the two deputies.

Malloy answered with several uh-huhs before saying, "I'll be right there. Tell the kids Daddy's coming."

"We'll be here." Tommy hung up. "He's not happy. I can tell."

Helga smiled at Tommy. "Leave him to me. I can handle him."

56

Malloy shook his head as he resisted the temptation to slam the receiver back in its cradle. "My youngest woke up sick. Wife panicked and drove her to the ER. Paged me, but I didn't respond so she called the governor. I'm sure I'll hear all about it in the morning." The dispatcher grunted, before returning to his magazine.

Malloy rushed back to Milenburg's office and checked the top of the file cabinet where his pager sat several hours ago. No longer there. Did it fall off? The cabinets were tight against the wall so he knelt to search the floor. Not there, either.

His face went slack when he remembered. Around ten o'clock, he took a short break and talked to that deputy for a few minutes before his partner joined him. The partner must have entered the office, read the open files, took his pager, and warned Sinclair.

Malloy needed to secure the files. *Can't leave them lying out now.* He found an old flap-over style briefcase in the closet and crammed the files inside, debating whether or not he should hide it back in the closet. He chose to carry it with him.

At least I'll have these files for evidence. No telling what might happen after I leave.

As he drove to Rausburg, Malloy's anger grew with each mile.

I gave Peterson a simple task, and he blew it. Where the hell was he? I assumed he'd stick to Alicia like glue. Now we're forced to take over the whole department so they don't destroy any questionable records and hang us out to dry. Those bastards will get away with murder.

Malloy screeched to a stop by Tommy's front door and burst into Tommy's office.

"What's going on here? What have you done? I told you to watch Alicia. Are you trying to ruin this case?"

Helga jumped out of her chair and planted herself in front of Malloy. "You sit and listen, mister. Those creeps from Mineral Ridge kidnapped and almost killed Ali. Tommy saved her life and got shot because you used her as a decoy. The killer is behind bars. It's Sheriff Sinclair, and he bragged that Lynch is involved, too."

Malloy said nothing.

Ali sprung out of her chair and waved her finger at Malloy. "I stayed of my own free will to assist you, and I chose not to have Tommy watch me. Bad decision, but don't you dare blame Tommy for doing his duty. He saved my life."

Malloy's nostrils flared once. Ali lowered her hand and Malloy turned toward Tommy. "All right, Peterson, fill me in."

After Tommy, Ali, and Helga replayed the evening's events, Malloy had the whole picture. He rubbed his forehead. "I never suspected Sinclair would be that brazen. That was a brave thing you did tonight, Peterson. Good job, thinking on your feet."

"Where were you? We've been trying to page you for the last two hours," Helga asked.

"A deputy stole my pager and alerted Sinclair, so I'm to blame for this mess."

"You sure are. What are you going to do about it?"

Malloy held his hand up. "Give me a moment."

He gazed out the front door into the night. *I don't need to squeeze a deputy or secretary into implicating Sinclair. I can go the opposite way now. With Sinclair in custody, the underlings will talk. I can still build my case, but we need to seize control now before Lynch guts the files and destroys all physical evidence of his wrongdoings.*

"Time to rally the troops. This morning the State of Wisconsin will commandeer the entire Kickapoo County Justice Department, jail, sheriff's department, and courts. Eight hours from now, I'll oversee the county's legal system while Lynch is incarcerated in his own jail. Peterson, I need to use your phone. Let's get the ball rolling."

Malloy caught Fred, in Madison, in the middle of his deepest sleep. Malloy gave him a few seconds to wake up. "We have to strike now. My true purpose in being here is known. Sinclair is in custody along with two deputies. When he doesn't show later this morning, the situation will deteriorate rapidly. You have everything ready to go, right?"

"We do."

"Place the calls, and keep me informed at this number."

Malloy hung up and leaned back in the chair. "My team prepared for this possibility, but I hoped it wouldn't be necessary." Silence enveloped the room.

"Alicia, I need one more favor from you. I need to build a stronger case against Lynch."

"What is it this time?"

"I need to arrest you and put you in Mineral Ridge Jail."

"What? After everything I've been through, you're arresting me?"

"It's a diversion."

Ali snapped. "That's what this whole weekend's been about. I almost died for your diversion. Forget it. I'm free, I'm leaving, and I'll never come back here again."

"You'll be subpoenaed to testify."

"We'll see about that," Ali said before storming out the front door.

When Malloy rose to follow her, Helga grabbed his arm. "There's a better way."

He glared at the sweet, mild-mannered woman. Normally he would have shaken loose and told her off, but something made him listen.

"You had your chance. You'll only drive her away again."

"After all this, I can't..."

"Hush."

After Malloy fell silent, Helga snapped at Tommy. "What are you waiting for, an engraved invitation? If you love her, go after her. If you don't, she'll never come back."

Tommy sent his chair flying back against the wall as he pushed off and bolted out the door.

————

Ali stormed down Main, determined to throw her things in the car and leave Rausburg forever.

I wish I'd never listened to Val. Make peace with your past. Learn to trust more. What a joke. The whole village wants me to be the killer so they can go back to their mediocre lives, content that no one achieves more than they do. Malloy treats me like a worm on a hook. Why should I help him? He was perfectly willing to arrest me and destroy my career.

"Ali, wait!" She spun around to see Tommy running after her.

"Don't waste your words, Tommy Peterson. All week it's been stay, stay, stay, I'll prove you're innocent, but there's always something else. Well, I'm over it. I won't stick around and take it like I did eight years ago. I'm not the same person as before."

Tommy stopped in front of her. "Yeah, you aren't the same person. You've changed. That's for sure."

Ali put her hands on her hips. "What do you mean by that?"

"I mean, the Ali I remember wouldn't walk away from a fight about right and wrong. Now you're all me, me, me. I guess you do belong in San Francisco because you sure don't belong here."

When Tommy took two quick steps back to his office, Ali chased after him. "Hold on there, mister. Are you calling me a quitter?"

Tommy faced her. "Yep. You aren't the same girl who fought for that field trip to the Milwaukee Zoo or ran the baby seal fund-raiser. You left that person behind."

"How dare you say that. I've done more than my share. Malloy can arrest Lynch without my help. He put you in harm's way, too."

"He might convict Sinclair without your help, but not Lynch. Lynch will claim he knows nothing about the murders and let

Sinclair take the fall. You don't think he's stupid enough to write it on his calendar, do you? Remind Sinclair to buy bat and gloves for murder next week?"

Tommy threw his hands up in frustration. "But that's all right because you aren't coming back. Now you'll have a good excuse. You'll be afraid to show your face in Kickapoo County because you'll know Lynch is free and waiting to finish the job." Tommy dropped his hands.

Ali looked Tommy in the eye. *Tommy saved my life. He has my best interests at heart. Maybe he's right.*

"I didn't consider that," Ali said. "What if Mom gets sick?"

"She's managed without you for eight years. At least now she knows you care."

Wow, that stings.

"Maybe I was hasty. I may need to return, and I don't want to be watching over my shoulder for Lynch to finish the job. I pose a threat to him now, don't I?"

"Yes, you do. If you let Malloy arrest you, Lynch will charge you. When Malloy links him to the murders, your testimony will hammer his deceit home. Your words will carry weight because of your position and success. Any jury will believe you, and a few years from now you won't hear about Melanie's baby standing in front of that tyrant because she made a slight teenage mistake."

Twice this week Melanie gladly embraced Ali. Chet welcomed her at the grocery, Mr. Farmingham was nice to her at school, along with a few others. If Ali didn't follow through, she'd let them down along with her Mom. Ali didn't like to disappoint people.

Ali pursed her lips. "Okay, I'll stay and finish the job."

Tommy took her hand. "I told you that I'd stand by you, and I meant it. We'll go through this together."

As they strolled back Ali said, "Just so you know. You were wrong about me changing. I'm the same person you knew, with some deep scars."

"I'll help you with those too if you let me."

"Promise you'll be there through this scam and you'll make sure I'm not risking my life needlessly."

"Promise."

"Good, let's tell Malloy what he wants to hear."

As Ali entered Tommy's office, she avoided Malloy and faced Helga instead. No words passed between them. Helga looked apprehensive. Would Ali leave for good or would she submit to the fake arrest? Either way, Malloy was out of options and at her mercy.

"Okay, Malloy. I'll do it. If we don't nail Lynch now, I'll never be safe in Rausburg again."

Helga stood and wrapped her arms around Ali. "You're sure?"

"I'm sure I want to see my mother in her own home whenever I darn well please. I'm not excluding you from my life again."

"Oh, Ali." Helga squeezed Ali hard.

———

Malloy was eager to start but smart enough to wait until Helga pulled away. "Okay. Back to business. Alicia, I'll guard you at home while you get ready. Doc, after you patch up Peterson, stay until my people arrive in case of a medical emergency. Peterson, if a prisoner needs to be removed, cuff them and keep them in your sights. I'm sure Sinclair's plotting his escape as we speak."

"What about me?" Helga asked.

Malloy faced her. "Peterson could use a little motherly love. Shooting another person places a heavy burden on a man's mind. Stay and reassure him that he did the right thing. These two need to hold it together until this nightmare ends. We'll be back soon. I'll keep your daughter safe."

———

Ali sat on the passenger side of Malloy's car with her arms crossed and her face impassive.

"I'm better at interrogations than small talk," Malloy said as he pulled away from the curb.

Ali looked out the side window. "No surprise there."

When he swung onto Colfax a few moments later she said, "If you're worried I'll renege on our deal, don't be. It's in my best interest to see this through."

"Your word is good."

"Like Thursday night when you accused me of murder?"

In the dark, Ali felt Malloy tense as he straightened in his seat. "We don't have to be best friends. When this is finished, I'll go my way and you'll go yours. We'll probably never see each other again."

"Probably."

Ali let out a deep sigh, wondering if he was this dense with his ex-wife.

"What?"

She waved him off. Apologies and gratitude were apparently not Malloy's strong suit.

Once they were parked in the driveway, Malloy leaned over the steering wheel. "Good. Your mother left the lights on. Stay behind me while I sweep the house."

With his gun drawn, Malloy searched the entire house before permitting Ali to shower and change. Several minutes later, she was clean and dressed in a fresh blouse and jeans. With the door open she combed her hair while Malloy talked her through the upcoming charade.

"I have a demand for my court appearance this morning," she said.

"Oh?"

"I want Tommy in the courtroom when I'm there."

"No problem. He might notice details we wouldn't know about."

"Make it your idea. I don't want him to know your request came from me."

"Done."

Malloy stayed with Ali, Doc, and the prisoners at the office while Tommy went home to shower and change. Helga tagged along and made scrambled eggs for him, which he inhaled along with toast and coffee.

Helga washed dishes as Tommy finished his coffee. "Well, whatever you did to change Ali's mind…"

Tommy swallowed. "She asked me to stay and protect her."

"That's a good start," Helga said, patting his shoulder.

Before they left, Helga saw Tommy rest his hand on his parents' picture by the backdoor. Helga turned away to give him privacy and failed to see concern sweep his face.

Tommy gave Helga a half smile. "I forgot something. Have a seat. I'll be a couple minutes."

57

The shower and breakfast fully revived Tommy, and when he and Helga arrived at his office, things were happening. Fred called to report the night shift sequestered in Mineral Ridge while replacements waited to surprise the day shift.

"Did you fly there?" Malloy asked.

"Ha. Deserted roads, no traffic. Sunday night is a good night for this operation. We should remember this if we ever do it again."

"Don't even suggest that."

After Malloy finished the call, Tommy's office remained quiet. Since they were too exhausted to string words together, there was little to be said.

"You should go home now and rest," Malloy told Helga.

"Thanks, but I'll stay."

"There's nothing more you can do, and I don't want you in Mineral Ridge. What we're doing is dangerous enough without risking you too."

Helga folded her arms. "I'm not deserting Ali. Besides, won't Lynch be suspicious if I'm not there?"

"The arraignment will go quickly. I doubt he'll notice your absence."

"You don't have to go, Mom. I'll be fine," Ali said.

Helga pointed a finger at Ali. "I'm going and that's that. No point in discussing it further."

Malloy opened his mouth but shut it before saying anything.

———

Two troopers escorted the paramedics as they wheeled the gurney through Tommy's office to the back room. One trooper raised his shotgun and stood slightly back as his partner opened the cell, pointed at Sinclair and said, "You first. On the gurney."

"Do you know who I am?" Sinclair spat out.

"An alleged killer who misused his office for his own personal gain?"

Sinclair shook his head. "I'm the sheriff. Elected to uphold the law in Kickapoo County. Peterson broke the law and shot me. Arrest him. Malloy, too."

"Not this time. Now I need you to lie quietly on the gurney."

The trooper stepped back and pointed to the gurney, giving Sinclair a wide berth.

"Okay, boys, follow me and we'll arrest Malloy and Peterson." Sinclair stepped out of the cell and tried to shoulder his way by the trooper.

The trooper slammed him against the cell bars, while his partner brought his shotgun to eye level and aimed it at Sinclair. "Ow! Damn it, I'm injured."

"Lie on the gurney," the trooper said through gritted teeth before he stepped back.

"You're making a big mistake by backing the wrong side. It'll be your badges."

The trooper smiled. "I'll chance it. Get on that gurney and shut up."

The shotgun remained trained on Sinclair until he was securely strapped down. "Okay boys, he's all yours," the trooper said, motioning the paramedics inside.

"You going to cooperate?" the trooper asked Dave after Sinclair was wheeled out.

Dave climbed onto the gurney without comment.

After Sinclair and Dave were taken away, Malloy went in the back room to interrogate Leslie.

Tommy was filling out paperwork in his office when Malloy returned, shaking his head as he took a seat. "With those two bozos gone, I had hoped to flip her, but she's keeping her lip buttoned."

Ali lifted her head from reading a magazine. "Is she locked in the cell?"

"Not for long. Transport's on the way."

Ali stood. "She might talk to me. Strange as it may sound, we bonded for a few minutes back in the car. She didn't shoot Tommy, either."

Malloy rose. "I'll go with you. If you want to try—"

Ali put her hand out, motioning for him to sit. "No. I'll go alone. Don't worry, I'll stand back from the cell. She can't hurt me now."

Malloy glanced at his watch. "Don't take long. Things will pop soon."

When Ali entered the back room alone, Leslie averted her eyes. "Come to gloat?"

"For years, I dreamed of humiliating you like you humiliated me." Ali sat in the folding chair. "Taking advantage of my inexperience. Denying me the basic rights of a prisoner to suit your boss's whims. Many nights I laid awake imagining what payback would feel like."

Ali looked away. "But I can't do it. It isn't right."

Ali crossed her legs while shaking her head. "We do have something in common now. We're both women working in a man's world. You didn't want to participate tonight, but Sinclair didn't give you a choice. You've let him manipulate you for years, all because you like women instead of men."

Leslie bowed her head. A tear fell and left its mark on her jeans.

"Sinclair's finished. Malloy will nail him along with Lynch. There's no need to share their fate. You don't deserve that. Talk to

Malloy. God knows I had my fill of him this week, but he keeps his promises."

Leslie sniffed. "Doesn't matter. I'm going away. And when I get out, I won't be wearing a uniform. Who'll want to hire me? I'll be no better than the skanks who end up in jail year after year, writing bad checks because they're broke, drinking to forget their miserable lives."

"You don't have to become one of them. I wanted to teach, but my conviction forced me into a new occupation. Now I'm happier than I ever imagined possible."

"Really?"

Ali shrugged. "This past week wasn't so great."

Leslie managed a solitary laugh.

"I don't know what sentence you'll receive, but if you cooperate and keep your nose clean, I'll help you get an entry-level position with Robel's when you get out. If you work hard, you can advance and have a good life. After a couple years of exemplary service, you could work for another company if you wanted to."

Leslie looked at the floor. "After what I did to you, you'd do that for me?"

"I've been in your situation, facing incarceration. Don't misread it. I'm not trying to hit on you."

"I know. You're in love with Baby Face."

In love? Ali wasn't sure about that. "I'll help you, but you need to tell Malloy everything. You could save a life."

Leslie raised her head. "Guess it couldn't hurt."

"Good. Let's call him back here."

Ali stayed while Malloy questioned Leslie, who confirmed that as the weekend progressed, more people grew suspicious. A deputy noted the files Malloy studied and placed a call to Lynch, and he gave Sinclair the go-ahead to end the situation. "Sinclair woke me up about midnight. Wanted the arrest to appear legit. I didn't want to do it, but he has dirt on me, and I couldn't refuse. I didn't know he planned on killing her until we drove away. Should've bailed when I had the chance, but I chose not to. Another bad choice."

Leslie's tears flowed freely now, so Malloy passed her a tissue. "Lynch suspects I'm onto them?"

"I believe so. Sinclair knew."

"Lynch expects to show up at work today, learn of Ali's death, dismiss me, and get on with his life. Is that about it?"

"I believe so," Leslie said, holding her hand out for another tissue.

Malloy passed her another. "Thank you, deputy. You'll be taken to Madison, where you'll have an in-depth interview later. When we see where you fit in all of this, we'll cut the deal. You'll be treated decently."

"Fair enough."

Ten minutes later, two troopers escorted Leslie to the waiting squad car. Ali watched her climb in, cuffed and humiliated. Malloy rapped on the roof, signaling the car to go. Ali shivered, and Helga put her arm around Ali's shoulder.

"Not as enjoyable as I imagined," Ali said, leaning in.

Helga gave Ali another squeeze. "At least it's not you in that car."

"No, but I'm next."

58

Monday, October 22, 1984

Ali and Malloy both jumped at Tommy's siren blip. Tommy and Helga were following Malloy's unmarked car in Bernice as they sped along the interstate toward the Mineral Ridge exit. Malloy swerved back into his own lane.

"Should I drive?" Ali broke the silence from the rear of Malloy's unmarked.

Malloy glanced in the mirror. "I haven't slept in twenty-four hours."

Ali wouldn't admit her own distraction, remembering her last Mineral Ridge trip before the trial and surprise incarceration. At least today she could change her mind and cancel this charade, but she wouldn't.

Better finish the job so these false allegations don't follow me to the grave.

Malloy glanced into the rearview mirror. "Alicia, there's something I should tell you because..." Ali met his eyes in the mirror before he focused on the road. "...I might not see you later."

"If you're apologizing for the false accusations, I understand. You were doing your job. The evidence pointed at me."

"That's not it, but you're right. I am sorry about that." Malloy shifted in his seat. "I know why Orville Luetz testified against you and how Lynch justified the maximum sentence eight years ago."

Ali gazed through the window. Sinclair had gloated about Luetz's deal after her failed appeal and proposed one of his own. If Ali had given him what he wanted, he promised to make her time easy and arrange for her early release to start college on time. His offer disgusted her, and she didn't believe him anyway so she refused and her stay became virtual solitary confinement. That night at the Ranch House, when many people saw her altercation with Mr. Luetz, she had leaned over and whispered, "I know about your dirty little deal." That's when Luetz berated Ali, prompting her to curse at him and stomp off in disgust, setting her up so no one would believe her allegations.

Malloy looked in the mirror again. "...a few days before your trial, Margaret Luetz was arrested for DUI in Mineral Ridge. Lynch connected your principal with the drunk in the holding tank, saw an opportunity, and offered a deal. Luetz supplied testimony to justify the maximum sentence for your crime. Lynch made the papers and secretly dropped the charges against Margaret."

Ali's eyes narrowed.

"Milenburg intended on using that information when he ran for judge. Someone pulled your case file, found the letter you wrote Milenburg from jail and used it to forge the note Peterson found with Orville Luetz."

"Sinclair bragged about that in his car last night."

"Then we'll find the original letter when we search Sinclair's home and office later today."

"You'll also find a signed confession that he forged my signature on."

Malloy glanced over his shoulder. "Don't worry. After last night, I would have assumed the signature was forged anyway."

They were both silent for a moment. "So, Tommy was right about the note derailing the investigation."

"Appears that way. If you hadn't returned, a few calls to the West

Coast would have established your alibi. Tommy would have surrendered the case to Sinclair, which would have guaranteed it would go cold while they blackmailed Milenburg to keep quiet."

Ali's brow furrowed. "Sinclair killed Milenburg because I came home for a visit?"

Malloy's eyes darted toward the mirror and watched Ali turn her head to the side but not before a tear rolled down her cheek. "No, they killed him because he threatened Lynch's empire. After reading page after page of transcripts, it's obvious to me Lynch manipulates trials to get the outcome he wants. I'm sure Milenburg knew many other secrets. Yours was the most convenient."

Ali sniffed.

Malloy dug out his handkerchief and passed it back to her. "Go ahead, let it out. You'll feel better."

Ali took it, but she refused to cry in front of Malloy so they traveled in silence until Malloy pulled into a vacant used car lot on the edge of town.

He got out and opened her door. "Hands behind," he said. She stepped out and he cuffed her. At least this time it was voluntary.

Malloy gently spun her around. "I appreciate your help."

"Ha. Coming from you, that sounds like a presidential citation."

He chuckled. "You aren't going to get sick, are you?"

"Only if you put me in a cell."

"I'm sure we can avoid that. Listen. When we get there, I'll treat you like a criminal until we get inside. I won't hurt you, but anyone watching has to be convinced this is real."

"I can scream 'police brutality' if you want."

"That won't be necessary."

Ali smiled. "No, but it might be fun for me."

Malloy pointed toward the back seat. Ali glanced over her shoulder to make sure Tommy and Helga were still following them. They both looked somber, watching from Tommy's car parked behind. Ali climbed in, Malloy shut the door and they continued on.

A shiver raced up Ali's spine as Malloy parked by the jail, grasped her arm, and whisked her inside. He opened the door and the institutional stench hit her nostrils, making her stomach roll as they came to a desk with a woman standing behind it.

Malloy nodded in the woman's direction. "This is my teammate, Betty Fowler. She's in charge."

Tommy and Helga caught up with them after parking across the street. Malloy pointed at Tommy. "Peterson, you come with me. Helga, this is Betty. You can stay here with her."

Malloy and Tommy left. Betty removed Ali's cuffs before handing her an orange jumpsuit. "Change in the inner office. Leave your clothes there. We'll come back for them."

Betty reached under the desk to open a cooler and pull out a ginger ale.

"Malloy warned me you might become queasy. Take your time changing. Court convenes at nine. Once you step out here, I'll need to shackle you for appearance's sake. Helga, you can wait with me if you like. We'll walk over once we get the signal."

"You're doing the right thing, dear." Helga took Ali's hand to reassure her. "Soon it'll be over and we can forget this mess."

Ali managed a weak smile. Helga had often said the same thing before her trial. She took the orange jumpsuit and ginger ale and went inside to change.

59

"I've got a job for you," Malloy told Tommy on the way to the conference room. Tommy suspected Malloy included him in the task force meeting to prevent him from creating any more problems.

Malloy opened the conference room door. Several veteran officers sat around the table, silent and focused, the gravity of the situation muting any excitement they felt at pinning on the badge. Fred stood at the head of the table and offered his hand to Tommy.

"Good work. These bastards aren't playing around, are they?"

Tommy shook Fred's hand, but before he could answer, Malloy said, "Gentlemen, this is Chief Tommy Peterson from Rausburg. Last night Tommy saved a woman's life and brought to light the corruption that plagues this department. He's why we're all here. Since he knows this department better than we do, I'm stationing him at the front desk to handle any emergencies that might arise before we complete the procedure.

"Peterson, secrecy is crucial until Lynch charges Alicia. If a civilian calls or enters seeking assistance, you keep them from becoming suspicious. A leak now will spell disaster. If regular staff report to the front desk, tell them there's a mandatory meeting and escort them here. Act upset with me so they'll sympathize with you.

"When we're ready, you'll accompany me to the courthouse. In the meantime, your presence sells the charade and your knowledge guarantees we miss nothing. Can you do that?"

"Yes, sir."

Malloy offered his hand. "I trust your judgment. Frank's working the front desk and dispatch right now. I told him that you'd handle any problems."

Tommy shook Malloy's hand before heading for the front desk.

———

"Jesus, don't you ever sleep?" Wendell Ferguson asked as Malloy stood in his doorway. Before Wendell moved a pile of papers on his desk, Malloy glimpsed a warrant, now hidden underneath.

"I bring good news. Arrested Alicia Thorein last night."

"What? I didn't think... I mean, it seemed like you—"

"The lab worked overtime. They placed her at the scene of Milenburg's murder. Peterson locked her in his cell, and I brought her over first thing this morning. If we get her in front of Lynch right away, I'll be out of here by noon."

A perplexed Wendell tapped the top of his desk. Malloy was sure Alicia's warrant waited for Sinclair on Wendell's desk. Wendell maintained his composure but looked confused as to why Sinclair hadn't come for the warrant.

"Why don't you give Judge Lynch the good news yourself? I'll be ready when court convenes if he wants to get her initial appearance out of the way."

"Happy to. He'll appreciate your efficiency in this matter."

Malloy contained his grin.

When he entered Lynch's chambers, Malloy learned the judge was aware of Alicia's arrest. "Did I hear right? You changed your mind?"

"Yes, your honor, I did. The lab found conclusive evidence, so there's no reason to drag this out. She's in jail, pending her initial appearance."

Lynch's forehead creased, and he hesitated a moment. "I have a full day planned, but I'll process her first. You must have other ongoing investigations."

"I do, and I appreciate your timeliness."

Lynch leaned back in his chair, staring at Malloy and making him uncomfortable for several seconds while he digested this new information.

"Is Sinclair in the loop on this?"

"Funny thing. I was headed to Rausburg early this morning when Peterson radioed me that he locked her up. Sinclair overheard and responded, too. Must be a real night owl. Anyway, she's in jail. My job is done here. As soon as she's charged, I'll finish the paperwork and head back to Madison. I may be heavy-handed, but now you have an open-and-shut case. Even with Justin Green as her attorney, she'll spend years in prison."

Lynch offered his hand. "Justice is served in the long run. Thanks for your help on this case. See you in court."

Yes, you will. Malloy took the judge's hand. *It'll be the last case you ever preside over.*

60

Frank shook Tommy's hand. "So, you're the guy who started this mess."

Frank's grin gave him away. "I guess."

"Good work. I'm counting on you to avert any disasters until this operation's complete."

They chatted while monitoring the radio. A call came from a school bus driver reporting a defaced stop sign on his route. Tommy asked Frank to call Ken Steiner at county highway and report the matter.

Precisely at eight thirty, Malloy stopped by with a staff list. After Tommy confirmed all the detained staff and deputies, Malloy checked his watch.

"Right on time. We'll wait here. Don't want to get chummy with court personnel. I met briefly with Lynch."

"Lynch bought the story?" Tommy asked.

"It's plausible enough. Sinclair could have heard us while he headed over. We wouldn't know if he was in his car, and it's not uncommon for a sheriff to have a base station at home."

"He has one," Tommy said.

"Even better. We're all set."

Tommy hid his skepticism. He was certain Lynch had called Sinclair this morning to find out why he hadn't arrested Ali himself. *What did he think when Sinclair failed to respond?*

Malloy reviewed the rest of his plan as they crossed the street. "Two retired troopers are already waiting over there. One's tall with reddish hair, and the other's squat and bald. We called them Mutt and Jeff. Good men. They'll take the clerk and bailiff. You escort the court reporter out, I'll get Wendell, and Judge Symington will handle Lynch. We may have to assist him. I doubt Lynch will leave easily."

Leon, the bailiff, guarded the courtroom door. Tommy knew little about him other than he was counting the days to retirement. Leon spotted the bandage on Tommy's ear and the angry red mark beneath it. He pointed to it.

"Have an accident there?"

Tommy smiled. "Yeah. Some trouble Saturday night." He stepped ahead to enter.

Leon stuck his arm out, stopping Tommy. "Need your weapons, gentlemen."

Malloy glared at him. "We're sitting in the back to watch this first arraignment. Nowhere close to the prisoner."

Leon stretched to his full height of six feet and crossed his arms. "Sorry, Judge's orders. No weapons in court today. If you want to sit inside, they have to go in the lockbox."

Malloy didn't want to pull rank and risk tipping his hand. No one else would be armed, so he surrendered his sidearm.

Tommy handed his sidearm to Leon and said to Malloy, "I'd better hit the can first. You go on ahead. Save me a seat."

Malloy grimaced but entered alone.

After a short time, Tommy took the seat next to him.

"You okay?" Malloy asked.

Tommy nodded. "Nervous, I guess."

"Me, too. Don't worry. We'll nail Lynch."

Tommy remained skeptical, knowing Lynch ran his courtroom

with an iron fist. He doubted Lynch would stand by and peacefully accept his arrest. Tommy slowed his breathing, as he had been trained to do on the target range, and focused on the long gaps between breaths when time felt infinite.

Whatever happened next, Tommy was ready.

61

Ali waited with Betty and Helga almost an hour before the phone rang. Betty answered, listened for a moment, and announced, "It's time. We'll meet our escorts in front. You remember your part in the courtroom?"

Ali patted her stomach and nodded. "I plead not guilty and try not to puke."

Betty grinned. "All kidding aside, do what I tell you. I'll risk my life to protect yours."

Ali's brow furrowed. "You expect trouble?"

"Unlikely, but I'm prepared."

Ali's stomach rolled when Betty put the shackles on, but the ginger ale kept her from getting sick. It didn't keep her from being scared and as Ali approached the two waiting troopers, she froze. The older one glanced left and right before winking at her and taking her arm. Betty took her other arm while the other trooper followed behind with his hand on his pistol.

Betty patted Ali's arm. "Shackles are hard to walk in. We're not in any hurry. Helga, we'll see you in the courtroom."

Helga went ahead while Ali shuffled across the street to the court-house. With her escort maintaining stiff postures and stern faces, it appeared the troopers were escorting the killer she pretended to be to her final destiny.

The holding room brought back another set of unpleasant memories. After her sentencing, Sinclair cuffed her before whisking her there and ordering her to sit. When a deputy clamped on the shackles, she told Sinclair she felt sick. He laughed and stood back to watch her puke all over her best dress before he hustled her across the street to jail, tripping and stumbling. When pedestrians stopped to stare, Sinclair joked, "What stinks?" His deputies laughed.

Her last visit to the holding room came at her appeal. After a month of incarceration, her attorney found precedents for adjusting her sentence to time served. An inmate on trial for assault awaited his fate along with her. She experienced nausea then too, but she entered the courtroom hoping her nightmare would end and she could start college in a few weeks.

That day, Lynch belittled her lawyer for wasting his time before dismissing her appeal. While she was alone in the holding room, Sinclair squeezed her arm and whispered, "You're mine now, Sweetmeat." She puked outside in the grass but kept it off herself.

No other prisoners shared the room with her today as she sat alone and anxious, surrounded by guards.

After a few minutes, the bailiff opened the metal courtroom door. He scanned the room and straightened to his full height. "Where's Leslie?"

"She's home sick. I'm Betty."

He scowled. "Okay, Betty, take her to the far table. Prisoner stays shackled, judge's orders." He stared at the troopers. "I'm surprised Sinclair is missing this one."

"Flu's going around the jail. Got a late call. Had to hustle."

"Well, you'd better hustle back and bring the next one. Lynch doesn't like to wait. He'll reprimand you in front of the whole courtroom without batting an eye."

The courtroom hadn't changed in eight years. Helga sat close behind the rail on the defendant's side, sniffing and dabbing her eyes while Malloy sat behind the prosecutor's table. He locked eyes with

Ali for an instant and lifted his chin. Tommy avoided her eyes alto-
gether and appeared ill at ease. Several spectators sat in the gallery,
but no one stood out as law enforcement.

As she sat in chains, the reality of the situation overwhelmed her.
In a few minutes, she would be charged with two counts of murder in
the first degree. If convicted, she would spend the rest of her life in
prison.

Ali's breathing became shallow as her heart pounded.

*What if Malloy doesn't have jurisdiction? Maybe Tommy found out the
truth. That's why he's nervous.*

An image of Malloy sneering through iron bars flashed in her
mind. *Gotcha!*

She jumped when Betty squeezed her hand under the table.

"Don't panic," Betty whispered.

Wendell Ferguson entered, nodded to Malloy, and glared at Ali as
he dropped her paperwork on his table.

"All rise," the bailiff announced. The entire room rose as Judge
Lynch entered. Ali's stomach rolled when she noticed Lynch's flushed
complexion made him appear on the verge of exploding. Ali shivered
while staring blankly ahead.

"Sit," Betty whispered, tugging Ali's sleeve.

After the clerk announced the case, Lynch asked the attorneys to
identify themselves.

Wendell Ferguson stood and announced the State of Wisconsin
was charging Alicia P. Thorein with two counts of first-degree
murder. Ali swallowed hard.

It's official. I've been charged with two murders I didn't commit.

Lynch addressed Ali. "I see you lack representation. It is my
understanding that you are not indigent. Therefore, you represent
yourself at this hearing. What is your plea?"

She struggled to her feet. "Your honor, I haven't been allowed to
contact my attorney yet."

Lynch glared at her. "It doesn't matter. The outcome will be the
same. The murder of two upstanding citizens is a crime I can't take

lightly. You'll have plenty of time to confer with your attorney later. How do you plead?"

"Not guilty, your honor."

"Figures. Alicia Thorein, I charge you with two counts of murder in the first degree. You are remanded to the county jail to await trial. Bail is to be determined later." He banged the gavel.

Ali fell into her chair as her knees buckled.

62

Tommy's heart ached as he watched Ali play her part. He could imagine her emotional state. Even though he was assigned to handle the elderly court reporter, he focused his attention on Lynch and the bailiff, Leon. Any resistance would start with them.

Malloy sat next to him smiling, and Tommy wished he could act more assured, but he suspected things weren't what they appeared. In a small department, word travels fast. Lynch must know of the massive changes across the street by now.

After the gavel banged, Malloy glanced to his right and a distinguished older man stood and advanced to the bench. Lynch's focus remained on Ali's paperwork, so he didn't notice him at first. As Judge Symington approached, Lynch looked up and scowled.

"What are you doing in my courtroom?"

Symington flashed his ID. "Removing you from the bench. This is no longer your courtroom. You are relieved of your duties, pending impeachment. You, sir, will enter custody on two charges of felony murder and one count of attempted murder. You have the right to remain—"

Lynch rose, his face a vivid red now. "Get out. You have no authority here."

While Lynch argued, Malloy led Tommy and the two troopers through the gate before they split in different directions. Malloy got his hand on Wendell's arm first and informed him of his own suspension, pending investigation.

Mutt and Jeff flashed their ID's at the surprised bailiff and clerk. The reporter's head swiveled to Tommy, eyes wide as he approached. Tommy forced a smile to appear friendly, but Lynch diverted his attention by clawing at his robe.

Tommy raised his eyebrows at the flash of metal. Behind him a woman yelled, "Gun," which was followed by chairs scraping and a loud thump.

"Everyone freeze," Lynch yelled. "This is my courtroom, and I will shoot anyone who defies me here."

All motion stopped.

"Stand down. I mean it."

63

"I mean it," Lynch repeated. "I'm in charge here. This is my courtroom, and I will maintain order."

Tommy stood closest to the bench and recognized the long barrel Smith & Wesson .44 magnum, the most powerful handgun in the world. Lynch could inflict much damage with it.

In the dead quiet, Malloy's soft footsteps dominated the courtroom. When Lynch swiveled in the direction of the sound, Malloy froze and Tommy jammed his hand into his jacket pocket while angling toward the bench.

Malloy took another step, hands out, his palms facing Lynch. "Put your gun down carefully before it goes off. Fight this in the courts, not today."

"You lack the proper authority. Bailiff, arm yourself and prepare to take these men into custody," Lynch shouted.

Tommy doubted Leon would defy Lynch, and his receding footsteps confirmed that belief. With Leon armed and Lynch empowered, the chance of a peaceful resolution disappeared.

Time to act.

"That's what I told him, your honor," Tommy said as he swung around to face the judge. "It's not right that he pokes his nose in here and takes charge."

Tommy took two steps to the center of the room, pointing at Malloy with his left hand as he raised his voice. "It's time you got your wings clipped. You pushed us around all week, and I'm sick of it. We were solving this on our own until you pushed your way in and walked all over us. We didn't need you butting into our business."

Tommy froze. The courtroom was silent.

"Well, Peterson, you are on the right side. I had my doubts," Lynch said.

Tommy let his left arm droop. "I've always known, your honor. It's time to take a stand for justice."

The court reporter cringed at the flash of blue steel when Tommy drew a small revolver from his right jacket pocket while pivoting in Lynch's direction and taking the classic stance. Two pops echoed through the room as Tommy shot on either side of Lynch, forcing him to duck and cover his head.

Before Lynch could respond, Tommy stepped closer to the bench while aiming at Lynch's forehead. Tommy's tone remained firm and measured.

"That was a warning. Next one goes between the eyes."

"You wouldn't dare," Lynch snarled.

"I'll do it. Sinclair and Dave found out the hard way last night. Slowly lower your weapon."

Silence was a powerful tool, and Tommy had mastered its effective use long ago. Both men locked eyes while considering their next move. With Lynch's gun pointed at the ceiling, he didn't have a chance to fire first.

As Tommy stood firm, Lynch's arm sagged and his hand went limp, allowing Tommy to snatch the gun from his grasp. "Malloy, you can continue now."

Malloy remained frozen for a few seconds before taking charge. "All officers of the court are suspended from their duties pending further investigation. Any resistance will be dealt with accordingly.

Gentlemen and lady, if you wish to avoid prosecution, I suggest you cooperate or you may find yourself in a cell with your former boss."

Everyone stood or sat quietly while Mutt retrieved the guns from the lockbox. After the court officers were whisked away, Lynch plopped back in his chair, slowly shaking his head and narrowing his eyes. Tommy stood steadfast in front of the bench, his .38 aimed straight at the judge, oblivious to everyone else.

Malloy approached Lynch from the side. "Stand down, Peterson. I've got this." Tommy relaxed and dropped his stance.

"You can't do this. I'm a district court judge. I'm innocent, she's the criminal," Lynch shouted, shaking off Malloy's grip.

"I've read your court transcripts, and I know better. This is your last chance to leave with a shred of dignity. I'm not asking again."

Lynch swiveled, raising his hand to point at Malloy. "I'm in charge here."

Malloy grabbed Lynch's wrist, twisting and pulling the judge's arm to bring him out of his chair. In one swift motion, Malloy bent Lynch's arm behind his back. Lynch gasped in pain.

"Peterson, grab the door," Malloy said.

Tommy ran to the door, barely getting it open before Malloy shoved Lynch through.

───────

While helplessly lying on the floor under Betty, Ali listened. When the door swung shut behind Malloy and Lynch, the courtroom released a collective gasp, and Betty rolled off and helped Ali to her feet. As she took her seat, Judge Symington stepped behind the bench and a gray-haired woman from the gallery strode to the reporter's desk and sat.

"Are you ready, Joyce?" Symington asked. She nodded.

"Effective immediately, the state has taken over District Court 19, relieving Judge Phillip Lynch of his duties. I, Frederick Symington, have been appointed acting judge until a new permanent judge is elected.

"All charges brought in the State of Wisconsin against Alicia P. Thorein by District Attorney Wendell Ferguson and ruled upon by Judge Phillip Lynch on this date are dismissed. In addition, Ms. Thorein's June 1976 misdemeanor conviction and her subsequent sentence are ordered expunged from her record. Let the records show Ms. Thorein assisted the governor's task force, led by Agent Dirk Malloy, by agreeing to her arrest and indictment on false charges.

"Alicia, the State of Wisconsin thanks you for your help and patience. You are free to go. I declare this court adjourned for the day. We will reconvene at nine a.m. tomorrow and continue with the scheduled docket."

Betty fished the key from her pocket and removed Ali's shackles and cuffs. "Wait here. I'll take you back after we clear the courtroom."

Ali leaned over the rail, receiving the best Mom hug she could imagine while tears flowed for both.

"It's over. It's over," Ali repeated while the courtroom cleared.

64

With Tommy following, Malloy hustled Lynch to the detainment room and handed the judge to two burly state troopers at the door. "Pat him down, and cuff him. This one pulled a weapon in court, so be cautious. Don't give him a chance to cause more harm."

The entire sheriff's department and court staff filled the room and sat in silence while watching the troopers manhandle Lynch.

Malloy stepped into the middle of the room. "Here are the facts. Sheriff Sinclair framed a young woman from Rausburg for the murders of two men, your co-worker Dan Milenburg and Orville Luetz from Rausburg. Two deputies aided him last night in kidnapping and almost killing her in cold blood. All three are now in custody. Sinclair committed those crimes on orders from Judge Lynch. I have enough proof to convict, and I will arrest anyone standing in our way."

Malloy surveyed the room, letting his words sink in. "You all face an important decision now. The state will punish those willfully misusing the office. Help return law and order to Kickapoo County and you may keep your job. Hold back to protect the guilty and you will face the consequences. It's that simple. My staff will give you details before dismissing you.

"Fred, they're all yours. Peterson, step into my office." Malloy held the door open to the hallway.

Well, this is it. Ali's free. I'll take courses at the technical college, find a new career. Maybe join her in San Francisco.

As Tommy pulled the door shut, Malloy scanned the hallway. They were alone.

"Do you ever follow orders? Do you even know what it means to be part of a team?"

Tommy started to remove his badge for the second time that week.

Malloy grabbed Tommy's wrist to stop him. "Jeez, enough with the badge," Malloy said as he released Tommy's wrist. "You saved our butts in there. I won't take that away from you. Tell me, how did you know Lynch would pull a gun?"

Tommy's hand dropped. "I didn't. In my house, my parents' picture hangs by the back door. I always touch it for good luck when I leave, but today I… I can't explain it." He pulled the little pistol out of his pocket. "Ma taught me to shoot with this one. This morning, when I touched their picture, I could hear her saying, 'someone threw a monkey wrench into it.' She used to say that when things went wrong, like last night. Made me think. When Leon forced us to check our guns at the door, I became suspicious but couldn't say anything without blowing our cover."

Malloy smiled. "How did you sneak it in?"

"Taped it to my upper thigh back at the house. Been wearing it for the last few hours. No deputy would ever check there. After we surrendered our weapons, I stopped in the restroom and transferred the gun to my jacket pocket. Leon never suspected, so I got away with it. Walked right past him with it in my pocket."

Malloy laughed once. "Well, the simplest approach is usually the best. Your outburst caught me off guard. It took guts to do that, especially with the judge holding that cannon."

"After last night, I doubted he would give Ali a fair chance. Couldn't live with that, so I made sure he wouldn't get another opportunity."

"You were lucky Lynch didn't pull the trigger when you shot at him."

Tommy studied the little pistol. "Shyness has its advantages. I spent most of my youth observing people. Lynch is a coward like all bullies. I knew he didn't have the guts to pull the trigger, and I didn't give him time to reconsider. Actually, he's the lucky one."

"How's that?"

"I missed on purpose. At that range, I could have saved you the cost of a trial."

"We'll keep that part of the story between us." Malloy rested his hand on Tommy's shoulder while his smile faded. "I've been rough on you this week, but you're one hell of a good cop. You saved this whole situation. I'd be honored to buy you dinner sometime and get to know you better as a friend."

"I'd be honored, too."

"There's one more thing I need from you."

"Name it."

Malloy took his hand off Tommy's shoulder. "Accompany Lynch and the troopers while they lock him up. They'll do all the paper work. You make sure Lynch doesn't cause any trouble. You can take the women home after he's squared away. Good luck with Alicia. I hope things work out for you two."

"Is it that obvious?"

Malloy's smile returned. "Oh, yes. That's what made me suspicious. Fortunately, you both proved me wrong."

Malloy opened the door. "Joe, Steve. Bring the judge here."

The troopers appeared with Lynch cuffed between them, his face wet with tears. "This is Police Chief Tommy Peterson from Rausburg. He'll assist you in escorting the judge to his cell. Tommy will follow several feet behind. If the judge tries anything stupid, hit the deck. Tommy's an expert marksman. He'll make sure the judge doesn't hurt anyone."

After the troopers shook hands with Tommy, Malloy said, "Okay, boys. Take him away."

65

Betty put the phone down. "Takeover's complete. All uniforms are now ours."

"I'm relieved that's over," Ali said.

"Me, too," added Helga. "Tommy's taking us home, right?"

"He'll be along in a minute or two. I'll stop by your house tonight to take both your statements, otherwise you're free to do whatever," Betty said.

Ali gave Helga another squeeze. "Not sure what we will do now. All week long the cloud of suspicion hung over us and put a damper on our social life."

"Whatever you decide, I'll come by this evening to record you. The state prosecutor's office will contact both of you soon and take over from there." Betty handed each of them a card.

"If you have questions, call me. Otherwise, I speak for the whole team when I say how much we appreciate your help and understanding in solving this case."

Ali took the card. "No one's happier than me. Now if we're done, I'd like to get out of here." Ali opened her arms and gave Betty a hug before stepping outside.

———

Ali and Helga paced in front of the jail for another fifteen minutes before Tommy arrived.

"Sorry. Got hung up," he said as they slid in Bernice.

Ali closed her door. "No problem. I enjoy hanging around jails. You meet the most interesting men here."

Tommy grinned, glad to see old Ali from high school was back.

Helga sat in back while Ali rode shotgun as they drove away. Ali turned to face Tommy. "Shooting a sheriff and a judge. Will you come out unscathed?"

"I'll go before the state review board. May get reprimanded for withholding that note, but nothing serious. Malloy promised to put in a good word for me."

"They should give you a medal or citation for saving my life. I never suspected little Tommy Peterson had that in him."

"You always said I could be whatever I wanted. Was that just talk?"

Ali smiled. "No, I guess not. I was thinking more like a regular job, though. I never dreamed you'd become a cop."

"Disappointed?"

Ali laughed. "No, not at all. You're the cop I'd want to protect me in my home."

"This is your home."

Ali had no answer to that.

"Tell me what happened while Betty had me tackled on the floor. I never saw a thing."

Tommy snickered. "Covered you pretty good, didn't she? Well, when Lynch pulled his gun..."

Ali studied Tommy as he relived their courtroom experience. The cute, shy boy she remembered from her childhood had blossomed into a handsome young man, possessing an inner strength many overlooked.

Bet Malloy doesn't consider Tommy some small-time rube anymore.

Despite the turmoil thrown at her, she found Tommy to be a

calming influence she wanted to know better. That feeling surprised her. She didn't hate men. But because she was forced to compete with them, Ali rarely dated. Too bad Tommy wasn't another executive in San Francisco. They might have a solid future together. But as an underpaid cop in Wisconsin, their differences seemed insurmountable.

She had vaguely promised they could date when the dust settled, and she planned to honor that promise, but visits home would not be often enough to develop a real romantic relationship. Maybe she could help him see that and encourage him to seek a mate elsewhere. Yes, that would be the kind thing to do.

As they crested the ridge north of Rausburg, Tommy slowed to a crawl and flicked his light bar on before blipping the siren twice.

"What are you doing?" Ali asked.

Tommy pointed ahead. A small crowd of people lined Main Street in front of the school.

"What's wrong?" Helga asked.

"Nothing's wrong. It's a parade. A 'Welcome Home Ali' parade."

Ali gaped at the crowd "You're kidding."

"No. I made a few calls and suggested we have a chance to say we're sorry and we'd better take it. This will always be your home. It's about time you faced the truth."

Several people hoisted a homemade sign. *Welcome Home Ali.*

The entire school stood outside and as Tommy approached, the school band formed to lead the one-car parade and played the school song with more enthusiasm than accuracy.

Tommy drove into the school parking lot as a small crowd lined the driveway, waving and cheering. Ali waved back, tears dampening her cheeks as they parked in front of the school.

"Don't sit there," Tommy said when Ali failed to move. "Better say hello to your friends. Eight years is a long time. They've missed you."

Tears flowed as people she grew up with came to shake her hand and apologize. Many asked, "Can you forgive us?" while she nodded in return.

Chet shouted, "Cake and ice cream in the gym," and the crowd swept Ali inside.

Once everyone was inside, Harv Middleton called for silence. "Ali, please excuse the small size of our party here. You deserve a bigger celebration, but timing is more important than size today. We didn't want you to leave without showing you how we feel about you.

"Rumors flew all morning because you three were missing. No one knew what was going on until Tommy called and told us about your ordeal. I speak for everyone here when I say we're sorry the first time you came home to visit, you had to go through that."

A round of applause interrupted Harv.

"Eight years ago, many of us made a big mistake, one we've deeply regretted. We sat back and let events run their course. After your trial, we couldn't help, and we were ashamed we failed you after all the good you did for the school and community.

"When you came home that fall, the shame we carried made us appear hostile, which drove you away. We're sorry for that. We always expected to straighten this out, but we hurt you so much you didn't come back until now. On top of that, we've been dealing with the tragedy that took place last week.

"We all owe you an apology and hope you can find it in your heart to forgive us and let us make things right. We want you to feel welcome here." He flung his hands out. "I'm not the most eloquent. Maybe someone else can do better."

A chorus of 'Well put' and 'Me, too' echoed from the adults present while the children stood quietly, stunned by so many adults admitting bad behavior.

Ali still carried resentment. Visiting the jail and courthouse that morning stirred those memories. Not all the village residents shared Harv's sentiments, either. Fern Johnson and her friends were nowhere to be seen.

But Chet, Harv, Melanie, Mr. Farmingham, and her former teachers were there. Many times, she dreamed of confronting the entire village and berating them for deserting her, but today she couldn't do it.

"I'm sorry, too. For bringing dishonor to our home and putting you on the spot. Didn't mean to, but that's what happened. I could have written and let you know I chose to live elsewhere, but I didn't. In the last few days we all went through events new and foreign to us. Thank you for welcoming me back. It's nice to be home."

Her friends applauded, and Harv held his hand out to shake hers.

"Not good enough," she said, hugging him like she used to as a little girl. Both had tears in their eyes when she pulled free.

Harv announced, "Break out the ice cream. Today we celebrate the return of a valued member of our community."

Curious about the day's events, many people had questions for Ali, but Tommy stepped in. "We can't discuss the specifics until we've given our official statements. I can tell you last night Sheriff Sinclair and two deputies kidnapped Ali and almost killed her to cover up Mr. Luetz's murder."

"Sinclair? Why?" Harv asked.

Tommy bit his lip, but Ali helped him out. She carried anger and resentment for the man responsible for her incarceration but tarnishing his memory would hurt Margaret more. "Mr. Luetz had information that would have cost Lynch his job. He planned to come forward but didn't get the chance. Sinclair assumed I was in California when he made it look like I killed Mr. Luetz. After he found out I was here, he killed Dan Milenburg and abducted me."

Tommy continued. "But the real mastermind is Lynch. Agent Malloy will continue the investigation. Based on what we witnessed this morning, we'll elect a new judge and sheriff next year."

"Is that why your ear is bandaged?"

Tommy nodded. Ali wouldn't let him downplay his heroics. "Tommy received that while saving me. He risked his life to save mine."

"Just doing my job. Let's serve the cake and ice cream and celebrate."

As Chet and several of the teachers served, Tommy gently pulled Ali aside. "I have to fill out a mountain of reports. I'll leave you here to enjoy your day."

"Oh, please stay. This party is for you as much as me."

"No, this is your celebration. Many people have missed you. I want you to know that before you leave. I'll swing by your house later when Betty comes over. You enjoy yourself. That's an order. You've had a rough week and deserve all the fun you can handle."

"Promise you'll come over later?"

"Promise."

"Okay, go fill out your paperwork."

They looked at each other for a moment before Ali threw her arms around him. He held her tight.

"Thanks," she whispered. "I can't say it enough for all you've done."

"It's been my pleasure. Now go. I've got work to do. Crime doesn't take a holiday for cake and ice cream."

66

Tuesday, October 23, 1984

The temperature had dropped below freezing overnight, giving Rausburg its first hint of the coming winter. While Ali's car idled in the driveway, the defroster cleared the windshield. Inside the house, Helga and Ali shared the last few awkward moments all grown children experience when leaving their childhood home.

"Feels like I just arrived," Ali said.

Helga's eyes were moist. "For me, too. I'm so glad you came. My home will always be your home, no matter what."

Ali hugged Helga and rested her head on Helga's shoulder, taking her time, unlike their last goodbye at the bus station eight years ago when the bus heading west for Dubuque, Iowa was ready to pull out. At eighteen and still suffering from the biggest trauma of her life, Ali rushed to buy a ticket and board before she changed her mind, leaving Helga and the past behind with nothing more than a wave.

Ali lifted her head and looked at her mom. "Should have resolved this years ago. I missed you more than I cared to admit."

Helga brushed a hair away from Ali's cheek. "When will I see you again?"

"I'll come home for the trials, if not sooner. We're in my busiest season now. Once that's past—"

Helga sniffed. "Call me tonight? I'll worry until I know you made it back safe and sound."

"I'll call. I won't cut you out of my life again. I won't repeat that mistake."

Helga squeezed Ali once more and released. "Please be gentle saying goodbye to Tommy."

"I will. He turned out great, and I owe him my life, but—"

Helga put her finger on Ali's lips. "Keep an open mind. You can have a career and a family. If not with him, then with someone else." Helga smiled and took her finger off Ali.

"Things will be different now. This last week brought back good memories too." Like Rausburg's *Young Citizen of the Year* award, now resting in her suitcase. That plaque was the crowning achievement of her childhood. Better it hung in her apartment or office to serve as a reminder than remain buried in a box.

After Helga followed her to the car, they hugged again before Ali got in. Helga gave a slight wave, shivering from the cold. Ali rolled down her window, held her arms out, and Helga gave her a last short hug. "Drive safe."

"I will, Mom."

Ali backed out while Helga followed her out the driveway to the street, waving until Ali disappeared onto Main.

———

Tommy sat in his squad car, Bernice, by the speed limit sign on the north ridge, visible to everyone while avoiding the kids and their endless questions. Normally he loved talking with them, but today he worked to avoid sensationalizing his actions. Young boys might assume shooting people made them a hero, and Tommy didn't want that.

Besides, Tommy knew Mr. Farmingham had scheduled an assembly today to tell students the facts about Mr. Luetz's death.

Yesterday Farmingham stopped by Tommy's office after Ali's reception, questioning him and taking notes to accurately answer student questions.

Tommy hadn't asked if the deal Luetz made to gain Margaret's freedom for Ali's maximum sentence would come up. He wasn't sure how to explain it himself. As much as he blamed Luetz for ruining Ali's life and driving her away, he couldn't bring himself to tarnish the dead man's reputation further.

Farmingham was also announcing the construction of a sign in front of the school, jointly funded by the village board, advertising school and other community events in Rausburg. People already knew these things, but that wasn't the point. As Farmingham told Tommy, "We're telling our students their extracurricular efforts matter by letting the rest of the world know we're proud of them."

Tommy thought the sign was a great idea, symbolic of the change that had taken place this last week. Ali's party yesterday was another good sign that attitudes were changing in Rausburg. After her warm reception, he hoped Ali felt welcome and would visit more often, giving him a chance to romance her. Already she had agreed to meet him at the diner in another hour. Later tonight he hoped to get her alone and kindle a real relationship.

A few stragglers remained at the crosswalk when Ali's white Ford Tempo appeared on Main, earlier than planned for their date at the diner. He flashed his lights, expecting her to park by the diner and wave him down, but she drove on. She passed his office too, slowing for the crosswalk before continuing north until she pulled over and parked opposite him across the highway.

Tommy jogged over as she rolled down her window. "Sorry. It's important I get back to San Francisco."

After taking Ali's statement, Betty Fowler pointed out that reporters would see Ali with Tommy today and realize she was the Jane Doe mentioned at Malloy's press conference yesterday. "I can't phone my boss and tell him I was charged with two counts of murder. We need to meet face to face."

Tommy imagined a knife sticking out his back. His relationship with Ali was destined to be a challenge. Crouched by her open window, he said, "I hoped we'd have time together, without all the accusations, so we could be ourselves."

When Tommy grabbed her car door's windowsill to steady himself, Ali rested her hand on his. "I know. I'm sorry." Even through his gloves, he felt the spark. Maybe someday she would feel it as well.

"You have lots of vacation time, don't you? Maybe you could take a long weekend over Halloween and I could visit you in San Francisco."

She squeezed his hand. "This is my busiest season of the year. Don't waste your money on a plane ticket just to spend a couple hours with me. Halloween is too soon. I've got a ton of work to catch up on."

"Thanksgiving?"

She cocked her head. "That's a possibility. I'll call. I have your number now."

"I can call you, too."

"I'll be on the road more now, so you'll have trouble reaching me. It's better if I call you since your schedule is more stable."

Can't catch a break with her, can I?

He stood and rubbed his knees, hiding any signs of his frustration with Ali's need for dominance.

She looked up at him. "I'm calling Mom tonight to let her know I arrived safely. I can call you too."

She does have beautiful eyes.

"I might be at Helga's anyway. We usually eat together on Tuesdays."

"Great. You can tell me how your press conference went." Malloy had scheduled an afternoon press conference so the media could meet Tommy and question him.

"Thanks for the reminder."

Ali squeezed his hand. "You're not a shy little boy anymore. You're a hero for saving my life. Picture the reporters in their underwear, and you'll be fine."

"Right."

Ali removed her hand from Tommy's. "I've got a plane to catch. I'll call tonight. Promise." She put her car in gear.

Tommy stepped back. "I'll be waiting."

Ali smiled at him before checking her mirror and pulling away while Tommy stood in the road, watching her leave. One final wave passed between them before she disappeared over the ridge. His big chance to show Ali how he changed was finished. Years of waiting and planning were now over.

Tommy sat in his car, surveying the village he protected. When the final school bell rang, there weren't any kids visible so the crossing guard headed home, stop sign lowered, her temporary importance gone. Tommy's mind wandered, reliving the special moments he and Ali shared this past week. He would hang on to them, treasure them. She would have to testify at the trials. At least he would have more opportunities to show her the great life they could share.

His radio squawked. "Chief Peterson? Are you available for a stalled car at G and 72?"

Tommy grabbed the mic. "Be there in a minute."

Despite his disappointment at Ali's unexpected departure, his normal routine was comforting. As he pulled onto the highway, he switched on his light bar to warn everyone he was driving over the limit and hurried to help whoever was having car trouble that morning.

IF YOU ENJOYED THIS BOOK,

please consider leaving a review on Amazon. Your honest input helps me write better books and positive reviews help others find this series. Thank you for sparing a moment of your time.

Mailing List

If you would like updates on new releases as well as notifications of deals and discounts, please join my email list. No spam will be sent and you can unsubscribe at any time.

Click here to subscribe at:

gfhunnauthor.com

ACKNOWLEDGMENTS

You write and write, and write some more until you feel your story is worthy of someone else's time before you release it to a select few, cross your fingers, and hope that someone else likes it. I had the nicest crew of beta readers when the time came for feedback. Thank you Rebecca, Tina, Julie, Charlyene, Tim, Dana, Nina, Jody, and Sheryl for your compliments and observations.

My good fortune continued as I was led to the best editor imaginable for this book. Martha Hayes, thank you for educating me and leading me to write a better story than I could have imagined.

ABOUT THE AUTHOR

G. F. Hunn comes to writing after a long career as a musician. Once he discovered the thrill of performing could be obtained through great writing, he was hooked, and this book is the first result. Originally from Indiana and Wisconsin, G. F. Hunn has resided in Florida for many years with his lovely wife, Linda, and a small menagerie of pets.